THE FIXER

JOSEPH FINDER is the *New York Times* bestselling author of ten previous novels, including *Vanished* and *Buried Secrets*. Finder's international bestseller *Killer Instinct* won ITW's Thriller Award for Best Novel of 2006. Other bestselling titles include *Paranoia* and *High Crimes*, both of which became major motion pictures. He lives in Boston.

JOSEPH FINDER

THE FIXER

First published in the United States in 2015 by Dutton, an imprint
of the Penguin Random House Group

This edition first published in the UK in 2015 by Head of Zeus Ltd

9 7 5 3 1 2 4 6 8

A CIP catalogue record for this book is available from the British Library.

Designed by Leonard Telesca

ISBN (HB) 9781784081294
ISBN (XTPB) 9781784081300
ISBN (E) 9781784081287

Printed and bound in Germany by GGP Media
GmbH, Pössneck

Head of Zeus Ltd
Clerkenwell House
45–47 Clerkenwell Green
London EC1R 0HT

WWW.HEADOFZEUS.COM

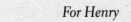

For Henry

1

On a lovely West Cambridge street this 1903 Queen Anne home is on a large level lot with many mature trees. Graciously proportioned rooms and elegant millwork. Pocket doors and two working fireplaces with original ceramic tile. The house is in need of updating, please see attached home inspection report.

The house was a dump. There was no way around it. The listing had been online for seven months, and it had generated a flurry of interest at first and one offer so lowball that the real estate agent refused to dignify it with a reply. The agent had written the ad himself and was justifiably proud of it. It was a great ad. It was also a steaming pile of horseshit, as everyone eventually discovered when they got a look at the house. An absolute lie. The place was a disaster. A money pit. Potential buyers usually fled after spending a minute or two stumbling through the decaying interior.

So Rick Hoffman, who'd left the family house on Clayton Street in Cambridge seventeen years ago, solemnly vowing never to return, was now camping out in what used to be his father's study, on the second floor. December in Boston could get awfully cold, but he'd turned off the heat, which was ridiculously expensive, so he was sleeping fully clothed in a sub-zero expedition sleeping bag on the old leather couch, next to a space heater. The study smelled vaguely of cat piss. Glassed-in legal bookcases lined the walls, tall and rickety. On his father's desk was an ancient IBM PC, in early-computer ivory, that belonged in the Smithsonian, and an Oki Data dot-matrix printer. If the 1980s ever came back, he'd be all set. His old bedroom, where he'd lived until he went off to college, had become a storeroom for broken furniture and cardboard boxes of files. So he slept on the leather sofa in a room as cold as a meat locker with the faint aroma of cat urine in the air.

This was, he realized, the lowest point in his life.

He had nowhere else to live. A week earlier he'd been forced to move out of the Back Bay apartment he'd shared with his (now) ex-fiancée until Holly had announced she no longer wanted to marry him. He'd spent a few nights in a motel on Soldiers Field Road in Brighton, but his money was running out fast. He had no income anymore. He'd sent out his résumé to dozens of magazines and newspapers, with no reply. He'd sold his watch, a nice Baume & Mercier, on eBay and unloaded most of his fancy clothes on a website that let you buy or sell "gently used, high-end" clothing.

His money was almost gone. He was lucky he had a place to crash for free. But it didn't feel so lucky, sleeping in the cold hovel on Clayton Street, the house he and his sister had grown up in.

Wendy, three years younger than Rick, was living in Bellingham, Washington, with her partner, Sarah, who owned a vegan restaurant. "Just sell the damned place," she'd told Rick. "The house is shit, but the land's got to be worth a couple hundred thousand bucks. That's money I could use."

Until Holly had broken off the engagement and kicked him out of their apartment on Beacon Street, that had seemed like a decent plan. But Rick needed a place to live, at least until he found another job, got back on his feet.

Two months ago, he'd been the executive editor of *Back Bay*, a glossy magazine devoted to the rich and the famous in Boston, the movers and shakers. It had just enough slavish coverage of celebrity chefs and posh weddings and best bartenders to ensure a nice, fat magazine, and just the right dash of snark—a knife-edge balance, really—to hook covetous and aspirational readers who considered themselves smart and sophisticated but actually weren't.

Seven or eight years ago, a local private-equity maestro named Morton Ostrow took over the joint, infusing *Back Bay* with cash, made it slicker and glossier, a rich man's plaything. He ushered in a golden age of big salaries and almost unlimited expense accounts. You had to spend money to make money! he liked to say. He moved the magazine's offices from a cramped but elegant redbrick town house on Arlington Street in the Back Bay to a converted mill building on Harrison Avenue, in the newly desirable, artist-infested SoWa district in the South End. Brick and beam, huge nineteenth-century industrial windows, and polished concrete floors. Parties at dark, bunkerlike clubs no one could get into, sponsored by Ketel One or Stoli Elit.

Rick, who'd rented the movie *All the President's Men* at an impressionable age and had been obsessed with it, had always wanted to be Woodward or Bernstein, an intrepid reporter who specialized in ferreting out high-level government fraud and conspiracy. He went to work for *The Boston Globe* in the Metro section and got a lot of attention for an exposé he did on private, for-profit prisons. He did an article about corruption in the city's taxi business and a series on how easy it was to get out of drunk-driving charges in the state. He might, he told himself, have been on the upward trajectory toward Woodward-and-Bernsteinism if he hadn't met Mort Ostrow at a book party in Cambridge. Ostrow, a short, squat frog of a man, liked Rick right away. He was hired away from the *Globe* at a ridiculous salary to beef up *Back Bay*'s coverage of the "power elite"—scandals at Harvard, intrigue at the State House, gossip among the pashas of the hedge funds. He was given license to puncture and skewer.

He acquired a big apartment on Beacon Street and a beautiful blond girlfriend to go with it. He and Holly went out to parties or dinner almost nightly. He could get a table at the tiniest, most exclusive restaurant, the kind that's booked months in advance (not years; this was Boston, after all), at half an hour's notice. When he wore suits, they were made by Ostrow's tailor (working buttonholes on the cuffs, Super 130s, fully canvassed), at the friends-and-family rate. He had a weekly breakfast with Mort Ostrow at Mort's regular table at the Bristol Lounge at the Four Seasons.

While it lasted, it was a pretty nice life.

The space heater buzzed and snarled. He heard something . . . *scurrying* somewhere within the walls nearby. A soft commotion, a rodent scrabbling. Mice? Rats? Squirrels? Anything could have gotten in through the chimneys or vents in the long years the house had stood unoccupied. Rodents or birds could be living in the walls. He got up from the couch, listened in silence for a moment, heard the muted scrabbling sound from inside the study's back wall—then slammed the wall with his fist.

There was a great crash as one of the bookcases toppled, hurtling its contents to the floor, its glass front shattering.

"Shit," he said. At least the scrabbling sound had stopped.

Broken glass was scattered everywhere, jagged shards twinkling in the morning light. Red bound volumes of *The Massachusetts Law Reporter* were arrayed on the floor. Rick's father, Leonard, had been an attorney, a solo practitioner whose clientele included some sketchy characters: strippers, porn purveyors, club owners. He'd rented an office on Washington Street in downtown Boston. But he'd always kept a duplicate set of his law books in his home study.

Rick went to fetch a broom and a dustpan to sweep up the broken glass. The broom closet was off the kitchen, down one floor.

A thick blanket of dust and debris had collected on the wooden stairs, including some crumpled Narragansett beer cans and a discarded foil condom wrapper. Teenagers had gotten into the house—hence the broken window—but probably not squatters. No long-term residents. The house had been rented for most of the eighteen years since Len's stroke. But as the place slowly deteriorated and repairs were left undone, the quality of the renters deteriorated along with it. The last ones were so rowdy and degenerate that the neighbors started complaining. Three years ago Rick had given up renting the house altogether.

The hallway was dark—the lightbulbs in the ceiling fixture were burned out—but he knew the way by heart. He could navigate the house blindfolded. He found the broom closet and located a tangle of plastic shopping bags but no brooms. And an old carpet sweeper that, even if it still worked, wouldn't pick up most of the shards of glass anyway. He looked around the kitchen. More beer cans here, and beer bottles, and discarded Big Mac cartons.

"Don't move, asshole!" someone shouted.

Rick jumped, startled. He spun around, saw a tall, skinny, balding man in a barn coat, jeans, and boots.

"Oh, it's you," the man said. "Hey, man, good to see you, Rick!"

"Oh, hey, Jeff." He smiled with relief. "Been a while."

"Sorry, dude, didn't mean to scare you. I thought it was those damned Rindge and Latin kids again." He held up a key ring and jingled it. "Wendy gave me a set of keys a couple, three years back and asked me to keep an eye on the place."

"No problem." Rick shook his head. "And listen, I really appreciate it."

Jeff Hollenbeck lived next door, had grown up there and inherited the house after his parents' death. He was a year or so younger than Rick. He and Rick weren't friends, exactly, but used to play a lot of one-on-one basketball in Jeff's parents' driveway using the hoop mounted to their garage. Jeff, always tall and skinny and athletic, usually won. When Jeff went to Rindge and Latin, the local public high school, Rick had gone off to the Linwood Academy, a private school, so their already minimal friendship had been attenuated further. Also, Jeff began to make fun of Rick's "faggoty uniform"—the blue blazer, white shirt, and striped crimson-and-gray repp tie. All legitimate grounds for ruthless teenage mockery, but not great for their friendship either.

Apparently, Jeff had gone through a druggy phase in high school, came close to being expelled once, but straightened up in time to go to Bunker Hill Community College. Rick didn't remember what Jeff did for a living—something in the construction trade, maybe? His balding head was close-cropped on the sides. As a teenager he'd worn it down to his shoulders. Now, as if to compensate for the hairlessness up top, he had a goatee, wiry, gray-flecked. His eyes were a watery blue-gray.

"I think the word got around the high school that the house is empty, and there's this gang of kids who use it for partying and screwing and whatever whatever. If I ever hear them, I show up and shoo 'em away. How's your dad doing?"

Rick smiled sadly, shook his head. "Same."

"Same, yeah? I guess he's—still in that nursing home?"

Rick nodded. "He eats and gets parked in front of the TV all day and that's his life, you know . . . ?" It was beyond sad, actually. It was heartbreaking the way his father had ended up.

"Wendy still out in Oregon?"

"Washington, but yeah."

"And you're the grand pooh-bah of *Boston Magazine?*"

Rick shrugged, too weary to correct Jeff on the name of the magazine, which would also mean setting him straight on Rick's job title, which was no longer any title at all. Plus, there was something enjoyable about being out in the real world, where the news of his firing actually hadn't made it. It was refreshing to visit a place where no one could hear the low beating of the tom-toms.

Which he himself hadn't heard until it was too late.

He was the last person to figure out he was going to get sacked. His numbers—subscriptions and newsstand sales, anyway—were looking great. He'd told Holly he was expecting a raise. There was even talk of end-of-the-year bonuses if the magazine was "ahead of plan."

Later, of course, he found out that the gossip that his days were numbered had been burning up the wires for weeks. Mort had made a couple of disastrous market calls. He'd lost a big bet on a gold mining company and a Chinese timber firm. His fortune had gone poof, just like that. Or so the rumors had it.

Rick found out over breakfast at the Four Seasons, after he'd ordered, before he'd finished his first cup of coffee.

It wasn't that he was being fired, that wasn't it at all; *his job was being eliminated.* Mort was discontinuing the print edition. He could no longer afford the fat salaries and the expense accounts. Anyway, the luxe strategy wasn't working. The ad guys were always having to discount to fill the pages, too obviously stuffing the remnant space with house ads. Time for some disruptive innovation! He was slashing the payroll, letting his overpaid editors go. Staffers were getting converted to freelance, paid by the piece, meaning by the post. Rick was certainly free to pitch stories to the new editor/publisher, a loathsome little squirrel in Chuck Taylors and Ben Sherman and ironic Buddy Holly glasses whom Rick had hired as a web editor a year earlier.

By the time his prosciutto-and-roasted-asparagus omelet had arrived, Rick had lost his appetite.

"Still living across the river?" Jeff said.

"Nah, I'm moving out." Rick didn't want to get into the gory details. Not with Jeff Hollenbeck, anyway.

An arched brow. "Moving in here?"

Rick shook his head. "I mean, for a little while, yeah, but it's time to sell."

"They've been showing it for a while now. I guess no bites, huh?"

Rick spread out his hands. "We got one lowball offer. Place is a shithole."

"Definitely needs work. But it's got good bones. Someone wanted to invest some time and money into it, it could be sweet."

"That's sorta what I'm thinking. Maybe get a carpenter in here, a plasterer, sand the floors, new paint. . . ."

"You're not thinking of doing it yourself, are you?"

"No way. Not my skill set."

"You hire someone yet?"

He shook his head again. "Bank account's a little light. Maybe a couple of months down the road." He said it in an offhand way, as if it was only a matter of time before a tsunami of money started pouring in.

Jeff shifted his weight from foot to foot. "I wouldn't mind taking a crack at it. You know that's what I do, right?"

"Oh yeah?"

"Yeah. Builder, carpentry, gut renovations, the whole nine yards." He pulled a business card from the front pocket of his barn coat and handed it to Rick. It said JEFF HOLLENBECK BUILDERS. "Got a couple guys working for me now. I don't know what kind of quotes you're getting, but I don't mind giving you a break, you know—childhood friends, all that."

"Huh." He'd never thought about Jeff as a serious adult, let alone a successful builder.

"You wouldn't believe what houses on this block are selling for, man. It's crazy. It's like—you know the D'Agostino place across the street?"

"Sure."

"I think they got one-point-five mil for that place, and it's not nearly as nice as this . . . could be, I mean."

"A million and a half bucks? For that dump?"

"I know, it's crazy. I mean, you put some good work into this place, you could get two mil easy. More, even."

"I don't really have the . . . liquidity, I gotta be honest with you."

Jeff nodded. "We could do a deal, maybe. Like, my company does the work and I get a cut of the sale. Work out something that's good for both of us." He took out a pack of Marlboros and a Zippo. "Mind?"

"You kidding? Anything to get that cat piss smell out of my nostrils."

Jeff chuckled as he lit a cigarette. "Luckily I don't smell it."

"Upstairs in my dad's office, that's where it's bad. Plus, we've got critters living inside the walls."

Jeff exhaled twin plumes of smoke. "So what do you think?"

Rick was quiet for a long moment. He thought, *What the hell*. This could be fairly painless. "When could you start?"

"Anytime. Like now."

"Business slow?"

"Always slows down in the winter. I mean, I've got a couple of big jobs lined up starting March or April. . . ."

"It's an interesting idea. If we can work it out, I mean."

"Well, so think about it. Meanwhile, let me check out what that smell is upstairs. I got a pretty good idea I know."

Jeff followed Rick up the stairs. "Jeez," he said, toeing the condom wrapper. "Can't even clean up their own shit."

When they got to the study, Jeff said, "So that was the crash I heard." He snorted. "Oh yeah, I smell it now. That's nasty. Hold on, I'll be right back."

He galumphed down the staircase. Rick was picking up the larger pieces of glass when Jeff appeared in the doorway, a shop broom and dustpan in one hand and a crowbar in the other.

"Thought you could use this." He handed Rick the broom and dustpan. Then, waggling the crowbar, he said, "If you're serious about doing work on the place, I can open up the wall and see what the problem is."

Rick shrugged. "Go for it, why not."

Jeff walked carefully to the middle of the room, weaving around and through the broken glass. Then he stood, head cocked, listening. A moment later, the rustling started up again. Jeff followed the sound to the back wall, then stood still for a few seconds more. He opened the closet door, heavy and paneled, with an ornamented brass knob. He noticed the dangling string, the pull cord, and tugged it to switch on the bare bulb mounted on the canted ceiling.

Jeff nodded, smiled. "They're in the crawl space. Squirrels, I betcha. They get in through roof vents or they chew holes in the soffit. Evil little buggers."

He hoisted the crowbar and slammed its hooked end into the back wall of the closet. A chunk of the wall came away with a screech. It wasn't plaster and lath, Rick saw, but a flat piece of plywood, ten or twelve inches across, a couple of feet long.

"Here she comes," Jeff said. "Easy."

Jeff stepped aside as the long board toppled to the closet floor in a cloud of plaster. A tall hole had opened in the back wall of the closet, too narrow to get through, but enough to glimpse the dim interior. There was a *scree* sound and a quick pitter-patter, like rain on the ceiling, the mad scrambling of small creatures.

"Squirrels," Jeff announced. "Knew it." He coughed. "Whoa. Gross."

Rick stepped closer to get a look.

"Hate squirrels," Jeff said. "Nothing more than furry-tailed rats."

Then he jammed the crowbar into the wall once more and ripped out the adjoining board. It squealed as it came out, nails screeching against wood, and clattered to the floor.

"No plasterboard here," Jeff said. "Strange. Like they just painted over this plywood."

"What is it, a nest?" Rick asked. "I don't want the goddamned squirrels running around inside the house."

"Nah, if there's a nest, it's probably on the other side of the house. This right here is their latrine."

"Latrine?"

"Squirrels don't soil their own nests usually."

"Think they're still in there?" Rick asked.

"Maybe, maybe not. If they've got babies in the nest, they're not leaving."

"So now what?"

"Trap 'em, that's the best way. Or chase 'em out of here. Then seal up the holes with hardware cloth or steel mesh."

Rick could now see into the crawl space a little more clearly. In the faint, dappled light—from a lot of little holes in the roof, he guessed—a pile of some sort was silhouetted, a heap a few feet tall.

"Careful where you walk, there, dude," Jeff said.

Rick took a few more steps, through the opening, into the crawl space. He hunched over—because of the steeply pitched roof, there wasn't enough room to stand.

"You know," Jeff said, "if you want to open up some of these walls up here, we can get some more square footage on this floor. Bedroom nook, a kid's room, whatever. Could even put in skylights—that would be nice. I've had good luck with Velux Cabrio balcony roof windows."

As Rick's eyes adjusted to the dark, he moved closer to the pile. A black plastic tarp, on top of what were probably boxes. Now the boarded-up section of the closet wall made sense. At some point in the century or so of the house's history, the crawl space, normally wasted space, was used for storage. Maybe it was accessed through the closet. A trapdoor, a removable panel, was put in. Maybe it was part of the original construction.

"Careful in there," Jeff said. "I've seen squirrels attack people, you know. They don't even have to be rabid. You invade their nest . . ."

Rick tugged at one corner of the tarp, but it wouldn't lift up; it was stapled to another piece of tarp. He yanked harder this time, and a couple of staples popped and sprinkled to the floor, and now he could see inside.

"Jesus," he said.

He looked again. What he saw didn't register.

"You get bit?" Jeff said with a cackle.

The light in there was bad, but there was just enough to make out the engraved number *100* and Ben Franklin's face. It seemed a mirage. He stuck his hand into the hole in the tarp and pulled at the first thing he could grasp.

A wad of hundred-dollar bills, it looked like. A band bisecting the packet, printed twice with the number $10,000.

His hand was actually trembling, he realized.

"Dude, what is it?" Jeff said.

"Nothing," Rick said.

2

His first instinct was to conceal. Without even thinking about it, he swiveled, placing his body between Jeff and the tarp-covered heap, blocking Jeff's view.

. . . view of what?

Whatever was in that hulking pile, a couple of feet high by maybe four feet wide, Rick knew what was on top of it: packets of money. Packets of hundred-dollar bills. Maybe not the whole pile; that would be crazy, flat-out inconceivable. Packets of money atop . . . what? A pile of papers, maybe files.

The whole pile couldn't be cash. That wasn't possible. He tossed the packet back onto the heap.

He couldn't think clearly. He needed to look again, but without Jeff around. Because what he'd seen had blown his mind. He'd held, in his very own hand, ten thousand dollars. A hundred hundred-dollar bills. In one single packet. And that was just the top of the pile.

Money that obviously wasn't his father's, because Len had no money.

"Looked like cash you were holding there," Jeff said. Something about his tone, lower and insinuating, had changed. He sounded more aggressive.

A shadow obscured his face. Rick couldn't see his eyes.

Rick tried to give a dismissive chuckle, but his mouth was dry and it came out *hah*, more scornful than he intended. "I wish." He clambered out of the opening in the wall, forcing Jeff to back up out of the way. "Bunch of old register receipts is what it is."

"Well, let's drag it out here into the sunlight."

"Another time." Rick sounded weary and bored. He glanced at his watch. "I'm going to need to get going."

"Well, now, hold on a sec—do we have a deal?"

"In principle, yeah. But we've got to talk about what kind of work you'll be doing, how long it's going to take, all that."

"Well, sure."

"I'm not thinking a gut renovation, just so you know." Rick put a hand on Jeff's shoulder, on the coarse cotton duck of his barn coat, guiding him out of the room and toward the stairs. "Minimal destruction. Repairs and improvements, mostly. Second and third floors. Paper over the cracks."

"I don't know as I agree about that, Rick. There's rotten wood all down through the middle of the house. Serious water damage. Probably from a worn pipe boot—water's been leaking into the ceiling for years. Or maybe it's from stopped-up gutters or leaking chimney flashing. Rain's been seeping down into the house for years, making wet spots. Causing wood rot and mold. Gonna have to cut out the rotten wood and plaster in some parts. Not everywhere. Just some parts."

Rick groaned. "You serious?"

"I'll take you through and show you."

15

Rick shook his head. "I believe you. But I'm gonna want you to draw up a plan. Put it down on paper so there's no misunderstanding."

"Sure, sure."

"How soon could you do it?"

"I could get started on it tonight. Like I said, it's slow, this time of year."

"Sounds good," Rick said.

As soon as he'd gotten Jeff out of the house, Rick rummaged in the kitchen drawers and found a flashlight. He clicked it on but its batteries were dead. He found a D cell battery nestled among an assortment of stray Ziploc sandwich bags and swapped it for one of the old ones, and that provided enough juice to generate a feeble light.

He went back upstairs to his father's study. Its window looked out onto the Hollenbecks' yard, which meant that Jeff could see into the room. But pulling the venetian blinds closed would cast the study into darkness, and the overhead light was burned out here, too. It also would look strange for him to pull the blinds, as if he were trying to hide something from Jeff.

He left them open and returned to the crawl space. It still smelled of squirrel urine, but now he barely minded. He directed the sputtering beam of watery light at the tarp-covered pile. He yanked at the tarp, hard, and popped some more of the staples. He pulled the flap back and shone the light to see what was there.

It was a neat square stack about a foot and a half tall and maybe two or three feet per side. It gave off a musty odor. From what he could discern, by directing the failing light back and forth over the pile and lifting random packets, it was all banknotes. Top to bottom.

He was able to count 398 packets before the flashlight died. Most of them—290 packets—were hundred-dollar bills; the rest—108 packets—were fifties. He found a dog-eared gas station receipt in his wallet and scrawled a calculation on it. The total was 3,440,000 dollars.

More than 3.4 million dollars.

He felt a strange vertiginous sensation, as if he were plummeting headfirst into space. His head was spinning, swimming. He picked up one of the packets of hundreds and rifled through it with his thumb. He inhaled its musk. He could smell mildew and tobacco, solvent and ink and sweat. Some of the banknotes looked as if they'd never been circulated: They were crisp and unmarked. Others were dog-eared and creased.

He glanced at the off-center engraving of Ben Franklin on the front of the banknote, with shoulder-length hair and a constipated expression. It certainly looked legit, not counterfeit, though he was no expert.

How long had this pile been walled up here? The bills looked new—uncirculated, anyway—but they'd probably been inside the wall for a few decades.

He only knew he couldn't leave them here.

3

He grabbed a handful of plastic supermarket shopping bags from the broom closet—a couple from Star Market and a couple from Whole Foods, from the old days, when they used to give out plastic bags. The packets of cash fit into six bags, but when he tried to lift one of them, the bag broke and the cash tumbled to the floor. He doubled each bag, then hauled them downstairs two at a time, handling the flimsy bags gingerly. When he'd gathered them at the foot of the staircase, he tested carrying two at a time. Not possible; the weight he could manage, but the cash was too bulky. He didn't want to risk a bag failure between the house and the car, cash spilling across the driveway.

Especially if Jeff were watching from next door. Why the hell wasn't he off on a job somewhere, renovating a Watertown condo or building a spec house? What did he do all day when he didn't have a job scheduled?

The trunk of his old red BMW 3 Series—the red had been a mistake, one of a long line of mistakes; cops really did go after red cars more often—was stuffed with crap. A gym bag, a pile of magazines he'd optimistically planned to read on the elliptical trainer, a set of jumper cables. He rearranged the junk, jamming old *Entertainment Weeklys* and *Back Bays* as far back as possible, until there was room for the six bagsful of cash. Then, after looking around outside to make sure Jeff — or anyone else — wasn't for some reason watching, he trundled the bags carefully to the trunk.

Then he got into the driver's seat and sat there, thinking for a moment of where he might take 3.4 million dollars for safekeeping. The obvious place, of course, was a bank. A safe-deposit box. He didn't have one; all he knew about safe-deposit boxes was what he'd seen in the movies and on TV. He seemed to remember a standard size of a few feet long by maybe eight or ten inches wide. Did they come in larger sizes? He assumed you could request a larger one if you wanted.

His bank had a branch office in Harvard Square. He started the car and maneuvered down Clayton Street to Huron Ave, and then over to Garden Street toward the square. He'd begun to think more clearly now, and he started having second thoughts about carting six grocery bags of cash into the Bank of America. Was it even legal to store cash in a safe-deposit box? He pulled the car over to the shoulder in a no-stopping zone and switched on his blinkers.

He loaded the Safari browser on his phone and searched. The answer wasn't clear. Banks had to notify the IRS of any deposits of more than ten thousand dollars. But that referred to deposits into bank accounts. Not stashing away packets of cash.

Still, in this post-9/11 age, banks probably had to pay close attention to the movements of large quantities of cash, right? In case it was connected to ill-gotten gains? Maybe the US government could even confiscate your cash if it thought you were engaged in criminal activity. He wasn't sure, but it wouldn't have surprised him if that were true.

If he wandered into the Harvard Square branch of the Bank of America toting six shopping bags full of cash, mostly hundreds, that was as good as blowing a trumpet and announcing to the world that he was a coke dealer. He would be observed, no question about it—how could any banker who wasn't too busy texting or checking her Facebook page *fail* to observe him carrying in a load of cash? Then the teller would summon the assistant manager, and . . .

It no longer seemed like such a good idea to bring all this cash into a bank.

In fact, it didn't seem like such a good idea to carry his cash anywhere in those crappy supermarket bags. Not just because of the risk of the bags' splitting, but also because anyone could see their contents. That was just asking to get mugged.

He turned off his blinkers and pulled back into traffic and headed back the way he'd come, then over to Mass Ave, where he found a 7-Eleven. Parking the car in a space he could monitor from inside the store, he quickly bought a box of Glad trash bags (ForceFlex, black, extra strong) and returned to the car. Standing at the trunk, about to pop the lid, he suddenly became aware of how exposed he was.

Any passerby, anyone peering out of a car in the honking, snarling traffic, would be able to see into the trunk. All that cash—that insane, scarcely believable quantity of cash—wasn't something you wanted to put on display.

He pulled the car out of the space, turned it around, front end out. Safer this way. Now maybe someone inside the store could see, if he happened to be looking. But there seemed to be no one in the 7-Eleven except the cashier. He pressed the button on the remote and the trunk opened, and there they were, six bulky overstuffed shopping bags, the diaphanous plastic strained to the breaking point. He glanced over his shoulder for the third time, reassured no one was watching, and set to work pulling a big opaque black trash bag over each smaller one, jammed with legal tender.

Then he slammed the trunk closed.

He looked around again, just to make sure no one had seen anything, and then he glimpsed a truck lumbering by with COSMOS SELF STORAGE painted on its side, and he had an idea.

Cosmos Self Storage was a tall boxy cinder block building on a short block of matching cinder block buildings off Fresh Pond rotary, a faceless row of automotive glass companies and plumbing supply firms. It looked freshly painted, bright yellow, like a Crayola box. He parked right in front and locked the BMW when he entered. Inside it was cavernous, warehouselike. The storage units were rows upon rows of converted industrial pallet racks. Sitting at a desk behind a window was a young guy with big eyelet piercings in each earlobe. He answered Rick's questions in a tone that made it clear he'd rather be doing anything other than sitting in a box in a self-storage facility. He slid a clipboard through the slot.

Ten minutes later, Rick had rented the smallest storage unit available. It was located on an upper level, like all the smallest units, reachable only by means of a rolling steel ladder.

Motion-sensor lights came on as he went down the aisle looking for the locker. He found number 322 and pulled the ladder over to it, climbed to the top platform, and tried his key. The lock came open, but it took him a while to figure out how to open the roll-up steel door. *Calm down, man,* he told himself. He took a deep breath, then surveyed the space. The unit was maybe four feet wide by five feet high by six feet deep. More than enough space. Its interior was clean and dry.

It would do just fine. An anonymous locker in a building where no one seemed to be paying much attention to anyone.

He rolled a dolly out to the parking lot and unloaded the trunk.

Ten minutes later he'd moved all six black trash bags into the storage unit. Even though there didn't seem to be anyone else loading or retrieving stuff, no one here but the guy with the big holes in his earlobes, Rick still was careful not to open the bags until he was crouched down inside the unit. Not that he needed to. He just wanted to see if the money was still there, if it was still real. He resisted the urge to count it again. Looking around—the coast was clear—he reached into one of the bags and pulled out a few packets and slid them into the inside zippered pocket of his Mountain Hardwear down jacket. Then he grabbed more packets, stuffing one into each of the four pockets. His ski parka was now worth a hundred thousand dollars.

A little spending money.

When he was finished, he rolled down the steel door and locked the Master Lock and glanced around, his heart pounding, sweat droplets breaking out on his forehead. He tugged at the lock a few times to make sure it was secure.

There was probably only one person who would know how the hell all that cash ended up in the house on Clayton Street, walled up in the crawl space. How it got there and what it was doing there.

Only one person.

And that guy—Rick's dad—couldn't speak.

4

The whiteboard sign mounted outside Leonard Hoffman's room said, in big flowery purple letters:

*Leonard was a lawyer in Boston
has 1 son and 1 daughter*

A sign like that hung outside every resident's room at the Alfred Becker Nursing and Rehabilitation Center. It was meant to remind the nursing staff that their charges were real people with real families and lives, give them something to chat about.

All the nurses and health care aides acted as if they liked Len a lot, probably because that was part of their job, to make visiting family members think that each Dad or Grandma was their very favorite. Which had a certain piquancy to it. Because if Leonard Hoffman did have the power of speech, they'd all love him for real.

He'd had what people called an outsize personality. He was endearing, funny, corny. He loved women, flirted with them in a way that was flattering, that didn't seem at all icky, especially coming from an older guy. Women were always "girls" to him. They were "honey" and "sweetheart" and "doll." If a massive stroke hadn't robbed him of his ability to wheedle and charm, he'd have the nurses glowing around him, wagging their index fingers, mock chiding. He could never resist a pun or a groaner. Leonard, in full command of his speech, would have asked the squat dark-haired nurse Carolyn, with a wink, "You sure you're not Greek? 'Cause you look like a goddess to me!" He would have told the sloe-eyed nurse Jewel, the Saint Lucian beauty, "You must be Jamaican—Jamaican me crazy!"

And they would have loved it.

He'd been something of a lady's man, in his day. He was always a flamboyant dresser, favoring bold striped shirts and double-breasted pinstriped suits like Al Capone might have worn and bright ties with matching pocket squares.

Now he wore drawstring pants and a pajama top.

But life wasn't like *To Kill a Mockingbird*. Lenny wasn't exactly Atticus Finch, and Rick wasn't Scout. There was nothing soft-focus about their relationship. It was tense, distant, frustrating.

"You haven't touched your lunch," Rick said.

The meat loaf was a revolting beige, the peas a hideous electric green. Len, pre-stroke, would have patted his food with his fingertips in response and said, "There, I'm touching it."

But Len now just looked at Rick balefully. His expression rarely changed. He had a penetrating, almost horrified stare, as if he'd just glimpsed something blood-curdling. Rick visited his father almost every Sunday, had done so as often as possible since the stroke, but he still couldn't get used to his father's harrowed expression.

"Actually," he said, "I don't know how they expect you to eat that shit. But they're not going to let me give you any ice cream if you don't eat your meat loaf."

His father turned his head toward the window and watched the Brookline traffic, a gob of spittle on the left side of his mouth. Rick took the napkin from his lunch tray and daubed the spit away.

It had been a bumpy ride since Len's long-suffering, loyal secretary, Joan, had discovered him sprawled out on the floor in his office after lunch one day eighteen years ago. An ambulance had rushed him to Mass General, where they determined he'd had what they called a "left-side blowout." His left internal carotid artery, stiffened and gummed up from seven decades of steaks and ice cream, had burst, cutting off blood flow to most of the left hemisphere of his brain. He had a huge lesion in the frontal, temporal, and parietal lobes.

They put him on a ventilator, explained that he was likely now a global aphasic—meaning he couldn't speak, probably couldn't read or write, and they didn't know how much he understood of what was said to him. Rick figured his father would be a vegetable. Wendy, being younger, deferred to her brother on all decisions.

After a week, Leonard was shunted to a rehab facility, where he seemed to make progress for a while. An occupational therapist had taught him to walk again, which he did now in a frantic, staggering way, swinging his stiff right leg around in a circle. Most of the time he used a wheelchair. His right arm didn't work anymore. The right side of his face drooped. A speech pathologist, a large black woman named Jocelyn, tried in vain to get him to communicate. It didn't look good.

Then one day, Jocelyn grabbed Rick in the hall outside his father's room and said, "He understands. I know he does."

She pulled him into the room and demonstrated by putting some objects on the table in front of Len. A key ring, her watch, her glasses. "Leonard, would you please look at the watch?" she said.

Len moved his eyes to the right and stared, unmistakably, at her pink Fossil.

There was, Rick thought sadly, someone inside there.

But apart from that one parlor trick, Len seemed to make no progress, and a month later he was moved to the nursing home to sit in a wheelchair all day in front of the TV. Rick still had no idea how much his father understood when you talked to him.

He was unshaven this morning, or maybe just poorly shaven, clumps of gray beard scattered here and there like tumbleweed on his chin and his sunken cheeks. His fingernails were long and ridged and yellow, badly in need of clipping.

"Hey, Dad, I'm having some work done to the house."

Len turned and looked in his direction. His expression was hostile, disdainful, the way he constantly looked these days.

Talking to his father felt like talking to himself, except that Rick kept some topics—Holly and all that, the flaming wreck of his career—carefully off-limits.

"You remember Jeff Hollenbeck next door? He's a contractor now, and he's going to give me a good price."

Len stared, blinked a few times.

"Remember I said we're going to sell the old place, now that no one's living there anymore?" He sidestepped the fact that he was sleeping on Len's couch. That was too depressing to talk about; Len didn't need to know.

"So I wanted to ask you something." He watched Len's eyes. "I found

26

something inside . . . inside the house." He waited a beat, glanced back at the door, then back at his father. "Inside the walls. Next to your study."

"I *thought* it was Rick!" a loud female voice exclaimed. Rick turned, saw the aide he liked the most out of all of them, a heavyset blonde named Brenda, swoop into the room. She was probably fifty and wore her thick glossy hair in a pageboy. She wore baby-blue scrubs and had rhinestone-speckled harlequin glasses, which seemed to be an artsy affectation. The rhinestones glittered in the light from the ceiling. She smiled her big gummy smile. "Wait, it's not Sunday, is it?"

"Nah, decided to shake things up a bit."

"Phew, I guess I'm not losing it after all."

"My dad treating you okay?"

"Your dad's a sweetie," she said. "We all love Leonard." They both knew that Brenda had no idea what Len was like, whether he was a sweetie or an ogre. The man didn't talk, didn't even react. But Rick appreciated her saying it just the same.

She glanced at her watch. "It's almost time for *Judge Judy*, and I know he doesn't like to miss that."

"Dad and I are going to talk just a little more." His father had never watched *Judge Judy* or any other court show, back when he was able to voice his opinion; he doubted Len liked it now. And if he did, he had no way of letting anybody know.

"Leonard, what about your lunch, honey?" she said. "Not hungry today?"

"I don't think he's a big meat loaf fan."

As Brenda began to leave, Rick asked, "Do you have a pair of nail clippers?"

"Of course." She swiveled to one side and plucked a pair of clippers out of a dresser drawer, handing them to Rick with a flourish.

"Let's see your hands, Dad." He took hold of Len's left hand and began to clip his father's thick, grooved nails, and Brenda drifted out of the room.

Rick clipped slowly. His father held out each hand, one at a time. It felt oddly intimate. It was like taking care of a small child. He thought about how everything sooner or later comes back around. He realized with a jolt that his eyes had teared up.

He stopped clipping. "Jeff and I were doing some exploratory demolition," he said quietly, "and we opened up the wall next to your study, at the back of the closet." Len's mouth was frozen in that haughty expression, but his watery eyes seemed anxious. They followed Rick's. "There was money back there. A huge amount of money. Millions of dollars. How did it get there, any idea?" Rick swallowed, waited. "Is it yours?"

Len's restless eyes came to a stop, looked directly into Rick's.

"Is it?"

The old man's eyes bore into his. Then he began to blink rapidly, three or four times. Nervously, maybe.

"Are you signaling me, Dad?" His father was able, at times, to blink: once for yes, twice for no. But not always, and not consistently. Did he sometimes lose the ability; did it wax and wane? Or did he grow weary of trying? Rick had no idea.

The blinks stopped, then resumed after a few seconds.

"How about you blink once for yes and twice for no. This cash I found—is it yours? Once for yes, twice for no."

Len looked straight, unblinking, into Rick's eyes, held his gaze for a few seconds.

Then blinked twice.

"No," Rick said. "It's *not* yours, correct?"

Nothing. Then one blink.

Yes.

"Okay, we're getting somewhere." Rick's heart rate began to accelerate. "Do you—do you know whose cash it is?"

Nothing. Five, ten seconds went by, and Len didn't blink. He looked away, then blinked a few times, but it didn't seem to mean anything.

"Dad, who does it belong to?" Rick asked, before remembering he couldn't ask a question that didn't have a yes or no answer. "Let me try again: Do you know whose cash it is?"

Now Len blinked rapidly, not just once or twice. Many times, too many to count.

It was hard to tell, but he looked frightened.

5

He had a hundred thousand dollars in cash burning holes in his down parka and no room on his credit cards. His Citicard MasterCard, his Bank of America Visa, his Capital One MasterCard—all maxed out, all as worthless as Confederate dollars.

He was carrying around an insane amount of cash, with many times that sitting in a storage locker, in a world where fewer and fewer people took cash anymore. Who used cash in any serious quantity? Drug kingpins and Mafiosi. Criminals. The infamous Boston mobster Whitey Bulger, hiding out in Santa Monica, paid his rent in cash, Rick had read somewhere. Sure, you tip bellhops and parking valets with real money. But buy an airplane ticket with cash and you'll have Homeland Security crawling up your ass.

He drove to Harvard Square and circled around for ten minutes, looking for a parking spot, before he realized he could now afford to park in that damned overpriced parking lot on Church Street. At the Bank of America branch next to the Harvard Coop, he deposited nine thousand dollars into his checking account. Then he opened an account at Cambridge Trust bank, across the street, and deposited nine thousand five hundred dollars into it. As long as he kept deposits under ten thousand bucks, he'd be fine. He saw a sign for Citizens Bank on JFK Street and stopped in there.

Now he had 28,500 dollars in three separate bank accounts, with temporary checkbooks to go with them. It seemed like a small fortune.

By the late afternoon he was back at the house. The side door off the driveway, which opened into the kitchen, was unlocked. Strange. He didn't remember leaving it unlocked. He wondered if Jeff had.

When he opened it, he noticed a file folder that had been shoved under the door. He picked it up and flipped it open. It contained a stapled thatch of papers on Hollenbeck Construction letterhead.

It was a construction proposal, clearly done on some template, listing the scope of work. Demolition and renovation, the dates when work was to begin (tomorrow!) and completed (the end of March). A lot of legal gobbledygook.

And a standard payment schedule, including deposit. The cost was reasonable, but there was no mention of any sort of barter deal. Nothing about his doing the work and getting paid from the proceeds of selling the house.

All payments to be made in cash, starting with "Deposit: $8,000."

If there was any doubt about whether Jeff had seen the cash, there wasn't any longer.

He hesitated, thought about arguing with Jeff, then decided it wasn't worth it. He pulled out a pen and signed each copy of the agreement. Then he stepped outside. Jeff's house had been unimproved for decades, except for an exterior paint job not that long ago. The side door to his house also opened into the kitchen. Jeff's kitchen, with its sheer curtains on the door

31

and yellow wallpaper patterned with miscellaneous fruits, its Kenmore range and refrigerator, looked perfectly preserved, identical to the way it had looked when Rick and Jeff were kids. Rick slipped the copies of the contract under the door, along with a check written on one of the new bank accounts. He thought about knocking on the window and asking about the change, the money terms they hadn't agreed to, but decided it was better not to get into it. Jeff had seen something; he'd seen the money, that was obvious. But it was only a glimpse. He had no idea how much there was.

Rick was already zipping up his sleeping bag and arranging himself uncomfortably on the couch when the realization hit him, like a clap of thunder: He didn't have to stay here anymore. He didn't have to live like the impoverished, scraping person he used to be. He could stay in a hotel. He could stay in the Four Seasons if he wanted to.

Tomorrow he'd find someplace decent to stay. Tonight he'd relish his last night in the sleeping bag on the leather sofa in his father's office. Now that he had a choice whether to sleep here or not, he could think of it as slumming, as camping out.

He got back off the couch and walked through the rooms on the ground floor. It smelled faintly of natural gas down here—not squirrel piss—but not alarmingly so. An odor put out by the gas stove, maybe a minuscule leak from the pilot. Behind the stove, the wallpaper was scorched where there'd been a cooking accident years ago. A grease fire from when Wendy had experimented with deep-frying a turkey.

He found the place outside the kitchen pantry where his and his sister's growth was recorded in horizontal lines made with pen or marker. They'd stopped measuring by the time he and Wendy got to high school. Maybe he and his sister had refused to submit to the indignity any longer, the ruler on top of the head, all that. He didn't remember anymore.

He had no nostalgia for the house but couldn't help feeling a slight pang when he saw those lines. <u>RICK—MARCH 2 '85—50"</u> . . . <u>RICK—NOV. 14 '92—64"</u> . . . Between the ages of seven and fourteen he'd had his major growth spurt. The marker on the pantry wall showed it. Soon that would be gone, the wallpaper stripped off, the walls repainted, along with the scorch mark in the kitchen and the divots and dings and scrapes of a house where two kids had grown up.

He went back upstairs, turning off the lights behind him. He cranked up the space heater and settled down to sleep on the leather sofa.

In the middle of the night a creaking noise woke him up.

He opened his eyes. The only light in the room came from the streetlight on Clayton Street. The noise had sounded as if it came from inside the house, maybe down one flight.

Someone on the stairs?

He waited, listened. The house was old and had always made odd, random settling sounds throughout the day, like an old person sitting down stiffly in an armchair. You noticed it more at night when everything was quiet. That was probably all it was.

He turned over, closed his eyes. The leather sofa squeaked as he moved.

He heard it again, and this time it definitely seemed to be coming from the stairs. The sound of a footstep, a heavy tread taken carefully. No mistaking it.

He sat up, felt his heart start clattering, slipped out of the sleeping bag, and then got to his feet softly, quietly. He listened.

Another creak.

It sounded as if it was coming from right outside the closed door to his father's study. He slid barefoot along the floor, carefully—the floor in here creaked just as much as the stairs—until he reached his father's desk. He looked for a weapon, or something that could function as a weapon. There was his father's ancient computer, an IBM, under a plastic dust cover. He slid open the center drawer, looking for something, a pair of scissors, a paper cutter, a stapler, something heavy or sharp. Nothing— just some old pencils. A sharp pencil could be used as a weapon, but you had to get close up, if it came to it, and that he preferred not to do.

He spotted a bronze bust on the desktop behind the computer. A bust of someone his father idolized, probably Henry David Thoreau. Or was it Ralph Waldo Emerson? He grabbed it, cold in his hands, and substantial, and shushed over to the study door. There he stood and waited for another sound. Thought about switching the overhead light on, then decided not to.

He heard another sound. The high school kids from Rindge and Latin? But they wouldn't be sneaking around. When they broke in, they did it because they were sure no one was home. Thus, no reason to be quiet. They'd be noisy. Drunk and noisy. Boisterous.

These were careful, furtive footsteps. He stood back from the door and off to one side. If anyone opened the study door, he'd have the jump on them. Slam them with the bronze bust.

He waited, breathing slowly, quietly. Another creaking sound, this one no closer than the last. He listened, heart pounding, and tried to locate the sound, decided it was coming from upstairs. He could hear the steady creaking overhead now, a sound more interior and muted, the sound of old cracked floorboards compressing, protesting underfoot.

Whoever was in the house—because there *was* someone—was climbing the stairs to the third floor.

He breathed steadily, listening. The sound grew more distant.

The intruder was upstairs.

He turned the doorknob and pulled the door open slowly, steadily, bracing for a squeaky hinge, prepared to stop if need be. He got the door halfway open, just far enough to sidle out, not wanting to risk opening it any farther and causing a telltale squeak.

When he was in the hall, he went still and just listened for thirty seconds, which seemed an eternity. He wanted to make sure the sound was indeed coming from upstairs, not the second floor. His chest was tight and his breath was short.

And the sound was coming from the landing upstairs, the small steady squeak of a heavy tread crossing the wooden floor, moving steadily yet carefully.

He knew which steps creaked and which did not. His bedroom, and Wendy's, had been on the third floor, and he had gone up and down this staircase innumerable times. He'd sneaked upstairs late at night, occasionally drunk or stoned, in high school. He knew how to climb the stairs noiselessly, and he could walk it blindfolded.

It wasn't Jeff—he wouldn't be sneaking around the house, or at least not now that he knew Rick was staying here. Or would he?

What if it was Jeff?

He'd seen the money but said nothing about it, not yet. Maybe he was back to see if there was any more secreted in the house. But then Rick realized: That was farfetched. The money had been behind a closet wall. If there was more to be found, it would be walled up somewhere, behind plasterboard, and reachable only by doing some destruction. No way would Jeff be skulking around the house at two in the morning.

Then who was it?

Rick had a fleeting, paranoid thought. Someone had seen him, despite his precautions, with all that cash. But who? Had he been followed home from the storage unit? But who could have seen him there? Just the kid with the big holes in his earlobes who was barely paying attention.

Maybe someone in the neighborhood had seen him carrying the plastic bags of banknotes out to the trunk of his car. He no longer knew most of the neighbors here. It wouldn't be impossible that someone had been watching, someone brazen and criminally inclined enough to break into the house. Maybe someone had got hold of a front-door key. Maybe someone had broken in before and had figured out how to do it quickly and quietly. A high school kid, maybe.

The more he thought, the more anxious he felt.

If he was going to do anything, it was time to move. Now.

Clutching the bronze bust, he started up the stairs, staying to the front of the first step, then to the back of the second, avoiding the noisy spots where the old boards had warped or shrunk over time, or both. A pallid moonlight shone in through the window. He looked up the staircase, didn't see anyone there.

A board squeaked under his foot, and he froze. He stood still, waited and listened. He heard the footsteps upstairs, still moving along the floor.

He climbed a couple more stairs, silently. Waited and listened. Finally reached the third-floor landing.

His eyes had adjusted to the dim light. He looked around for a shape, didn't see one.

"All right," he said. "Whoever's up here, come out now."

He raised the bronze bust, cocked his arm, ready to slam it if need be, but equally ready to stay his hand if the intruder were just some high school kid, sheepish and apologetic.

From out of the darkness, something slammed into his gut, doubling him over in pain. He toppled, his head hitting the wooden floor, the bust clattering. He tasted blood, metallic and warm. Loud footsteps behind him. He tried to catch his breath, but he'd been hit in the solar plexus, and the pain was sharp and exquisite, as if someone were sitting on his chest, he couldn't breathe, he spat blood. Someone was running, thundering past him and down the stairs.

From downstairs came a crash and a thud and the sound of a door slamming, and the intruder was gone.

Now he knew he had no choice. He had to get out of there.

6

He walked to Harvard Square, limping slightly, his head pounding, and into the Charles Hotel. The pain had subsided considerably. He'd been kicked, or hit, or walloped with something. His abdomen was tender and bruised. His rib cage hurt, mostly when he breathed. He'd bit his lip, hard, when he fell. Other than that, he was unharmed. By the time he'd gotten to his feet and gone downstairs, his attacker was gone.

He had no idea how the man—he'd assumed it was a man—had gotten in. But he had no doubt the man was after the cash. The house wasn't safe.

"I have a deluxe king for three ninety-nine," the clerk—midtwenties, neatly trimmed beard, tweezed brows—said.

"I'll take it." He hesitated. "You take cash, right?"

"Of course, sir, but I'll need to take an imprint of your card for incidentals."

He handed over one of his useless credit cards and hoped the clerk wouldn't run it.

It occurred to him that he could in fact take the Presidential Suite, if the Charles had one. The most expensive suite in the hotel. But for now, just staying in a nice hotel room felt like an outrageous splurge. At least until he determined who this money belonged to, he'd be . . . prudent, as he liked to think of it.

He went to his room and felt relieved to bolt the door behind him. He felt safe. Later he'd bring a suitcase over. He took the packets of money out of his ski parka and locked them in the hotel safe. He took his MacBook Air out of his shoulder bag and did some quick research.

His father's secretary—she'd been more than that, actually; she was his adviser and traffic cop and praetorian guard and personal assistant— was a woman named Joan Breslin. A no-nonsense platinum-haired woman with a South Boston accent, a brusque manner, a tart tongue. And clearly the patience of Job, having put up with Len's shenanigans for all those years. As far as Rick could recall, she had retired after his father's stroke. She was living in Melrose or Malden or Medford, one of the M-towns north of Boston.

He had her phone number but didn't remember where she lived. Switchboard.com was no help. There was a long column of Breslins in Melrose and Malden, none of them Joan. She was married, Rick was fairly sure, or widowed, and she was of the generation of women who usually listed themselves under their husbands' names. So she'd be under John or Frank or whatever, probably not Joan. ZabaSearch .com was more helpful, since it listed ages. Eventually he found a Joan Breslin, age seventy-two, in Melrose, listed under her husband, Timothy.

A woman answered the phone on the fifth ring. He imagined a tan wall phone in the kitchen, a long gnarled coiled cord.

"Is this Joan?"

"Who's calling?"

"It's Rick Hoffman. Leonard Hoffman's son."

A pause. "Oh, my goodness, Rick, how are you?"

"I'm good. And . . . Tim?"

"Yeah, you know . . ." She suddenly sounded worried. "Oh, no, is it—Lenny?"

"Dad's fine. I mean, he's the same."

"Oh, good. I paid him a visit a couple years ago, Rick, but it's hard, you know. Seeing him like that."

"I know."

"I can't. It—it tears me apart."

"Me, too," he said. "Me, too. Thanks for that." He paused. "I haven't heard from you in a while, so I assume everything's okay with the insurance, right?" She'd set up long-term care insurance for Lenny and very generously volunteered to handle all the paperwork for him as long as he was alive.

"Everything's fine, nothing to worry about."

"Joan, I wonder, if it's not too much of an inconvenience, whether I could come by and talk to you for a bit. I have some questions."

An inconvenience. Like your schedule is crowded, Rick thought, between mah-jongg and trips to the supermarket and to the post office to buy stamps, one at a time.

"Talk? I don't know what I—"

"Just some loose ends concerning my dad's law practice. It's about . . . Well, I don't know anything about how law firms operate. Things like escrow accounts and how he dealt with cash and all that kind of thing."

"Escrow? Is someone complaining they never got their retainer back? Because—"

"No, nothing like that. It's a bit . . . involved. Could I drive out to, ah, Melrose, and maybe we could have a cup of coffee?"

"I've got houseguests," she said. "Can this wait?"

Rick agreed to call her back in a couple of days, after her guests had left. But Rick wasn't particularly optimistic. She hadn't sounded defensive or squirrelly on the phone. If she knew something about a vast quantity of cash, she'd sound different, he decided. Evasive, maybe, if she'd been involved in covering something up. Or frightened. Or at least *knowing*, somehow.

He went out to get some supplies for the next few days.

Half an hour later, in line at a supermarket on Mount Auburn Street, pushing a cart full of cold cereal and milk and yogurt, plus some junk food, SunChips and Tostitos Hint of Lime, he heard someone call his name. He turned around.

"Rick? That *is* you. Oh my God."

"Andrea." His face lit up.

He'd barely noticed the woman in line behind him, wearing sweatpants and a long puffy white down coat, scraggly hair pulled back in a kerchief. At first glance she looked like some overscheduled Cambridge mom racing through her checklist of errands.

Andrea Messina had been his girlfriend senior year at Linwood. They'd gone out starting with the winter semiformal, continuing into the summer after graduation, when he'd broken things off before heading to college. He hadn't seen her since. Just seeing her now gave him an uneasy pang of guilt. He'd been an asshole and had never paid the bill.

He hugged her, gave her a kiss on the cheek. She kissed the air. She smelled of a new, different perfume than he remembered, something more sophisticated, but after two decades a woman had the right to change perfumes.

On second glance, he realized that despite her general dishevelment, she was attractive, strikingly so. Even more than in high school. She'd always been cute, doe-eyed, winsome, graceful. A dancer. Her brown hair had honey highlights. Now her face was thinner, more contoured. She still had creamy skin; she'd always had, but in a woman in her midthirties it was particularly noticeable. She'd grown into her beauty.

"Great," she said. "I haven't seen you in like forever and I look like a bag lady." She adjusted her kerchief and finger-combed a few tendrils of hair behind her ears. He noticed she wasn't wearing a wedding ring.

"Not even close," Rick said. "You look terrific. You live around here?"

"Off Fresh Pond, yeah. Don't you live in Boston? Not around here . . . ?"

"I'm doing some work on the old house on Clayton Street."

"Is your dad still . . ."

"He's still alive, yeah. In a nursing home."

"I heard he had a terrible stroke."

He nodded. "It sucks, but it is what it is." He hated that empty phrase — what did that mean, anyway, *it is what it is?* — but it had just slipped out. It was what it was. He'd once done an interview for *Back Bay* with a local hip-hop celebrity who kept saying *It is what it is* and *haters gonna hate* and *I just want to live my life.* "Your mom and dad okay?" he asked.

"Charlie and Dora are still Charlie and Dora, so . . . yeah."

He looked at her grocery cart full of Goldfish and graham crackers, juice boxes and applesauce, peanut butter and Fruit Roll-Ups. "Crazy guess here, but you've got a kid?" He bypassed the question of whether she was married or not; the absence of a wedding ring seemed conclusive. "Or maybe you've just gotten into snack foods in a big way."

"Evan is seven." She smiled. "It even rhymes. But not much longer—he's about to turn eight."

"Evan eats a lot of Goldfish, I see. The five-gallon carton."

"He's having a birthday party. And you're still a health-food nut."

"You mean Tostitos aren't a basic food group?"

"It's got the hint of lime, so you're getting your vitamin C."

He squinted, tilted his head. "Why did I think you were in New York?"

He remembered she'd gone off to the University of Michigan but lost track of her after that. He thought she might have made the obligatory postcollege migration to Manhattan.

"Yeah, I was with Goldman Sachs for about like two seconds."

"Goldman Sachs?" Not what he'd expected. He'd pegged her for a more modest career track, working for the state or an insurance company. Less high-powered, anyway. Goldman Sachs seemed pretty high-test for the Andrea he knew.

"Yep. How's the magazine business?"

"Eh, I've moved on, I guess you'd say."

"Oh yeah? What are you doing?"

"Bit of this, bit of that." He put his Golden Grahams and Cheerios and Tostitos on the conveyor belt and put the green plastic divider bar at the end of his items like a punctuation mark. He glanced back at her again and smiled. "Hey, are you ever free for dinner? Like maybe tonight?"

"Tonight? I mean . . . no way I could get a babysitter last-minute." She blushed. He remembered now: Whenever she was embarrassed or excited, she blushed. Her translucent skin displayed her discomfort like a beacon. She could never hide it.

"Tomorrow night, then?"

"I could . . . I could ask my sister . . . but the thing is, I can't stay out too late. My day starts ridiculously early." She fingered a tendril of hair. "How about I let you know?"

Usually, he knew, that formula meant *no*. But something about her told him that this time it meant *yes*.

7

Rick's ex-fiancée, Holly, had a small studio apartment on Marlborough Street in the Back Bay. She'd moved back into it once their engagement was broken. He should have realized from the glaringly obvious fact that she insisted on holding on to it even after they got engaged that she'd always had one foot out the door. She'd claimed one day they'd be glad "they" had the extra space, for storage and such. Maybe an office.

They'd lived together in a spacious three-bedroom condo on Beacon Street, in the same building where Tom Brady, the Boston quarterback, had once lived with *his* fashion-model partner. When Rick and Holly broke up, neither of them could afford it. They could scarcely afford it even when Rick had a job.

Holly's tiny apartment was lovely, elegant, and jewel-like, like the woman herself, though also a bit cramped and impractical, like the woman herself. Or so he thought when she opened the door in a toxic cloud of recently reapplied Chanel No. 5. He was not in a forgiving mood.

She'd insisted he come over and take away his Wilson Audio floorstanders or else she'd sell them to the building super. She didn't want those giant loudspeakers, and she was in a hurry. The movers were coming tomorrow to pack and move her out. She was moving to Miami. She worked in the fashion division of a luxury branding agency, and they'd offered her a promotion and a big raise, and besides, her mother and sister lived in South Florida.

"Oh, hi," she said as if she didn't expect him. As though he were a salesman, a nuisance interrupting her day. "Come on in."

She'd taken her lunch hour to meet him here and didn't look pleased about it either. She was dressed for work: a black leather motorcycle jacket over a white top that draped at the neck, skinny black jeans and studded black leather booties. Her ass was perfect.

She'd also recently reapplied her lipstick, so clearly she cared what she looked like to him, even though she had pointedly not kissed him. In her business, everyone was always kissing each other's cheeks, even strangers'.

"I've got plenty of bubble wrap if you need it." She waved vaguely toward a few big rolls in the corner next to her vanity. Her nails were painted ruby red. He rolled in the hand truck he'd borrowed from Jeff, navigating a fjord between cliffs of neatly packed and labeled boxes.

"Also, Rick, I'm sorry to have to ask, but you owe me like a thousand bucks."

"For what?"

"The Amex bill. Remember, we had to use mine because your cards were full up?"

"Oh, right."

"I'm sorry it's come down to this. You can give it to me when you've got it. It's not due until next week."

He took out his wallet. "*Like* a thousand?"

"Eleven twenty-five, to be exact. One thousand, one hundred twenty—"

"I can do math." He shucked out eleven hundred-dollar bills, searched for a twenty, found a fifty instead, and handed her the sheaf.

"Whoa, someone's flush all of a sudden." She smiled, displaying her perfectly upturned upper lip, her perfect teeth. Her parents had not stinted on their two beautiful daughters' orthodontia.

"Sold some of my dad's stuff." He began wrapping each speaker in bubble wrap and then fiddled with a complicated packing-tape dispenser, gave up trying to make it work, and scratched the end up from the roll of tape. "Congrats on the promotion," he said. *Doing whatever it is you do, but for more money.* "What's the new gig?"

She did something involving "brand positioning," developed "brand voices" for her clients, doing image and messaging revamps for fashion designers. Solving for a brand's "challenge," delivering an "impactful" message, working on the engagement strategy and developing actionable plans to deliver agreed-upon goals.

Or some such mumbo jumbo. It was all just verbal Styrofoam anyway. Packing peanuts of meaninglessness. It was a job, something that paid the rent between modeling gigs, which weren't all that plentiful in the Boston market. Her company's motto was brilliantly stupid: "Simplify." Maybe he should have paid more attention: When it came to their relationship, her "engagement strategy" had been to simplify him out of her life.

"I'll be—" she started. Then: "Like you're actually interested."

"Of course I'm interested." A car alarm went off somewhere nearby.

"Anyway," she said, "it's a lot more responsibility and a thirty percent bump in pay, and I get to move back to Miami so I can be there to help out Mom."

"How is Jackie doing? Is the lupus flaring up again?"

"Rick, okay, you can stop now."

"Stop what?" He slid the hand truck's nose plate under one bubble-swathed speaker and realized this was going to take two trips out to the car.

"Pretending you ever gave a shit."

"Not this again," he said with a groan.

"I'm sorry, Rick, but you were so not ready for marriage. I have no idea why you even proposed." She'd sold the diamond engagement ring for not much money to a jeweler downtown. He thought they should have at least split the proceeds, but he was too demoralized to wage battle over it.

"Because I wanted to spend the rest of my life with you. Which, by the way, you were totally into until the paychecks stopped."

"Oh, please." She put one hand on her slender waist. She was in even better shape than when they lived together. Mourning their engagement obviously hadn't kept her from Pilates. "You couldn't have been less interested in my inner life. I was an . . . accessory. Every time we walked into a party or a fund-raiser it was so clear I was just your arm candy. You were so into the way other people were looking at me. You showed me off like I was your goddamned fire engine–red midlife-crisis Ferrari Testarossa. *Eat your heart out, look who I'm tapping.*"

He bristled a bit. "You just didn't want to live in poverty, and you finally figured that out."

"No, Rick, I figured *you* out. You were always clocking who's up and who's down. I was that tall blonde who looks great in tennis whites. You loved the idea of making other people jealous."

"That's not true. I loved you."

"No, Rick. You loved *that*."

He shook his head and scowled, but something acid at the back of his throat told Rick she might have a point.

8

Music was blasting from the house on Clayton Street by the time Rick pulled up in his red BMW the next morning, angry-sounding rap, so loud it was distorted. He parked behind an old Ford flatbed truck, a beater with DEMO KING TRASH-A-WAY painted on its side, and not by a professional.

The front door was wedged open. Plaster dust was everywhere. Three guys in white polypropylene coveralls and white plastic helmets, wearing respirators, were tearing off chunks of wall. Plaster chips were flying. The floors were covered with Masonite panels duct-taped together. A gray plastic trash barrel was heaped with scrolls of ancient wallpaper and scraps of lumber with nails sticking out.

A radio blared: *You ain't gotta like it 'cuz the hood gone love it.*

"What the hell?" Rick said, but the guys in the white suits didn't hear him. One of them was prying off a door casing, the nails screeching a protest as they pulled out.

I'mma kill it . . . I buy a morgue in a minute.

"There he is! You better put one of these on." Jeff handed Rick a dust mask, a white cup with elastic loops. "You don't want to breathe that shit."

"Where's all the furniture?"

"DeShawn and Marlon and Santiago have been working since seven—they moved stuff into the basement. Put tarps on it and all that." He reached down and shut off the radio or CD player. The guys in the white suits turned to look. "DeShawn, Santiago, Marlon, this is Mr. Hoffman. He's the owner."

The three workers were huge, tatted guys, two black and one Hispanic, one bigger than the next. One of the black guys thrust out his hand. "Marlon."

"Rick."

The other two just nodded, regarding him suspiciously.

"Demo crew?" Rick asked Jeff.

"Construction, too. They do everything for me. I don't use subs. Keeps the costs down." He pointed toward one of the trash barrels. "You see the black mold on that plaster? It's bad." Then he pointed to a big section of the wall that was open. "The old lath-and-plaster construction. They put horsehair in the plaster, which makes it a real pain in the ass when it comes to demo. I get hives."

"How long is this going to take?"

"Demo, a week, maybe. Most of the house gets left intact. But you're not staying here. I, uh . . . I notice you didn't spend the night here."

"Glad I didn't."

"Back to your apartment across the river?"

"I stayed . . . with a friend. You got a minute? We need to talk."

Jeff looked at him curiously, shrugged. "Sure."

One of the guys, either DeShawn or Santiago, flicked the boom box back on. The angry rap blasted: *Get out the way, bitch, get out the way.* They resumed hurling chunks of plasterboard and scraps of timber out of the second-floor window into the Dumpster below.

Rick signaled outside and they stepped onto the front porch.

"I signed the contract," he said, "but that wasn't our deal." Rick wanted it out in the open. He wanted Jeff to acknowledge it.

"These guys need to be paid," Jeff said.

"I thought you were planning to front the money."

"I don't normally do that, front the money. Anyway, things have changed."

"Oh yeah?"

"Look, I didn't want to say anything about this, but you know, we've been helping out your family for years. All those years, Meghan and I kept an eye on your house. When you had those sketchy renters, we let you guys know. I used to shovel the driveway when the snowplow service didn't show up."

Rick blinked a few times, surprised. He knew Jeff and his medical-receptionist wife, Meghan, had been vaguely helpful, but didn't know the specifics. He wondered if this was going where he feared it might be going.

"I appreciate all that, Jeff. A lot. You guys have been great."

"I'm just saying. All these years, we never said anything about it. Plus the guys. They need to be paid."

"What happened to our arrangement?"

"Like I said, things have changed. You can afford a hell of a lot more than forty thousand bucks for the job, and you know it."

"Jeff, I don't know how much you—"

"You really want to have this conversation?" Jeff's eyes glittered, as if maybe he did.

Rick felt his stomach flip over. He heaved a sigh.

"I'm thinking maybe I'm owed a little . . . consideration," Jeff said.

"Consideration."

"You know what I'm saying."

He paused, decided to change the subject. "Let me ask you something. You see anyone around the house a couple nights ago? I mean, middle of the night."

Jeff shrugged, shook his head.

"The kitchen door was unlocked. You weren't in the house, were you?"

"I don't know what you're talking about."

"Someone came in, was snooping around."

"Didn't see anyone. Sorry."

Rick noticed that one of the guys in the white suits was standing at the front door, watching them. The guy pushed open the glass storm door and said, "Jeff, you want us start filling up the Dumpster?"

"Yeah, Santiago, you and Marlon cart out the scraps. DeShawn can keep at what he's doing."

Santiago peered at Rick, then over to Jeff, and said something in Spanish. Jeff answered him in Spanish, sounding fluent. Santiago laughed gutturally and said something back, this time clearly looking at Rick as he spoke. He was gesturing with his hands. Then he turned and headed back inside, letting the storm door slam behind him.

Rick didn't know Spanish, but he understood one word Santiago had said.

Dinero.

9

Jeff knew about the money. He'd seen it, that was clear. But how much did he know? Jeff was smart, no question about it. He had a builder's gift of space perception—had he somehow extrapolated, based on his glimpse of the hundred-dollar bills, how much was there?

Though they'd known each other since they were both kids, Rick didn't know Jeff well. But Jeff had always struck Rick as basically honest. Salt of the earth. A Good Samaritan, maybe. He wasn't going to do anything threatening or violent, Rick was confident.

Nearly confident, anyway.

The guys in the demo crew Rick wasn't so sure of. They were huge, and their tattoos looked like prison ink. If they found out about the cash, they could be serious trouble. Greed brought out the worst in people.

Back in his hotel room, his mind went to Andrea Messina, and he opened his laptop. A quick Google search turned up a LinkedIn profile, showing her employed at Goldman Sachs in New York as a banker. The entry had to be out of date. He could imagine the rest of her story line. She marries a fellow investment banker or a trader at Goldman, gets pregnant, has a baby—and then the marriage implodes. The Goldman guy's an asshole. Not exactly front-page news. She gets divorced and moves back home to Cambridge, where her mother's available to be part-time babysitter. Or something along those lines, anyway. Hubby visits his kid two, maybe three times a month. She's used to pulling in big bucks at Goldman, and now she's living at home with Mom. A long slide down the razor blade of life. Welcome to the club.

His feelings toward Andrea were complicated. He was surprised at how attractive he found her. He also felt a considerable degree of guilt. He'd been a jerk in high school. He wanted to apologize, but it was twenty years too late.

At least he could try to make it up to her. He called the best restaurant in Boston, a place called Madrigal. *Back Bay* regularly ran pieces on the chef and reviews, and he knew that you had to call them a month or more in advance to get a reservation. If you were lucky and had strings to pull. Plus, it was preposterously expensive, rivaling New York spots like Per Se or Masa. The girl on the other end of the phone had no idea, when he identified himself as Rick Hoffman from *Back Bay* Magazine, that he'd been fired. They knew his name. They might have cared more about what Zagat or Michelin thought, but they preferred to stay on *Back Bay*'s good side, even if it was now only a website.

He got a table for two that evening at eight.

The problem was—though it really wasn't much of a problem at all, he realized—that he didn't have anything decent to wear on his date with Andrea tonight. His good clothes had been sold. What remained in his few suitcases was mostly jeans and casual attire, the stuff he couldn't sell online, not what you'd wear to Madrigal.

And he wanted to look good for her. He was fronting, he knew: He wanted to look successful even if he felt like an enormous failure.

He debated taking his car into Boston. Then he thought about the difficulty of finding a parking space in the Back Bay and settled on the easiest, if most expensive option. He'd take a cab, reminding himself he didn't have to worry what it cost.

He got out on Newbury Street in front of one of the few stand-alone buildings on the street, which was lined mostly with three- or four-story row house brownstones. This was a magnificent redbrick mansion, originally built in the nineteenth century as a single-family residence. Now it housed the most exclusive men's clothing store in town, Marco Boston. Marco was where Mort Ostrow was outfitted, at least until his calamitous financial blunder.

Ostrow had taken Rick in here a couple of times. Rick had seen a pair of socks selling for a hundred dollars, a baseball jersey selling for twenty-three hundred dollars. He'd seen cashmere jogging suits and ostrich vests and lizard-leather boots and a kangaroo-hide jacket. The price tags had commas but no decimals.

Inside, the store was spare and imposing. The floors were polished concrete. There were no clothing racks; items were brought out and displayed with hushed reverence. Here and there were austere floral arrangements, white calla lilies and orchids. A ten-foot-long library table had exactly three sweaters on it, each folded into a perfect square. An antique tapestry hung on one wall. An immense crystal chandelier twinkled overhead.

A couple of clerks—*sales associates*—were murmuring off to one side as he entered, a slender man all in black and a severe woman in a black pencil skirt and a charcoal cardigan. The woman drifted toward him and asked, "How may I be of service?" Then she cocked her head in recognition. "Welcome back."

"Thanks." She was good. Now he remembered her waiting on him the last time he was here, in the lower-priced section of the store, on the top floor. That was where they sold the Marco's Own line. Which still wasn't cheap, not even close, just not as ridiculously expensive.

"Mr. . . . Hoffman, isn't it? Sheila."

Surprised she remembered, he smiled. "Nice to see you again."

"Shall we take a ride to the fourth floor?"

"Sure. Actually, you know what? The hell with that. Maybe I can find something I like on this floor."

He sat in an antique leather French club chair in his own private changing-room suite, while Sheila rounded up a couple of blazers and shirts and pants she thought he'd like. Meanwhile, a white-gloved butler served him a flute of excellent Champagne. Rick half expected to get a foot massage ("Care for a bit of reflexology?") as he compared Massimo Bizzocchi ties. He could have been the sultan of Brunei.

Sure, he could have picked up a jacket and a pair of pants at J.Crew or at Brooks Brothers, down the street. But somehow that felt lame. It felt . . . inadequate to the occasion. He was going on a date with a lovely and intelligent woman at the fanciest, most expensive restaurant in Boston, and he'd rather not look like a suburban dad driving the carpool to soccer practice on Saturday morning.

This would be his first date since Holly had kicked him out. And it wasn't just with an ex-girlfriend. It was with a woman with whom he'd clearly screwed up. No, that wasn't even it. He'd been a jerk, plain and simple. He felt a twinge of embarrassment, of shame, remembering what he'd been like as a high school senior, what an asshole he'd been. He was going to Northwestern, to the Medill School of Journalism, and then he was going to become the next Bob Woodward. Whereas Andrea was sweet and pretty, but she wasn't going anywhere. Or so he'd thought. When he broke things off after graduation, he explained they were moving in different directions. He was going far and fast and wanted to travel light. He didn't want to check any baggage. Back then, with a young man's arrogance and obliviousness, he hadn't wanted the entanglement. He was ambitious, and she didn't seem to be, didn't seem to fit the profile. She wasn't right for him.

Truly: What an asshole.

And almost as bad: He'd completely misread her. He'd got her completely wrong. He'd underestimated her. She wasn't just some around-the-way girl; she was a Goldman Sachs woman. She was a go-getter. She was one of those high-powered women who appeared in the photos *Back Bay* magazine used to run. And she was smart. And lovely.

He wasn't going to misread her again, and he wasn't going to screw up again. He was going to take her out to have an amazing meal at a romantic, high-end restaurant, and he'd be damned if he was going to look like some zhlub. He thought about how gorgeous Andrea was in the supermarket, and that had been without makeup, after running. He was going to look great, stylish, no matter what the cost. He wasn't just going to look like his old self; he was going to look better. And *he wasn't even going to look at the price tags.*

Sheila returned with another associate, their arms full of hangers. A good number of the items were immediate rule-outs, the ones that were so fashion-forward they were silly. He had no use for rib-paneled denim biker's pants or polka-dotted trousers or monk-strap A. Testoni shoes made of alligator skin, and some of the jackets looked as if they could have been Soviet-era Red Army surplus. But once Sheila understood that he wanted to look elegant and understated and not like a pimp or a Russian oligarch, she started to bring out the right things. An old Cole

Porter song was running through his head like a soundtrack to his life, something he'd heard someone cover—was it Jamie Cullum, or maybe Michael Bublé? "I'm Getting Myself Ready for You." He was so over feeling and looking like a loser. Maybe he was unemployed, but now all of a sudden he was rich, unequivocally so, and it was time to look like it.

"All right," Sheila said, materializing again with yet another garment on a hanger. "With your physique? This unstructured cashmere blazer would look *fabulous*."

The butler brought a second flute of Champagne, and Rick took it with a crooked smile. This was a nice life. He could get used to it.

On his way out, clutching a couple of chocolate-brown Marco garment bags and a large brown cloth shopping bag, he heard someone calling his name.

"Rick? Is that you?"

It was Mort Ostrow, entering the store as Rick was going out. Ostrow drew back and gave Rick a gimlet-eyed appraising look. "Doing a little clothes shopping?"

With a polite smile, Rick said, "Hi, Mort."

Ostrow actually stroked one of the garment bags as if it were a cherished pet. "Well, you certainly seem to have landed on your feet."

"I'm doing okay." Rick was suddenly at a loss for words. His brain had frozen.

"Quite a bit better than okay, I'd say."

Rick shrugged, felt his cheeks get hot.

Ostrow smiled thinly. "Looks like someone's paying you too much, and I don't think it's us." He gave a jovial chortle, or at least his idea of a jovial chortle, but his jocularity sounded forced, and something in his tone struck Rick as almost ominous.

10

The town car pulled into the driveway in front of Andrea's house, a handsome classic colonial on Fayerweather Street, buttery yellow with glossy black shutters, slate roof, and dormers. Rick rang the bell, and she came right out as if she'd been sitting there, waiting. He almost gasped when he saw her. She was transformed. Stunning. No more puffy white down parka. Under a black pea coat she wore a red dress with an asymmetrical plunging neckline. Now she had makeup on—very red lipstick that matched her dress—and understated jewelry, pearl earrings and a gold chain around her neck so dainty it nearly disappeared. Her hair was up.

"You look great," he said, giving her a kiss on the cheek.

"Thank you. Nice jacket." She looked over his shoulder at the black sedan. "Uh, what's this?"

"I didn't feel like driving into Boston."

"So . . . I mean . . . wow." She turned around and yelled into the house, "Evan, come kiss mommy good-bye! . . . Evan?" To Rick, she said, "He was upset I was going out, so I let him watch *SpongeBob*, and now he can't tear himself away from the TV." She turned back and yelled again, "Good night, sweetheart—Mommy's leaving!" She waited a moment, ear cocked. "I think I should escape while I can."

As they walked to the town car, he said, "Lived here long?" It was a step up from her parents' three-decker on Huron Ave where she'd lived in high school.

"Since I moved back."

They sat in the spacious back of the sedan as it purred through the Cambridge streets. "I don't think I've been in a town car since Goldman," she said. "Look at this. And you actually got a reservation at *Madrigal*? You must know someone."

Rick shrugged modestly.

"Of course you do. You know everyone in town." She said it with a level gaze, in a lightly mocking tone.

Madrigal's interior was dramatic and industrial-chic—it was located on the site of an old factory—with the obligatory exposed brick, vaulted ceiling, and rustic beams. It had cast-iron chairs, a poured concrete bar, scarred dark wood factory floor, and big rusted chains and gears and rigging placed here and there as decoration. The menus were heavy, fashioned from large copper sheets, and the edges threatened to slice off your fingertips if you weren't careful. The lights were so low, the pinpoint lights so sparse, they could barely read the menu anyway.

While they were deciding what to order, their waiter poured them each flutes of the house Champagne and another one brought over amuse-bouches that looked like tiny ice-cream cones wrapped in little white napkins on a small silver tray. They were hard tuiles filled with salmon tartare and red onion crème fraîche, buttery and savory and amazing.

61

"Oh my God, Rick," she said, eyes widening.

He smiled. "My *bouche* is definitely amused."

As soon as they were finished, a couple of people materialized at their sides to take the napkins from their hands. They each ordered the chef's tasting menu—*champignons à la grecque*, butternut squash "porridge," Wagyu beef tartare, quail *pressé en croûte*, halibut confit, and so on. Earlier that day, Rick had phoned the restaurant to make sure they still had the appetizer they were famous for, an outrageously extravagant concoction called beggar's purses: crepes stuffed with beluga caviar, tied up with chives as purse strings, and topped with real gold leaf. He'd read about them in one of the many pieces *Back Bay* had done on Madrigal. They did still have them, he was assured. He put in a request to have an order of each of them presented before the entrée. A special surprise. "Oh, and can you use osetra instead of beluga?" he'd said.

"Certainly, sir," he was told.

Rick scanned the wine list, as thick as a Tom Clancy novel. "We'd like the 1990 La Tâche," he finally said.

"*Excellent* choice, sir," the man replied, and he patted Rick's shoulder. With a wink, he said, "I think you'll be extremely pleased with the La Tâche."

When the waiter had left, Andrea said, "Hold on, did you just order the DRC?" She was using insider shorthand for Domaine de la Romanée-Conti, the wine producer in Burgundy generally considered one of the very finest in the world. Also one of the most expensive. The only reason Rick knew about DRC was a piece he'd written about a Boston hedge fund manager's wine grotto at his McMansion in Weston. He'd never actually tasted the stuff. The fact that Andrea was on such intimate terms with DRC that she used its nickname, its initials, though—that was disorienting. This was the same Andrea Messina who, when last he knew her, didn't know how to use a corkscrew. *We all grow up*, he thought. Even high school girlfriends. Maybe especially high school girlfriends.

He nodded.

"Seriously?"

"Hey, you only live once."

"That's like . . . four thousand dollars!"

He shrugged. Like it was nothing. A pittance, a bagatelle. He felt more than a little uncomfortable about it.

She gave him a sidelong glance. "Did you just rob a bank? Or does journalism pay better than I thought?"

"And they say print is dead," Rick said, smiling.

"I hope this is on *Back Bay* magazine's expense account. Oh, wait, you said you moved on. Who are you working for now?"

"I've got a number of things going on," he said vaguely. "Online start-ups and so forth." The less said about his employment situation, the better.

There was a gleam in her eye. "What kind of start-up?"

Rick shook his head, as if it was just too boring to explain. He didn't want to lie to her, nor dig himself in deeper.

"Nineteen ninety La Tâche." She nodded appreciatively. "So . . . let's see . . . the grape crushers were getting jiggy to M. C. Hammer's 'U Can't Touch This,' I'm thinking."

He laughed. "How was Evan's birthday party?"

"It was nice. It was sweet. Loud. Nine seven- and eight-year-old boys."

"His dad . . . is he in the picture?"

"Vance lives in New York, so not much. Luckily."

"Vance. Hmm. Didn't end well?" She was divorced, he reminded himself; of course it didn't end well.

"We were oil and water. Chalk and cheese, as the Brits say."

"Goldman Sachs guy?"

She shook her head, clearly uninterested in talking about her ex. "We met at Wharton."

So she'd gone to business school before Goldman Sachs. "And you? When you're not being a mom?"

"I started a little venture called Geometry Partners." She spoke as if he must have heard of it.

He nodded as if he had. She'd left Goldman Sachs to start her own investment firm. A go-getter for sure. He really hadn't known her at all, back in the day.

"Tell me about Geometry Partners."

"You first. I want to hear about these 'online start-ups' of yours."

He drained his flute. A slight commotion caught his eye—their waiter standing at the maître d's podium near the entrance, consulting with someone in a dinner jacket, maybe the maître d', who had an air of authority. They both glanced over at Rick's table, and then the authoritative man came walking over.

"Ah, yes, Mr. Hoffman, may I have a word?"

Rick knew right away what it was. The damned credit card he'd given them to guarantee the reservation. Normally they wouldn't have run the card before the end of dinner, but he'd just ordered a four-thousand-dollar bottle of wine. Maybe they wanted to be sure he was good for it.

This was best handled away from the table. "No problem," Rick said. "Why don't you take me to your wine cellar?" As if the problem had to do with a wine selection they were unfortunately out of.

The manager, or maître d', smiled uneasily. This was awkward and unpleasant for him. The two of them walked to the back of the restaurant near the kitchen, then stopped. "Is there a problem?" Rick asked quietly.

The man bowed apologetically, moving his head close to Rick's. "Would you happen to have another credit card? This one was, er, declined."

"You know, I just remembered—I canceled that card. My bad." He reached inside the breast pocket of his preposterously expensive new sport coat and pulled out a sheaf of hundreds, flashing a wad of Benjamins as if it were a gangster's bankroll. "In any case"—and he rifled through the banknotes like a blackjack player with a deck of cards—"I'll be paying cash tonight." He slid a single hundred-dollar bill off the wad, folded it between forefinger and thumb, and slipped it to the man. "Sorry for the trouble."

"Absolutely, sir—my apologies for the, uh, misunderstanding."

When he returned to the table, Andrea was looking at him with a half smile, her head tilted. "You know, I always thought you were going to be the next, you know, Woodward and Bernstein."

"Me?"

"Isn't that what you always wanted? The crusading investigative journalist? Unmask conspiracies, flush out corruption, all that?"

Rick shrugged. "Well, I don't think I really was—"

"But that was the plan, right? Sunshine's the best disinfectant, all that?"

"A guy's also gotta earn a living."

The tilted head, the half smile. She looked skeptical. Almost as if she could see right through him. Her smile turned a little sad, and she shook her head. He could almost hear her words: *That's too bad.*

"Remember when you almost got Dr. Kirby fired?" she said, smiling. "That whole plagiarism thing?"

He shrugged modestly. "More like, I almost got myself kicked out of school."

In his junior year at the Linwood Academy, Rick became editor in chief of the *Linwood Owl*, the student newspaper. One of the first issues he published contained a bombshell. It accused the legendary, and much feared, Latin teacher (and Classics Department chairman), Dr. Cadmus Kirby, of plagiarism. That June, Cadmus Kirby had given the commencement address to the graduating class of 1994, entitled "Why Study Classics?" Dr. Kirby had passed out copies to all his Latin students. It turned out to have lifted passages directly from a speech by the president of the University of Chicago decades earlier. The only reason Rick knew that was that he was going through a book of Great Speeches he found in his dad's study, in prep for that fall's debate competition, and he came upon some very familiar prose.

Working almost single-handedly, he put out a special issue of the *Linwood Owl* with a seventy-two-point headline on the front page: OWL QUESTIONS ORIGINALITY OF DR. KIRBY'S COMMENCEMENT ADDRESS. In the piece he ran chunks of Dr. Kirby's speech alongside identical chunks of a speech by Robert Maynard Hutchins.

It was as if a bomb had gone off at the school. The response was swift, but it wasn't quite what Rick had expected. Rick was suspended from school for a week for failing to submit the issue to the headmaster's office in advance. Rick had deliberately ignored protocol because he knew the headmaster would kill the issue. Dr. Cadmus Kirby got off easy by blaming "some accidental borrowings" on his eidetic, or photographic, memory. An honest slip.

Rick got a C- in Latin that fall.

"My God, the hell you raised at school," Andrea said. "You were fearless. Nothing ever stopped you. Your dad must have been so proud of you."

"Dad? Want to know what he told me? He said, 'You didn't play by the rules, Rick.' And he smiled. Like he was watching a bloody scrimmage on *Monday Night Football. You didn't play by the rules?* You call that pride?"

She shook her head. "Well, *I* was impressed."

Pleased, he said teasingly, "You must have been easily impressed."

She gasped comically. "Thanks a lot! Hoffman, do you remember what you did to Mr. Ohlmeyer?"

"Not really." Mr. Ohlmeyer was a sadistic teacher who used to stroll through the dining hall stealing food off students' trays. He had a particular fondness for the little bags of barbecue potato chips the school served with sandwiches.

"The way you pranked him with the potato chips?"

"Oh, right." One day Rick took a potato-chip bag home, razor-bladed it open, sprinkled the chips heavily with cayenne pepper, and carefully sealed the bag up. He brought it to the dining hall, and sure enough, Mr. Ohlmeyer stole his bag of barbecue chips, tore it open greedily, and raced out of the dining hall, roaring in pain. A round of applause broke out in the hall.

With a crooked smile she added, "You were always so ballsy, Hoffman." She shook her head. "I bet you haven't changed."

"I've grown up since then. So how'd you like working at Goldman?"

She shook her head. "Hated it."

He was surprised. Not what he'd expected. "It's a pretty high-testosterone place, I imagine. Strip clubs and steak dinners, right?"

"Look, I *like* steak. And I don't mind the strip clubs, really. I mean, so the traders need to blow off steam, and one way is to pay women with silicone breasts to do lap dances for them, since their wives won't. That's fine, I get it. I can deal."

"But?"

"But in a lot of ways it felt like a frat house. Most of the inside jokes are from dumb comedies. If you never saw *Caddyshack* or *Fletch*, you miss half the jokes. 'Just put it on the Underhills' tab!' Like that."

Rick shook his head. He knew they were classic dumb comedies but he'd never seen them either.

A sommelier arrived with the wine and the whole elaborate ceremony: the display of the bottle, the careful extraction of the cork, the presentation of that cork, the tasting, the nod, the decanting.

"Would you like to wait for the wine to breathe, sir, or would you like me to pour some now?" the sommelier asked.

Rick looked at Andrea, who nodded. "We'll have some now."

The wine glasses were as big as a baby's head. He swirled his wine, watched it run down in legs along the side of the glass. It smelled a bit musty, almost barnyardy. He took a sip, sucking it in as if he were drinking through a straw. He'd gone to wine tastings, written about them. He knew good wine in theory. A wine person would probably say this one had a *complex nose*. Exotic hints of anise and soy sauce, floral and herbal notes, and a long finish. At least, that's how the wine gurus would probably put it. He decided the wine was probably excellent. It had to be. It cost a thousand dollars a glass.

Andrea was watching him, her head tilted, a wry smile, amused. He noticed her crooked tooth in the corner of her smile, and he smiled back. She used to be cute. She'd become gorgeous. She was also confident in ways she'd never been before.

She took a sip and nodded. "I'm sure it's great. But it's definitely wasted on me."

Four thousand dollars and neither of them was experiencing a sensory orgasm. *At least*, he thought, *it's not my money.*

"So you didn't get the jokes," Rick said, back to Goldman Sachs.

She shrugged. "You play along. So you're trading credit derivatives. Credit default swaps. You're basically betting against some poor cash-strapped company and hoping they go down the tubes so you'll get rich, cashing in your death-spiral convertibles—oh, sorry, I meant 'floating convertibles.' You're inside the donut machine making . . . synthetic collateralized debt obligations and selling them to rich schmucks. Arcane, exotic financial instruments no one understands. And so what?"

Rick didn't understand most of what she'd just said. She might as well have been speaking Serbian. He took another sip of wine. He could taste a little cherry, some tannin in the aftertaste. It was actually quite good. It was definitely opening up. "But at least you're making good money."

"Crazy money. Ridiculous money. Enormous amounts of disposable income. But you know what? You've got no time to spend it anyway. Because you're working a hundred hours a week or more and that's all you're doing. You have no life."

Rick nodded. "I get it." He took another sip. He noticed a grapefruit note, and something dark and dusky, almost bricklike. It was truly a spectacular wine.

"I mean, you spend every minute of your day buying and selling shit for someone else. Really. That's all you're doing. Meanwhile, you're looking at the hedge fund guys and thinking, how come I don't bring home *that* kind of money? If they ever stopped to think about it, which they usually don't, they'd consider it a waste of a life. I mean, I think that's why some of those guys throw their money away without even thinking about it, so they can at least have something to show for all that wasted life. So they can feel their life has some kind of meaning. So they can tell people they saw Paul McCartney or Sting on the beach at Saint Bart's. Or they'll go to Per Se and dump thousands of bucks for a single bottle of . . . of freaking fermented *grape juice*, you know?" She lifted her giant wine glass. "It's stupid. It's *obscene*. It's gross." Then she smiled. "No offense."

Rick smiled back, starting to feel a little queasy. "So Geometry Partners is, uh, what, a hedge fund?"

"Oh," she said with a quick, musical laugh. "Oh, God no. It's—well, I took some of the money I made in the Distressed Opportunities Fund at Goldman and started this little nonprofit. We try to make low-income kids fall in love with geometry."

It was his turn to laugh. "So you mean *actual* geometry."

She nodded. "I did Teach for America for a year before Wharton, and, well, I liked it, but I figured I could do a lot better someday. Just dealing with math—you remember how much I loved math, right? I mean, geometry is so concrete. It's so visual. It's real world. It's buildings and houses and rockets and baseball—the angle of a pitch, right?—the sun and the moon. And if you bring it to them that way, kids *get* it. They love it. They realize they might actually be good at math, and that gives them the confidence to do well in school."

Rick nodded, took another sip of the four-thousand-dollar wine, which was starting to taste a little like a horse barn.

"We bring in math teachers and train them how to make math fun—we pay them for it, of course—and then we get the kids in there, and the damn thing is, it *works*, Rick. Like today—there's this kid Darnell who goes to this school in Dorchester, and the teachers all hated him because he was so hostile. His brother's in prison and his mother has a drug problem. I mean, Darnell's exactly the kind of kid the gangs would love to sweep up, help them count keys of coke or cash or whatever. You can just see him disappearing into the life. But today I was showing him this math game on the iPad? And I could see him transform before my eyes—that hostility, that wariness—it was all gone. He was *into* it. He felt empowered. And I think—I don't know, maybe I'm crazy, but I think this kid might . . . just might . . . make it." Her eyes were moist, shining. "Distressed opportunities? One day it just popped into my head: How about public education? Isn't *that* a distressed opportunity?"

Rick had fallen silent. He was fairly drunk by now from the Champagne and the wine, and his head was reeling. He hadn't just underestimated Andrea. He realized he never knew her.

A couple of waiters appeared with golden plates, which they set down in front of Andrea, then Rick. Rick peered bleakly at the obscene display, crepes stuffed with caviar, tied up with chives, actual gold leaf on top of each one. They were loathsome now to look at, and besides, Rick had lost his appetite.

"Sir, madam? Your beggar's purses. Osetra instead of beluga, just as you requested!"

"Thank you," Rick said weakly.

Andrea glanced from her plate to Rick's eyes. Her smile now seemed chilly. "Beggar's purse, huh?" she said.

11

When he got back to his king-size bed at the Charles, he was unable to sleep. He was drunk. The hotel room tilted on its axis, wobbled, and capsized. He thrashed around the bed as he replayed the evening over and over, agonized. How could he have been such a buffoon? Jesus! What the hell was he thinking, throwing money around like that? He saw himself through Andrea's eyes, and it was painful. He might as well be one of those Goldman Sachs dicks she despised. The ridiculous beggar's purses. *Beggar's purses*—could there possibly be a more offensive name? And that . . . *four-thousand-dollar* bottle of La Tâche, wasted on both of them.

He could almost hear her words playing in an echo chamber. *They'll go to Per Se and dump thousands of bucks for a single bottle of . . . of freaking fermented* grape juice, *you know? It's stupid. It's* obscene. *It's gross.*

He was no better than one of those swaggering, splurging, callow investment bankers whose life was hollow and meaningless. He was just the kind of asshole she was railing about. Exactly the sort of guy *Back*

Bay magazine used to publish worshipful profiles about. With only one difference: He had less money.

He'd been trying to impress a girlfriend he'd once dumped, to win her over with a fraudulent optical illusion of his "success." When that was the fastest way to repel her. And he'd repelled her for sure. He could see it in her face, now that he reviewed the tapes of the evening, the way her smile had gone from sweet and nervous and hopeful to amused and then cloyed and finally outright disgusted. She saw him for what he was: a tool. A pompous, pretentious, affected jerk.

Yesterday, that three and a half million dollars had been a vast, almost incalculable fortune. And then? Between his fancy duds from Marco (ten thousand dollars), paying Jeff, and the seven thousand bucks he'd dumped at Madrigal, his fortune—which was how he thought of it now, *his*—had been depleted by twenty-five thousand dollars. If he kept up spending at this rate, after a month and a half he'd have nothing left.

He awoke late the next morning, head thick and pounding and mouth tasting like asphalt, as though a truck had driven through it, farting its foul exhaust. He got up carefully, balancing his throbbing head as if it were a fragile globe made of gossamer-spun glass, and made it to the toilet just in time to throw up.

That made him feel a little better.

He went down to the small lobby gift shop in T-shirt and gym shorts and bought a little bottle of Advil and a couple of bottles of water and gulped down four pills right there in the shop. He went back upstairs, changed into jeans and a button-down shirt, and went to the restaurant attached to the hotel and had some black coffee. He was still too queasy to eat anything. A sip of fresh-squeezed orange juice was a mistake; it hit his stomach like battery acid. Eventually he was able to eat a croissant, dry.

Moving slowly and gingerly, he took the elevator down to the parking garage beneath the hotel and looked for his car.

It was on the second underground level, parked a little crooked. And he'd been mostly sober at the time, except for a couple of flutes of Champagne at Marco. When he thought about how roaring drunk he'd gotten last night, he was glad he'd hired a limo.

Then he remembered: Hadn't his father indicated that the money wasn't his?

Then whose was it?

He knew what he had to do today. He had to find out where this money came from, how it had ended up sealed in the walls of his father's house.

Where to start? His sister, Wendy? She'd have said something after all these years. And she'd have been looking for it: If she *knew* there was money hidden there, she wouldn't be insisting on selling the house. No way did she know about the money.

But someone did. Whoever had broken into the house and attacked him was looking for something, that much was clear. It couldn't have been a coincidence. Once again he ran through the list of possibles. Someone at one of the banks where he'd made deposits? The guy from the storage place? A neighbor?

Jeff? One of his guys?

Rick had been so careful, up until last night, anyway. Because he knew having too much cash always makes you a target.

He'd seen enough movies to know what happens to people who find large quantities of loot. Rarely did it end well. Brother turns against brother, Humphrey Bogart goes stark raving mad. A psychopathic killer with LOVE and HATE tattooed on his fingers comes to town. A lunatic with a nail gun pays a visit. But he didn't want to be in a noir film. He wanted a happy ending. He wanted *Brewster's Millions*, not *The Treasure of the Sierra Madre*.

He took out the BMW's keyless remote and thumbed the button to unlock the car.

Maybe Len's old secretary could help figure it out. He'd have to be cagey about the amount of cash—she might well try to insist that some of it rightfully belonged to her. She'd worked for Len for more than thirty years, after all. And even if she knew nothing about the three million–plus, she could still be invaluable. She'd have appointment books and calendars and ledgers. Somewhere in there would be the name of a client or a friend or—

He heard a quick scuffle, and something moved behind him and then everything suddenly went dark.

Some kind of rough cloth was smothering his face. His throat was vised in a strong grip: Someone had come at him from behind, thrown something over his face, and grabbed him round the neck. He tried to swing his fists, dropping the car's remote in the process, but didn't connect. He tried to free his neck from the crook of his assailant's arm, someone much bigger than he, someone who stank of sweat and mildewed clothing and something that reminded Rick of a barbershop. He struggled, but it was useless. Something was binding his wrists together, some kind of plastic restraint, pulled tight. A hand was clapped over his mouth, atop the cloth.

His legs were free, though, so he kicked out in front of him, hit the steel of the BMW, painfully. Then something slammed into the backs of his knees, and he crumpled to the ground in excruciating pain, but his screams were muffled.

On either side there were voices, male voices, talking fast. In English but with an accent—Irish, maybe. The hand was still flat against his mouth. He tasted something bitter and dirty and organic, maybe burlap. He jammed his heel into something that wasn't steel, something probably human. He heard an *ooof*, a man's low cry. He managed to grab some of the burlap in his fingers and move the hood up far enough for him to see his attacker's hand, a green blob of a tattoo on the inside of his wrist. He heard a car trunk popping open, and then he was slammed against the concrete floor of the parking garage and he could taste blood, his own blood, dark and metallic.

He kept struggling, but with his wrists bound, and being unable to see anything, it was useless. He was hoisted and pushed and gripped and then dropped like a sack of rice into the trunk of a car. He could feel the steel lip of the trunk as his ankles crashed against it. He swung his bound hands upward and hit something hard, unyielding: steel. Frantically now he kicked, hit more steel, felt the lid of the trunk.

Then he heard the guttural growl of a car's engine roaring to life, the dull vibration against his face, and he knew the car was taking him someplace.

And wherever it was, it would not be good.

12

At first Rick was aware of very little beyond the obvious. He knew he was in the trunk of a car, he knew he was being driven somewhere. Gradually he recognized textures and smells—besides the normal automotive smells, familiar scents like Coast soap and Speed Stick antiperspirant. He felt a jug of some sort of fluid rolling around, a nylon gym bag, and an assortment of magazines, and knew then that he was in the trunk of his own car.

His heart raced, his body crackled with adrenaline, he was damp with sweat and terror.

He remembered having dropped his car's keyless remote. His attackers—he could tell by the voices that there'd been two at least—had retrieved it and now one of them was presumably driving the car. Taking him somewhere in his own car.

He struggled to remove his hood. His feet were bound, and so were his hands—but in front, fortunately, which made it possible at least to tug and yank at the hood. But it was secured fairly tightly around his neck. Tied, maybe.

He slid to one side of the trunk as the car took a sharp left turn. The back of his neck slammed against something, but the quick slash of pain subsided quickly. For the moment, he gave up on the hood and concentrated on feeling around the interior of the trunk, with his bound hands, looking for a way out.

There had to be an internal trunk release, a button or a toggle switch or a handle. Didn't all cars have them now, by law? He felt around the lid and the sides of the trunk, feeling for handles or buttons, and he pushed and tugged at everything that seemed like a possibility. But nothing popped the trunk open.

He was weak with terror, and the terror came from uncertainty, not knowing why he was here and what was about to happen. The money, of course—that was obvious: It was the money that put him here. But what his abductors planned to do with him he had no idea. That was even more terrifying, the not knowing.

Though he knew this much: It had to be the construction crew. Who else could it be? Who else besides Jeff—who he was fairly certain wouldn't take part in something like this—knew what he'd found? They'd been talking about the *dinero*. Jeff must have told them, must have given them a sense of how much money was there, or a wild approximation, an exaggeration. The goddamned *dinero*. The hood was their way to ensure Rick didn't identify them to Jeff, their employer. It was crude, and intimidating, and it worked.

Did they somehow know where he'd stashed the money? Were they taking him to the storage place to make him unlock the unit? But if they *knew* where he'd put the cash, they could simply have grabbed his keys. They wouldn't need him along. So that made no sense. Unfortunately, ruling that out meant something a lot scarier. They were going to *make* him hand it over, make him tell them where he'd put it.

He'd forgotten their names but he remembered their tattoos, their muscles, their menacing attitudes. One Hispanic and two black guys, all three immense.

The car slowed and came to a stop, and he heard the car doors open and slam shut. The trunk came open, and hands grasped him roughly and pulled him, stumbling, out. He careened to one side, his knees cracking against something hard, and he crashed to the floor.

He was in a cold, echoey place that smelled strongly of something rotten. A garage or a warehouse. There was a kind of musky, ripe, fatty odor, rancid and — like meat, he realized. Like a butcher shop. And it was cold. He shivered.

He was sprawled on one side on a hard floor. He tried to get to his feet, but he couldn't, since they were bound at the ankles. He managed only to sit, knees splayed.

A voice was speaking to him, at him, now.

"Your rich uncle die on you, Mr. Hoffman?" A man's voice, deep and commanding and resonant, echoing in this garage or warehouse or wherever he was. This butcher shop.

Rick didn't reply. He turned his head toward where the voice was coming from.

Louder now: "I said, you have a rich uncle die on you, Mr. Hoffman? You come into an inheritance, is that it?" A baritone, precise enunciation, very reasonable sounding. A fairly strong Irish accent. And not Boston Irish either. Irish from Ireland. Not a voice he recognized. A guy speaking calmly, not raising his voice, maybe ten feet away.

"I don't know what the hell you're talking about," Rick said, his voice muffled by the hood.

"Cute hoor, isn't he, though?" said the voice. "Who told you about the money, Mr. Hoffman?"

"I don't know anything about any money. You've got the wrong guy."

"I'll ask you again. Who've you been talking to? A simple question, Mr. Hoffman. Because your father doesn't speak. So it's someone else."

"You've got the wrong guy," he said again.

A gusty sigh.

"Let's try again. Who told you about the money?"

"What money?"

The hood over his head was coarse, scratchy against his skin. He heard footsteps on a hard surface far away, echoing in what seemed a cavernous space.

Now the reasonable voice was very close, so close that Rick could smell the eggy breath. "They tell me you're a literary man, Mr. Hoffman. A scribbler. You write on the computer? Type with both your hands?"

"What?"

"My question is very simple: Do you use both hands when you type on the computer? Or do you dictate?"

Rick didn't know what his questioner was getting at, and he didn't reply.

"You know the poem 'Does It Matter,' Mr. Hoffman? Hmm? No?"

"No, I—"

"It's a grand poem. You should know it. We learned it by heart in school." Then he declaimed: "*Does it matter, losing your legs? For people will always be kind.* Surely you know it, Mr. Hoffman. A great poem, and you're a man of the word. *And you need not show that you mind.*

When —" he hesitated — *"the others come in after hunting to gobble their muffins and eggs."*

His abductor was some kind of lunatic, Rick realized with a cold spasm of fear. Completely out of his mind.

"Gents, hoist him up, will you, please?"

Someone grabbed him from behind at the ankles, and someone else grabbed him by his wrists. He bucked violently to throw them off, managing to land one heel in something soft and he heard a snarled epithet before his ankles were grasped again, and then he was lifted, wriggling and torquing his body, and slammed down, his face on something cold and hard and metal.

Then there was a click and a high-pitched whining sound, a sawing sound, quite unmistakable, the sound just a few inches away. A power saw.

"I've yet to meet a man who could stand up to the Butcher Boy. Tell me, Mr. Hoffman, are you left-handed or right-handed?"

Rick unloosed a torrent of obscenity.

An adenoidal laugh, a smoker's cough. "The lip on this one! But you'll want to answer me, because I'm giving you a choice this time. It's your choice. It's up to you. Which one's your better hand, Mr. Hoffman? Left or right? I'll only take the one this time."

Suddenly, Rick found it hard to catch his breath. Panic flooded his body. The power saw whined shrilly maybe twelve inches from where his cheek rested on cold metal. He tried to wrench his hands free, but the grip was too strong. He smelled rancid meat again, and the dark odor of motor oil.

"He's right-handed," the Irishman said. "Let's do him a kindness and take the left. Leave him his right."

"No!" Rick shouted. "God, *no!*"

His hands were yanked across the hard metal surface, the saw shrilling just inches away. "No!" he said, unable to jerk his hands free, and then something cold and sharp sliced through the puffy parka sleeve and into his wrist—and the saw's whine became a shriek, and then there was silence, except for the echo of Rick's own screams.

His left wrist was hot and sticky with blood.

"Mr. Hoffman," came the voice, "my father used to tell us kids, 'The first time you get a talking to. The second time it'll be the strap.' Well, you'll wish it was the strap, Mr. Hoffman. So I want you to think very hard because we will speak anon. Anon we will speak, Mr. Hoffman. And if we find you've held out on us, next time I won't be asking 'left or right.'"

Rick was drenched with sweat, his heart galloping, and all of a sudden he was grabbed by the knees and the hands again and dumped back into the trunk.

He heard the engine's dull roar and the car was moving. With the fingers of his right hand he felt the cut on his left wrist. There was a lot of blood but the cut seemed superficial. The blade had cut through the sleeve of his parka. He could feel the tufts of down spilling out of the slash. Then he noticed that the saw blade had nipped partway through the plastic flex-cuff restraint. He twisted his hands around in opposite directions and yanked them back and forth and finally the plastic broke through and the cuff came apart.

Now that his hands were free, he tugged at the hood and managed finally to get it off. He jerked at the restraints securing his ankles, but what he needed was something sharp, and he succeeded only in tightening the cuff still more.

Sometime later—he could no longer keep track of time—the trunk lid was popped open and he heard the roar of traffic close by. He bucked, thrusting his feet first in one direction, then the other. It was dark, and he couldn't see well, but two bulky men, both with shaven heads, were grabbing him. One got hold of his left ankle and the other grabbed his right wrist, then his left, and he was swung into the air and was dropped hard onto grass.

He could hear car doors open and slam and heard the gunning of a car's engine. He scrambled to his knees, stumbled and tipped to one side, keeling over into the soft turf. He took a gulp of air and saw that he was sitting on the grassy median of a busy highway—he didn't immediately recognize his whereabouts—and that his BMW was parked partly on the shoulder, partly on the grass, nearby.

13

With the notched side of one of his house keys, he was finally able to saw through the plastic flex-cuffs binding his ankles. He stumbled into his car, found the keyless remote, which had been left on the driver's seat. He felt his left wrist, noticed that the bleeding had stopped.

He drove back to the Charles Hotel, but he knew he had to move. He'd been abducted in its parking garage, after all, which meant he'd been followed, which was how they knew he was staying there. And they'd be back. In forty-eight hours, if the Irishman was telling the truth.

If he'd been followed to the hotel, they'd probably follow him *from* the hotel, too. He had to be mindful of that. He had to find someplace else to stay but take care not to be followed, to the best of his ability.

He bought some bandages at the hotel gift shop and, back in the room, applied a few to his cut wrist. Then he took the elevator down to the lobby, then switched to the separate bank of elevators down to the parking garage.

That brief moment, those twenty seconds when he was changing elevator banks was a time of potential exposure. He assumed there were people watching him at the hotel. How else could they have known that he'd parked in the underground garage? He had to assume there was still someone, or several someones, watching him. Probably watching the front desk. He hadn't noticed anyone, but then again, he hadn't been looking for anyone.

As far as he could tell, he hadn't been followed into the garage. No one had jumped into the elevator cab after him. Just to be safe, he'd pushed the buttons for both garage levels. In case someone was watching the lobby elevator banks to see which level he chose.

He remembered there was an Avis desk inside the hotel. But it was in the lobby. If anyone was waiting in the lobby to watch his comings and goings, they'd see him talking to the Avis desk and immediately figure out what he was up to. So he left the hotel through the garage exit and took a roundabout path to the nearby Hertz. There he rented a gray Ford Focus, the most anonymous-looking vehicle in their fleet. Then he drove through Harvard Square and up and down Mass Ave in Cambridge, looking for a place to stay, and soon found a bed-and-breakfast on Mass Ave a few blocks out of Harvard Square called the Eustace House. It was an old gray Victorian converted into jaggedly shaped guest rooms; it had creaky floors and the pervasive sweet floral smell, lilies and chrysanthemums, of a funeral home. He checked in under a false name: Jacob Clayton. He wasn't sure why he used an alias. Maybe because it made him feel safer. He had no luggage.

Then he took a taxi back to the Charles Hotel and asked the cab driver to enter the garage. He returned to his room, retrieved the packets of cash from the safe, and packed it in his suitcase. He called for the bellhop and asked him to take the suitcase down to garage level 2, where the taxi was waiting, while he checked out. Then he headed back to the B&B. Once in his room, he took off all his clothes and climbed into the creaky bed and fell asleep for hours, a clammy, feverish sleep. His nerves were jangled. In his sleep he relived the abduction, over and over, in jolting fragments, a grim slideshow. He awoke at around midnight, then again at four in the morning, at which point he couldn't sleep anymore. He switched on the bedside lamp.

He ached all over. His knees were bruised and tender. The bleeding from the gash on his wrist had stopped. Only the psychological terror had remained, the feeling of powerlessness. Of not knowing whether he was about to be dismembered, or killed, at any moment. The hood over his head. The icy charm of his unseen interrogator, the poetry-loving man with the Irish accent.

He knew he was in this thing deep and that now everything had changed for him. His abductors had somehow found out about the money. But how?

All he knew for certain was that he was no longer safe, and what had happened to him in that warehouse or butcher shop or whatever it was could easily happen again, but with a much worse outcome. It seemed more important than ever to find out where the cash had come from, whom it actually belonged to.

And that search started with the money itself.

He took the packets of banknotes from his suitcase and set them down on the quilted coverlet of the bed. Some of the bills were old, a few were new. He slid one of the new hundred-dollar bills from a packet and for the first time looked at it closely. Printed to the left of Ben Franklin's big head were the words SERIES 1996.

He pulled out his MacBook Air and searched for a wireless signal.

Eventually he connected with a fairly weak Eustace House Guest signal, which got stronger the closer he got to the door of his room. He sat on the edge of the bed and Googled US currency redesigns. In 1996, he discovered, the hundred-dollar bill was redesigned for the first time since 1929. Various anticounterfeiting measures were added: a watermark of Franklin, a security thread that glowed red under ultraviolet light, color-shifting ink.

The newest of the bills in the stash was dated 1996. The redesigned hundred-dollar bill had come out in March of 1996. Lenny had had his stroke in May. Which meant that the money could have been stashed in the house any time after March, and as late as May 27, the day of his stroke. That was a window of three months. So who was his father doing business with between March and May 1996? Who were his clients?

His secretary would know that. Twenty years later she might not remember all the names, but she'd know some. He'd have to push her to recall whatever she could.

When the sun came up and he began to hear creaks and low mumbling from the floor above, he went downstairs and got coffee from a thermal carafe in the front sitting room, near where an elderly couple were eating breakfast and reading tourist guides to Boston. He half expected to see someone waiting for him in the sitting room, someone muscular and formidable. But there were only the elderly couple and another old codger reading a Lee Child novel in a wing chair.

Rick hadn't been followed to the B&B, he was still sure. Then he went back to his room and called Joan Breslin. He left the B&B, down the front steps, saw a few passersby, but no one seemed to be looking in his direction. The rented Ford was parked halfway down the block.

An hour later he was pulling into the driveway of Joan Breslin's house in Melrose.

14

Rick took a left into the housing development and, to be sure he hadn't been followed, circled around the block. Maybe the rent-a-car tactic had worked. For now, at least. Though soon enough his watchers would discover that he was no longer a guest at the Charles Hotel.

Joan's house was a tidy split-level ranch painted an unexpected turquoise. To the left of its pristine driveway, recently reblacktopped, was an immaculate patch of brown lawn, dormant for the winter. A welcome mat made of coco brush the same color as the lawn said THE BRESLINS. The doorbell chimed like church bells in a town square. This was the residence of a couple who took pleasure in order and neatness and routine.

"Rick Hoffman," she said, smiling, her hands out in a gesture of welcome. "Were the directions okay?"

"Perfect," Rick said. "Thanks so much for seeing me."

"I've been trying to guess what the questions are you want to ask me. You've got me in suspense."

Joan Breslin's lipstick was ever so slightly off the outline of her lips. It looked as if she'd applied rouge to her cheeks, though Rick wasn't sure if women actually used rouge anymore. Her hair was shorter than Rick remembered. Instead of platinum blond, it was now a snowy white.

She was wearing a brilliant emerald caftan. Rick had a sense that she rarely had visitors and had gotten dressed up for this meeting. A special occasion, maybe the high point of her week. He smelled freshly perked coffee.

He hadn't seen her for eighteen years, since a few weeks after Len's stroke, when he'd had to sign various legal forms closing down the law practice. Years earlier, Len had drawn up a Durable General Power of Attorney and Designation of Pre-need Guardian, documents that designated Rick as his guardian in the event of his father's incompetence or incapacity. That meant that it was Rick's job to dissolve the firm and close the checking account and all the other annoying little details he'd never imagined actually having to do. Joan had been cooperative and efficient, and she'd seemed nice, and that was about all he recalled.

The house was just as immaculate inside as out, almost oppressively so. Not a single piece of mail on the demilune mail table in the hall. Turquoise was the color scheme: everywhere, the walls, even the wall-to-wall carpet, which showed the fresh tracks of a vacuum cleaner.

She poured him weak coffee in a mug that said GATE OF HEAVEN PARISH. She asked again if Len were "all right," which probably meant whether he was still alive.

"It's funny," she said. "You look so much like him. The way he looked when I first started working for him."

"He's lucky you didn't quit on sight."

They both laughed. "No, no," she said. "He was a handsome man back then."

Rick eased into a conversation about the nursing home and how nice the nurses were, how sometimes Rick thought his father could understand what people said to him and sometimes didn't.

"Your dad was one of a kind," she said. "They broke the mold when they made him, that's for sure." She had a smoker's raspy voice, but he didn't smell any smoke. She'd probably quit some time ago.

"For sure. So I found some records in Dad's study at home that I wish I could ask him about. Notes about quantities of cash he was given to hold on to, something like that."

"Cash?"

"I figured if anyone knew what my dad was up to, you would." He found himself going right into investigative reporter mode, an old groove but comfortable. His reporter's instincts told him to come in at a slant. To be oblique in his questions. This was a lot of money he was asking about, and money like that did funny things to people. It could make them greedy and uncooperative. He remembered that line, a classic, from *The Treasure of the Sierra Madre:* "I know what gold does to men's souls," says the old prospector.

There was also the possibility—the likelihood, he thought—that the money was connected to something illegal. Maybe something she'd been involved in, too. Until it was proven otherwise, he knew he couldn't trust her.

"I don't know how much I can help you," she said. "We're talking almost twenty years ago."

"If a client gave him cash, you'd be the one who'd handle it, right?"

"Well, I was the one who made the bank deposits most of the time. And I had the combination to the safe."

"He obviously trusted you implicitly."

"He did. But I can't speak for what he might have done, or gotten, outside the office, when I wasn't around."

"Right, sure." He gave a slow, easy grin. "Some of dad's clients were kind of . . ."

She raised her eyebrows. Pretending she had no idea. She wasn't playing along.

". . . Sketchy," he finished.

"He defended a whole range of people. And yes, some of them were, well, unconventional. He certainly had his pet projects, your father did."

"Strip clubs, adult bookstores, that kind of thing."

"Our office was a few blocks from the old Combat Zone," she said uncomfortably. The Combat Zone was Boston's red-light district, an area of porn houses and hookers, that by the 1990s was mostly gone. "Your father was a strong believer in the First Amendment."

"I know." Leonard Hoffman: the Clarence Darrow of pole dancing. "Those are cash businesses. I assume some of those clients preferred to pay him in cash, right?"

She seemed to flinch and was now regarding him warily, as if she were a witness on the stand and he were a prosecutor. He wondered why she was being so defensive. She wasn't just protecting his father's image. It was something else.

"It's legal as long as you declare it as income," she said. "You could get disbarred if you don't report your income truthfully."

So maybe that was it. "I'm guessing he didn't report all of his cash income."

"What does any of this have to do with—I mean, why are you asking?"

"Joan, I'm not with the IRS. I have no interest in getting him, or you, in trouble."

91

"I always told him to make sure to report all the cash."

"I'm sure you're the one who kept him in line. But some of his clients were drug dealers, maybe?"

She shrugged. "As they say, everyone's entitled to legal representation." She said it as though she didn't mean it.

That sounded like a confirmation. "Joan, my father was in possession of a significant quantity of cash, and I'm trying to figure out where it might have come from."

Her nostrils flared. "Are you asking if I held on to money I wasn't entitled to? Because I resent the implication—"

"Not at all. Don't misunderstand me. I'm wondering whether he might have been given a lot of money to keep for someone else."

She looked away, peering off into the middle distance. She was silent for ten, fifteen seconds. She inhaled. For the first time, Rick became aware of the muted ticking of the mantel clock. Finally she said, "Your father was a wonderful man with a big heart."

"I know."

"You know, things . . . they don't always turn out the way you want. He might have done some things he wasn't proud of. Let's leave it at that. There's no use in rehashing the past. What's done is done, and that was a long time ago."

"I'm only asking for his sake."

She shook her head slowly. "Your father always tried to protect me. He didn't tell me everything."

"You were the one person he confided in."

She hesitated. "He never confided in me. And I'm sure there were some things he wouldn't want *you* to know about either."

"You and I both want the same thing," Rick said. "To protect Len.

Because he's not able to protect himself. But if I'm going to really protect him, I need to know what we're dealing with."

She expelled a long, rattling sigh. "Look, it's a dirty business, this—this world. The adult entertainment industry, I mean. You know, the police and the city inspectors, they were always shaking down those places for bribes. Massage parlors, you know—lot of times they had to give the cops . . . sexual favors to keep from getting hit with code violations. Sometimes just cash. Shakedowns, that's all it was." She rubbed her thumb and forefinger together in the universal sign of filthy lucre.

"So I'm not sure I understand. Dad handed out payoffs to city officials and cops?" The term for that kind of thing was *bag man*, Rick thought. His father was a bag man.

He thought about his father's reproach when he published the plagiarism exposé in the high school newspaper: *You didn't play by the rules, Rick.*

What were the rules that Lenny was playing by?

She hesitated. "That's how it started. Money went to the liquor board, public health, fire department, all that . . ."

"We're talking maybe a couple of hundred bucks here and there, I'm guessing."

She nodded. "Or more in some cases. With the bigger strip clubs. Lenny just sometimes had to go in and grease the wheels. I guess he came to be known as—well, as a guy who got things done. He was really good at sorting out disputes. Private arbitration, you might call it. He was what you'd call a fixer."

"Was it mostly city officials he paid off?"

"Not just. If someone wanted to build a nightclub and the owner of the neighboring building was being difficult, he'd, you know . . ."

"Pay off the owner."

A shrug. "He handled cash transactions between businesses, too. He'd meet clients for lunch at Locke-Ober's or Union Oyster House and they'd give him envelopes or brown bags, and . . ." She closed her eyes, kneaded them as if she had a headache.

"The day of his stroke," Rick said. "May twenty-seventh. Do you remember if he was supposed to deliver a payment to someone?"

She looked at Rick, squinting a *you can't be serious* scowl. "May 27, 1996? You really think I can remember what he was doing on May 27, 1996? Do *you* remember what you were doing on May 27, 1996?"

"The day of his stroke. When you found him—that day, was he about to make a large cash delivery to someone?"

She looked away slowly now, but not evasively, as far as he could tell. She appeared to be searching her memory. A long moment went by.

Finally she shook her head. "I'm sorry. I can't remember. It's possible."

Rick waited. The mantel clock ticked.

She scratched an itch on her left shoulder. "I have some of the old office files in the basement. The old datebooks and such. Do you think those might help?"

15

Her basement was neat and precise and orderly, more like a laboratory's supply room than the sprawling junk heap that was the basement of the Clayton Street house. Gleaming stainless steel shelving units held blue plastic storage bins and immaculate rows of white cardboard banker's boxes, everything neatly labeled in black Magic Marker, in architect's lettering. There was a faint bleach smell.

"You saved all the office files?" Rick asked.

"Just the financial records. In case he got audited. The client files I shredded."

"Shredded?"

"I asked you guys, don't you remember? You and your sister? You said you didn't want them."

"So how would I find out who he met with on a particular day . . . ?"

"The red book, I'd say. It's like a client diary." She pointed to a cardboard box, and he took it off the shelf—unexpectedly heavy—and set it on the high-gloss-painted cement floor. She bent over carefully, one hand splayed on her lower back, and lifted the box's lid.

Inside were thick red hardcover books, each the size of the Manhattan phone book.

Each red book was titled *Massachusetts Lawyers Diary and Manual.* It was like a desk diary combined with reference book: municipal directories, statutes, directory of judges, all that kind of thing. Kind of like a farmer's almanac for lawyers, only more boring. He picked one up for the year 1989, flipped through it. The parts that interested him were the daily diary and monthly planner. A page for each day. Clients' names and times of meetings, written in what he assumed was Joan's neat handwriting.

In another box he found the book for 1996. He turned to the page for May 27. A fairly light schedule, it appeared. Only three appointments for the day. One in the morning, one at noon, one late in the afternoon. He didn't make the afternoon one, of course, since he had his stroke right after lunch. But the twelve noon appointment he presumably did. On the line for 12:00 it had no name, only an initial: "P—."

Rick pointed at the entry, his eyebrows questioning. "That was his last appointment before his stroke. Who's 'P'?"

Joan took a pair of reading glasses hanging on a chain around her neck, put them on slowly, peered at the page. "Oh, I don't know who that was, 'P.' That's all he told me—someone he met with once in a while." She pushed the glasses down her nose and turned to him. Stiffly she added: "I hope you don't mind my saying, I always assumed it was a girlfriend."

Rick smiled. "Did he always meet with 'P' at lunchtime?" A midday assignation at a cheap hotel—that sounded like Len. Patty, Penelope, Priscilla, Pam. He wouldn't have been cheating on his wife, Rick's mother: She'd died three years earlier, when Rick was fifteen and his father was forty-four. Not exactly an old man, and the guy had a sex drive, much as Rick didn't like to think about it. There'd been a few girlfriends, but no one for very long. His parents' marriage had always seemed contentious. Maybe being married once was enough for Len.

"Sometimes after work. But never at the office. That's why I assumed . . ."

"He never asked you to order flowers for 'P,' did he?" He said it jokingly, but she took it seriously, frowning and shaking her head.

"But if 'P' was a client, there'd be bills and files and such, right?"

She nodded. "She wasn't a client, honey."

"You know this for a fact, or you're guessing?"

"Woman's intuition."

"I see." He hefted the big red book. "Mind if I borrow this?"

She hesitated. "Okay, I suppose."

"The financial records are here?"

She tapped a box labeled CLIENT INVOICES 1969–1973. There was a row of six boxes of invoices covering the years 1969 to 1996, the years Len's practice was active. "Have at it. Take whatever you want. Just tell me what you've taken, all right? Is there enough light for you here? I think Timmy has one of those clamp lamps on his workbench."

"I should be okay, thanks."

After Joan left, he took down the box labeled 1994–1996. It was organized not chronologically but by client, which was sort of annoying. He wanted to zoom in on the period right around May 1996 to see what kind of legal work his father was doing in the weeks before his stroke. But there was no easy way to do it. So he sat on the immaculate polished basement floor and began pawing through the folders of invoices.

Some of the clients were people, some were businesses. Most of the names he didn't recognize. A few he did: notorious strip clubs and X-rated theaters whose flashing neon signs once lit up the night in the four-square-block sleaze district next to Chinatown. By 1996, most of the "adult entertainment" establishments had closed. But a few remained, some of them Len Hoffman clients. Their names were on folders here: the Emerald Lounge, Club Fifty-One, Pleasures, the Kitty Kat.

So what kind of legal work had his father done for them? He pulled out the Kitty Kat folder and found what looked like monthly invoices to the Kat typed on Leonard Hoffman letterhead ("Law Offices of Leonard Hoffman, P.C." Offices plural. As if it were a multinational firm). A couple were for twenty thousand dollars, some for less. A few for twenty-five thousand, one as high as fifty thousand dollars. Some of them said simply "for services rendered." Others said things like "Board of Health dispute" and "Liquor license suspension."

Rick began to feel a prickle at the back of his head. It was as if the old investigative reporter juices, long dormant, were beginning to flow again. He knew he had a great head for investigative work, and he enjoyed it more than any other kind of journalism. There was something here he couldn't quite figure out, some kind of story here, if he could only puzzle his way into it.

The way in, he was convinced, was to compile a list of all Len's clients around the time of the stroke. If he dug in deeply enough, he might find the client—if indeed it was a client—who was the mysterious "P" that Len saw at noon that day.

Systematically, he plucked out all invoices dated May 1996, for all the client folders. Maybe one of them was this "P"—.

Then he reconsidered. Why not take the whole box with him and cross-check thoroughly? In the front of the box, he found a floppy disk marked BANK ACCOUNTS. It was an old computer disk 5 1/4 inches square. They were the latest technology in the 1980s, but was anyone using them in the 1990s? Maybe people who weren't at the cutting edge of technology, like Len and Joan.

Maybe, just maybe, these files would solve the mystery of where all that money had come from.

16

The city of Boston kept all of its old records in a large, bunkerlike building in a remote part of the city called West Roxbury. Back in the day, when Rick had been an investigative reporter for *The Boston Globe*, he'd had occasion to drive out to the City Archives. It was a giant warehouse that wasn't open to the public. You didn't just show up; you had to make an appointment. Pretty much every historical document or transcript or filing was here, going back to before the city was founded by the Puritans in 1630. Rick had no idea who frequented City Archives apart from historians. Some newspaper reporters didn't even know about the place.

As he drove back to Boston, he called City Archives and asked for Marie. Marie Gamache had been there forever and had a buoyant good nature that distinguished her from her more introverted colleagues. She also had a tenacity that Rick admired. She could find anything, any scrap of paper, in the sprawling warehouse. She took on every search like a personal challenge, refusing to give up. Very few of the city's documents before the year 2000 were available online. They were stored in gray archive boxes on shelves that went on for miles. You couldn't do a computer search. The only search engine was in the heads of the archivists, and none, in Rick's experience, was better than Marie.

"Hey there," he said. "Rick Hoffman."

"Oh my God, Rick Hoffman! It's so great to hear your sexy voice!"

"Well, you might not be so glad to hear from me once you hear what I want."

"Uh-oh."

"I'm going to need a bunch of records from 1996. Buildings Department, Board of Health, Licensing Board, Inspectional Services."

"Hold on, let me get a fresh yellow pad."

"You're still not using computers?"

"Oh, hush. Nothing's better than a pad and a pencil, and you know I'm right."

He pulled over to the side of the road and read off to her a list he'd scrawled down in Joan Breslin's basement.

When he finished, she said, "And I suppose you want them all first thing tomorrow morning."

"What about this afternoon?"

"I hope that's a joke."

"I'm serious. Possible?"

"I think the mayor's office is ahead of you in line, and they've got me pulling registry records for days."

"Who's more important, me or the mayor?"

She laughed. "You have a point. Give me three hours."

"You're a doll." As he spoke, he winced. He could hear his father speaking the exact same words. Charming women the same way. He was indeed Lenny Hoffman's son, for better or for worse.

His next stop was a computer repair shop on a quiet side street in Allston. He knew he'd be laughed out of the sleek Apple Store if he went in with a floppy disk from the 1980s. But the Computer Loft had repaired Rick's computers for years and they seemed to be able to fix anything fixable, and it was at least worth a try.

A rotund young man, probably in his midtwenties, emerged from the back. He had mouse-brown hair down to his collar, a full reddish beard, and a small hoop in his septum.

"Help you?"

Rick held up the disk. "You have a computer around that can read this?"

"What is it?"

Rick sighed. "Is Scott around?"

The bearded man ducked his head and returned to the back of the shop, and a minute later the owner, Scott, emerged. He was tall and bald and wore a black-and-white bowling shirt that said HOLY ROLLERS.

"Well, look at that," Scott said. "A real, honest-to-God floppy disk."

"You got a machine that can read it?"

"Rick, there hasn't been a machine made that can read them for twenty years at least. I mean, I think the Apple II used them, back in the early nineties."

"Do you happen to have one of those around?"

Scott shook his head. "Maybe at the Computer Museum. Isn't there still a computer museum somewhere? Otherwise, I think you're going to have to look on eBay. Look for one of those old IBM PCs, a 286 or whatever. You might get lucky. People sell all kinds of shit."

Rick suddenly remembered the IBM computer on his father's desk. "Actually, I think I know where I can find one."

On the way to his father's house he made a stop at Tastee Donuts, an old-fashioned place that served up hand-cut donuts that were still warm when you got them, and bought a box of a dozen assorted.

He noticed a black Escalade idling double-parked outside Tastee Donuts, halfway down the block. He couldn't see inside; its windows were tinted. He thought he might have noticed a similar black Escalade behind him on the expressway. But such vehicles were common. There was no reason to believe this was the same one.

By the time he got back to his car, the Escalade was gone.

17

City Archives was a half-hour drive away along the winding Riverway that went from the Fenway section of Boston past Jamaica Plain and ended in West Roxbury. He parked in the visitor lot, was buzzed into the main entrance, and followed the signs to the reading room.

Marie Gamache was behind the counter: short, plump, her short brown hair in a pixie cut. She was talking to a slim man with black curly hair and thick wire-rimmed glasses. She beamed when she saw Rick. "I've still got some more to bring out, but you can get started right now if you're ready."

He turned in the direction she was pointing and saw a long blond-wood library table covered with gray archival boxes.

"Oh, boy," he said tonelessly. "Well, first things first." He handed her the box of donuts. "For you."

"From the Tastee? God, I haven't had one of those for years! But I'm gluten-intolerant now. I can't. Oh, this is torture!"

"I'm not," her curly-haired colleague said, taking the box from her. He opened the box and pulled out a glazed donut.

"God, I miss bread," Marie said. "And pizza. And donuts. But I do feel so much *cleaner* without wheat."

It was mind-numbingly tedious work, going through the minutes of the Boston Licensing Board for 1996, scanning through hundreds of filings. His father had billed Club Fifty-One twenty-five thousand dollars for legal work connected to a "liquor license suspension." It was probably pretty routine work. Maybe the place got caught serving minors or just serving after the legal hours. The club's license would be revoked or suspended. A lawyer—in this case, Len—would go before the board and appeal to get the license reinstated.

But after an hour of combing through the records for 1996, he didn't find a single mention of Club Fifty-One. He went back to the invoice. Sure enough, it was dated May 1996. But there was nothing about it in the files. Which was bizarre. He wondered whether something in the archives was missing.

He moved on to another invoice, this one made out to "Jugs DBA LaGrange Entertainment" in the amount of thirty thousand dollars for a "Board of Health matter." Jugs was a strip bar, a popular place for bachelor parties, or it used to be. He had no idea if it was still in business. The city had all sorts of intricate laws regarding strip clubs, such as requiring there always be a three-foot gap between performer and customer. No touching allowed. Even if you paid extra for a private dance in the Champagne room. Sometimes undercover officers would go into the clubs, pretending to be customers, to make sure the laws were being followed. If not, they'd slap a fine on the club or suspend their license for a day or two, which meant closing down briefly.

Rick pored through the archives, looking for "LaGrange Entertainment" or "Jugs" or "Leonard Hoffman," but there was nothing in April or May. This was beginning to bother him. He went back to the counter. "Can I get the Licensing Board records for all of 1995 and 1996?"

Marie groaned. "Really?"

"Really."

Half an hour later she rolled a library cart stacked with twenty more archive boxes up to his table. "Go crazy," she said.

Two hours later he'd gone through all the board of licensing records and still hadn't found any mention of his father making an appearance or filing a plea. He'd billed eight separate clients a total of 295,000 dollars in May 1996. This was big money for a small-time lawyer. Yet nowhere was there a record of Len actually doing the work he'd billed his clients for. Board of Health appearances, zoning variances, liquor license suspensions . . . all those jobs billed for—but none of it, apparently, done.

Sherlock Holmes had once deduced the identity of a thief from the fact that a dog didn't bark. Sometimes the thing that *doesn't* happen is more important than the thing that does.

Leonard Hoffman had billed almost three hundred thousand dollars for work that he apparently didn't do.

So what did that mean? Either his father had been a master scammer and his clients had been dupes—not likely—or something else was going on. Some kind of tricky arrangement involving large sums of money.

So did this mean that his father had not only billed for work he didn't do—but he then hadn't gotten paid for it?

It was time for some good old-fashioned gumshoe work. It was time to go to the old Combat Zone and find out which, if any, of his father's clients, the strip clubs and adult bookstores and such, still existed.

And start asking questions.

18

In the mid-1970s, the mayor of Boston, seeking to contain the spread of prostitution and "adult entertainment," declared a four-square-block area of downtown Boston next to Chinatown the red-light district. Teeming with peep shows and strip clubs, adult bookstores and prostitutes, it became known as the Combat Zone, probably because of all the sailors and soldiers it attracted. It looked like a miniature version of the old Times Square in New York City before it was pasteurized and homogenized.

But as Boston's downtown became more desirable, the big real estate developers moved in and began buying up property, and the next mayor campaigned to shut the Combat Zone down. He succeeded.

Now all that remained of the Combat Zone was one adult bookstore and a couple of strip clubs. The oldest and best known of them was Jugs. Jugs had a big pink sign outside that proclaimed WHERE EVERY MAN IS A VIP. He wondered how Jugs and the other place were able to survive the eradication of the Zone, the way cockroaches are supposed to be able to survive a nuclear war. He wondered if it was under the same ownership now as it was in 1996. Back then the owner was an entity called LaGrange Entertainment. No names. But he needed a name. Sometimes the easiest way to find something out was just to ask.

It was late afternoon and the sun was shining bright. A sign on Jugs's front door said PROPER ATTIRE REQUESTED. WE RESERVE THE RIGHT TO REFUSE SERVICE TO ANY CUSTOMER. NO PHOTOS ALLOWED.

Inside it was dark. It took his eyes several seconds to adjust to the light. Behind the long bar he saw a stage where a young black woman in a G-string gyrated around the pole. She was wearing the proper attire. Mounted high on the wall were three flat-screen TV sets, one tuned to a basketball game, one to *Access Hollywood,* one to something else, the sound off. Music was thumping, a Lil Wayne hip-hop song.

Rick was one of maybe five patrons, two at the bar and three in booths. Each of them was sitting next to a dancer wearing only a G-string. He sat down at the bar. A sour-looking Asian man with large bags under his eyes asked him what he wanted.

"I'll have a beer," Rick said. He noticed the refrigerators under the stage filled with Bud Light and Blue Moon and Sam Adams. "A Blue Moon."

The bartender slapped a coaster down in front of Rick. "Ten dollar," he grunted. He sounded almost defiant. Ten dollars for a beer—that was probably more than they charged at the Ritz-Carlton, only a block away. But that was the price of admission, and it was also the price of information. Rick shrugged. The bartender took a bottle from the refrigerator and thumped it down in front of him. Rick watched the dancer. She was doing what looked like isometric exercises with her butt cheeks, which were firm and round. Probably because of all the isometric exercises. She was wearing only a G-string and sparkly platform heels.

Someone came up and sat at the stool next to his. It was one of the dancers, clad in a skimpy thong and black leatherette bra with tens and twenties sticking out of her right cup. "Hi," she said, extending her hand with her elbow crooked, mock-formally. "I'm Emerald." She was cute and small, with a diamond stud in her lower lip. Her skin was mocha and her tits were small. She looked Hispanic. Her eyebrows looked as if they'd been painted on.

"Hi, Emerald, I'm Rick."

A pause, then she said, "Is this your first time here?"

"Yep. You been dancing here a while?"

A woman behind the bar, with black hair cut into bangs high on her forehead and very red lipstick, interrupted them. "You want to talk to Emerald," she said in what sounded like a Russian accent, "is thirty dollars."

Rick nodded and took a twenty and a ten out of his wallet and set it down on the bar. The price of admission had gone up.

"I'll have a Dirty Shirley," Emerald told the bartender. He went to work filling a tall glass with ice and some kind of soda from the bar and vodka from a Grey Goose bottle and grenadine. Rick assumed the vodka was water. They weren't going to waste Grey Goose on a dancer. Probably not even alcohol.

"I've been dancing here for a year," Emerald said, taking a sip of her drink. "But I've been dancing since I was eighteen."

"They treat you well here?"

"Uh-huh. Where're you from, Rick?"

"New York. She doesn't own the place, that woman?" he asked, pointing with his chin at the black-haired woman.

"No, she's the manager."

The music segued bizarrely from Lil Wayne to Nickelback doing "Photograph." The dancer left the stage and another one, white with bleached blond hair, took her place. She had a spray bottle in one hand and a white rag in the other, and she was cleaning the pole while undulating to the rhythm.

"Is the boss around, or does he come in later?"

Emerald smiled uncomfortably. "There's a couple of bosses. Why you asking all that?"

Rick shrugged. "Just making conversation." He'd come on too hard with the questions. He was out of practice; his investigative skills were rusty. But that was okay; he didn't seriously expect to learn much if anything from her. She might know the name of the owner or owners, sure, but he hadn't been counting on it. He mostly wanted to get the lay of the land. When the right moment presented itself, he'd be ready to ask questions of the manager or the owner, under the guise of being an undercover city inspector. "Maybe I'm looking to buy the place."

She laughed, not sure whether to take him seriously.

Rick looked around. The sour Asian man was taking glasses out of a dishwasher built into the end of the stage. The black-haired Russian woman was talking with a man in a black fleece at the far side of the bar. He didn't look like a patron. They were speaking with an easy, joking familiarity. Maybe he was an owner or one of the owners. The man nodded at someone in back. Rick turned to see who he was nodding at. It was another man, tall and wide, with a blond buzz cut, emerging from the dimly lit recesses at the back of the bar. He looked like a bouncer type.

At the back of the bar he saw a restroom sign. Maybe the bouncer was coming from the restroom, or maybe that's where the employees' entrance was.

"I'll be back," he told Emerald, getting up from the stool. He went toward the back. He passed the women's restroom, then the men's. He glanced down the narrow hallway and saw a couple more doors. One was painted steel with a push bar on it and looked as if it led outside. Another was ajar. Light from the room flooded out into the hall. Probably an office of some kind.

He looked around, didn't see anyone coming, then shouldered the door open. It was indeed an office, a metal desk piled with papers and mail, a framed poster of a stripper, signed with a Sharpie in flowery script. The *I* was dotted with a heart. On top of a dented black steel file cabinet was an old Mr. Coffee coffeemaker and a few reams of printer paper.

No one here. He scanned the heap on top of the desk, saw a Comcast bill in a window envelope. So maybe he'd get lucky, find a letter or a magazine addressed to the owner, by name. He took the Comcast bill and saw it was addressed to "Jugs DBA Citadel LaGrange Entertainment." That wasn't a name, but it was something. He shoved it into his back pocket.

Something or someone slammed him up against the wall. He turned just in time to see the crew cut bouncer, his right hand pincered on Rick's throat, choking him. With his other hand the bouncer pinioned Rick's right hand against the door.

"What do you think you're doing?" he said.

Rick gagged. He looked down at the bouncer's left hand, saw a green blob on the inside of his wrist. It was familiar. Then he remembered: He'd seen a similar tattoo on the wrist of one of his abductors in the Charles Hotel parking garage. It was actually a clover leaf, not a blob. A three-leaved shamrock. On each leaf was the number 6, making it 666. The number of the antichrist.

Rick kneed the man in the groin, thrusting hard. The man groaned and doubled up and Rick was able to break free of his grip. He lunged into the hallway, spun around, then slammed a hip against the push bar on the steel door. The door made a bleeping sound, and Rick could feel a rush of cold air. He stumbled, scraping a knee against the asphalt ground. The bouncer lurched through the door after him, shouting something, but Rick was already out of the alley and down the street and racing as fast as he'd ever run in his life.

19

He arrived at the offices of *Back Bay* magazine with scuffed jeans and a big rip at the knee. He'd torn his jeans in the alley and didn't feel like going back to the B&B to change. He didn't particularly care. He wasn't going for a job interview.

Rick was still officially on the staff of *Back Bay.* Shortly after Mort Ostrow had fired Rick, after the shock had worn off, he'd swallowed his considerable pride and accepted Ostrow's offhanded offer: If Rick agreed to post at least one piece a week, he'd get to keep access to the usual databases and receive a salary of sorts. A pittance. Next to nothing, but not nothing. It was useful to have access to the databases and be able to say he was calling from *Back Bay* magazine. That might come in handy now, too. He didn't have to come in to the office to post things, so he'd stayed away. In fact, only once since Mort Ostrow had delivered the bad news had he been in to the office, and that was to pack up his desk.

His stomach tightened as he approached the glass door to the office suite. He dreaded meeting up with his colleagues. Ostrow had let go all the editors over the age of thirty except Darren Overby, the new editor in chief, and Karen, the managing editor, but she'd been part-time since the birth of her son, four years ago. They might still be here, though, slaving away on freelance pieces, taking advantage of the free office space to work until the magazine, which was really just a website now, downsized to whatever minuscule closet it was moving to and then disappeared altogether, like a wisp of smoke. Rick didn't look forward to making small talk (*The job search is going great, thanks! Updating my LinkedIn page as we speak!*).

Then he remembered the pile of cash in his storage unit and he immediately felt better about everything. The money was like a suit of armor. It protected him against insults and indignities. Yes, he didn't have a real job, but no longer did he have to worry about money. Except, he reminded himself, for worrying about protecting it. Keeping it safe from whoever knew he had it. Keeping himself safe, too.

Nine people were seated around the big cherrywood conference table. Rick recognized only two of them, the remaining two editors, Karen and Darren—so perfect a team they even rhymed! The other seven were a fresh-faced assortment, all in their early to mid twenties, hipster lumberjacks dressed so similarly they might have been wearing uniforms: bulky cable-knit sweaters or checked flannel shirts, a few of them wearing big chunky eyeglasses. They had to be freelance writers, here for a story meeting. All of them looked hopeful and optimistic. They weren't yet cynics. They weren't writers, really, either. They were *contributors*. They repurposed content from blogs and websites, and they were paid by the click.

But more than that, they were survivors. Looking around the conference table, Rick couldn't help but think of a painting he'd once seen in the Louvre called *The Raft of the Medusa*. It depicted a small gang of desperate, dying people clinging to a raft in a turbulent ocean.

The painting was based on a real historical event, a French naval ship that had run aground, leaving a couple hundred survivors hanging on a raft, enduring weeks of starvation and thirst and savagery, the stronger killing the weaker, throwing each other off to the sharks, and eventually resorting to cannibalism, until only a dozen or so were left to rescue.

The survivors of *Back Bay* magazine were clinging to the raft in their fashionable cable-knit sweaters.

Darren, in his heavy black glasses, was holding forth at the head of the table, drinking a stevia-sweetened green apple soda. "We're not getting the uniques, people," he said. "Every time you turn in a piece I want you to come up with twenty-five possible headlines. Then we're going to A/B test the best ones. The headline is an *itch* the reader has to *scratch*. I want superlatives, okay? I want, I don't know, *'What This Chef Does with Lamb Is Amazeballs!'*"

"What about '. . . *Will Change Your Life'* instead?" suggested an earnest bearded guy in red-and-black buffalo plaid.

"Sure," Darren said. "Or *'Rock Your World.' With* me, people? Hit them right in the feels."

"Numbers are always good," Karen put in.

"Numbers!" Darren said. "*'Seven Facts about Wellesley That Will Blow Your Mind.' 'The Five Best Power Breakfasts in Boston.'*"

"For the one about the Fall River city administrator's resignation, how about this: *'Her First Sentence Was Moving. Her Second Sentence Brought Me to Tears.'*"

"Excellent!" Darren barked. "I love it. Do we have any photos of puppies from the animal shelter? Or GIFs? Any GIFs?" He noticed Rick slipping quietly into the room. "Rick Hoffman!" he sang out with false joviality. "Welcome! Joining us?"

He shook his head. "Doing a little research."

"Research!" Darren said it as if research were something exotic that most people didn't actually do themselves, like baking croissants or overhauling their car's transmission. "Can't wait to hear the juicy details! Oh, Rick, your piece on craft beers, we're going to post that tomorrow morning. But you know, there's going to be that groundbreaking for the Olympian Tower in a couple of weeks, and we'd really like you to do a Q&A with Thomas Sculley; could you do that?"

Rick shrugged. "What are we talking about?"

"Just fifteen hundred words. You know, give him the full Rick Hoffman treatment?"

"Sure, uh, fine."

The Rick Hoffman treatment: Man, was that an expression Rick had come to detest. It meant an adoring, adulatory profile. The sort of mindlessly positive piece—usually a Q&A—that its subject, usually someone rich, powerful, or famous, could only love. Nothing hard-hitting, honest, or blunt. In other words, just the sort of article Rick had once promised himself he'd never do. At *Back Bay*, it had become his skill set. Thomas Sculley was one of those Boston billionaires the magazine made a specialty of covering with wet kisses.

"Excellent," said Darren. "Also, Mark Wahlberg's new movie starts filming at Fenway next month, so there's that. And apparently the new dean of Harvard Law School, Ronald Proskin, has a twenty-thousand-bottle wine collection—David Geffen offered to buy the whole thing outright."

"Great," Rick said. "Lots of possibilities." He excused himself and walked past his old office, which was still empty, just a desk and a credenza and power cables and snowdrifts of dust. The company computer had been removed. The desk and the credenza and the fancy Humanscale office chair all had SOLD tags on them.

The hall outside was lined with cardboard boxes. The lease on the Harrison Avenue space was up in a few weeks. He found a cubicle that looked unused—there were a lot of them—and signed on to the magazine's intranet. His user ID and password still worked. That was something, at least.

He overheard Darren saying, "Everyone loves chocolate-chip cookies! The ten best chocolate-chip cookies!"

First he pulled up a half-written plug that had been moldering on his hard drive about an artisanal cheese maker who had a shop on Tremont Street. He came up with a line—"Rumor has it that the good stuff—the *raw* stuff—is hidden away in the back, like the hard cider in Prohibition days"—and zipped it off to a mellow snowboarder on the copy desk named Dylan Scardino. Dylan also served as "web producer," which meant he was the guy who uploaded the files and put them up on the Internet.

Then he took out the cable company bill he'd filched from the strip club. The bill was for high-speed Internet and a generous cable package for their wall-mounted TV sets. It was made out to "Jugs DBA Citadel LaGrange Entertainment." No wonder he hadn't pulled up any corporate records on LaGrange Entertainment. The name had been changed. There was any number of reasons why it might have been done. A change in ownership, maybe, or an attempt to duck a lawsuit.

Darren's voice: "Is it *awesome?* That's the only criterion—it has to be *awesome!*"

He entered "Citadel LaGrange Entertainment" in one of the corporate records databases and pulled up exactly . . . nothing. A P.O. box was listed, but no names.

The story meeting broke up and the freelancers scattered. The bearded guy in buffalo plaid sat down at the cubicle next to Rick's.

Rick looked up the phone number online for the Massachusetts attorney general's office and called the number. "I'm looking for some records on a business that's incorporated in Massachusetts."

"What sort of records, sir?"

"Corporate filings. Ownership records."

"You might want to try the Division of Professional Licensure."

"Could you transfer me?"

A click. "Licensure, Reilly."

"Yes, Mr. Reilly, I have a client, an exotic dancer, who's looking to sue a strip club in Boston called Jugs for wrongful termination. I've been searching high and low for ownership information, but I'm stumped. I'm wondering if you could be so kind as to pull the records."

"You said Jugs?"

"That's right. Maybe the name of the president . . . ?"

Tappa tappa tappa tappa tap.

"I don't have a Jugs, sir."

"You might want to try their corporate entity, Citadel LaGrange Entertainment."

Tappa tappa tappa tappa.

"I'm sorry, sir, I don't have anything on that."

"Thanks for trying." Rick hung up, then rested his chin on his palm and looked at the monitor.

The bearded freelancer's head popped up over the partition. "So, you're working the *telephone*, huh?" he said with a derisive smile. "Like, an actual telephone. With the curly cord and everything. That's so, I don't know, *normcore.*"

"Normcore," Rick said. "That's a new one."

Then he had an idea and started going through corporate records for past years. When he got to Citadel LaGrange's filing for 2007, he found a name. Just one: that of a corporate secretary, Patricia Rubin. She was listed in 2006 as well, and for years going back. After 2007, no one was listed.

But "corporate secretary" didn't mean owner. At least he had a name. That didn't mean she'd know the real story, why Leonard Hoffman had billed Jugs for thirty thousand dollars' worth of legal work he hadn't done. If he could find her, though, she'd certainly know the name of the owner. If she was still living, anyway. He entered her name in the LexisNexis Public Records search database, clicked dutifully through the legal disclaimer about the electronic communications privacy act, and came up with a phone number and address in Acton, Massachusetts.

So she was alive.

Rick stared at the computer monitor and thought. He could just call Patricia Rubin and ask who owned Jugs, but that was a risk. There was probably a reason the owner's name wasn't listed. Maybe the owner of a strip bar just preferred to keep a low profile. Maybe he didn't want to be sued. Whatever the reason his name wasn't public, Ms. Rubin probably wasn't going to give it up readily.

Not unless she had a good reason to.

He thought some more, then did some quick Googling and found the right website. He entered a credit card number, the Citicard MasterCard he'd just paid down, and bought a subscription. Then he looked up the telephone number of the Internal Revenue Service's office in Andover, Mass. He knew that was one of their big offices because he'd been ignoring numerous mailings from the IRS with an Andover return address. Their phone number was an 800 number that ended in "1040," which was probably supposed to be clever. Tax humor.

Then, on an outside phone line, he punched in the number of the phone-number-spoofing website he'd just subscribed to, and after the tone he entered the IRS number. When the call went through, the phone number that would show up on the caller ID would be the IRS's.

"Ms. Rubin, please? Patricia Rubin?"

A woman's voice. "Who should I say is calling?"

"This is Joseph Bodoni from the Internal Revenue Service in Andover. I'd like to speak with a Patricia Rubin."

A pause. The same voice. "Speaking."

"Ms. Rubin, I have your name down here as corporate secretary of the Citadel LaGrange Entertainment company; is that correct?"

"What? No! I haven't been connected with that place for years!"

"I'm sorry, you're no longer the corporate secretary?"

"Not for years! Not since I got divorced from that jerk."

"'That jerk' is the owner of the business?"

"Yeah. Joel Rubin. So?"

"Well, we need to reach your ex-husband, then. We have a refund of thirty thousand dollars that needs to be personally signed for by the president of the Citadel LaGrange Entertainment company. I'm going to need a name and a telephone number."

"Yeah, great," she said bitterly. "Give that asshole even more cash to squirrel away from me. Just what he needs."

Rick paused for a few seconds. He realized he'd just screwed up. She wasn't going to give up her ex-husband's phone number if she thought it meant he'd get a chunk of money. "Huh. Busted. Okay, Ms. Rubin, I gotta come clean. I'm not with the IRS. I'm a process server, and I've got a summons to serve your ex-husband. He's being sued for a lot of money in Suffolk County court."

"Oh, yeah? Well, am I ever sorry to hear that!" She cackled. "Call me Patty. You want his home number or his cell?"

After Rick hung up the phone, the bearded freelancer's head once again rose from behind the partition.

"Were you just pretending to be from the IRS?"

Rick shrugged.

"You can do that? That's not . . . illegal or something?"

"It's not *illegal* as long as you don't do it for the purpose of defrauding someone. But most newspapers or magazines would fire you for doing it, so don't try this one at home, kids."

"She gave up the name and phone number?"

Rick nodded as he got to his feet.

"Huh," he said. "Cool."

"It's just reporting."

"That's so *retro*, you know?" the guy said. "Like out of a noir film? I didn't know people still did that kind of stuff anymore."

20

Joel Rubin, the owner of Jugs, lived in a condo in Lynn, an unlovely town ten miles north of Boston. The condo building was a tall, ugly blond-brick structure with jutting balconies on Lynn Shore Drive near Nahant Beach. It looked like something you might see in the old East Berlin. The Atlantic was right across the busy street.

Rick parked in one of the numbered spaces in the parking lot, probably taking some resident's space. When he got out of the car, he could smell the ocean, the seaweed and the salt. The waves crashed rhythmically. He could hear the squawk of a seagull. A plane flew by low overhead. Logan Airport was close.

Inside the narrow lobby was a call box. He scrolled through a seemingly endless list of residents' names, found Joel Rubin, then pressed his four-digit unit number.

A full minute later a man's voice said, "Yeah?"

"Rick Hoffman."

Another long minute, then the plate-glass inner door buzzed open. He took an elevator to the tenth floor.

Rick was expecting some degree of hostility. On the phone, Rubin had barked at him, "Do I know you?"

"You knew my dad, Leonard Hoffman."

There was a long silence. Then, slightly less hostile: "Where'd you get my number?"

"Patty."

A sigh. "Figures. There some kind of problem?"

"No, not at all. There's something I need your help with. It would be a lot easier if we talked in person. I'll explain."

Rubin was willing to meet, though grudgingly. Rick made a mental note not to start out asking about the bouncer at Jugs. That would certainly make the guy retract like a terrapin on high alert. He rang the doorbell. A shadow darkened the peephole and the door came open quickly.

Rubin looked to be in his sixties. He was bald on top with a cascade of gray-blond ringlets behind that reached his shoulders. He was skinny and had a small potbelly like a spare tire. He wore a bright orange African dashiki and scruffy faded jeans with new bright white sneakers. There were big dark circles under his eyes. He stuck out his hand and gave Rick a limp moist handshake.

"Sorry, I was doing dishes. Come on in." He stopped short. "Jesus, you look just like your dad! It's amazing." He put a hand on each of Rick's shoulders and squinted, tipping his head from one side to another. For a long moment, he didn't speak. His eyes were bloodshot. He looked like he might be buzzed. "Yeah, you know, I thought you were just yanking my chain, but you're Lenny's son, all right. It's written all over your face."

The apartment was brightly lit. A set of glass slider doors looked out onto the shore road and the ocean. There was light blue wall-to-wall carpeting and a set of furniture—sectional couch and matching chairs—that looked as if they'd all been purchased on the same shopping trip to a low-end home store. The whole place smelled of rotting fruit and old bong water.

He offered Rick coffee, but Rick shook his head. "How'd you get to Patty, if you don't mind my asking?"

"I found her number in some of my dad's old papers," Rick lied. He didn't want to provoke any more suspicious hostility by telling him about searching old city archives.

"You saw what that bitch looks like, right? Would you believe she was, like, a zipper-ripper when I first met her? I hired her as a bookkeeper, but I kept telling her she shoulda been a dancer. That girl had a body as hard as Chinese arithmetic, I kid you not."

"We just talked on the phone."

"What's this about? Isn't your dad . . . I mean, I heard he's in rough shape."

"He had a stroke like twenty years ago, yeah. Lost the ability to speak."

"Yeah, you know, what happened to him—man, that sucked. Nobody should have that happen to him."

"Well, he really left his financial affairs in a mess. He owes people money, he has clients who owe him money—"

"Hey, I don't owe him a dime."

"I know you don't," Rick said quickly. "I know you were one of his biggest clients, and I need some help unwinding his business affairs. What kind of work did he do for you?"

"We did business together." There was a petulant, evasive note in his words. His eyes narrowed in a cartoon gesture of suspicion.

"What do you mean?"

"I think you know."

"I wish I did."

"Seriously?"

"What kind of business? I know he billed you for a bunch of jobs."

Joel looked away. "Yeah, well, that was twenty years ago and I was doing a lot of coke at the time, okay? It's all kind of a blur."

"I know he billed you, and it doesn't look like he got paid."

"Huh? Oh, he got paid, believe me."

"I believe you. But from what I can tell, he never did the work. I mean, I'm asking you because I can't ask him: He billed you for thirty thousand dollars' worth of legal work in a month. Sure seems like he was scamming you."

Joel was quiet for a long moment. A motorcycle ripped by on Shore Road, ten stories below. He clenched and unclenched his jaw, then shook his head. His voice trembled. "What your dad was into, it was kind of complicated, but there was nobody—*nobody*—people trusted more than him. Or respected. Your dad was the salt of the earth. You dig?"

"Then maybe you can explain to me what kind of business you and he were doing."

Joel gave an odd-looking smile. "You don't want to know."

"I do."

"You think you want to know, but you don't, I promise you. You really don't."

"Tell me what I'm missing here."

Joel shook his head. "Your dad was so . . . Hey, listen—do you get high?"

"Uh, sure." Rick hadn't smoked marijuana in a long time. He didn't like it, what it did to him. It made him jittery, sort of paranoid. But he had a feeling, just based on the rhythm of the conversation, that this was his best way in, maybe his only way in. That if he got high with Joel, he'd talk. It was a kind of barter.

Joel brought out a sleek piece of machinery with a conical base that looked like a high-tech Waring blender. Not the bong he'd expected based on the swampy smell in the apartment. It was a vaporizer. Rick had heard about such things but had never used one.

"I liked your dad a lot," Joel said as he busied himself breaking up a ball of weed into small buds on top of a CD case, then tipped the buds into a small stainless steel manual grinder. "He was a cool dude. Worst sense of humor in the world, but . . ."

"That's for sure," Rick said, laughing ruefully.

"But I felt for the guy." He turned the grinder to pulverize the buds, then dumped the powder onto a folded dollar bill and used it to slide the herb into a filling chamber. He put that piece on the vaporizer base and then what looked like a limp plastic sandwich bag on top of it. The whole process was as elaborate as a Japanese tea ceremony.

"You felt for him . . . ?" Rick prompted.

"The way he ended up." The plastic bag began slowly to fill up with white smoke like an oblong balloon.

"You mean his stroke?"

Joel shook his head, took the inflated balloon off the vaporizer base and attached a mouthpiece, then handed it to Rick.

"Nah, nah. I mean his broken dreams, you know? Kind of sad."

"Broken dreams?" Rick drew in a shallow breath. He couldn't fake it, not with Joel watching. He had to make a dent in the balloon. Then he handed the balloon back to Joel, who sucked in a lungful of smoke.

"Yeah, you know, the Black Panthers, the Weather Underground, all that?"

Rick kept the smoke in his lungs and managed not to cough before exhaling.

"Black Panthers . . . ? I don't know what you're talking about."

"He never told you about that?" Joel said in a little strangled voice through a mouthful of smoke.

"You sure we're talking about the same Leonard Hoffman?"

"He didn't tell you about his badass civil liberties days?"

Rick shook his head.

"Oh, man. I can't believe he never told you about it. He defended Bobby Seale, back in the day. The Black Panther trial in New Haven. The New Haven Nine, right?"

"My dad?"

Joel let his breath out slowly, reluctantly. "Yeah. Yeah. That was what he was gonna do, fight the Establishment. He was a total idealist. I mean, that's what he really wanted to do in life, stick it to the Man. Change the world. But it never happened for him. He had to give it up."

"How come?"

"You."

"Me?"

"He had kids. He needed a job that paid the bills. You get it?" Joel took another lungful of smoke, depleting the balloon.

Rick nodded slowly, distracted. He began to feel the first rush of the marijuana. He felt dizzy, vertiginous, disoriented. He was surprised, and unexpectedly saddened, to hear this. That his father had had a whole life he'd never talked about. Leonard Hoffman aspired to be a very different kind of lawyer than he turned out to be. The kind who fought for civil liberties, who argued before the Supreme Court. A hero who defended the downtrodden. An idealist, as Joel had said. Not a vaguely disreputable small-time lawyer who defended strip clubs and porn shops.

"Wow," Rick said, more to himself than to Rubin. "That's . . . heartbreaking."

"Right?" Joel said. He was already beavering away at another fist-size hunk of marijuana, plucking apart the buds, crunching it up onto the CD case. His bright orange dashiki began to vibrate. Rick studied the ornate pattern that made a V at the neckline of the dashiki, mesmerized by its paisley whorls and squiggles. This ganja was definitely stronger than whatever he'd occasionally smoked in college. "I mean, I get it. I totally get it. This is just, like, what happens when you grow up. You never end up where you thought you would. You think I wanted to be sixty-three and the owner of a titty bar? You think that was my dream in life?"

The paisley pattern in Joel Rubin's dashiki had begun to squirm like a nest of snakes. It was fascinating but also repellent. Rick realized that Joel was waiting for him to say something, so he said thickly, "What was it? Your dream, I mean." An ambulance raced by down below, its siren crescendoing and Dopplering before it faded away, leaving a slug trail of sound shimmering in the air.

"I was, like, reviewing concerts for *The Real Paper* when I was at Brandeis, you know. I was a concert promoter. When I wasn't turning on, I mean." Joel chuckled. He tipped out the ashes from the filling chamber and filled it up with new, freshly ground weed, then put it expertly on top of the vaporizer. "I was selling dope. The kind of crap we were peddling back then, you couldn't even sell it today. I was gonna be, like, the next . . . who's that guy who's the big concert promoter?"

Rick shook his head. The dashiki was starting to gross him out, so he was forcing himself to look away, to stare outside through the glass sliders, at the metallic sky and the very blue ocean, which was actually kind of beautiful.

"Know who I'm talking about? That big concert promoter guy? You'd definitely know his name!"

Rick shook his head again, slowly. "Don't know."

The balloon inflated with white smoke, and Joel took it off and put on the mouthpiece. He passed it to Rick, who shook his head. "I gotta take a break," Rick said.

A pigeon landed on the railing of Joel's narrow balcony. It was strutting, bobbing its head in a regular, steady beat, as if to an internal metronome.

Joel inhaled greedily. Then, through a mouthful of smoke, he said in a fuzzy voice, "Man, I can't . . . it'll come to me . . ."

"Anyway, you were going to be a concert promoter," Rick reminded him.

Joel nodded, held a forefinger in the air, telling Rick to wait. He expelled the smoke after holding it in for ten seconds. "I was like—" Then Joel raised his arm and stuck out his middle finger. "Stick it to Tricky Dick."

"Tricky Dick?"

"Tricky Dick Nixon. You're either on the bus or off the bus, dig? I got a job in the old Combat Zone working at a newsstand, you know, selling *Screw* and *Hustler* and *Swank*, right . . . it was a gas. Then the opportunity came up to buy the place. And one thing leads to another and all of a sudden I own a couple of titty bars in downtown Boston. And now it's down to just the one."

"You were about to tell me about the business you did with my dad."

Rick's brain had slowed down to a crawl. He was fighting to maintain a grasp on the conversational thread.

"Jugs was mostly a cash business. Guys don't want wifey back home in Newton looking at the credit card bills and figuring out hubby wasn't at a client dinner, you dig? I had tons of it coming in, and I guess your dad knew someone who wanted cash and was willing to pay a premium for it."

"You sold him cash?"

Joel grinned. "Capitalism, man. That's capitalism reduced to its essence, you know? Distilled to its purest form. Like"—his eyes lit up— "a paradigm. A beautiful thing."

"So he gave you bills you could write off as legal expenses and you paid him in cash," Rick said, realizing all of a sudden how it worked. Finally he understood the big-ticket invoices without commensurate bank deposits. His father was buying, and probably selling, cash. Most of Len's clients were cash-rich businesses. Now it made sense.

"Who was he doing it for?" Rick asked. His mouth had dried out. His tongue was cleaving to the roof of his mouth.

"How would I know? He wanted cash, I had cash, everyone's happy. The circle of life. I must have given him half a million bucks over the years. A lot of other guys in the Zone got in on the party, too. I wasn't the only one."

"He never told you who it was for?"

"What kinda lawyer would he be if he revealed his client's name? Anyway, you didn't ask. You didn't look too close."

"You don't have a guess? That's a lot of cash."

"When was this, back in the 1990s?"

Rick nodded.

"You remember what it was like back then, back in the nineties? You grew up in Boston, right? You remember the Big Dig?"

Rick nodded again. "Of course."

"I mean—you've never seen such a swamp of graft and corruption. It was like pigs at the trough. The greatest boondoggle of the twentieth century! Wasn't it like forty billion dollars, all told? I mean, you could have a couple of wars for money like that."

The Big Dig was an immense, infamous construction job that transformed the city of Boston. Back in the bad old days, a highway called the Central Artery had slashed through the middle of downtown. As the city grew, the traffic jams became ridiculous, hours-long. Then in 1991 a massive project began to sink the Central Artery deep under the city, in tunnels through Boston Harbor, beneath the towering skyscrapers. It was supposed to cost 2.6 billion dollars but ended up costing more than 24 billion. It was supposed to be finished in ten years but ended up taking twenty. The Big Dig was bigger than the Panama Canal, bigger than the Hoover Dam or the Alaska Pipeline or the pyramids.

Len's secretary had said Len was a "fixer," that he knew the right people to pay off to get things done.

But who was he fixing *for*? Not for the strip clubs and the massage parlors and such. Those places, which brought in a lot of cash and knew who to pay off themselves—the cops threatening to arrest a dancer for getting too close to a patron, the health inspector who wanted an extra payday—those places didn't need a lawyer to do that.

But the Big Dig . . .

Now, that was interesting.

"He handled payouts for, what, contractors bidding on jobs in the Big Dig?" Rick said.

"If you were a big construction company and you wanted in on the Big Dig, you either had to know the right decision makers in the city or the state . . . or know whose palms to grease. Though why palms get greased, I never understood. A really strange expression, that one."

Three and a half million dollars in cash had been hidden inside the walls of the house on Clayton Street, and now at least Rick knew where it had come from: from cash-intensive, high-liquidity businesses like Jugs, most of them in the old Combat Zone.

So . . . whose cash was it?

Someone who'd resort to violence to get it back, that was for sure.

"Man, there was so much cash washing around in those days, it was like Iraq after Saddam Hussein. It was like the fall of the Roman Empire. I mean, there were contractors and subcontractors and sub-subcontractors and *sub*-sub-subcontractors . . ."

"Joel?"

"Right. Right. So anyway, yeah. I don't know who it was for, but Lenny must have had someone going through cash like veggies through a Vitamix."

"He had a client, I think—I don't know the name, just an initial. P. You have any idea who that 'P' might have been?"

Joel laughed. "I told you, I had a drug problem in those days. Half the time I was wasted." He went to work crunching up some more marijuana on the CD case. "I could barely remember my *wife's* name. Now I wish I could forget it."

Something was tickling at the back of Rick's brain, something niggling and uncomfortable, something unpleasant. His thoughts were floating and drifting like clouds. But then he remembered the shamrock tattoo and it all came rushing back to him. The terror of the hood being slipped over his head, the quiet insistent voice. And then the remembered fear became something much closer to anger.

"Hey, so your bouncer gave me a hard time," Rick said, trying for a casual tone.

"Who, Padraig? Yeah, he's a hothead."

"He's Irish?"

"As Irish as Paddy's pig."

"I think I've seen him around before." Rick wondered if Joel was trying to maintain a poker face. But Rick's perceptions were off. Joel might not be.

"Yeah?" Joel didn't seem much interested. He slid the herb into the grinder and turned it a few times.

"Yeah, I'm pretty sure I recognize that tattoo."

"What, the shamrock?"

"Right. With the 666."

"You see it here and there. Bouncers and other tough guys in the clubs downtown. Those are the guys you hire. Kind of like the Teamsters, you know? Don't have a choice. I think someone high up in the state has the power to get those guys visas and stuff. Anyway, you want to stay in business, you hire the guys you're told to."

"Told to by who?"

"The PTB, man."

"PTB?"

"The powers that be."

"Like . . . who?"

Joel tamped down the powder. "You know what?" he said. "Almost thirty years in this business and I've learned two things. You can't fight the powers that be, and you don't ask questions."

21

It had been a mistake getting high. He felt a low-level paranoia starting to come on, like a migraine's aura. The sky was iron gray and swollen. It was windy and cold and he felt disconnected from the world around him, the cars whooshing by, horns smearing the air. It wasn't a pleasant feeling. A tractor-trailer blasted a cloud of diesel exhaust. A cold ocean breeze sliced through his jacket. He couldn't find his car.

It took him several circuits around the condo building parking lot before he remembered he was driving not his red BMW but a rented Ford. He got in and turned the ignition and sat behind the wheel for a minute or so, gauging his ability to drive. Not good, he decided. He needed, at the very least, a cup of coffee before attempting the drive back to Boston. He got out, crossed the parking lot, and walked along the highway until he reached a Dunkin' Donuts. There was another one directly across the street, too.

A sign at the counter announced they wouldn't accept fifty- and one-hundred-dollar bills "because of fraudulent activity." He mostly had one-hundred-dollar bills, taken from one of the packets in his suitcase, and had to search his pockets, and every compartment in his wallet, before he eventually found a crumpled ten-dollar bill.

He bought two large coffees and downed one of them sitting at a sticky, crumb-strewn table. He felt his heart rate start to accelerate. He was, if not sober, at least more attentive, in a thick sort of way. The donuts smelled good, and he had a bad case of the munchies, so he returned to the cash register and bought a half dozen and carried the box with him along the road back to the condo parking lot, devouring two, one after another, pausing only long enough to swallow. When he got to the car, he realized he needed a little more time to sober up, or at least try to.

So he crossed the street—it took a couple of minutes to find a gap in the traffic—and sat on a wooden-slatted bench facing the ocean. He watched the waves churning, crashing into the narrow bar of sand. A seagull dive-bombed, then soared upward, cawing and shrieking triumphantly. A particularly big swell sent spray over the low concrete wall. He could feel the fine droplets of mist. After a while the surf's white noise melted into the fizzy whoosh of the tires of the passing cars. A bicyclist came riding past, a big guy in a David Ortiz jersey and Red Sox cap.

And he thought about his father. He drank coffee and thought about Len's aspirations, his broken dreams, which was news to Rick. There was another Leonard Hoffman, whom Rick didn't know, had never known. A Leonard Hoffman who wanted to be something else besides what he ended up.

And then for a moment Rick was sixteen and bored out of his skull, trudging through the overpolished ceremonial halls of the Supreme Court on a family field trip to Washington, DC. His father's idea, this family excursion, a way to put the pieces back together, to mend the torn fabric of their little family, six months after Ellen Hoffman had died of ovarian cancer. Mom had been the glue that kept the family together, Rick had come to realize. Then for five months it was her illness, then her death, and then everything seemed to fly apart. They each occupied their own separate sphere of solitude, barely talking to each other, knocking up against each other only when necessary. Rick was surly and unpleasant to be around, just by virtue of being a teenage boy. But his mother's death had curdled something inside him, had given him permission to let the ugly fly.

It was also the last thing Rick wanted to do, spend a week of his spring break with his father and younger sister slogging through the monuments of our nation's capital and admiring the cherry blossoms, when his prep school and neighborhood friends were staying at home sleeping late and watching TV and hanging out in Harvard Square.

The visit to the Supreme Court was the pièce de résistance of this sad little trip. Lenny hadn't been able to get them into the courtroom itself, an actual argument session, a failing about which he seemed sort of annoyed and embarrassed. Apparently you had to know someone in Congress, or so he claimed. Anyway, he didn't know anyone, so the family had to take what he called "the schmucks' tour."

Washington had been all of a piece with the Supreme Court—wide malls, wide avenues, wide marble hallways lined with statuary and plaques. History everywhere. Squirming fellow teenage hostages with their families reading plaques and listening to tour guides drone on. The Lincoln Memorial was crowded, and the Washington Monument was crowded and stupid. Only the Smithsonian National Air and Space Museum was cool, because of the space suits and stuff.

Wendy, a seventh grader, had brought along her best friend, Peg. The two girls did everything together and giggled at Rick and the exhibits and exchanged private jokes. The two of them shared a room at their cheap hotel off Dupont Circle, and both were vegetarians, which complicated meal issues.

A docent had given a canned lecture about America's Temple of Justice, which was in fact a Mausoleum of Tedium. From its marble walls and floors seeped chloroform. Even the gift shop, normally the one reliable fallback, had nothing Rick was remotely interested in buying. (Pewter baby mug! Supreme Court coffee mug! Why not Pez dispenser versions of the justices, he wondered. Or action figures, at least?)

They all stood around the John Marshall statue, a bronze figure of an arrogant guy in a bathrobe, or so it appeared, while Len went on at length about how important John Marshall was. Rick, burping up egg from the immense breakfast he'd eaten at the hotel, tried not to fall asleep standing up.

"The point," his father said, "is you can be anything you want! This guy was born in a log cabin on the Virginia frontier, the oldest of fifteen kids. Point is, if you can conceive it and you can believe it, you can achieve it!"

Wendy and Peg lurked at a distance while Len talked. They giggled and rolled their eyes at Lenny's earnestness. Len was so awkward at playing parent. He had no game. He didn't even know how to hug the kids. Rick could feel his father's self-consciousness: one hand or two, and do you do the back-clap thing? Len was like a skater who stumbles when he starts to overthink how he could stay up on his skates. And Rick found himself rooting for the old man: *C'mon, Dad, you can do this. C'mon, Dad. Be a dad, Dad!*

After Mom's death, the guy was trying so hard to be a father, to reach out to his two kids, to be the center of things, to replace Mom now that she was gone. He'd schlepped his kids to DC to fill up some space he'd seen in their lives, the Mom space that he could never occupy. But dammit, he was going to try. This field trip to DC was all part of that campaign. Neither of his kids wanted to be here, and he knew that, but he wasn't giving up yet.

An important-looking man in a gray suit came striding past and stopped. "Lenny? My God! Is that you?"

"David Rosenthal," his father had said, stopping midsentence. "Are you arguing before the court?"

The man nodded. "Just finished. My heart's still pounding." A few other men in suits stood back, waiting. "So what are you up to these days? Since New Haven?"

Len flashed his rabbity smile. "Oh, a little of this, a little of that." He looked strange, as if he was pleased to be recognized by this big-deal lawyer who had just emerged from the courtroom they hadn't been able to get inside. But at the same time, he looked as if he wanted to drill a hole into the marble floor and disappear.

Wendy imitated Len's aw-shucks mannerism with perfect vicious accuracy, mouthed the words *Oh, a little of this, a little of that,* but Rick refused to make eye contact with her. She wanted her older brother to roll eyes together with her, but he was having no part of her conspiracy of derision. He was caught by a feeling of almost parental protectiveness toward his father, though he knew it was topsy-turvy for a kid to feel that way, and, when he thought about it, that was probably more insulting to Len than his sister's snark.

The important guy gave Len a strange look. Rick was too young to identify that look: pity mixed with contempt. His father looked sheepish and queasily embarrassed by something. Maybe by who he was, or who he wasn't. Somehow Rick felt the embarrassment, too, mixed with a flash of irritation, and the fleeting moment of tenderness had evaporated.

He could see his sister's mockery out of the corner of his eye but didn't give her the satisfaction of acknowledgment.

Finally, he sidled right up to her and let fly the burp he'd been suppressing for a minute or so, right into Wendy's airspace, which led her to squawk vehemently. "Yuck!" she protested, theatrically loud, and Len's brow scrunched with the fleeting look of dark annoyance, and Rick could see him decide, no, he wasn't going to hold an inquiry into the incident; Len didn't want to know. He seemed almost relieved by the distraction.

Rick wondered about the regret or bitterness Len must have felt over the career he ended up with, as a bag man and a fixer, about as far removed from the legal heroics he'd once envisioned as you could get. He wondered if his father thought about such things anymore. If he thought about anything anymore. He wondered whether the stroke had wiped out his ability to think, along with his speech.

He didn't think Joel Rubin was lying when he insisted he didn't know who Len bought cash for. It made sense that his father would have protected his clients' identity, not just because of attorney-client confidentiality, but because his clients were almost certainly involved in something criminal. Joel had claimed he didn't have any idea who this mysterious "P" was, and Rick believed him.

But there had to be a way to figure out who "P" was, who he worked for. No one would know like a newspaper reporter. A real old-school journalist. Luckily, Rick still had contacts from his reporter days. A lot of them had accepted buyouts from *The Boston Globe* as the paper downsized and were now freelancing, just skating by, but at least one remained at the paper. Monica Kennedy was one of their star investigative reporters, a hard-bitten woman in her late forties with unkempt steel-gray hair and thick smudged aviator glasses. She'd won a George Polk Award for her series on sexual abuse in Boston's Catholic archdiocese, a lot of attention for exposing a state crime lab tech who'd faked hundreds of drug test results. Back in the 1990s, she'd done a whole series on cost overruns in the Big Dig.

He was still high, though less high than he'd been in Joel Rubin's apartment, and his thoughts were muddled. He wasn't thinking clearly. It took a great effort, but he scrolled through the contacts on his phone and eventually found it. Monica Kennedy.

He hadn't talked to Monica in probably ten years. The only number he had was her work phone number. But that was unlikely to have changed. He called it, let it ring. On the fifth ring he got her voice mail. He left a message, asking her to call him back.

Then he drained his coffee, tossed the cup into a trash can, crossed the street, and got into his car. By now he felt confident enough to brave the traffic. Maybe it was an illusory confidence, but after all, driving around Boston required far more guts than skill.

He inspected his face in the rearview mirror. His eyes were bloodshot, droopy, and glazed. His clothes reeked of marijuana. He wouldn't be fooling anybody. But he could always stop into a CVS, if he passed one, and buy some Visine. Maybe that would help.

He put the car in drive and turned right onto the Lynnway, past Meineke Muffler, a U-Haul, another Dunkin' Donuts, and then car dealerships, one after another. He drove slowly, cautiously, braking at yellow lights, infuriating the drivers behind him. Not the way he normally drove, and not the way you drive in the Boston area. But despite the big hit of caffeine, the marijuana's effects hadn't yet gone away. Everything around him seemed to be going fast, jittery and choppy.

He took his cell phone from the passenger's seat and glanced at it. He knew he shouldn't be using his cell phone while he drove. He pulled into a Shell station, filled up the tank, then parked in the side lot. He found "Recents" on his phone and redialed Monica Kennedy's number and got her voice mail again. He didn't leave a second message.

He continued on the Lynnway, eventually getting onto VFW Parkway, past the old greyhound track in Revere, Wonderland, now a shopping plaza. Soon the city of Boston loomed into view, its handsome glinting skyscrapers reminding him of the magical first time you glimpse the Emerald City in *The Wizard of Oz*.

Within a few minutes he was navigating a newly built series of roads, broad thoroughfares and rotaries built during the Big Dig. Then he entered the Ted Williams Tunnel, zipped through it. Everything did move faster around Boston now. Boondoggle or not, you had to give it that much: The Big Dig really had made the trains run on time.

He passed the airport, and the cargo terminal, and he continued on more new roads to *The Boston Globe*'s headquarters, a sprawling midcentury building on sixteen acres on Morrissey Boulevard, a no-man's-land south of downtown. Then he pulled into a visitor parking space and hit redial on his phone.

This time Monica answered.

"Kennedy," she snapped, the warning bark of a junkyard dog.

"Monica, it's Rick Hoffman."

"Oh . . . Hoffman, hey." She sounded distracted, unenthusiastic. "Yeah, I was about to call."

"Can I take you out to lunch?"

"Already ate at my desk."

"I mean, can I have half an hour of your time?"

An annoyed sigh. "You still at that crappy magazine?"

"Sort of."

"Heard you got canned."

"That would be more accurate."

"Hope you're not looking for something here. *Globe*'s not hiring."

"Nope."

"Does it have to be today?"

"I'd prefer it."

Another sigh. "After I file my column. Four, four thirty."

"Meet you at the *Globe*?"

"Liars." He knew she meant the Three Lyres, the official after-work bar for *Globe* reporters and editors and staff.

She hung up.

Monica wasn't a bad sort. Like most newspaper reporters, she didn't waste any charm on anyone who wasn't a potential source.

He didn't want to sit in the parking lot. He just needed to find some coffee shop with Wi-Fi nearby and do some online research. Then he realized he wasn't far from Dorchester, where Andrea's nonprofit, Geometry Partners, was based. Maybe she was there. She wasn't returning his calls, and he owed her an apology.

More than that, he owed her a do-over, another date, if she'd agree to it. He owed her another Rick, the real Rick, not the poser and fop and idiot with bundles of hundreds burning a hole in his pocket.

Ten minutes later he found the crumbling street off Dorchester Avenue and an old brick warehouse that had been converted cheaply into offices. The paneled door looked as though it belonged not on a warehouse but on a split-level ranch house in the suburbs.

Hardware-store stick-on numbers on the door said 14. A sheet of paper that said GEOMETRY PARTNERS in big computer-printed letters was taped just below the numbers. He suddenly had to pee. A lot of coffee had flushed through his digestive system and wanted out.

He knocked on the door awhile, then gave up waiting for someone to answer and just pulled it open. Inside was a small office crowded with two metal desks and a few people, looking like parents and kids, black and Hispanic. He approached one of the desks and asked the woman seated behind it, "Is Andrea Messina here?"

"She is, but she's tied up in meetings all afternoon. I'm sorry. It's nonstop."

He took one of Andrea's business cards from a tray on the desktop. It had her name and FOUNDER/CEO and the name GEOMETRY PARTNERS fashioned into a kind of colorful diagram, angles intersecting circles and dotted lines and points. He put it in his jacket pocket. Then he took another card and wrote on the back, "One more chance? Please?" and signed it "Rick."

"Could you give this to her when you see her?"

"Certainly, sir."

"One more thing. Could I use your restroom?"

"First door on the right."

A guy who looked like a gangbanger with sleeve tattoos down both arms, wearing a soiled white tank top, a so-called wifebeater, entered, holding a little girl by the hand. Father and daughter, presumably. He looked at once fierce and tender.

Rick found the bathroom and took a long, relieving piss. When he came out he bumped into Andrea. She was wearing a black pantsuit and a white blouse with a V-neck. The blouse wasn't cut particularly deep, but he could make out the cleft between the swell of her breasts. She was dressed conservatively but somehow looked sexy at the same time. Her hair was glossy and full and tumbled down to her shoulders.

"Oh, Rick," she said. "What—what are you doing here?"

She gave him a quick, chaste kiss on the cheek.

"I was in the neighborhood and just wanted to say hi. And apologize. And beg for a second chance. I left you a note to that effect."

"I'm sorry, it's been crazy," she said. She didn't sound convincing.

"I understand."

"Look, Rick"—she backed up into a tiny office, no bigger than a storage closet, which he could tell immediately, from the photos, was hers. "I wanted to thank you for dinner. It was . . ." Her nostrils flared as if she'd detected a bad smell. She peered suspiciously into his bloodshot, bleary eyes and asked, "Are you wasted?"

22

Not far from Geometry Partners was the Three Lyres. *The Boston Globe* reporters and photographers and editors who frequented the place called it, simply, Liars. The Liars Pub. The Liars Club. The walls were paneled in dark wood and the lighting was low. There were a lot of old pub signs mounted on the walls. The room was dominated by a big, welcoming U-shaped bar.

Monica Kennedy was waiting for him in one of the booths that lined the perimeter of the room. On the wall above the table hung an old Guinness sign of a toucan with a pint balanced on his beak. She had a beer in front of her in a pint glass, some brown ale with a round creamy head. Also an immense blooming onion, deep-fried to a perfect tan, as big and frightening as a sea creature, giving off a slightly rancid aroma.

"You hungry?" she said as Rick slid into the booth. "I'm starved. Missed lunch."

"I thought you ate at your desk."

"A yogurt doesn't count. Flag down the waitress and get yourself a beer."

She was hunched over the blooming onion, plucking out leaves like a surgeon. Her glasses were smudged, as always. Rick wondered if it ever bothered her, peering through clouded glasses, or if she got used to it, if she preferred it that way. She was wearing a grimy-looking maroon crewneck sweater over an ivory shirt with long collar points that stuck out like a nun's habit.

"Thanks for meeting me."

"Are they shutting it down totally?"

"What?"

"Your crappy magazine."

"Oh. Mostly. It's going to be online only."

"Sometimes they say that just to peel off staff." She produced a small squeeze bottle of nasal decongestant and squirted some into each nostril. Then she sniffed loudly. She was still an Afrin addict, apparently. "I still don't know why in the hell you quit real reporting to go to that rag."

"Money, why else?"

She looked up from the onion. She looked surprisingly, touchingly hurt. "But you were good."

He smiled, shrugged. "Apparently not good enough."

"What did you think, the *Globe* could match Mort Ostrow's offer? Not possible. You were the rising star here. I thought you wanted to be the next Sy Hersh." She meant the investigative journalist Seymour Hersh, who reported for *The New Yorker*, a legend in investigative journalism.

"Anyway, it was time for a change."

She shook her head, disgusted. "Have some onion."

"Maybe later." He managed to get the waitress's attention and asked for a Sam Adams.

He remembered a time when an ambitious editor had assigned him and a couple of other junior reporters to work with Monica on a team-written Pulitzer-fodder piece about a big chemical company that had been dumping a toxic pesticide, causing a cluster of birth defects in Western Massachusetts. Monica, competitive to the bone, was grudging and ungracious about having to be a "goddamn dog walker." But when Rick handed her his reporting file, she said, "Huh. Doesn't entirely suck." And Rick, realizing this was the highest praise from Monica, glowed.

"So what do you want?" she said.

"You ever come across my dad's name when you were reporting on the Big Dig?"

"I don't even know who your dad is."

"Leonard Hoffman. He was a lawyer."

She shrugged.

"He had a lot of clients in the Combat Zone."

She shook her head, turned her palms up.

"He represented strip clubs and various other establishments of the sort."

"Hey, someone's gotta do it."

"Apparently he bought cash from some of them. A lot of cash."

Her eyes widened and she smiled. Now he had her attention. "Really?"

"You know about this?"

She kept smiling. Her cheeks bunched up and lifted her glasses. She took a long sip of her Guinness. She set it down. "In theory. Wow."

"What?"

"It's like you just told me you saw the Loch Ness monster."

"Meaning what? You don't believe me?"

"Meaning it's something I've heard of for years and never could prove."

"Prove what?"

"The cash bank. Long rumored. Never spotted in the wild."

He raised his eyebrows. "The cash bank?"

"You need cash to pay bribes. No paper trail. But it's always a problem, how to get your hands on enough cash." She was nodding quickly, reflexively, examining the head on her beer. She never looked at you when she was thinking hard. She'd look at the floor or the cubicle wall or her (usually chewed) fingernails. "If you're not a cash business, and who is, anymore?" She made a tally on her fingers. "Convenience stores, restaurants, liquor stores. Parking garages. Nail salons. Back in the heyday of the Combat Zone, strip clubs and adult bookstores, places like that—I mean, talk about cash-intensive businesses. Any idea what quantity we're talking about?"

At least three point four million, he thought. "I have a feeling it was a lot. You never wrote anything about the cash bank."

"Look, it's like this." She pulled out her Afrin bottle, held it up. "What I *know* is this." She shook the bottle, which sounded mostly full. "But what I can *print* . . . is this much." She squeezed a dose into each nostril, snorted. "You remember, or maybe you don't. Maybe it was too long ago. But you always know a whole hell of a lot more than you can publish. Always. It's the hellish part of my job."

"So it's called the cash bank, huh?"

"Now, that would be a story, Hoffman. If you survived to publish it. Which you might not."

"'Survived'?"

"You write about that, you're messing with some heavy hitters who wouldn't want it out. You piss them off . . ." She shook her head.

"What?"

"Put it this way. You piss them off, they're not just gonna write angry letters to the editor."

23

He took Mass Ave straight through Boston and into Cambridge, and by early evening he'd returned to the Eustace House and lucked out, finding a parking space on Mass Ave right in front. As he backed into the space, he glanced at the passing traffic and noticed a hulking black SUV pass by, then pull over fifty feet or so ahead.

It was an Escalade. From a distance, and in the darkness, he couldn't tell whether its windows were tinted like the Escalade he'd seen earlier in the day, outside the donut shop. The odds of it being the same vehicle were small, he realized.

But if it was . . . He didn't want to be tailed to the B&B. Best not to take a chance. Forget about parking. He had to make sure he hadn't been followed.

He pulled out of the space, passed the Escalade, then signaled right. When he looked in his rearview he saw the Escalade moving back into traffic, behind him, and signaling right, too.

As if it were following him.

He turned right, and looked in his rearview, and the Escalade seemed to hang back. He caught part of its license plate: CYK-something. Then the vehicle made a right turn as well, and then Rick felt a prickle of anxiety.

He turned right again at the next block—and the Escalade didn't, and for a moment, Rick relaxed. He'd probably just been paranoid. He completed the circle around the block, this time passing the Eustace House without stopping.

Then, as he kept going down Mass Ave, the realization settled on him that maybe he wasn't in the clear at all. Maybe the Escalade had pulled away because its driver decided he'd been detected.

And as his stomach clenched, he tried to figure out how they'd found him, but he couldn't. He'd rented a car to avoid being tracked, and he'd been careful when renting the car not to be spotted. Or so he thought.

The fact was, Rick was an amateur, and he was dealing with professionals. He was dealing with relentless, possibly cold-blooded people. People who threatened him with dismemberment, threats that seemed all too plausible.

He thought he'd lost them at the Charles, and he was wrong. Somehow they'd found him again.

He had to take more extensive measures. He had to make sure.

He drove straight through East Cambridge to a shopping mall, the CambridgeSide Galleria. It was a perfectly ordinary, semi-high-end mall with a J.Crew and an Old Navy, an Abercrombie & Fitch and a Body Shop and a California Pizza Kitchen.

And a Zipcar office.

He parked on the second level, got out, went into Macy's and came right back out. He went down to the Apple Store and pretended to study the iPads. He went abruptly into Newbury Comics, where he acted as if he was browsing the DVD selections. He was anxious and trying hard not to let it show. No one seemed to be following him, but again, he couldn't be sure. There was no way to know. He went into Best Buy on one level, bought a flashlight, and exited on another level.

After forty-five minutes of this he felt jittery and paranoid and still not one hundred percent sure he wasn't being followed.

Then he rented another car at Zipcar. From the old car, he retrieved the file carton he'd taken from Joan Breslin's basement. Then, leaving the old rental car in the parking mall garage, he drove the new car out of the mall and across the Mass Ave Bridge near MIT into Boston. He found a bed-and-breakfast on Beacon Street in Kenmore Square that he'd seen a few times before, on his way to or from watching the Red Sox play at Fenway Park, and paid for a night in advance. He called Hertz to let them know where he'd left the Ford Focus. There would be stiff penalties for failing to return the car to a Hertz desk, but money was one thing he was no longer short of.

He wondered whether he was indeed safe. There was no way to know.

And then he realized he had to go back to the house on Clayton Street. And soon.

24

At two in the morning, Rick awoke, as if to an alarm, got dressed, and went down the dark stairs of the bed-and-breakfast to the empty street below. He'd parked on a side street a block away. The traffic lights were flashing yellow. The sidewalks were empty. The streets shone, slick after a late-night rain shower.

He took his keys to the house and the floppy disk from Joan's basement and the Maglite he'd bought at Best Buy.

He drove over to Clayton Street, past the house, and around to Fayerweather. The neighborhood was dark. A few porch lights were on, and the widely spaced streetlamps. He parked and rounded the corner back onto Clayton and stood at a distance, looking at the house. He felt almost silly doing it. There was no one in the house, of course, and no one outside of it. No one waiting for his return. Not at 2:20 in the morning.

He unlocked the back door and quickly entered, navigating the interior blindly, by rote, a route he'd taken countless times in high school, also in the middle of the night in the dark, hoping not to wake his ever-vigilant father or his sister.

He had to use the flashlight to get down the basement stairs without stumbling over the brooms and mops that hung on the stairwell walls. In full daylight, with the overhead lights on, this staircase was a trip hazard.

Down here it smelled of mildew and laundry detergent and something loamy, fungal. The furniture from upstairs was stacked high and covered in clear plastic tarps—couches, chairs, the kitchen table. Along the cinder block walls were old plastic shelves from Bed Bath & Beyond, heaped with junk: old toys, a bread maker, a food dehydrator, a sewing machine that probably hadn't been used since his mother was alive. Pots and pans and Igloo coolers and Tupperware containers. In the far corner was his father's workbench, rarely ever used, in front of a pegboard mounted on the wall, which was hung with rusty old saws and hammers and mallets and screwdrivers, an orange extension cord, a DeWalt power drill. Another shelf held turpentine and spray paint and cans of paint and wood finish.

He found the section where the furniture from Lenny's office had been relocated. His father's desk had been thoughtfully covered with a clear plastic tarp, now coated with a fine layer of white plaster dust. The plaster dust seemed to be everywhere, even down in the basement where no destruction had taken place.

He lifted the plastic tarp, then took an extension cord from his father's workbench and plugged in the old computer. He flipped the switch and was relieved to see it come to life, grunting and groaning. Green numbers and letters appeared on the monitor. It booted up slowly. As he waited for the computer to boot up, he looked around. There was all kinds of junk here on the plastic shelving—toys, appliances, old cell phone bills. His father never threw anything away.

He pulled a big box off the shelf that held stuff taken from Lenny's desk. There was that antique brass paper clip in the shape of a hand, which once belonged to Lenny's father. An envelope moistener, a blue plastic bottle whose yellow foam top had grown crusty with envelope glue and age. Did anyone use those anymore? A red heart-shaped glass paperweight, a gift from Rick's mom. A Swingline stapler. An empty tin can with rotelle pasta glued onto the outside and painted all over with light blue tempera—a crappy arts-and-craft project Rick had brought home from fourth grade. His father had always kept his pencils in it, though he had far nicer things to hold pencils.

Then he pulled out a large piece of white foam core with a lot of small rocks affixed to it. Rick's old, once cherished, rock collection. He was surprised to see it here. As a kid, Rick had for some reason collected rocks and minerals and had once painstakingly glued his best specimens to a poster board: rose quartz, obsidian, shale, mica schist. . . . Then he'd carefully labeled everything with one of those old-fashioned Dymo label makers, the kind with the alphabet dial and the embossing tape. (Click, click, click, *squeeze!*) But Rick distinctly remembered tossing it when he entered high school, purging his room of childish things. Len must have rescued it from the trash and brought it into his office, holding on to it for all these decades like a curator of Rick's childhood.

He found a silver desk clock, vaguely familiar. TIFFANY & CO., it said on the face. Then he noticed that its base was engraved:

FOR LEONARD HOFFMAN WITH THANKS FROM THE PAPPAS GROUP.

What was the Pappas Group, he wondered, that had given Lenny such an expensive gift?

He turned to the computer and saw the blinking prompt: C:>. Ready for him to type in text. My God, he'd forgotten about those days, when computers were first widely used. Rick had used a Macintosh for years and had gotten used to the ease, the friendly interface. Back in the day, you had to type in commands. He'd forgotten how.

But he knew how to insert a floppy disk. He pulled it out of its paper sleeve and slid it into the drive slot. The hard drive grunted some more, and after a few seconds some text appeared on the monitor.

It was a financial program called Quicken, and it was really nothing more than a record of deposits made into, and withdrawals from, two different Fleet Bank accounts. Fleet Bank hadn't existed in years, having been swallowed up by a bigger bank that was in turn swallowed up by an even bigger bank.

One was a regular business account, recording checks written to the electric company and other utilities, to the real estate company for the office rent, to Staples, that sort of thing. The other one was apparently a client fund account, a record of the checks Lenny had received from his clients.

All pretty standard and all pretty unremarkable. Rick wasn't sure if any of this would help him, but just in case it might, he plugged in the dot matrix printer, heard it clatter noisily to life, and made sure its cable was connected to the computer. It was. He clicked Print, and a minute or so later a long spool of perforated computer paper with little tractor-feed holes on either side came spewing out of the printer.

Sitting on the side of the desk he studied the sheaf of computer paper. It showed deposits and withdrawals for the last three years of his father's practice. He found the entries for the year 1996 and began scanning the columns slowly for deposits.

He found various deposits, in amounts ranging from fifty to thirty-two hundred dollars. Nothing bigger.

This just compounded the mystery. According to Lenny's office files, he'd billed eight of his clients 295,000 dollars in the month of May 1996. Yet according to the city archives, he hadn't done any of the work he'd billed for. And now he'd found that his father hadn't gotten *paid* for any of the work he'd billed for. Work he apparently hadn't done. So the bills were fraudulent.

He heard a noise from upstairs, a thump, and he froze.

He clicked off the flashlight and, in the pale moonlight, wove a path through the piles of chairs and the tarp-covered coffee tables toward the stairs. There he stood and listened again for the thump, and after another minute it came again, and he realized it was coming from the refrigerator in the kitchen directly above, cycling noisily on or off. He'd turned it on to use for cooling water and beer.

Keeping the flashlight off, he returned to his father's desk, grabbed the printout, and headed back up the stairs and out of the house.

Back in his room at the B&B, Rick Googled the Pappas Group.

It seemed to be some sort of public relations firm. Its website showed a bright photo of the gold dome of the Massachusetts State House, which was probably meant to symbolize power and access, the way a DC-based firm's website would probably show the Capitol. It disclosed little. There was language about "our expert tacticians" and "high-profile clients" and "discreet representation" and "reputation management." One page featured the logos of some of their clients—banks, restaurant groups, universities, shopping malls, radio stations, health clubs, and high-end retailers. All Rick gleaned from the website was that Pappas's firm was deeply entrenched and well connected.

The founder and CEO was Alex Pappas. His biography was spare:

"For almost thirty years Mr. Pappas has brought his unique media savvy and political acumen to bear in investigations, high-profile celebrity clients, and strategic advice on dealing with corporate communications challenges."

A Google search on Alex Pappas pulled up very little. A few passing mentions in the *Globe*, a blip in *Boston Magazine*. Everything was cursory and vague. Pappas had been a press secretary to a Democratic governor of Massachusetts years ago, ran the governor's successful reelection campaign, then left the public sector in a blaze of glory to start his own "strategic and crisis communications firm." It was as if he then decided to fly under the radar. You almost never saw mentions of him in the press. He'd all but gone into the witness protection program.

A search for the "Pappas Group" yielded more results. The firm was leading the public relations campaign on behalf of the Olympian Tower, a planned skyscraper in Boston that was sort of controversial, since it threatened to cast a long shadow over the Boston Public Garden. That was about all Rick was able to pull up.

What in the world was Lenny Hoffman, solo lawyer, doing with a Tiffany clock from such a high-powered firm?

In the morning Rick waited till ten before he called Monica Kennedy at the newspaper.

"What do you know about a guy named Alex Pappas?" he said.

"You're still on this cash bank thing?"

"Pappas is . . . the cash bank?" he said, surprised.

"Isn't that why you're asking about him?"

"Who is he?"

"I guess you'd call him a publicist."

"I'd never heard of him."

"Sure. He's so high-profile you've never heard of him. See, Rick, there's two kinds of publicists. The kind who gets your name in the paper, and the kind who keeps it out."

"What does he do? I mean, besides keep your name out of the paper?"

"Reputation management, crisis management, introductions."

"Introductions?"

"Back in the Big Dig days, Pappas was the guy to know if you wanted to land a contract. He introduced construction companies that wanted work to the people who hired. Let's just say he made a lot of state workers rich."

"You never did any reporting on him, did you?"

She sighed heavily. "To be honest, that guy was always too slippery for me to get a grasp on. Like nailing Jell-O to the wall."

And only then did it occur to Rick that Pappas began with the letter *P*.

25

He was never going to evade the watchers, as he'd come to think of them, entirely. That wasn't realistic. If he was careful, he could keep them from knowing where he spent nights. Theoretically he could change his rental car every couple of days, to make sure his vehicle wasn't tracked.

But he wasn't going to stop visiting his father, even though there had to be someone watching the nursing home, watching the comings and goings, waiting for him to show up at some point at the one place he was almost certain to go. So he'd have to take further precautions.

First he made a stop at Brooks Brothers on Newbury Street to pick up something for his father. He was there when the store opened, double-parked, and found a fluorescent orange parking ticket on the windshield of the Zipcar Toyota Prius when he got back. He didn't care.

Then he stopped at a costume shop on Mass Ave near the Berklee College of Music. It wasn't remotely Halloween time, but somehow this shop stayed open for business.

By a few minutes after eleven he parked a few blocks from the Alfred

Becker Nursing and Rehabilitation Center. He approached the tan-brick building with a heightened awareness and a low-level sense of anxiety. He wore a Red Sox baseball jacket and a black wig and a pair of aviator sunglasses. Anyone who wasn't looking too closely wouldn't recognize him.

Inside, he stopped at the men's room off the lobby and removed the wig and sunglasses. The woman behind the glassed-in counter seemed to take no notice of him. He wasn't sure what she was doing there.

"Twice in one week!" Brenda the health care aide said with a gummy smile when she saw him. "Dad's gonna be thrilled."

"Got something for him," Rick said. He stuck out the navy blue Brooks Brothers gift box.

"He loves chocolate," Brenda said.

"It's clothing. Don't get his hopes up."

She fell in beside him, joining him on the long walk down the corridor to Lenny's room. Rick was a little surprised. He didn't need an escort; he'd been coming here since long before Brenda started working here. He wanted to ask his father some questions, or rather, to give it another try, and he preferred not to have company.

He studied the wall-to-wall carpet underfoot, tan and beige and brown in a tight checkered pattern. The carpet was only a few years old. The Alfred Becker home took in a hell of a lot of money from its patients— its patients' families, actually—and could afford to keep the place up. Though it was really little more than a long-term parking facility for old people. They gave Lenny hardly any medical care, because his health was basically stable. In his case, six figures a year went to pay for the nursing home's staff and its terrible institutional food, which its inmates mostly didn't mind, probably, because after all they had no choice, and what was the use of complaining? The old people probably started off complaining vociferously when they first entered. But after a few months, they settled down and resigned themselves to their fate.

Lenny Hoffman wasn't much of a complainer, but Rick suspected that he, too, might be grousing if he were able to speak.

"There he is," Rick said heartily. Lenny was slumped in his big vinyl-cushioned chair next to his bed. There was a line of drool on his shabby old pajama top.

The TV was on—TV doctors in scrubs standing around a glossy set. "One cough—one sneeze—one million germs released into the air!" a gravelly voice-over said. The Chyron on the screen read, *Disease Cloud!*

His father lifted his head slowly, as if it were too heavy for his neck. Once again Rick was momentarily flustered by the outraged look on Lenny's face.

"Leonard!" Brenda called as if he were deaf, not just mute. "Look who's here again!"

His father moved his head warily in Rick's direction and then turned back to the TV.

"Next on *The Doctors*," the TV announcer said, "hybrid tummy tucks!"

"Thanks, Brenda," Rick said, dismissing her, or at least trying to. "Lenny, I've got something for you." He handed his father the Brooks Brothers box. Lenny took it in his left hand, the one that worked. It slipped from his grasp into his lap.

"Let me help you open it," Brenda said. She took the box from Lenny and pulled it open. Meanwhile, Rick found the TV remote and clicked Mute.

"Oh, aren't these handsome!" she said, taking out the navy blue

161

pajamas with white piping around the lapels, sort of nautical-looking. "That's exactly what he needs. We'll have to put them on after lunch."

"Hey, Lenny, how's it going?" Rick turned to Brenda, who showed no signs of preparing to leave. "I think we'll be fine now," he said pleasantly. "Time for a little father-son bonding." He sat at the end of his father's bed.

"Of course, of course, I completely understand," Brenda said, and with a curt nod she left the room.

Rick looked at his dad and found it hard to breathe. The air in the room was thick and oppressive. He smelled rubbing alcohol and cleaning solvent and nursing home food and something vaguely fecal. Something was pressing down on his chest. He could see a black hair sprouting out of a pore on his father's nose.

Lenny Hoffman, it turned out, harbored a secret ambition. He wasn't blithely satisfied with his sketchy job, his embarrassing clientele. He wanted more. He wanted something else. Maybe it was like his obsession with having Rick attend the Linwood Academy, that aspiration, that ache for something more in life.

There was nothing wrong with Rindge and Latin, the local public school. The mayor of New York City had gone there! So had Ben Affleck and Matt Damon! And the Linwood Academy was a mediocre prep school, for kids who couldn't get into Milton or Roxbury Latin or Belmont Hill or Buckingham Browne & Nichols. Sure enough, Rick hadn't gotten in to any of the good schools. He didn't interview well. He had no interest in switching to a prep school, but his father insisted. This was right after Rick's mother had died. Maybe Lenny wanted a school to take the place of a mother, give his kids the attention he couldn't. Or maybe there was something else going on, something even sadder. Like, if he couldn't be respectable, at least his kids could go to fancy schools.

"Dad," he said now. "The day you had your stroke you were scheduled to have lunch with someone. Someone whose name began with *P*. Do you remember who it was?"

His father looked at him, or at least seemed to be looking at him. Rick moved closer down the bed. His father's eyes remained fixed on his.

"Blink once for yes and twice for no. Do you remember?"

No response. Rick waited. A few seconds later Lenny blinked, but it seemed to signify nothing.

"Let me give you some names. See if you recall. Was it Phil Aronowitz?"

No response.

"How about Nancy Perry?"

No response. No blinks at all. What, if anything, did that signify?

"Was it Alex Pappas?"

Something seemed to come over Lenny's face. He looked agitated — even more agitated — and pained.

"The money — was it meant for Pappas? Blink—"

His father's left hand suddenly reached out and clutched Rick's wrist. Rick's heart seized.

"My God," Rick said softly. "You understand."

26

In the late afternoon, after moving to a new B&B, in Boston, Rick went back to the house.

He took measures—parked three blocks away and didn't get out of the car until he felt sure no one had taken notice of him—and carried a cooler of Bud for Jeff and the crew.

But everyone had gone home except Marlon and Jeff. Marlon was still working, framing, screwing in two-by-fours. The racket made it hard to hear what Jeff was saying. Jeff and Rick popped open cans of Bud and sat on the plaster-dusty hardwood floor next to a Sawzall and a discarded can of Red Bull.

"The city inspectors came by," Jeff said, popping open a beer.

"What for?"

"Make sure everything's going according to code."

"I assume we passed." Rick opened a beer and took a few cold sips.

Jeff shrugged. "They know me by now. You do enough work in the city, they get to trust you."

Marlon shouted, "Mind if I pack it in for the day? I'm finished up here."

"Go ahead," Jeff shouted back.

A moment of silence passed. Jeff scratched his chin. The goatee was probably new and he hadn't gotten used to it yet. He looked at Rick, tilted his head. "Ask you something?"

"Sure."

"How much money was there, inside the wall?"

Rick hesitated, but only for a minute. The question wasn't whether Jeff knew; it was how much he knew. He shook his head vaguely. "I didn't count it. Forty, fifty thousand, maybe? Maybe not that much. But, I mean, it was a lot." Because any found money was a lot, to him and to Jeff. Jeff, who worked hard for it. And Rick, who used to.

"It sure looked like more than that."

"I wish."

Jeff looked at him for a few seconds, but it seemed a lot longer. "Huh," he finally said. "Hope you're keeping it in a safe place."

"I think so."

"Good. I mean, that's a lot of money, and you wouldn't want anything to happen to it. People hear about that kind of money around, they do all sorts of extreme stuff."

"I know," Rick said uncomfortably. It didn't sound like any kind of a veiled threat, but he couldn't be entirely sure.

"You think your dad saved all that, or what?"

"I wish I could ask him about it."

"Does he . . . I mean, I know he can't talk or anything, but does he get what you say to him?"

"Well, that's the thing. I can't be sure, but I'm pretty sure he does understand."

"How do you know?"

Rick hesitated. "He grabbed my hand. When I said something about the money. Like he was warning me, maybe."

"Warning you?" Jeff sounded amused.

"Could be I was just imagining it, I don't know. Maybe it was nothing. I just get this eerie sense that he's not a vegetable. That there's someone home inside that head."

"You ever watch *Breaking Bad*?"

"Sure." He and Holly had spent several steamy summer weekends binge-watching that TV show about a high school chemistry teacher who becomes a meth cook, addicted, a couple of zombies sprawled on the bed, the air-conditioning on high.

"Remember the old guy with the bell? The—"

"Sure. You mean, could I do something with that kind of letter board they used on the stroked-out old guy? It's an idea, sure. But I'm not sure it would work. Years ago we tried that on him, but no luck."

"Can't hurt to try again."

"I can't get him to blink once for yes and twice for no, or whatever. He blinks, but I'm not sure what he's responding to. I need to get him seen by a good neurologist."

"You know what; I just did a remodeling job on this great old town house in Louisburg Square, belongs to the chief of neurology at Mass General. I could ask him."

"You stay in touch with him?"

Jeff nodded. "He's a great guy. He was happy with the work. It was pretty damned fine, if I say so myself. We did an awesome winding staircase on the main level."

"You think you could get in touch?"

"Happy to. He was telling me about all this crazy-ass new shit they've been doing at MGH with, like, magnets on the brain or something. Really wild."

"Like electroshock therapy?"

"Isn't that where they hook your brain up to a car battery or whatever whatever? Nah, I mean, it's literally like they put some kind of really strong magnet on your head." He tapped the side of his skull. "It makes depressed people undepressed, he said, and they're starting to use it on people with brain damage or stroke. It made me think about your dad."

"Put me in touch with him," Rick said. "I'll try anything."

27

Jeff put in a call to his former client, the chief of neurology at Mass General, Dr. Mortimer Epstein. Dr. Epstein had in turn called Rick and spent a good ten minutes on the phone asking about Lenny's condition. A generous act by a busy man. Rick could hear traces of an old Brooklyn accent in Dr. Epstein's speech, probably traces he'd tried to expunge, mostly successfully.

A few minutes into the conversation, Rick said, "So Jeff mentioned something about magnet therapy?"

"It's called transcranial magnetic stimulation," Dr. Epstein said. "TMS. It's been quite successful in treating depression, and it's shown some promising results in treating stroke victims as well."

"So it's a brand-new procedure?"

"There's nothing new about it. TMS has been around for thirty years. The great thing is, there's no downside. They basically place a magnetic coil on the patient's head and run an electrical current through it, pulsing it on and off for half an hour. If it works, great. If it doesn't— well, no harm, no foul."

"How long does it take to work?"

"It can take weeks and it can take days."

"Sounds a little sci-fi."

"That's what they said about anesthesia a hundred and fifty years ago. Anyway, look, TMS has become quite popular. There's a long waiting list of patients desperate to try it."

"How long a waiting list? I mean, are we talking months?"

Dr. Epstein let out a low chuckle. His Brooklyn accent came on strong. "Well, look, I'll try to pull some strings, get you moved to the head of the line. But how long has it been since your dad's stroke? I mean, not for nothing, but it's been like twenty years, right? What's the rush all of a sudden?"

Rick didn't know how to answer. *What's the rush all of a sudden?* The answer was simple and almost too ugly to admit.

A few weeks ago he didn't care that his father couldn't speak. The Lenny he'd grown up with was gone, replaced by a gaunt, spectral Lenny who bore no relation to his actual father.

So for the last twenty years he'd parked this replacement Lenny in a nursing home, just waiting for him to die a quiet and anticlimactic death.

Until it turned out that there was a lot of money at stake.

The next morning Rick showed up at the nursing home in an uberX car, a perfectly neat Mitsubishi. He'd brought a new set of clothes: a pair of khakis, a belt, and a blue button-down shirt. One of the attendants, a short, stocky Brazilian named Paulo, got Len out of his pajamas and into the new street clothes, which was a complicated operation. Also, the belt was too big; his father had lost a lot of weight over the years, largely muscle mass. Rick wheeled him out of the nursing home and into the wheelchair-accessible cab, with a lot of help from the taxi driver.

This was his father's first time outside the walls of the nursing home in eighteen years, and Lenny stared out the window, wide-eyed. By shortly before noon, they'd passed through the gates of the Charlestown Navy Yard, the two-hundred-year-old shipyard now part residential, part commercial, part historical preserve. It was the site where the British landed just before the Battle of Bunker Hill. Now, Marine barracks and paint shops and forge shops had been turned into condos; warehouses and rope walks and officers' clubs had been converted into outlying research facilities for Mass General Hospital. The cab pulled up to a brand-new-looking hospital building, the Sculley Pavilion, named for a rich benefactor, Thomas Sculley, the real estate magnate. Just seeing it gave Rick that unfinished-homework pang. The piece he'd been pretending to write.

When they got out, Rick could smell the tang of salt air and hear the cry of seagulls. They were just a few blocks from the Atlantic.

Getting his father out of the cab and into his wheelchair was an ordeal. Lenny's head lolled to his left, a thread of drool escaping the left corner of his mouth. His eyes came open as the chair scraped against the ground.

"You doing okay, Dad?"

Rick hadn't pushed a wheelchair for nearly twenty years. Gradually he got the hang of it as he searched for the wheelchair-accessible entrance. Even the simple process of wheeling his father up into the Sculley Pavilion and finding an elevator and getting him up to the second floor required reserves of patience Rick no longer had, if he ever did.

The elevator to the second floor required a building card-key—the research facility was security-protected—but people, he found, went out of their way to help. A woman in scrubs swiped the elevator keypad for him before taking the stairs herself. People passing by smiled at him as he wheeled his father out of the elevator and down the corridor. He was the good son taking care of his aged father. Everyone liked that.

"Well, Lenny, the guy we're about to meet is apparently some hot shit at Mass General. He's an expert in something called transcranial magnetic stimulation."

His father's eyes stared straight ahead.

"I know," Rick replied to his father's silence. "That's what I thought, too. But I figure it's worth a shot."

The director of the Laboratory for Neuromodulation was Dr. Raúl Girona, an associate professor of neurology at Harvard Medical School who had dark brown hair cut in high bangs and had a few days' growth of beard that looked deliberate. He wore tortoiseshell glasses that looked Euro-stylish instead of nerdy, a navy suit and a bright green tie and a red Pebble smart watch. He couldn't have been out of his thirties.

Meanwhile, in the next room, Lenny was being put through a battery of tests, all exams he'd no doubt been given years before, the greatest hits of stroke rehabilitation. He submitted to the tests docilely, as he did everything now, since he no longer had the ability to object.

"I should warn you," Dr. Girona said as they shook hands. "Your father's case is a difficult one."

"Because of how long it's been?"

Dr. Girona shrugged and sank back into his chair behind a small bare desk. "That concerns me less than the fact that your father does not speak at all. Most stroke victims are able to speak to *some* extent. They can make sounds, sometimes words or phrases. But your father's chart indicates that he is unable to phonate at all, correct?" He was from Spain,

171

according to his bio on the Mass General website, from Catalonia, but his English, though strongly accented, was remarkably fluent.

Rick nodded. "I'm not expecting miracles. I'm not expecting him to sit up one day and start talking about the Red Sox starting lineup with me. I just want to know what's possible."

"Well, your father has been categorized as a global aphasic. That means he can neither express himself nor comprehend when he's spoken to. But I take it you think that diagnosis is incorrect."

"I think there's a good chance, yeah. Seems like he understands when I talk to him. He just doesn't have a way of communicating what he wants to say."

"What makes you think he understands?"

"He sometimes blinks rapidly, like he's trying to tell me something. And when I asked him about something recently—something upsetting, I think—he grabbed my wrist."

"With his right hand?"

"His left."

"Ah, yes. His right side is immobilized. Well, perhaps so. More to the point, the question is, how *much* does he understand? And how can you know?"

"If he could write a note, maybe. Or type on a keyboard."

Dr. Girona nodded. "I'm sure your father's doctors and occupational therapists have tried all of the standard methods. The picture and symbol communication boards and so on. But the problem is, some aphasics don't *understand* speech at all. At most, they recognize familiar names."

"Can TMS help with that?"

"Perhaps. You know how a stroke affects the brain, yes?"

"Basically."

Dr. Girona went on as if Rick hadn't replied. "A stroke happens when something cuts off the flow of blood to your brain. The neurons in a certain area of the brain are starved of oxygen and they die. Now, the part of the brain where your father had a stroke was the left side, yes? And we know the left side of the brain not only controls the right side of the body but it's also where the dominant language center is—the left inferior frontal gyrus, where speech is produced."

"Okay." Rick nodded.

"Now, when one side of the brain is damaged in a stroke, the other side takes over. As if to compensate. But we want to make the left side start to work again, right? To grow back, you might say. And the way we do that is to use magnetic pulses to rewire the brain itself. We run an electrical current through a wire in a coil to generate a magnetic field. Depending on what kind of magnetic field we generate, we can either activate the brain cells or inhibit them. Make them either more reactive or less. Are you following me so far?"

"I think so," Rick said. "So you want to inhibit the right side to make the left side start doing work."

"Exactly! We place the coil over the posterior inferior frontal gyrus. To inhibit the right side of his brain. Which we hope will make the left side, the language side, start to work again. And gradually the brain begins to rewire itself."

"Will it hurt him?"

Dr. Girona shook his head. "At most, it may feel like a series of pinpricks."

"How long will it take to see some results?"

"A few weeks, most probably. But you need to have realistic expectations."

"What should I expect?"

"Expect nothing, and you won't be disappointed."

"I see. Well, anything would be an improvement."

"One more thing. And perhaps I should have started with this. This is a costly procedure, and it's not covered by any insurance."

"How costly are we talking?"

"You'll have to talk to our finance people."

"Ballpark."

"For a full course of treatment we're talking probably over a hundred thousand dollars."

Rick nodded, shrugged. "That won't be a problem."

28

Rick called Darren Overby, the editor in chief of *Back Bay*.

"Darren, how would you feel about a profile of Alex Pappas?"

"Alex Pappas . . . Remind me who he is again?"

"The Pappas Group. PR guy, fixer."

"Oh, *right*. That would be great. But not a full profile, of course."

"No, no. Nothing too serious. Just a Q&A, really."

"*Do* it! But when am I going to see the Thomas Sculley piece?"

"Yeah, soon," Rick said. Like never.

Then he called the Pappas Group, was connected to Pappas's office, and left a message with one of his assistants, a woman with an appealingly raspy voice and a posh British accent.

It was a long shot, but worth a try.

To his surprise, an hour and a half later he received a call from the assistant agreeing to an interview the next morning.

The game was on.

*   *   *

He called Monica Kennedy and managed to keep her on the phone for six minutes while he questioned her about Alex Pappas. Though she claimed to have very little information on the man, she did know a few interesting things. She knew that his clients included a couple of former governors and mayors and senators. They also included a judge caught in a bribery scandal involving the construction of a huge parking garage. A football player for the New England Patriots, accused of murder, had hired Pappas to handle the public relations fallout, not legal representation. A House Speaker charged with corruption but who maintained his innocence had used Pappas's services—again, not legal but in the realm of "reputation management." Improving the Speaker's image. A chemical company accused of contaminating the drinking water in a remote Massachusetts town, causing a sudden rise in leukemia cases among the children, had hired Pappas. The chemical company had had the charges dismissed, but that might have been the result of shrewd legal representation.

Alex Pappas specialized in crisis management, in "putting out fires," Monica said. In making scandals go away.

The more Rick learned, the sketchier Pappas seemed to be. He seemed to have his fingers in a thousand pies.

In the morning, after too many cups of coffee, Rick arrived at Pappas's offices, on the forty-second floor of the Prudential Tower in the Back Bay. He was apprehensive for some reason, probably because he didn't know what to expect. He had to keep reminding himself that he was ostensibly there to conduct an interview. A puff piece. That was the cover story, anyway.

On one side of the bank of elevators was a law firm. On the other side, behind glass doors, was the Pappas Group. The reception area was hushed and sterile. Dove-gray wall-to-wall carpet, low flat coffee tables perched in front of low white leather couches. A receptionist sat at a long mahogany desk. Rick gave his name and prepared to wait. Some interview subjects liked to keep their interviewers waiting, just to show them who's boss. The more reluctant the subject, the longer the wait, Rick had always found. The receptionist, a dark-haired Asian beauty in her midtwenties, offered him coffee or water. Rick took a bottle of spring water and sat down on one of the sofas. He took out his iPhone, switched off the ringer, and pocketed it again.

Arrayed on the coffee table were the local newspapers, the *Globe* and the *Herald*, as well as *The New York Times*, *The Wall Street Journal*, and the salmon-colored *Financial Times*. Rick was reaching for the *Journal* just as someone said, "You must be Rick Hoffman."

He looked up and saw a lean middle-aged man bounding across the reception area. The man had silver hair and thick horn-rimmed glasses and was dressed in a perfectly cut gray suit.

Rick rose. "Mr. Pappas," he said, offering his hand.

"Alex. Please." He had a pleasant baritone voice.

"Rick. Nice to meet you."

Pappas had a sharp, prominent nose like a hawk's beak, a deeply creased, tanned face, and a dazzling smile. His teeth were a shade of white not found in nature. He was a few inches shorter than Rick, a tightly coiled man, fit and trim and radiating energy. "Come," Pappas said, placing a hand on Rick's shoulder and guiding him across the reception area, down a hallway and into a big corner office. Here Pappas didn't seem a recluse at all. The walls of his office were lined with photographs of himself with the rich and powerful and famous, governors and senators and businessmen and TV stars. He obviously wanted visitors to his office to admire his proximity to the famous, even if he didn't like to talk about it to reporters.

They sat at a couple of chairs off to one side of his desk, a glass coffee table between them. The chairs were high-backed, overstuffed, comfortable. The whole office was arranged as carefully, as ceremonially, as the Oval Office. Rick placed his small black leather-bound reporter's notebook on the table. He considered taking out his iPhone and switching it to Record mode but decided to hold off. A running tape recorder—actually, most journalists by now used their phones to record—was a quick way to get an interview subject to clam up. And he wanted Pappas to let down his guard, unlikely though that might be. But for now, that was Rick's best hope. He'd prepared a set of questions for Pappas, all of them predictable, none probing or provocative. The sort of questions that would enable Pappas to spout boilerplate answers by the yard, the sort of questions that might get the man to lower his defenses. This wasn't going to be an interrogation. The point was to lull him into complacency.

"I'm sorry *Back Bay* stopped publishing the print edition," Pappas said. "It was a handsome magazine."

"Me, too."

"Well, that seems to be the future. Everything digital, everything online, no more paper."

"Seems that way."

"They laid off a lot of the staff. And yet here you are."

"Thanks for seeing me. I know you don't often talk to the media."

"I talk to the media all the time." He paused. "Just not about myself—and why should I? I'm *boring*! I may have some interesting clients, but that doesn't make me interesting."

"Well, you are Boston's crisis management king."

"Or so the *Globe* once called me." He smiled, relenting a bit. "Rick, I want to get a sense first of what you have in mind. I think it'll work best if we're both clear about where we're coming from and where we hope to be going."

So this wasn't an interview at all, Rick thought. It was a *pre*-interview.

"Sure," Rick said. "Well, I'm interested in the world of crisis management and reputation management. You've been at the center of some significant events in the last several years, yet you seem to be happiest staying out of the spotlight."

Pappas was silent. He pursed his lips.

Rick went on: "It's basically a character study. What kind of person has these skills and abilities?"

"I see," Pappas said. "You're onto something. I'm not the guy who uses up all the oxygen in the room. Which is why this little story of yours may turn out to be a nonstarter. It may be what neither of us needs. Let's talk about you, shall we?"

"Me?" Rick attempted a smile.

"You're no longer the guy who was writing stories about pension abuse or illegal chemical dumping in Western Mass, are you? Though your byline on that series was shortlisted for a Pulitzer; am I remembering correctly?"

Pappas was clearly remembering from five minutes ago when he read through some information file, probably in a folder on his desk right now.

"Very good," Rick said. "That's right."

"You gave up a high-powered career in journalism, and now you're in the soft-soap business," Pappas said. "What is it that you really want?"

"What *I* want . . . ?"

"You. I ask because I've hired people in the past from your line of work, often very successfully."

"What are you turning this into, a job interview?"

"Would that bother you?"

"That's not why I'm here."

Pappas leaned back in his chair and looked up at the ceiling. The lenses of his glasses were thick, distorting his eyes. "Here's the thing, Rick. I don't really want this piece to be written about me. And I don't think you actually want to write it. Let's talk about the real reason you made this appointment with me."

"Okay. What I really want to ask about is my father. You knew him, didn't you?"

"I sure did," Pappas said at once. "Leonard Hoffman was a wonderful man."

"Actually, he's still alive."

Pappas's BlackBerry vibrated on the coffee table. He picked it up, glanced at it. "I understand. He had a stroke. A very unfortunate thing."

"Going over his papers, I noticed a lot of phone calls between you two. Were you a client of his?" That was an out-and-out bluff, about the calls. Rick hadn't seen any records of phone calls. He was hazarding a guess. If the two of them met, Pappas was the kind of man who'd have put in a call, or several calls first. Or had his office place some calls.

"Did I call your father? Of course. I called when I needed his help." Guess confirmed.

"In fact, you were scheduled to meet for lunch on the day of his stroke."

"Is that so? It's been years." His tone flattened. "What can I help you with, Rick?"

"I'm curious what sort of work he did for you."

"Various legal errands. I can't say as I recall the details."

"But why him? You have access to any white-shoe law firm in the city. To be honest, I was surprised to discover you two knew each other. You move in . . . well, in very different circles."

"If I were to limit my reach to the usual suspects, the Ropes and Grays, the Goodwin Procters, the Mintz Levins—well, they all play in the same sandbox. Your father, on the other hand, was well connected in certain quarters."

"So what sort of legal work did he do for you?"

Pappas had become distant, wary. His eyes looked out of focus. "I'm sure it all falls under the general rubric of attorney-client privilege, Rick."

Now Pappas hunched forward in his chair and gave a great crocodile's smile. "Rick, we're both grown-ups. Why don't you tell me exactly what you'd like to know? Let me know how I can help you."

"It's just surprising that you'd have anything to do with my dad," Rick persisted. "You're the major league, and he was anything but."

"Your father provided services."

"By services, you mean . . . ?"

"Any number of things. Rick, I'm—"

"Did my father's services include something called the cash bank?"

He waited. Pappas was silent. He didn't indicate whether he recognized the term or not. Rick went on, inching up to the edge of the cliff. "To be blunt, my father procured cash used for bribery. So I'm wondering whether he provided cash to you. For bribery."

"Certainly not, but I'm glad to see you've retained the old think-the-worst instincts of an investigative reporter. Son, I don't swim in that lane." His BlackBerry buzzed again. He glanced at it and ignored it again. Then he looked directly at Rick, his eyes magnified in size, the expression dead. "But you believe your father did."

Rick met Pappas's stare unflinchingly. He nodded.

"Were his books a mess? Did he leave you cash you can't account for? The more I know, Rick, the more I can help you."

"It's clear my father was involved in dirty work of some kind. I'm trying to get a handle on exactly what it was."

Pappas was silent for a long while. A cloud scudded by over the Boston skyline.

"That's quite an accusation," he said. "I assume your father isn't able to speak, or you'd ask him. So you must have proof of some sort."

"A number of documents," Rick lied.

Pappas tented his fingers thoughtfully. "Be more specific."

"Let me put it this way. There's a pretty interesting trail there."

Pappas took off his glasses and massaged his eyes with his fingertips. The BlackBerry buzzed again but this time he didn't even look at it. With his eyes still closed, he said, "You're suggesting your father was a bag man?"

"A fixer."

Pappas let the word hover in the air. "I believe the usual term for guys like him is *expediter*. How they do what they do is their own business. I know nothing about it, and I don't judge. But I think you're being uncharitable."

"Uncharitable?"

"Your father, as you may know, was scorned in most legal circles. He was regarded as untouchable, the poor man. But I knew better. I knew the stuff he was made of. He was a stand-up guy. He was a good person. Now, did I send people his way? Sure. I looked out for him. So tell me something: Why in the world would you want to drag his name through the mud, a man in his condition?"

Pappas was far slipperier an opponent than Rick had expected. For a moment he faltered, unsure how to proceed. Finally he replied, "Don't misunderstand me. I have no intention of writing an article about my dad's business. I'm here to get some clarity on the mess he left behind. On the 'cash bank' and how it worked. For my own sake."

"I see. Simple curiosity." He said it in a gentle, thoughtful way, but Rick sensed a subtle sarcasm.

"That's all."

"The 'cash bank,' you say."

"Whatever you can tell me."

"Well, Rick, Boston twenty years ago wasn't exactly the cleanest town. A lot of money changed hands, true. None of this shocks me. You know what Robert Penn Warren said in *All the King's Men*. 'Man is conceived in sin and born in corruption, and he passes from the stench of the didie to the stink of the shroud.' Or something very close to that. Just because my hands happen to be clean doesn't mean I judge. I do not. So tell me what you've found. What amount of cash did he leave around—ten thousand dollars? Ten dollars? I can't help you if you don't let me know the particulars."

Rick shook his head slowly.

Pappas got to his feet and beckoned Rick with a flip of his right hand.

He turned and walked out of his office into the hallway, Rick following close behind. Pappas swerved through the open door of an empty office that had been cleared out. There was a big desk and a high leather chair behind it and a lamp and a cluster of chairs and a coffee table in front of it, just as in Pappas's office. The view over Boston Harbor was remarkable. But there were no papers or framed things. It was vacant. No one worked here.

"This was Cass Mulligan's office. He was just hired away from me by a K Street firm. I need to replace him with someone who's fast and skillful and savvy."

Rick nodded. "Okay . . ."

"Let's speak frankly." He placed a hand on Rick's shoulder as they both stood facing the Boston skyline. "Son, your life is shit. You left journalism behind, Mort Ostrow offered you a big pay package, and that worked out for a few years until it didn't. You were let go. Minimal severances were paid. You have no salary, no wages, no benefits. Your situation clearly cost you personally—you and your lovely fiancée split up, yes? Holly, was that her name?"

Rick felt something twist within his abdomen. Pappas had done his homework. "That had nothing to do with my job," he protested.

"Irreconcilable similarities, then, is that it?" Pappas gave a low chuckle. "The temperature sure seems to have dropped quite a bit since the days when you and Holly were enjoying umbrella drinks at Pink Sands on Harbour Island, hmm? You've got to be wondering about the decisions you made. Now, you know the media from the inside out. I've always thought there's no better defense attorney than a former prosecutor. You're just the sort of person I'd be pleased to see on my team. If this is a scenario that might appeal to you, we can have that conversation. But maybe you have other decisions in mind."

"I'm flattered," Rick managed to say.

"The question, Rick, is whether you're more interested in the past or in the future."

Rick hesitated. "Both, I suppose."

"Let me tell you a story," said Pappas. "When I was a kid, my old man kept a small home office—he was an accountant—with a file cabinet whose top drawer was always locked. Naturally, I was curious." He placed a hand on his chest. "Then as now, I liked knowing things. What could possibly be in that locked file drawer? What could my father possibly be keeping from me? I loved and respected my father more than anyone in the world. Well, one day a friend and I figured out how to pick the lock on that top file drawer, using a couple of paper clips. We managed to unlock it. And what sort of files do you imagine were hidden away in that drawer?" He smiled ruefully. "Alas, no files. No papers. Do you know what was in that drawer? Magazines. What you might call smut magazines. Magazines with photographs of women with big boobs, lots of leather, lots of chains. Women being dominated. Women being submissive. My father was into what's called BDSM. Bondage and discipline and sadomasochism." He seemed momentarily lost in thought. "This was a side to my father I wish I'd never learned. I didn't need to know this. It turned my world upside down. It made me lose all respect for the man. I wish to hell I'd never opened that file drawer, Rick."

He stared at Rick again with those enlarged, blurry eyes. Rick nodded.

Pappas went on. "It's my business to know things. To know as much as I can. But sometimes . . . well, every once in a while you learn something you later wish you could unlearn. But you can't. Though, by God, you wish you could."

There was a long silence. Rick said nothing.

Finally, Pappas said mournfully, "Do you really want to know what's in that file drawer, Rick?"

29

Alex Pappas hadn't been fooled by the interview ruse, not for a moment. He seemed to know why Rick was there even before he arrived at his office. He was the sort of man who prided himself on always being a step ahead. And he had been.

Rick had the uneasy feeling that Pappas had agreed to the faux interview because he wanted to meet Rick. He wanted to sound Rick out, to find out what he could about what Rick knew and how he knew it.

And to manipulate him, to shame him if possible, to discourage him from probing any further and to try to buy him off. Pappas had done deep research into Rick, to a creepy extent, and he wanted to make sure Rick knew it.

But though Pappas had seen right through it, the meeting had been successful, from Rick's point of view. For one thing, Rick had spotted Pappas's business cards in a holder on his desk, facing the visitor on the outer edge of the desk, and he'd slipped one into his pocket. More important, he'd learned a number of useful things. He was now certain that Pappas was the "P" in his father's appointment calendar. And he'd corroborated his theory that Pappas was connected to the "cash bank" Monica Kennedy had mentioned. Pappas's behavior, his blatant attempts at manipulation, had confirmed it.

But all Pappas's attempts at intimidation had failed. Rick didn't much care for Pappas's condescending attitude toward his father. Pappas had given him a warning, and Rick was never good with warnings. Warnings just egged him on. They awakened the long-dormant investigative journalist part of his brain. Pappas was afraid of something, and now Rick was determined to find out what.

In fact, the meeting with Pappas had emboldened Rick. He'd stuck his head into the lion's mouth and pulled it back out without any visible bite marks on his neck. Five days had gone by without his being abducted again by the poetry-quoting Irishman with a butcher's saw.

I'll ask you again, the man had said. *Who've you been talking to? A simple question, Mr. Hoffman. Because your father doesn't speak. So it's someone else.*

Maybe the Irishman had gotten the answer he wanted. Or maybe he'd decided Rick didn't know the answer.

Who've you been talking to?

The question wasn't *Where's the money?* It was *Who have you been talking to?* Who'd told him about the money?

The Irishman, and by implication Pappas—since they had to be a team—wanted to know *who* he'd been talking to.

You must have proof of some sort, Pappas had asked. Proof that Lenny had engaged in bribery.

The more I know, Rick, the more I can help you.

Pappas had wanted to know what Rick knew. Were there account books? Were there records? Was there proof?

Maybe Pappas had finally concluded that Rick knew next to nothing, that he hadn't been talking to anyone, that he had no records, no proof.

Nothing that would cause Pappas any kind of problems.

If so, that would mean that Rick was no longer a threat to Pappas. Which meant that Pappas wasn't a threat to Rick. And neither was the poetry-quoting Irishman.

That would mean it was safe for Rick to appear at the obvious, expected places. He needed to return to Clayton Street anyway, and it would be easier in the daytime.

On the way, he thought about what Pappas had said. *Did I call your father? Of course. I called when I needed his help.*

Rick had been bluffing, but the bluff had turned out to be the truth. Pappas had indeed called Lenny.

So maybe there were records of those calls. When you were doing investigative journalism, you amassed as many documents, files, records as you could, to try to spot the tiny anomalies that might reveal something unexpected. Investigative journalism wasn't like meeting Deep Throat in a parking garage. It was like mining for gold. You dug and dug, past the topsoil, down to the mineral layer, then you blasted the rock apart using explosives, then you trucked the rocks somewhere else to crush and process, and for every ton of rocks you went through, you'd get maybe five grams of gold. If you were lucky.

He was still digging into the topsoil.

He called his sister, Wendy, spoke for just two minutes, and hung up. Then he parked and entered the house. The crew was hard at work, their music blasting, nail guns rat-a-tat-tatting, power screwdrivers whining and squawking.

Rick gave Jeff a wave. Jeff replied with a thumbs-up.

Then Rick headed down to the basement, where it was quieter, and cool, and peaceful. He pulled the cord on the bare overhead bulb in the back part of the basement where the old files and records were kept. Within a few minutes he'd located the cardboard boxes from Staples in which Wendy had boxed up all the old files and papers left around the house after their father's stroke.

He found the box marked PHONE BILLS and took it down from the shelf. He took out a few bills and opened them.

They were useless. Each bill listed the menu of "services" the phone company had provided for the month as well as whatever long-distance calls Lenny had made. But local calls weren't listed. They never were. There was nothing here.

Then Rick found a thick envelope that changed everything. It was a bill from Cellular One, for Lenny's cell phone. Rick had forgotten that his father had a cell phone fairly early on. By 1996 cell phones were starting to become popular, especially among businesspeople and lawyers.

And in the early days of cell phones, the wireless providers were still sending thick bills detailing every single call placed.

He pulled out all the Cell One phone bills for 1996. He couldn't find any after August, but then he remembered that Joan Breslin had canceled his father's phone after a few months, when it became apparent that he wasn't going to recover. He opened the envelope for the February bill, which covered all calls for a month starting from the beginning of January.

And he began going through the statement, his eyes running down the lists of phone numbers, of calls placed and calls received. He was looking for patterns, particularly repeated calls to and from any phone number. The number listed most often by far was the number of Lenny's office, which was no surprise: Lenny would have called the office to talk to Joan multiple times when he was out and on his mobile. Then there was the family home number, showing calls between Rick and Wendy and their father at work.

Rick took out the June bill, detailing May's calls, and moved right to May 27, the day of the stroke. He immediately saw a lineup of three calls, all to the same 617 area code number. He pulled out Alex Pappas's business card and confirmed that it was Pappas's mobile number. The day before, there were five calls to that same number. Six the day before that. None for the two weeks previous.

So why all the calls to and from Alex Pappas on those three days between May 25 and May 27?

Something must have happened that required Lenny's services. Pappas had wanted something from Lenny. So what had happened on those three days?

He couldn't ask his father. He needed some other way. The simplest solution was to look through a newspaper from those days, an online archive. That meant returning to his B&B and getting back online. Taking not just the one phone bill but all his dad's Cell One phone bills back to the hotel and poring through them.

Still, Rick would take precautions, as usual, to avoid being tailed. He carried the four phone records boxes to the foot of the basement stairs and climbed the stairs, passed through the cloud of noise and plaster dust and back-and-forth chat and angry hip-hop—*What you know about thumbing through them hunnits, twenties, and them fifties?*—to the windows at the front of the house, and there he froze.

Across the street a car was idling.

Hear the twenties, fifties, hundreds, the money machine clickin'.

He'd noticed it an hour or so ago, a white sedan, an Audi, nothing out of place for the neighborhood. But there it still was, the driver texting on a smartphone, a plume of exhaust snaking around from the rear. Rick backed away from the window until he was out of the direct line of sight but could still see the Audi.

It was waiting for him, he somehow knew. Something about the way the driver was studiously avoiding looking out the window, or the way the car was parked just far enough down the street so as not to be too obvious, or the way the car hadn't moved in over an hour.

But he knew it was watching the house.

Theoretically he knew the neighborhood well enough, better than any watcher, to lose anyone trying to follow him in a car. He knew which backyards led to which streets and which houses had toolsheds in their backyards. He knew places to hide better than anyone who hadn't grown up in this part of Cambridge.

But maybe there was a better way to evade detection. He tapped Jeff on the shoulder, then asked him if it was okay if he hired Marlon and Santiago for a brief errand. Jeff shrugged. "Be my guest," he said.

"Guys," he said when Marlon and Santiago were standing around the file cartons, Marlon wiping his plaster-dusted brow with the back of a large hand. He gave Santiago the key to his latest Zipcar. "You guys mind carrying these boxes out to my car? It's a blue Prius, parked a couple blocks away, right in front of 39 Fayerweather."

Both of them seemed to hesitate a moment or two. Marlon glanced over at Jeff, who shrugged again, giving his permission. They clearly didn't want to do it, saw no reason to do it. They didn't have to brownnose the owner of the house, because they didn't work for the owner. They worked for Jeff. Rick pulled out a couple of hundred-dollar bills, one new, one not so new, and handed one to each of them. Their faces lit up like kids being handed chocolate. Marlon had a full silver grill. Rick hadn't noticed before. He was overpaying them for a simple errand, but he figured it might buy some goodwill. There was more where that came from.

"Just these right here?" Santiago asked, suspicious there had to be a catch.

"That's all. And one more thing."

Santiago looked at Marlon: *Knew it was too good to be true.*

"Could one of you move my car to that little lot next to Hi-Rise? The bakery?"

"On Concord right near where Huron comes in?" Marlon said.

"Exactly." He didn't bother to explain; he didn't need an explanation. He just wanted his car moved, for some idiotic reason, to another spot a few blocks away.

Marlon looked at Jeff. "Cool, we take a break now?"

"Don't take too long," Jeff said.

Ten minutes after the two guys set off bearing cardboard boxes, Rick left the house. He walked up Huron Avenue toward Fresh Pond, the opposite direction from which the two workers had gone. He clocked something moving in his peripheral vision behind him, behind him and to his left, and tried not to look to confirm it was the white Audi. But it was. The driver in the Audi had waited until he'd reached the end of Clayton and turned right on Huron, when he'd be out of range. The last possible moment, so he wouldn't be detected. Rick kept going up Huron Ave, studiously not noticing the car. Not until he reached the busy intersection of Huron and Fresh Pond Parkway did he have the chance to turn sideways, as if watching for oncoming traffic, and then he saw the Audi double-parked half a block down, waiting.

It was following him. But he was walking nowhere, with great purpose. He crossed Fresh Pond and headed into the park, where he and his friends had ridden their bikes, where he'd walked their black Lab, who'd been killed running out into traffic the same year his mother had died, the year from hell.

He walked around the reservoir. A few joggers ran past, talking. In here, within the wooded enclave of Fresh Pond Reservation, the Audi was at a disadvantage: unable to see, unable to enter. He had lost them. There were dozens of exits from the park. He chose one on the far end of the park, on Concord Avenue, flagged a passing cab.

Then he walked a few blocks down Concord Avenue to Hi-Rise bakery and looked in the small lot next door and didn't see his Zipcar. He turned, looked around Concord. Maybe the guys couldn't find a space next to Hi-Rise and just parked it where they could. But no Sea Glass Pearl Toyota Prius in sight. He rounded the corner onto Huron Avenue, still looking. Maybe they'd parked it as close to the lot as they could, and . . . But no Prius, not here.

It didn't seem at all likely that Jeff's crew would have stolen his car. Not a Toyota Prius, in any case. But it wasn't here, and neither was Marlon nor Santiago. He debated heading back over to Clayton Street and was in fact on his way over ten minutes later when a Prius pulled over to the side of Concord, horn blaring.

"There you guys are," Rick said. "What took you so long?"

Marlon, in the passenger's seat, smiled and said, "Homey had to do an errand."

Santiago got out of the driver's seat and came around to hand Rick the keys. "Sorry about that, bro," he said. "Had to pick something up."

He knew then what had taken so long. They searched the car for cash. They thought Rick had hidden some or all the cash in the Prius, under the seats or in the glove compartment or in the trunk. They'd taken the car somewhere and pulled it apart. They'd probably searched the file boxes, too. But they'd found nothing. That didn't mean they'd stop looking, though. The question was how far would they go. He'd thought that slipping them each a Benjamin would buy them off, neutralize their greed, but it had done the opposite. It had goaded them on. Like the mechanical rabbit at the dog track. Like giving a bloodhound an article of clothing, a scent: *ready, go!*

It had been a mistake he wouldn't make again. Jeff wouldn't do anything.

But these guys very well might.

30

He pulled into traffic and was at the offices of *Back Bay* magazine fifteen minutes later. He was taking a risk, appearing for a second time at the magazine. But the kind of search he had to do could be done only at the office. He needed to do an advanced search of LexisNexis by date. A conventional Internet search would take forever. You can search *The New York Times* or *The Boston Globe* or *The Wall Street Journal* for incidents or names but not by what happened during three days in May in 1996. For that he needed to use LexisNexis on site.

The office was empty when he arrived. His badge got him in the door, though, and he flipped on the overhead lights, jittery fluorescents. He logged into the magazine's intranet and found a nagging e-mail from Darren. *How's the Sculley Q&A coming?* he wanted to know. *He'll be at the gala at the Park Plaza on Wednesday—maybe a good chance to sit down with him?*

Rick didn't bother to reply. The best strategy with Darren was just to ignore him. Rick pulled up LexisNexis. He typed in the date range, which yielded hundreds of headlines.

He groaned. He was looking at everything that had happened in Boston and Massachusetts over those three days. Politicians in trouble in the State House, town officials accused of graft . . . CAMBRIDGE MAN HELD IN STABBING. A guy was stabbed in the neck and chest at the Portuguese Football Club. 86-YEAR-OLD MALDEN WOMAN SUFFERS SEVERE BURNS IN APARTMENT FIRE. A sprinkling of obituaries, minor sports and medical news, the Indy 500 winner, the Fire Department's annual ball at the Sheraton.

Nothing seemed to fit the profile: something that would require the services of a PR guy like Pappas. After a few hours of searching, his eyes were weary and his head had begun to ache. Then he noticed a story with Monica Kennedy's byline, *The Boston Globe*'s investigative ace.

JAMAICA PLAIN FAMILY KILLED IN TUNNEL ACCIDENT. A terrible story about a young mother and father and their fourteen-year-old daughter killed when their car hit the wall of the brand-new Ted Williams Tunnel. Rick knew the tunnel was part of the Big Dig, so he lingered on the article for a moment. A tragedy, but not something that would in any way involve his father or Alex Pappas.

So why was Monica Kennedy writing about a car accident of all things?

He looked at his watch. It was a bit after 7:00 P.M. *Back Bay* had cleared out, but Monica worked long hours. If she wasn't at her desk, she was on her way home. She was disturbable.

"Kennedy," she barked after one ring.

"Monica, it's Rick." He paused. "Hoffman."

There was a lot of background hubbub punctuated by the clinking of glasses or silverware. "Rick Hoffman! Coming back like a bad penny." Her words were garbled by a mouthful of food. "What the hell you want

197

now?" She said it jokingly, but Rick knew there was a sharp edge of truth in there.

"The Cabrera family mean anything to you?"

"The who?"

"A family from the Dominican Republic who lived in Jamaica Plain, Hyde Square. Daddy, mommy, teenage daughter killed in a traffic accident."

"I don't know what . . ."

"This is back in '96."

"Are you still playing investigative reporter for the *Shop 'n' Save Gazette* or whatever you call that piece-of-shit supermarket circular you write for?"

"The Ted Williams Tunnel—?"

"Oh, *that*, sure, sure. Awful story. Family of three wiped out in a car crash."

"But why were *you* on a traffic story?"

"Yeah, hold on a second." She chewed, then took a big swallow. "You know, I never got the goods on that one. As I recall, it went like: This guy and his pregnant wife and young daughter are driving through the Ted Williams Tunnel in the middle of the night—this is right after it first opened—and the guy drives his car into the tunnel wall and they're all killed immediately."

"Got that. What I don't get is what put *you* on the story."

"The Ted Williams Tunnel. The spanking-new, just finished Ted Williams Tunnel, man. The Big Dig, what do you think? Started out I thought I had something about shoddy construction on the Big Dig and it turned out to be just a plain-vanilla accident. Nothing there. Like my Afrin bottle. Wait a second, now I remember! Alex Pappas!"

"Pappas? What about Pappas?"

"For some reason he was all over the story, playing zone defense. He called me a couple times. Yeah, Pappas was doing reputation management for one of the construction firms that built the tunnel, and he was making sure the company's name didn't get dragged into it. But like I said, he had nothing to worry about, 'cause it was just driver negligence or whatever. The driver was drunk, I always figured. Nothing there."

Pappas, he thought. Reputation management. If Pappas was talking to a reporter for the *Globe* and also talking to Lenny Hoffman . . .

Was it so farfetched? Pappas wanted Lenny's legal help, maybe.

"You think you still have the file?"

"Somewhere. Somewhere. I don't throw anything away. When was that again?"

"Ninety-six."

"Probably in the file drawer at work. Now can I get back to my dinner, please?"

"I'll come by tomorrow."

Rick had parked his Zipcar in the big parking lot on Washington Street behind the building where *Back Bay*'s offices were, a lot that faced a sports club and the off-street patio of an Italian bistro. In the daytime the lot was always full, but now it was half empty. He pressed the Unlock button on the remote to pulse the car's flashers and remind him where he'd parked.

He got in the car and pushed the ignition button and drove toward the exit, when he felt something whispering across his neck, maybe an insect, a fly, and he reached to scratch it and felt something grab his left shoulder and heard a man's voice immediately behind him, from the backseat.

"Pull over, Mr. Hoffman, but *gently*, please, sir. What you feel against your carotid artery is a seven-inch Japanese *santoku*, a chef's knife made of molybdenum vanadium stainless steel. Ice-tempered and hollow ground and probably the finest chef's knife in the world."

Rick froze, his heart fluttering wildly.

"It slices with very little pressure. So bring your chariot to a stop gently, Mr. Hoffman. This is a rental vehicle, and it's damnably hard to get blood out of the upholstery."

31

His body jerked slightly, he couldn't help it, as he eased his foot down on the brake and guided the car to a stop. "Jesus," he said. He felt the blade hot against his throat, gasped involuntarily as it broke skin.

"How much do you want?" he said.

He felt the warm wetness, the prickle of blood, and at the same time felt an icy clutch deep within his bowels.

He didn't dare raise his hands, do anything to cause his attacker to pull the knife in any harder. He smelled that barbershop smell again and the odor of stale cigarette smoke. He sensed that his attacker was alone in the backseat of his car, and he sized up his chances for escape. They were limited. If only he could reach up and grab the wrist that squeezed hard against his neck, tight as a hug. But the blade would sink in a beat faster, he had no doubt of that. He inhaled deeply and felt the bite of the blade on his larynx and tears of pain came into his eyes. He would have to lull his attacker into momentary complacency and then move suddenly. But that sounded workable in theory; in practice, it seemed impossible.

"You want me to talk to you, it's a lot easier if you take the goddamned knife off my throat."

He knew what they were planning to do to him, and he knew he had to do everything in his power to get away.

In his peripheral vision he saw someone approach the driver's-side door and the door came open and a pair of hands thrust inside, grappling with a piece of cloth. The moment had passed. The hood went over his head and everything was dark. The knife edge remained poised against his throat. It smelled of burlap and was coarse against his skin.

"But I have information for you," Rick attempted.

"We're not talking," a voice finally said. Not the voice of the poetry lover. This was higher, raspier. In just a few words he could detect an Irish accent. "Now move over."

"I can't," Rick said. He gestured with his hands at the console that separated the driver's from the passenger's seat.

A pause. "All right. Get out."

The knife came away from his throat.

He did. Someone grabbed his elbow; the second man. He couldn't see anything but was pushed and yanked into the backseat of the Prius. He wondered if anyone in the dark parking lot could see what was happening. He hadn't seen anyone in the lot when he unlocked the car a few minutes earlier. If someone did see, would he or she get involved, say something, or not. In a city like New York, people didn't get involved, as a rule. But Boston was a smaller city, in some ways like an overgrown town. Maybe someone who saw something suspicious would call the cops.

If he yelled, would that make a difference? He thought about it and decided no. It would just provoke the knife. One of the men got in the back of the car next to him, and the other must have gotten into the front, because the car began to move.

"To the plant?" the driver said.

"Yeah," said the man next to him.

"Goddamned underpowered sardine can," the driver said.

The man next to him muttered something inaudible in reply.

"The man's gonna meet us there?" said the driver.

"Yeah."

Both had Irish accents.

He tried to listen to the traffic patterns to determine which way they were heading, but it wasn't as easy as he'd hoped. They were in traffic; that was all he knew. The Prius was quiet. They were going someplace where someone else, *the man*, would meet them.

The man would ask the questions. That was why they didn't want him to talk. Their job, maybe, was just to bring him to the man who asked the questions.

So what did they want? Information, it seemed—not necessarily the cash. Maybe not the cash at all. Last time they'd wanted to know who he'd talked to—who had told him about the money.

He wondered where they were going.

A plant, the man had said. He wondered if it were a meat-packing plant. Maybe that was where they'd taken him the last time. There was an area in the city—in Roxbury, actually, on Newmarket Square— where a number of wholesale meat processing plants were located. They butchered and packed meat for food service accounts, schools and institutions and restaurants. Maybe it was one of those plants.

When the car finally stopped moving, he heard the front door open. Someone got out. Then he heard the clatter of a steel overhead door rolling up on its tracks, the whine of a motor. A roll-up warehouse or loading dock door. Thirty seconds later the car door slammed and the car was driven forward a bit. Into a loading bay, he supposed.

Then the backseat car door was opened and he was grabbed by the shoulder and pulled into the night air. At once he smelled that slightly rancid, rotting smell he remembered from last time. The smell of decomposition. The smell of meat. He heard footsteps echoing in a cavernous, high-ceilinged space.

He heard cars whizzing by, the wheezing brakes of an old van or truck, the screech of a gull. "Walk straight ahead."

He walked but didn't know what direction he was going and he found it hard to keep his balance. He gestured toward the hood. "Is this really necessary?"

"Shut your bake, you fecking eejit." He was yanked even harder and almost stumbled. He resumed walking, his hands stretched in front of him.

"He's not here," one of the men said.

"Tie him up," the other said. "The pole over there."

The other one said something inaudible ending in "Get me something."

The steel overhead door rattled closed and the outside sounds grew muted. More echoing footsteps, the sound of metal scraping against metal. The blat of a motorcycle racing past outside far away.

He was grabbed and jerked a few feet to his left. Did they keep him hooded so he wouldn't know where he was, or how he got here? Both, maybe.

A mobile phone rang, a burst of tinny music.

"Yes, sir? . . . Okay, right, then."

"Where is he?"

"Awwright, this one's gonna have to wait here while we go get the man."

"You go, I'll watch this bowsie."

"Man wants both of us there."

"We just leave him here? This gobshite? He'll do a legger."

"Tie him up to that and tie him up good. Check his pockets for knives or anything."

"Stick your hands out," said the voice nearest him, punching him on the shoulder.

He stuck out his hands, then felt something being wound around his wrists, something coarse and prickly, maybe rope. Then something was wound around his ankles and around his legs and he realized he'd been bound to a stout steel pole.

He wondered what the hell they were doing to him now. All he could tell was that he was being tied up in order to wait for someone, presumably someone senior. Their boss. Whoever it was they called Sir.

Neither of his abductors spoke to him. They spoke to each other quietly, at the far end of the cavernous space they were in. After a few minutes he didn't hear their voices anymore. He heard footsteps in the distance. A door opening and closing.

He waited.

Another few minutes went by. He heard the distant buzz of traffic.

"Hello?" he called out.

The rope was uncomfortable at his wrists and ankles. He was restrained in a position that forced him to remain standing. If he tried to sit, the ropes on his legs tightened painfully. He tried to untie the ropes that wound around his wrists, but gave up after a few agonizing moments. His legs began to cramp.

"What the hell's going on?" he said, louder.

No reply.

He had no idea how much time had passed since he'd been carjacked. An hour, maybe? Two? He knew he was somewhere within the city limits, or just outside. In a meat-packing plant or food-processing place of some kind, near a busy road.

And he waited.

And the notion occurred to him suddenly that he was not powerless, not as helpless as he felt. "Hey," he said. "If you get me out of here, I can make you rich."

There was silence.

"Hey!" he said louder. "You know I have a lot of money, it's why I'm here, and if you cut me loose, I'll make you rich."

Silence.

Louder still, he said, "Hello? You hear me? Let's make a deal."

Silence.

"*Hello?*" He waited five, ten seconds more. "You hear me?"

But no reply. Either they were gone or they were untemptable.

He heard the squeal of brakes close by. Voices. Then the motorized whir and the metallic rattle of the overhead door opening. A rush of cold air.

"That's the car, man." A voice, no Irish accent.

Another voice: "*Jesús Cristo! Mira!* Look at the guy!"

"Shit!"

These weren't the guys with the Irish accents, not the ones who'd brought him here. Then who were they? The voices were vaguely familiar.

"Can somebody help me?" Rick said. "Get this hood off me?"

"The hell's going on here?" the first voice said, getting closer. "Look at this!"

"All tied up and shit. *Jesús Cristo.*"

Then, abruptly, the hood came off and Rick was momentarily disoriented, but a few seconds later he realized he was looking at two familiar faces. It took him another second to remember who they were.

The guys from Jeff's construction crew. Santiago and Marlon.

"Thank you," Rick said, gulping fresh air. "What—what're you guys doing here?"

"What happened to him?" said Marlon. "You're bleeding." He touched his own neck. "On your throat, like."

"Can you guys untie me?"

"You got a knife on you?" Marlon said. "Maybe a box cutter?"

"What happened to you, man? Who did this to you?"

"Hurry, could you?" Rick said. "They could be back here at any minute."

Marlon produced a utility knife and slashed at the ropes around Rick's wrists while Santiago untied the knots at his ankles, and within five minutes the three of them were crowded into the front seat of the Demo King Trash-a-Way pickup truck and on their way from South Boston to Cambridge.

"So how'd you guys end up here?" Rick asked. "I don't get it."

The two were silent.

"Were you following me in the car?"

Silence.

"Did you put a GPS on my car?"

Marlon said, "Tell him about your brother, Santiago."

Another pause, then Santiago said, "My brother works at the Chevy dealer in Arlington."

Rick remembered Santiago showing up late with his car, horn blasting. "You guys LoJacked my car! That's what took you so long!"

They both laughed uneasily.

"Son of a bitch," Rick said.

"We wasn't gonna rip you off," said Santiago. "We just know you got all this money and shit."

"And you wanted to find out where I put it," Rick said.

The two were silent again. He didn't know what to think about this. It was creepy, anxiety-provoking how easily they were able to find him, but he was hardly in a position to complain. They'd saved him from whatever the Irish gang intended.

He owed them something.

32

By ten o'clock the next morning, Rick was at the offices of *The Boston Globe*, the time he knew Monica Kennedy usually got there. He stopped at security on the ground floor and called Monica's desk. She told him to meet her at the top of the escalator.

He took the elevator up to the second floor, where the newsroom was located, and waited there for her. A sports reporter he knew from his time at the *Globe* gave him a wave and kept walking. Finally, Monica appeared, a brown folder in her left hand. She didn't hand it to him. Instead, she said, "What do you want it for, Hoffman?"

He shrugged. "Personal curiosity."

"You're not working on a story. If you've got some angle on this, it's my work."

"Who would I be writing it for—*The Shop 'n' Save Gazette*? Come on, Monica."

"You got something on Alex Pappas?"

He didn't want to lie to her. And if he did lie, that wouldn't be so easy.

Investigative journalists are skilled at seeing through lies, especially ones as good as Monica Kennedy.

"It's about my dad. Because I think he must have run into trouble on this."

"What kind of trouble?"

"I don't know. But in any case, this is personal. It's about my dad and Alex Pappas. But look, if anything interesting happens to pan out on this, any live story, we can share."

"Share?"

"It's an old, dead story that you looked into and found nothing on. I'm not trying to show you up and I'm not trying to compete with you."

"All right, all right," Monica said, her suspicion momentarily allayed. Now she sounded only annoyed. She handed him the file folder and turned away to leave.

"So tell me something," he said. "You know anything about any Irish gangs in Boston?"

"The Irish mob? In Boston? Not since Whitey Bulger's heyday. Twenty, thirty years ago. Nothing on them in years. Why, you got something?"

He shook his head. "Could we talk about this story for a couple of minutes? You got time for a quick cup of coffee upstairs in the cafeteria?"

"No, sorry, I don't."

"Okay, two minutes, then." He waited for a vaguely familiar-looking reporter to pass by, nodding at Monica. "What made you think there might be a Big Dig angle to it?"

"I don't know, the Ted Williams Tunnel had just opened. I figured something might have happened. And look, ten years later something did happen, right?"

She was talking about an incident in July of 2006 when part of the ceiling of another new Big Dig tunnel collapsed, wounding the driver of a car and killing his wife. After a long investigation it turned out to be a problem with the epoxy used to fasten the panels to the ceiling.

"True," he said.

"But when I talked to the cops, I figured it was probably a DUI. End of story."

He nodded. "So what would Pappas have to do with a DUI? What would he care?"

"The rumor in the Dominican community was that something had gone wrong with the newly built tunnel, and that's what caused the accident. I made some calls and got nothing on that, and then Pappas calls me. He's working for some consortium of businesses called the Boston Common Alliance—the businesses involved in the Big Dig—and he wants to make sure this story doesn't get misreported. Look, I knew what he was up to, and I approached him with the normal amount of skepticism, but he turned out to be a useful source. He got me the police report. He greased the wheels with Boston police, made sure I got callbacks right away. I wasn't going to turn away help like that."

"Okay."

"You find out something, you make sure to loop me in, right?"

"Right. Will do."

"I mean it."

"I got it."

He wondered if she could tell he was lying.

33

Rick sat in his car—a Ford Taurus rented from Enterprise Rent-A-Car in Central Square—in the *Globe* parking lot and read through Monica's file. It was thin, a collection of scrawled notes on scraps of yellow legal pad paper and pink While You Were Out phone message slips and photocopies of documents like the Boston police report on the accident. Her handwriting was atrocious. It took him a few minutes of studying the hieroglyphics before he was able to decrypt it. She'd done interviews with neighbors of the dead family, a schoolteacher who'd taught the fourteen-year-old daughter, and sources in the Boston police. Somehow she'd put together an article about the death of an immigrant family from the Dominican Republic in a terrible accident in the brand-new tunnel.

One of the clips in the file was a *Globe* Metro desk dispatch on the accident, the first report to hit the paper, a day after it happened. The article was only a paragraph long and was by a junior Metro desk correspondent Rick knew, a woman who'd accepted a buyout and left the *Globe* some years ago to write a novel but hadn't met with much success.

JAMAICA PLAIN FAMILY DEAD IN TUNNEL CRASH

By Akila Subramanian
Globe Correspondent

A Jamaica Plain family of three was killed in a single-vehicle collision in the Ted Williams Tunnel at about 2:15 a.m. on Monday, according to police. The driver, Oscar Cabrera, 36, of Hyde Square in Boston, was killed along with his wife, Dolores, 35, and their 14-year-old daughter Graciela. The cause of the crash was not immediately released. Speed did not appear to be a factor in the accident, police said.

That was all at first. The plain facts, but not too many of them.

Then Rick could see in Monica's notes her attempts to come up with some sort of investigative angle.

CRASH HOW?? was written in big letters on a yellow lined page ripped from a legal pad covered with doodles (mostly bad drawings of horses) and various phone numbers and phrases like *traffic signals?* and *Lane markings???* Next to that: *SINGLE CAR COLLISION— wall? Drunk?* Scrawled in her crabbed script on a While You Were Out message was *suspected DUI pending BAC.* That meant that the police were speculating the accident had been caused by drunk driving but they'd know for sure when the blood alcohol levels came back in the pathology report.

As he parsed her other scribblings, it became evident that Monica was stumped trying to figure out how a car could have crashed in the

213

tunnel without hitting another vehicle. Was the accident caused by something in the tunnel? Some problem with the lane markings or the traffic patterns? A concrete stanchion placed where it shouldn't have been? But her interviews had apparently turned up nothing.

Her piece—the other clip in the folder—was a longer article that ran two days later. The coauthor was the reporter who originally caught the story, normal newspaper etiquette. There was no investigative angle to it, but you could tell Monica wanted one. The story, instead, was framed as one of those unfathomable tragedies that just happen from time to time.

TRAGEDY STRIKES IMMIGRANT COMMUNITY

By Monica Kennedy and Akila Subramanian
Globe Correspondents

She was a graceful dancer and talented beginning pianist with a quick smile who loved to help her mother cook.

Family and friends wept openly as they recalled Graciela Cabrera, the 14-year-old Hyde Square resident who was killed in the early hours of Monday morning along with both of her parents when the 1989 Toyota RAV4 driven by her father, Oscar Cabrera, 36, crashed in the Ted Williams Tunnel.

Oscar Cabrera, who worked as an engineer at the Colonnade Hotel in Boston, was remembered as a modest, self-effacing man always quick to volunteer to shovel snow or carry packages for friends and neighbors here in the close-knit Dominican community. Dolores, 35, was recalled as a loving wife and mother and a skilled beautician at Hair Again, a hair salon in Hyde Square. The young family had emigrated from the Dominican Republic 8 years previously.

The outpouring of grief in this working-class neighborhood was matched only by the puzzlement among friends and loved ones as to how this tragedy could have happened.

Authorities are trying to determine what caused Monday's accident, which closed westbound tunnel traffic for hours until the mangled vehicle could be towed away. Preliminary investigations indicated that Cabrera's Toyota sustained major damage in the tunnel, but that no other vehicle was involved.

"This is a great loss to the Dominican community," said civic leader Gloria Antunes of the Hyde Square Community Partnership. "There are no words to express how sorry we are."

Rick decided to drive over to Hyde Square in the Boston suburb of Jamaica Plain and just start asking questions. Sometimes you could pick up details on the ground. His old boss at the *Globe*, a gruff editor who favored bow ties and boldly striped shirts with white contrasting collars, was always ordering his reporters to get out of their cubicles and get off their phones and their butts and start poking around. "Just showing up," he liked to say, "is half of good reporting."

It was time to show up.

34

The area around Hyde Square in Jamaica Plain was Boston's Latin quarter, with bodegas that sold mango puree and plantains, and shops advertising paycheck cashing and money orders. This stretch of Jamaica Plain had been largely German and Irish until the 1960s, when the Cubans and the Puerto Ricans and the Dominicans settled there and transformed it into Boston's Hispanic area.

His first stop was the office of the Hyde Square Community Partnership, an organization, according to its website, dedicated to creating a safe and strong community, "the beating heart of Latino life in Boston." It brought together local merchants and politicians and community leaders. Its founder and leader was Gloria Antunes. He'd underlined her name in the printout of Monica's article. He figured that Antunes would be his best way into the neighborhood. The HSCP was located on the second floor of a building on the first floor of which was a *variedades* store. He went up the stairs and found a door marked with a HYDE SQUARE COMMUNITY PARTNERSHIP sign and a sunburst logo. The door was unlocked.

Inside, sitting at a receptionist's desk, was a large woman wearing oversize tinted glasses. Behind her an open door revealed an inner office where someone—presumably Gloria Antunes herself—sat behind a bigger desk, talking on the phone.

"May I help you, sir?" the receptionist said.

"I'm looking for Gloria Antunes."

"Gloria?" she said, smiling broadly. "Of course. May I tell her what this is in reference to?"

He handed her one of his *Back Bay* magazine business cards. "My name is Rick Hoffman, and I wanted to talk to her about the Cabrera family."

She was jotting down notes on a pad. "The Cabrera family . . . Will she know what this is about?"

"They're the family that was killed in the Ted Williams Tunnel almost twenty years ago."

"Yes, sir, one moment, please."

The receptionist got up from her desk and went over to the inner office and knocked on the open door. Then she went inside. A moment later she emerged. "I'm sorry, sir, Gloria is tied up with appointments. Is there something I can help you with?"

"Not really, thanks. I just need to talk with her. It shouldn't take more than a minute or two. May I—" and he approached Gloria Antunes's office door.

"Sir, please wait here," the receptionist protested.

"Ms. Antunes," Rick said, "I just wanted to talk with you briefly about the Cabreras." Doorstepping her this way was an aggressive—some would say obnoxious—move, but he knew when he was getting the runaround. Opportunity doesn't knock, an old saying went; it shows up only when you beat down the door.

Gloria Antunes was a slim, elegant woman with short, curly salt-and-pepper hair, wearing a colorful silk scarf around her shoulders and large hoop earrings. She rose from her desk and said, "Yes, Mr. Hoffman, I got the message but I'm sorry, I have a full plate here. I just don't have time to talk."

"Understood. Can I grab five minutes of your time today or tomorrow? Shouldn't take any more than that."

She replied in an imperious tone, "Mr. Hoffman, what happened to the Cabreras was a terrible, heartbreaking thing, but I have nothing to contribute."

"Would you be able to guide me toward any of their survivors?"

"Mr. Hoffman, I told you, I don't have time to talk. Now, good day."

Gloria Antunes's hostility was puzzling. He'd expected a community leader like her to be welcoming, wanting to remember the dead. There was some reason she didn't want to talk, and he needed to get to the bottom of it.

Within an hour Rick had located the rundown triple-decker house, not far from a behemoth brick housing project, where Oscar Cabrera and his wife and daughter had once lived on the second floor, according to the police report. He sat in his car outside the house, painted olive green, missing shingles, its cement porch steps crumbling. "Now what?" he said out loud to himself.

The family had died eighteen years ago. Maybe someone was around who remembered them and knew something about how they'd been killed. Dolores had worked at a hair salon that was located on Centre Street. He drove around, past a butcher shop called, cleverly, Meatland, an off-brand mobile phone store, and a Latino restaurant whose sign featured a palm tree and a cooked lobster. He found Hair Again salon. It was a "beauty center," according to a sign in the window, "especializing in" perms, extensions, and highlights.

He asked the young woman at the front desk if anyone there remembered Dolores Cabrera. It took a while for him to be understood. Besides the language barrier, there was the strangeness of the query. But eventually the manager of the salon, an older woman with glossy black hair and high arched eyebrows, came out from the back. "Why you asking about Dolores Cabrera?" she demanded.

"I'm writing an article. Remembering them."

The woman seemed to soften at once. "She was a sweet girl."

"Did she or her husband leave any family?"

"Family? Yes, of course. Why?"

Five minutes later, Rick left the salon with one useful piece of information: Oscar Cabrera's relatives still lived in the triple-decker where the young family had lived. He drove back there and rang the bell.

For a long moment nothing happened. From behind the door he could hear a cacophony of voices, shouts muffled and shrill. Then there were footsteps and a couple of women's voices. The door opened a crack and a woman looked out. She wore green hospital scrubs and curlers in her hair.

"Sí?"

"Do you speak English?"

"Em, a little. Yes?"

She was a *tía*, she said, Oscar Cabrera's sister. The hubbub behind her, which had abated when she opened the door, resumed. Rick could hear water running and dishes clinking and at least one baby crying and screaming.

He gave her a version of the pretext he'd given the woman at the beauty salon, that he was a journalist writing a story on the deaths of the Cabrera family. He didn't explain why he was writing it, eighteen years later.

"No!" she suddenly said, waving a hand back and forth. "No! No talk about this!" She pushed the door closed.

Baffled, Rick rang the doorbell again. Had she misunderstood? The door opened again, just a crack.

"*No, yo no quiero hablar! Por favor, vete! Déjanos en paz! Por favor, vaya lejos!*"

Then she closed the door again.

He understood most of what she'd said. She didn't want to talk. She wanted him to go away. Obviously something had gone very wrong in the translation between Spanish and English. He turned to leave and saw an elderly woman standing at the foot of the concrete steps.

"You want to talk about the Cabrera family," she said. She was stooped, with steel-gray hair in a tight bun, a very wrinkled face. She must have been in her late eighties. "They won't talk to you. Come with me."

She told him she'd heard from someone who'd been at the beauty salon that he was asking about the family. She knew them, she said. Her name was Manuela Guzman and she knew them from church. She had also been the daughter's piano teacher.

The woman invited him into her apartment, in the basement of a triple-decker across the street and down the block. It was a small but neatly kept space fragrant of recent cooking, of onions and garlic and wood fires, and dominated by a grand piano.

She beckoned him over to a large wing chair and sat next to him on a couch that was protected with plastic sheeting.

"The family, they will never talk about the accident," she said in a near whisper. "But if you are writing something about them, I want to remember them for you the way they were, not what everyone says."

"Thank you," Rick said, uncomfortably. He didn't like lying to this sincere and very kindly seeming old woman. "But why don't they want to talk about it?"

"I will explain for you."

"Okay, thanks." He took out his reporter's notebook to make it look as if he were taking notes for an article.

"Graciela was my piano student. She was so talented. A sweet girl she was. She was working, trying to learn Beethoven's 'Moonlight Sonata' when she . . ."

She fell silent. He heard the faint ticking of a clock somewhere nearby.

"Tell me the story," Rick said. He was still grappling with how everything fit together. Why was Pappas so interested in this accident that he repeatedly called Monica Kennedy at the *Globe*—and persistently called Lenny Hoffman as well?

"There is no story," she shot back. "There is only sadness. Sadness and lies."

"Lies," Rick prompted.

"After they were killed, there was talk that Oscar was drunk." She pantomimed drinking from a glass. Then she waved a hand dismissively and frowned. "But I know this is not true. He did not drink."

"Then what happened?"

"Graciela was so excited about going to Santo Domingo with her

221

mother to visit her *abuela* and *abuelo*. Oscar went to the airport to pick up his wife and daughter, but their flight was late . . . delayed. In the middle of the night they are driving through this Williams tunnel and then suddenly they were all killed."

"But . . . Oscar wasn't drunk."

She held up a crooked finger. "Never."

"And the car crashed. How?"

"But you see, nobody knows. There is only stories and rumor."

"Such as?"

She shook her head.

"Was there, you know, grease on the pavement?" Rick asked. "Was there something wrong with the car? Something went wrong, that's for sure." Monica Kennedy's article didn't mention anything like that. Her notes indicated that she suspected drunk driving, but obviously that hadn't panned out or it would have been in her story. "Don't you think the newspaper would have reported something about this?"

"The newspapers didn't know the truth. But when people say Oscar was drinking, I tell them I know better."

"But I still don't understand why the family won't talk to me."

She leaned forward and held up an index finger and bounced it in the air. "Because they get paid."

"They get paid."

"They got money. To buy their silence. To say nothing and ask nothing. So they live in their house on the money they got."

"Money—from what? From whom?"

She frowned and shook her head. "Maybe even they don't know. But no one will talk about what happened in the tunnel. No one will say the truth about what killed Graciela. I want to show you something. Please?"

Rick's mind was reeling. Things were becoming murkier. Was the truth somehow concealed that night—and if so, was Pappas part of the concealment?

And Lenny Hoffman?

The old woman opened an armoire inside of which was an old TV and assorted other electronic components and then found a videotape cassette, which she put into a VCR. She fussed with a remote control, and the TV came on, blaring a Dr. Phil show. "Can you help me?" she said.

Rick came over and tried a couple more remote controls and eventually the video was playing on the TV screen.

"She's the first one," the woman said, taking one of the remote controls.

It was a tape of a piano recital, Rick realized, showing each of her students. It took place in what could have been a room in a church or school. Manuela Guzman, looking considerably younger and peppier, wearing a high-necked blue dress, with black hair in a bouffant, made some remarks to the audience members, who seemed to be mostly parents and family.

There was a round of applause and then an awkward girl in pigtails, dressed in a gauzy white dress with a big pink bow at the waist, came to the front of the room and sat down at the piano. She played energetically, moving her head a lot, emoting. Whatever piece she was playing she seemed to be playing it well. She made just a few mistakes. When she finished, there was enthusiastic applause, and she got up and bowed and curtsied again, but this time she gave a big gap-toothed smile.

Something about that smile, earnest and uncertain, achingly beautiful, made Rick's throat tight. He turned and saw that tears were running down the old woman's cheeks. There were tears on his own cheeks as well. She was smiling back at Graciela, and she hit the Pause button.

"When you write your article," she said, "I want you to remember Graciela."

"I will," he said, and he cleared his throat because it was getting hoarse.

"This is sad about Graciela, isn't it?"

Rick nodded. "It's a tragedy. It's unspeakably sad."

"Tragedy, yes. It's funny, he say the same thing when I show him this."

"Who did?"

"Your father."

35

As soon as I hear the news, I went to the Cabreras' apartment to try . . . to see, to help them," Manuela Guzman said.

"To console them."

She nodded. "Oscar's sister Estrella was there and also Dolores's brother Ernesto and his wife and everyone was . . . well, they were in shock, and everybody crying. How could this happen? Everyone is saying, how could this possibly happen? They were . . . upset and angry, out of their mind, you understand?"

"Of course."

"The police say maybe Oscar is drinking, but everyone knows this is not so. Oscar never drinks. Picking up his wife and daughter from the airport? Oscar is so careful! And then Dolores's brother Ernesto said he talked to Gloria Antunes, who is like leader in the Dominican community."

"I know who she is." How could he forget: the imperious woman who didn't want to talk to him.

"Gloria Antunes say she want to start an investigation, the accident is not what people say. But then a man come to the door, a man who look just like you. He must be your father, no?"

"It's possible."

"He say he's with chamber of commerce, and he say he want to do anything he can to help them out in this terrible time. He want to help them with funeral expenses. He say anything we can help you with, here's my card, you call me."

Chamber of commerce? Rick thought. It must have been someone else. His cell phone rang, but he let it go to voice mail.

"He want to help out. He was the nicest man. He called me 'doll.'"

Calling a woman "doll" was almost Lenny's signature. Maybe it was him.

"And then I take this man—your father?—to my house and I showed him Graciela's recital, just like I show you. And he start to cry. He say it is a tragedy. Wait. A moment."

She put a hand on his shoulder and turned around and began looking in a dim corner of the apartment, rummaging through a bookcase. She pulled out a small green plastic box, the kind used for index cards or recipes. "I know I have the card. Wait."

Several more minutes passed by. Suddenly she said, "Ah! Yes!" She handed Rick a dog-eared white business card that said, as he knew it would,

THE LAW OFFICES OF LEONARD HOFFMAN

He looked up at her. "That's my dad." It didn't say chamber of commerce. He had the decency not to use fake business cards. But he was dealing with immigrants who would be easily misled. A lawyer's business card had its own kind of authority. He gave a sad smile. "How did he want to help out, did he say?"

She shook her head. "The family will never talk about it. I think this man paid them money. Maybe a lot of money."

"For their silence?"

"No one talks about it. But all of a sudden"—she rubbed her palms together as if dusting them off—"No more talk about the car accident. They never want to talk about it. They live in that house, all three floors, all the family. I don't know what they do for work. And Gloria Antunes— suddenly the Hyde Square Community Partnership becomes this big thing with an office and a secretary. I think they gave her money, too. And even all this time . . . nobody talks."

As soon as he left the old piano teacher's apartment, he checked his phone. The call that had come in was from an exchange he recognized as Massachusetts General Hospital.

"*Mr. Hoffman, this is Dr. Girona from Mass General Neurology,*" the message said. "*Could you give me a call as soon as possible?*"

To Rick's surprise, Dr. Girona left his personal cell phone number.

Standing outside a convenience store, Rick called the doctor back.

"Yes, Mr. Hoffman, thanks for calling," Dr. Girona said. "I've just been looking over the new MRI scans we ordered for your father, and I'm troubled by something."

"Okay?" he said.

"Your father's chart indicates a hemorrhagic stroke, obviously. But the scans we just got back—well, they're quite a bit more sophisticated than the scans we got twenty years ago—and they indicate the legacy effects of forceful traumatic brain injury. I mean, consistent with grievous battery."

"I don't understand." Rick felt his mouth go dry.

"I'm saying that we're picking up something that was entirely overlooked when he first was admitted back in 1996. The likely cause of his condition."

"You're telling me he was beaten," Rick said.

"I'd say so, yes."

"I'll be right over."

36

Driving to the Charlestown Navy Yard to meet Dr. Girona, he thought about his father. About the mystery of Leonard Hoffman. The more Rick learned, it seemed, the less he knew.

His father was beaten? This didn't gibe at all with Leonard's secretary's account. She had found Len slumped on the floor and called 911. Not lying in a pool of blood.

His entire understanding of the last two decades had tipped to one side. His father had placed a bunch of cell phone calls to Alex Pappas over a period of three days before . . . before he was beaten. Rick imagined a baseball bat to the side of his father's head. One blow and his father slumped to the floor, immediately suffering a stroke. Maybe not what the attacker had intended.

So who could have attacked Leonard, if indeed he was attacked? And what was going on during those three days?

Rick now knew that his father had come to pay off the Cabrera family survivors for some reason and then had seen the same videotape that Rick had just seen, and cried seeing the little girl, just as Rick had done.

Rick now knew that at some point shortly after that, Leonard had been beaten, badly enough to bring on a stroke.

But who had done it? And why?

Rick wondered whether his father's secretary, Joan, might have some idea.

And he thought about the cash hidden in the house, the three million dollars now in storage. If that was money Lenny had bought from places in the Combat Zone to use for bribes, then it was money he hadn't yet paid out. He must have given money to the Cabrera family—

Unless he hadn't.

Unless for some reason his father had held on to the money, not paid it out, and maybe that was why he was beaten.

At a stoplight, Rick glanced at his watch. His father would just be starting his treatment about now. A nursing home aide had begun driving Lenny to Charlestown for the daily treatments in a nursing home van. This was the way they preferred to do it.

Rick reflected that the more he dug, the more rot he was exposing. He couldn't help but think of the work that Jeff and his crew were doing on the old house, ripping out the decayed wood and plaster.

As Rick drove, his mind wandered, but he kept coming back to one question: Why did his father offer to pay off the Cabrera family? What was it about the accident that required silence? He thought and thought and kept coming up empty. Finally he called Monica Kennedy at the *Globe*. She answered after one ring, with her customary bark: "Kennedy."

"It's Hoffman," he said. Without checking first whether she had time to talk, he plunged ahead. "You've got a note in your file about a DUI. You wrote 'pending BAC,' which I assume means you were waiting to see when the blood alcohol concentration results came in from the toxicology reports. So what made you suspect drunk driving?"

"Whoa, whoa, whoa, slow down. 'Pending BAC' . . . Okay, right. That must have come from the cops."

"Not from Pappas?"

"Probably from him first, yeah."

"So why didn't you run with that? You don't mention it in your piece."

She sighed. "Because toxicology reports take sixty days to come in."

"You could have reported it anyway."

"No Afrin in the bottle."

"No confirmation."

"You don't report that about a father who's just died with his wife and teenage daughter unless you have the facts, and I didn't."

"Nice," he said.

"Come on, man," she said. "Even I have standards."

"I heard something about an investigation? A community leader talking about stirring up an investigation into what really caused the accident?"

"So did I, which was why Pappas was all over this. Look, believe me, the city and the state and every single company involved in building that tunnel were deathly afraid of a lawsuit. Everyone was afraid of community pressure for an investigation."

"But you didn't report anything about an investigation."

"Because there wasn't one! There was nothing to report. Pappas was making sure I didn't report something I wasn't going to report anyway."

"So who was he working for?"

"Something called the Boston Common Alliance, or like that. Didn't I tell you that?"

"You said it was a coalition of firms involved in constructing the Big Dig. You happen to know which ones?"

"I don't think it exists anymore, but I'm sure you could find out. Look, Hoffman, I gotta go."

"Thanks," he said, but she'd already hung up.

His father was still undergoing TMS treatment by the time Rick arrived.

He was escorted by a lab assistant into the darkened room where Lenny sat upright in what looked like a dental chair, canted back a bit.

A white cloth cap had been placed over his head, which was nestled within the arms of a tall contraption. "He has a few more minutes left," said a doctor or lab tech who seemed to be running the procedure. His father's eyes slid toward Rick, who gave him a wave. A loud rat-a-tat sounded, like the muted sound of a machine gun firing. Rick waited. After a pause, the machine gun sound went off again. Lenny didn't appear to be in pain. He looked straight ahead, occasionally glancing over at Rick. He looked somehow more engaged, more present.

After another few minutes, the noise stopped. The lab tech or doctor lifted the arms of the contraption up and away from his father's head. "Everything all right, Mr. Hoffman?" she said.

Lenny raised his left hand, his thumb sticking up in a sign of agreement.

Rick stared in amazement. His father hadn't done that in almost two decades.

The door to the room opened and Dr. Girona entered. He nodded at Rick. They would talk in private.

As he shook the doctor's hand, Rick couldn't help blabbering, "He just gave a thumbs-up! I don't think I've seen him do that since his stroke."

"He's been doing that for a couple of days now."

The woman who'd been in charge of the treatment said, "I'm Rachel. I'm the clinical research coordinator."

"Rachel, nice to meet you," Rick said, extending his hand.

"You're Mr. Hoffman's son, is that right?"

He nodded.

"Well, Mr. Hoffman is a great patient. He's got a session now with the speech pathologist. Were you planning to join him?"

"Is that okay, Dad?" he said.

Lenny gave the thumbs-up as he was helped into his wheelchair.

"Dr. Girona," Rick said, "do you have a minute?"

Girona nodded. "Of course," he said, escorting Rick into his office across the hall from the treatment room.

"You think my father was beaten, and that was the cause of his stroke?"

"He suffered traumatic brain injury, that much I can say for certain. He appears to have been struck with something on the left side of his skull. There's evidence of bone fractures precisely where the blood vessel burst. The only explanation I can think of is that he suffered a blow to his head, which triggered the hemorrhagic stroke."

"But how come no one noticed that in '96?"

"The scans back then weren't of nearly as high a resolution as they are nowadays. I'm sure they found evidence of a stroke and left it there. He didn't present with external signs of trauma—no blood, for instance. Right?"

"Right."

"So there would have been no reason to look further. The stroke was apparent."

"He could have had an accident, right?"

Dr. Girona shrugged. "Certainly a possibility. There might not have been external signs like blood or bruising. But in one way or another, he suffered cerebrovascular damage to his head, to his brain."

"He never indicated anything about it."

"Maybe he will now," Dr. Girona said.

A few minutes later, Lenny was seated at a table by a wall-mounted whiteboard in a small room. Rick sat across the table, and the speech-and-language therapist, an Asian woman in her midthirties, sat next to Lenny.

"Do you think I could have a few minutes alone with my dad?"

"Sure, of course!" the therapist said. She immediately rose from her chair and left the room, closing the door behind her.

"Dad, I need to ask you something," Rick said.

His father turned to look at him.

"I need you to help me out. Maybe save my life, okay?"

Leonard turned and looked directly into his eyes. He was listening.

Rick pondered for a moment. He could ask yes or no questions. But based on what the therapist had just done, he also knew he might be able to ask open-ended questions, too, as long as Lenny could answer with the letter board.

"I figured out about the cash you hid in the house. I know you were in charge of collecting it for the cash bank. To pay people off for Pappas.

Dad, this happened almost twenty years ago, but now there are people out there who are trying to hurt me. May be trying to kill me now, I don't know. Okay? So I need you to talk. To help me out. Okay?"

His father was still looking him in the eyes, and there seemed to be something in his glance, something besides fear. Maybe it was dread, or something like that. At least a great reluctance. He didn't turn his thumb up or down, but he was watching and waiting. His left hand rested in front of him on the table. His right hand was curled uselessly on the arm of his wheelchair.

"You're afraid of Alex Pappas, aren't you?"

Lenny slowly turned his left thumb up.

"Did he beat you?"

The thumb turned down.

Rick thought a moment. "Did he . . . have you beaten?"

Lenny's thumb slowly, hesitantly, turned up. Then he tucked his thumb back in and placed his hand flat on the table.

"Who did it?"

Lenny's left hand remained flat on the table.

"Who beat you?" Rick said.

Lenny's left hand slid across the table for the letter board. Rick moved around the table in his chair until he was next to the whiteboard. He picked up a green marker and prepared to write down letters as Len pointed to them.

Len curled his left hand with his index finger stuck out, a pointing pose. He slid his finger across the row of letters and stopped on *D*. Rick wrote the letter *D* in green marker on the whiteboard. Then he moved down to *O*, and Rick wrote *O* on the board. Then *N*. Then *T*.

The word on the whiteboard was DON'T.

Lenny made a slicing motion with his fingers, which Rick assumed meant "end of word."

Then Lenny touched R, and Rick wrote an R, and then E and within a minute the phrase on the whiteboard spelled out DON'T REMEMBER.

"You don't remember," Rick said.

Lenny slowly raised his thumb.

He didn't remember. That wasn't surprising, if he was telling the truth. A bad beating to the head, bad enough to induce a stroke—no wonder his memory was faulty.

He tried another question. "Dad, who was all that cash for? I need to know this."

For a long while his father didn't move. Rick wasn't sure whether Lenny understood, so he repeated the question: "Who was all that cash for?"

Another long pause. Then his father slid his left hand across the letter board, his index finger landing on the letter I.

Rick erased "I don't remember" on the whiteboard and in its place wrote an I.

His father's finger moved to W, and then A, and then N. A few seconds later his index finger moved to the T.

Rick wrote the letters on the board. IWANT. Realizing that these were two words, not one, he erased them and wrote them again with a space between the I and *want*.

Slowly picking up speed, Len's index finger moved to T and then O. Rick had written on the whiteboard, I WANT TO.

Rick spoke the words aloud: "I want to . . . What do you want, Dad?"

His father's index finger moved up the letter board to D and then I, and then Rick realized what his father was saying and tears came into his eyes as he finished the phrase:

I WANT TO DIE.

Rick put his hand over his father's useless right hand and tried to look into Len's eyes again, but his father was pointedly looking away, a tear coursing down his left cheek.

37

L eaving Charlestown, Rick had the uneasy sense he was being
followed.

It wasn't a certainty. A vehicle had been behind him all the way from
the hospital parking garage to Storrow Drive. Not a black Escalade or
Suburban but a gray GMC Yukon. Was it a tail, or just a coincidence,
someone else traveling from Mass General to Boston?

Maybe it was nothing, but he had to be careful. Where he was going,
it was crucial he not be followed.

He saw the exit for Copley Place and decided at the last minute to
take the exit. When he turned off Storrow and the Yukon followed, he
realized he wasn't imagining things.

A quick left and straight down Arlington Street and a few blocks later
he came to the Park Plaza Hotel. He remembered there was a gala being
held there, the one Darren from the magazine wanted him to attend.
It had probably started already. He'd had no intention of going, but his
name was on the guest list. Which gave him an idea.

He pulled up to the valet and the Yukon double-parked across the street. He wondered whether they wanted him to notice the tail, as if that was part of a strategy to unnerve him, cause him to do something stupid.

Well, they could follow him into the hotel, but not into the gala.

He got out of the car, handed his keys to the valet, and entered the hotel without looking back.

It was easy to find the banquet room where the event was taking place. The usual crowd was gathering, bunched at the entrance by a sign for the SCULLEY FOUNDATION LITERACY INITIATIVE, as attractive young women in headsets, holding iPads, checked off names.

He was wearing jeans and a fleece pullover and was seriously underdressed for the occasion. But they weren't going to kick him out for not wearing a jacket and tie. All he needed to do was spend thirty, forty-five minutes here, long enough for his watchers to give up and leave. He'd pretend to be on assignment from *Back Bay*. Which shouldn't be difficult, since he actually was.

Someone grabbed hold of his elbow. It was Mort Ostrow. "I like your idea of cocktail attire," he said. "Didn't I just see you at Marco?"

Rick shrugged. "Hello, Mort."

"Sculley's right over there. Isn't he on your dance card this week?"

"That's right."

"Listen, Rick, I want you to give him the real Rick Hoffman treatment."

He winced. "Sure." The truth was, Rick could write the lede to the Q&A in his sleep: *He may own several of the most iconic buildings in the Boston skyline, but when you talk to the billionaire builder Thomas Sculley, he'll tell you it's people, not buildings, that he's built his fortune on.*

"Let me introduce you," Ostrow said.

"Mort, how about we do this another time, I'm—"

"Two minutes." Ostrow sidled in close and confided: "Sculley and I are in talks. I think he's about to buy the magazine. Though I'm calling it a vertically integrated media company. I want him to experience the full Rick Hoffman treatment. There he is."

Thomas Sculley was talking to an elegant fortyish blonde, but when he saw Ostrow, he turned. He had craggy, rough-hewn features and looked to be in his seventies.

"Thomas, I wanted you to meet one of our ace reporters, Rick Hoffman."

Sculley gave him the big-man handshake-and-biceps grip-and-grin. "Oh, yes, Mr. Hoffman, why don't we have our little talk right now?"

"I'd love that, but I don't think these folks would forgive me if I took you away." Rick gestured vaguely toward the throng. "Maybe you can find a few minutes next week?"

"Certainly," the man said, crinkling his eyes.

A few minutes later Rick managed to escape Ostrow's clutches. He walked around the perimeter of the ballroom, which was crowded with tables set for dinner, and exited via one of the doors at the far end. He emerged from the hotel at the cabstand and got into one of the waiting taxis. "Government Center, please," he said.

38

Rick had met FBI Special Agent Ernie Donovan a few times, but it hadn't been for at least seven years. Donovan hadn't changed. He was ex-Marine and took pride in maintaining the look, the high-and-tight hair and the physique. Donovan's black hair was peppered with gray now. That was the main difference.

Eight years ago Rick had worked on a piece on interstate sex trafficking of minors and had, in the process, gotten to know Donovan. The FBI is always finicky in its dealings with journalists. It views them as unreliable, uncontrollable, publicity-seeking loose cannons, which is largely true. Journalists view the FBI as hidebound, bureaucratic, and legalistic, which is also largely true. But when their needs overlap—when the bureau wanted a story out—the relationship could be harmonious.

They met at a Starbucks across the street from the Boston field office. Donovan turned down Rick's offer of a drink after work. He had four kids and had a long drive home from Boston.

Donovan met Rick in line. The agent's grip was very ex-Marine. They made small talk until they were seated with their coffees at a table. Rick told him about what he was investigating, the covered-up accident. "Did that ever come across your radar screen?"

"You're talking about the Big Dig. The radar screen got awfully crowded those days."

"So nothing about this accident in particular? A cover-up?"

"I don't have anything for you, Rick."

"Meaning you can't tell me, or you don't have anything to tell?"

Donovan smiled. "If I had anything, I couldn't tell you."

"You'd know if an investigation was ever opened."

"And officially I'm not supposed to tell you that no investigation was ever opened."

"Got it. Thanks."

"I remember the accident well. Off the record, it always troubled me."

"But not enough to open an investigation."

"A lot was going on back then. Whitey Bulger had just vanished in Boston the year before. A lot of fingers were being pointed. But if you find something, let me have a look."

"Maybe I will."

"Listen, Rick. You're digging in a swamp. It's Boston and the Big Dig and corrupt contractors and a lot of people don't want the muck raked. Be careful out there, okay?"

39

"You're right on time," Joan Breslin said as she opened the door. "I've just baked some scones."

Lenny's secretary had been surprised to hear from Rick again, but she agreed, though sounding somewhat reluctant, to meet with him again. She was dressed more casually this time, in a gray cardigan over a pink button-down shirt.

The house smelled deliciously of her fresh-baked scones. She led him into her kitchen, which was wallpapered in a turquoise paper with a white trellis pattern. The kitchen table, set with two plates and butter and jam, was turquoise-painted wood, the chairs painted turquoise as well. She lifted several scones with a spatula off a wire rack on top of the oven and slid them onto a serving platter. Then she served one to Rick and one for herself.

"Please," she said, indicating the scones. "Tell me how I can help you."

"It's about my dad, obviously. When you found him, right after his stroke—is it possible he was beaten?"

243

"Beaten? For heaven's sake, why would you ask that?"

"Because his doctor had a new set of MRIs done and found unmistakable evidence of traumatic brain injury. He thinks that's what caused the stroke."

Her eyes widened and she shook her head. "He was slumped on the floor when I found him. A bunch of things from his desk were on the floor. I always assumed he fell and hit his desk on his way down."

Rick hesitated a moment. "You never said anything about that."

"I told the doctor."

"Is there anything else you can remember? Did he look like he might have been beaten?"

Her eyes searched the ceiling. "It's been so long. How long has it been, twenty years?"

"Just about. So no blood or other signs that he might have been attacked?"

"No, nothing. Who would attack Len?"

"That's what I wanted to ask you. Whether he had enemies you might have known about. You said he did business with sketchy people from the old Combat Zone, didn't you?"

"I don't know as any of them were violent, really."

He took a bite of the scone. It was still warm from the oven. Then he almost choked. It was as dry as a mouthful of sand. It took a good slug of coffee to get it down. "Mmm," he said. "Delicious."

"Oh, good. It's my mother's recipe. Irish soda bread scones. Please help yourself to more. Timothy doesn't care for them." She took a dainty bite and apparently had no problem swallowing it.

"I'm good," he said, and he took another gulp of coffee.

"But some of your father's clients from the old days—well, I just kept my mouth shut, since it wasn't my business, but before he started, um, working in the Combat Zone, he had quite a few of what I call the shaggy-haired America-bashers, you know. I imagine some of them might have been dangerous."

"America-bashers?" He took another long swig of coffee.

She pursed her lips. "Those students who wanted to overthrow the government. With their long hair and their 'power to the people' and their demonstrations." She made a fist and wagged it in the air. "The less said about those clients, the better. Your father and I agreed to disagree."

"What do you mean, Joan? Were there disagreements? Any threats?"

"Who knows with those people."

"You don't remember whether he had any enemies? Did he confide in you about any people he might have been afraid of?"

"I told you, your father didn't really confide much in me. He had a lot of secrets but not many people he confided in. I don't know as he had many friends, to tell you the truth."

That was true, Rick reflected. His father had his work, his clients, and then he'd come home and sit in his study. He seemed to have no social life.

"I don't think he had a lot of friends," Rick said. There were none that Rick could think of.

"There was that odd fellow in New Hampshire. He used to call from time to time."

"New Hampshire?"

"One of those scruffy people. A short name? Kent or Jones? He drove up to New Hampshire a week or so before his stroke. I think he was visiting this friend. Clark?"

"Clarke, right!" Rick said. "Paul Clarke."

"Clarke. I think he was a friend."

Rick had a sudden recollection of driving up to New Hampshire when he and Wendy were kids, visiting an old friend of Lenny's who had a maple syrup farm. Paul Clarke, the name was. He lived in an old farmhouse with a barn. Rick remembered playing with a Victrola with a magnificent horn that was kept in the barn, playing 78 rpm records. Lenny and Paul used to disappear into Paul's study and have long, deep talks for hours at a time, while Wendy and Rick and their mother explored the house and played in the barn or outside in the snow. Or they'd check out the sugar house where Paul made the syrup. They'd go sledding down a steep hill.

"Do you have his phone number by any chance?"

"It would probably be in the old Rolodex. Let me go down and see if I can dig it up. You help yourself to another scone, why don't you."

"I'm still working on this one. I'm trying not to be a pig."

While she went down to the basement, Rick looked around the kitchen. He noticed a framed needlepoint sampler on the wall that said ERIN GO BRAGH in yellow letters against a green background. The words were surrounded by sprigs of shamrocks. Rick didn't remember what *Erin go Bragh* meant, just that it was an Anglicization of some Irish expression. He thought of the "666" shamrocks on the wrist of one of his attackers.

Boston was, in a lot of ways, an Irish town. There were more Asians and Hispanics in Boston, by percentage, but the Irish had dominated Boston for more than a century. They came over in the mid-nineteenth century to escape famine and found themselves an oppressed minority. Old-line Bostonians hired the Irish immigrants as their servants, paying slave wages. The Irish did all the jobs no one else would do, mopping the gutters and scrubbing the laundry and butchering the hogs and taking care of the babies. They could get no other work. Signs in shop windows said NO IRISH NEED APPLY. But by the late nineteenth century the Irish had begun to organize and get elected to political office, and for a hundred years, most of the mayors of Boston were Irishmen.

"Here we go," Joan said when she returned. "A 603 area code; that's New Hampshire." She was carrying a big Rolodex wheel that must have held a thousand cards. The cards looked yellowed. She set it down on the kitchen table, open to a card with "CLARKE, Paul" typed in the typescript of an old manual typewriter. The e's were filled in. The card had a 603 phone number and a post office box address in Redding, New Hampshire.

"Could I take this?" Rick said.

After a moment's hesitation, Joan said, sitting down, "I suppose so," and she detached the card from the wheel and handed it to him.

"Thanks," he said. "Let me run another name by you. I think he's the mysterious 'P' that Dad was scheduled to have lunch with on the day of his stroke. Alex Pappas?"

She blinked once. "Alex Pappas. Sure." She looked as if she didn't want to say anything further.

"You know him?"

She shrugged. "Through your father."

Strange, he thought, that she never suggested his name when he'd asked who "P" might have been.

"I wonder whether Pappas, or people working for him, came to the office. Maybe they threatened him. Maybe someone hit him. I know that Lenny's afraid of Pappas."

Joan gave a sharp, mirthless laugh. "*Afraid* of him? You don't know

247

anything, do you? Who do you think's been taking care of him all these years?"

"What do you mean? I thought it was Medicare . . . no?"

"The Donegall Charitable Trust," she said. "They've been paying all of his expenses since his stroke."

"Donegall Charitable . . . Whose money is that?"

"I don't know. All I know is that Alex Pappas made the arrangements. So before you accuse Alex of having your father beaten, put that in your pipe and smoke it."

Donegall was probably a place in Ireland, Rick thought. "I don't understand . . . Why did Alex Pappas arrange to pay for his care?" Pappas had never said anything about that.

"Because Alex Pappas is a loyal man. Your father did a lot of business for Alex, and Alex took care of him when he needed help."

"The . . . cash-bank business, you mean. Collecting cash and giving out bribes and such."

She shrugged. "I suppose I made deposits of cash in the bank when I was asked to. Sometimes I put cash in the safe. But the whole business didn't concern me, and I asked no questions," she said with an almost prudish, defiant air. "Your father protected me."

"What do you know about the Donegall Charitable Trust? Do you have an address or a contact name?" Rick recalled the late-model Audi in Joan's driveway and wondered whether the Donegall Charitable Trust was taking care of her as well.

"It all happens with wire transfers and such, and I don't concern myself with the details. They've never been late with a payment, and there's never been a problem."

"So you don't have a name?"

"You're a persistent one, aren't you?"

"I never give up. Like father, like son, right?"

"I wouldn't say so."

"You wouldn't?"

"Wasn't your job all about uncovering secrets?"

"It was."

"Well, your father was all about keeping them."

40

Rick returned to the bed-and-breakfast in Kenmore Square, packed up his suitcase, and checked out. He drove maybe half a mile to a DoubleTree on Soldiers Field Road and booked a room. After checking in, he went online and looked up the Donegall Charitable Trust and found nothing.

Then he pulled out the Rolodex card Joan had given him and looked at Paul Clarke's phone number in area code 603. Was it still a valid number? For some reason he imagined that people in rural areas—and Paul Clarke's house was in a rural part of New Hampshire, that was for sure—moved around less often than people in large cities.

He thought about Clarke. He remembered a tall man in faded blue jeans and a barn coat, a man with silver hair and dark eyebrows. He remembered liking the man. He recalled the continual look of slight amusement on Clarke's face, as though talking to you was like watching a mildly amusing sitcom. Clarke seemed somehow too elegant to be a maple syrup farmer. He seemed out of place in the old farmhouse.

Rick had no idea how old Clarke was, just that he'd been around the same age as Len. To a kid, thirty-five and fifty all look the same. Would he still be alive? If he was approximately Lenny's age, he'd be anywhere from seventy-five to eighty-five. He might well still be alive.

If Lenny had driven up to New Hampshire to see Paul Clarke the week before his stroke, maybe he really had confided in him what he was worried about. Maybe Clarke would know something useful.

Rick took a breath and called the number.

It didn't even ring. A recorded message came right on, a woman's voice: *"You have reached a number that is no longer in service. Please check the number and try again."*

So maybe the man had died. He went to his laptop and Googled Paul Clarke, looking for an obituary. Nothing came up. He tried ZabaSearch, typing in "Paul Clarke" and specifying New Hampshire on the pulldown menu. A result came right up:

Found 1 record for Paul Clarke
Paul Wayne Clarke, 82, Redding, NH

That indicated that Paul Clarke was probably still alive. The town was right. He called directory assistance in New Hampshire. A robot voice said, *"Say the name or type of business."* When he said Clarke's name, the robot said, *"Let me transfer you to an operator."*

An operator came on a few seconds later. "Yes, in New Hampshire, how may I help you?"

"In Redding, can I have the number of Paul Clarke?"

The operator clicked away at her keyboard. "I'm finding a Paul Clarke, but the number is unpublished."

"But there is a number."

"Unpublished, sir."

He hung up. Then he called his sister's cell number. She answered right away. She was in some noisy place, probably the back of the vegan restaurant her partner ran. "Do you remember Paul Clarke?"

"Who?"

"Clarke. Paul Clarke."

"Isn't that a friend of dad's, lives out in the boonies someplace?"

"That's the guy."

"The maple syrup guy! He used to scoop up snow from the ground and put maple syrup on it and make us eat it?"

"He didn't make us eat it. We couldn't get enough of it."

"Maple syrup on snow. That's like the most disgusting thing ever, so why were we so into it?"

"We were kids."

"He and Dad used to go off and have these deep talks and we weren't allowed to interrupt them, right? And he had this pencil trick he used to do that we couldn't figure out?"

"Oh yeah. But he eventually taught me how. Anyway, I'm trying to reach the guy."

"What for?"

"I'll tell you about it sometime. Soon. For now, I'm just wondering whether you know where Dad might have put his phone number."

"Did you ask Joan?"

"The number she has is disconnected."

"Probably in his study someplace."

"Which is empty now. They're redoing some of the plaster work and repainting."

"I have no idea." In a mournful tone, she said, "I guess you can't ask Dad."

"Not exactly. Though he's making progress." He told her about the transcranial magnetic stimulation and how it seemed to be working. He didn't tell her about Lenny's "I want to die" message.

"What? You're kidding me! Amazing. Do they think he'll be able to talk eventually?"

"They don't know. It's all pretty experimental, and it's early. Don't get your hopes up."

A few minutes later he hung up and decided to take a drive to New Hampshire.

41

He took precautions.

It had become almost second nature to him now. He'd traded in the Zipcar—after removing the GPS tracker from the rear left wheel well and sticking it on a nearby car—for a Suburban from Avis. When he returned to Boston, he'd check out of the DoubleTree and find some other place, maybe in one of the towns outside Boston, like Newton.

But he had to keep moving, had to avoid comfortable habits and routines, until . . .

Until he'd found out who was going after him and why.

He welcomed the long drive up 93 North to New Hampshire as an opportunity at long last to think. The driving was repetitive and dull, and his mind wandered; he couldn't help falling into a reverie.

He found himself thinking about what Joan Breslin had revealed, that Pappas had been taking care of Lenny all these years. For what possible reason? It couldn't be out of the goodness of Pappas's heart.

And he found himself wondering what Joan was hiding. She'd never volunteered Pappas's name when Rick had asked who "P" might be.

That couldn't have been an oversight. She was covering something up, he felt sure. He wondered if she, like Lenny, was afraid of Pappas.

Such payments could be made to buy silence. Maybe hers had been bought. Then why pay off Lenny, who couldn't talk anyway?

After about an hour and a half of driving, the expressway cut a swath through the White Mountain National Forest, dense with pitch pines and red oak and cinnamon fern. It reminded him of the woods on Paul Clarke's property, which must have been twenty or thirty acres at least. The sugar maples, when they visited one winter weekend years ago, all had spouts dug into their trunks, dripping clear sap into tin buckets. Mr. Clarke, tall and silver-haired and distinguished-looking, showed them how the full buckets of sap were collected.

Rick remembered walking into the sugar house where the sap was boiled down in the giant evaporator over a roaring fire, the sensation and the aroma of being hit by the wall of steam heavy with the sweet smell of maple syrup. It took forty gallons of sap, Clarke had said, to make a gallon of maple syrup.

Paul Clarke had seemed oddly hip and handsome for a friend of Dad's. He looked, in his barn coat, more like a senator running for reelection than a farmer. They'd gone out for dinner at the only pizza place in town. Over pizza, Mr. Clarke showed Rick a trick with a pencil. He started with his hands together as if in prayer, a pencil grasped under both thumbs. Then somehow he swiveled his hands around and suddenly the thumbs pointed down, the pencil underneath his hands. It looked simple, but it was impossible to do. Wendy and Rick tried repeatedly. They asked him to do it slowly. No matter how many times he did it, they were unable to replicate it. Naturally they kept nagging him to show them how he did it.

"What's the trick?" Rick had demanded.

"There's no trick," Mr. Clarke had replied with a poker face. Only later did Rick come to understand. It looked like a trick, but it wasn't a trick at all. It was all about technique. Nothing was hidden. What you saw was what you got. No trick.

He remembered his father and Mr. Clarke going off for long conversations in Mr. Clarke's book-choked study. Rick and Wendy and their mother were left to read or hike in the woods. Rick, budding investigative journalist at age eight, got curious and stood outside the study door, listening, unable to make sense of their low voices. Rick woke early the next morning and found Mr. Clarke in the sugar shack, hard at work with the buckets of sap. At breakfast he finally persuaded Mr. Clarke to show him how to do the pencil trick, and he went around the house crowing to his younger sister, "I know the trick! I know the trick!"

But to this day he had no idea who Mr. Clarke was, this man who was one of his father's closest friends. With the typical obliviousness of kids, Rick and his sister couldn't be bothered to learn how Dad and Mr. Clarke were connected. Classmates? Colleagues? Was he an old client? What, exactly? They had no idea and never asked. For some reason Lenny had stayed in touch with Paul Clarke, had even gone to see him the week before his stroke. Rick wondered why.

When Interstate 93 emerged from the White Mountain National Forest, he drove past Franconia, then exited at Littleton and took 116 northeast along the curves of the Ammonoosuc River until he reached the town of Redding, New Hampshire.

All he knew was that Paul Clarke lived in Redding. He didn't know where. He had nothing more than a post office box. But as he drove through the town, he began to recognize landmarks. They'd visited

Clarke a few times, long ago, but it had been often enough that Rick remembered the town, in a sketchy sort of way.

He drove past a book barn that looked familiar, and next to it a general store. He remembered his mother and father browsing in the book barn for what seemed like hours while he and Wendy had gone to the general store nearby and shopped for candy and comic books. Then came the strip of storefronts, the art gallery, a children's clothing store, a coffee shop, a place offering web and graphic design services.

He stopped into the coffee shop, called Town Grounds, bought a cup of Sumatra—fancy artisanal coffee, even in rural New Hampshire!—and asked the young woman at the counter if she knew where Paul Clarke's house was. She smiled apologetically and said she had no idea. When he came out of the coffee shop he saw, across the street, Town Pizza. It looked like the same one where they used to go for dinner when they visited Clarke, who was a bachelor and didn't cook much.

He crossed the street and entered the pizza parlor. Behind the counter, a middle-aged bald guy was sliding a pizza into an oven with a wooden peel. He looked as if he might be the owner.

"Do you know Paul Clarke?"

"Paul? Sure."

"Do you know where he lives? I'm an old friend."

"I think I have a pretty good idea," he said, and he drew a map on a paper place mat.

Rick got back into the Suburban, drove past a white-steepled church, then a small town hall building, then an off-brand gas station. There he turned left and continued on straight for a mile or so until he dead-ended at Chiswick Road. He turned right and drove along a tree-lined road with modest wooden houses set back from the street, every quarter mile or so.

Then he came to a big, unpainted aluminum mailbox that said CLARKE in large stick-on letters.

The mailbox stood at the mouth of a narrow unpaved road that disappeared into thick coniferous forest. But there were also plenty of maple trees, he knew. He saw the ruts of large tires in the dirt that looked fairly recent.

After only a moment's hesitation, he turned into the private road, which twisted through woods for what seemed close to half a mile and then opened out into a gravel drive bordering a scrubby lawn and then a sprawling white farmhouse. Stones popped under the Suburban's big tires as he drove over gravel. A couple of well-worn vehicles were parked side by side, a Ford F-150 truck and a Subaru Outback.

If nothing had changed in the years since the family had last visited, Clarke lived here alone. So the odds were good that he was at home.

He parked and got out of the car.

Suddenly he heard a gunshot, and a tree trunk just a few feet away exploded. Startled, he ducked. "What the hell?" he said aloud, realizing in a moment that a bullet had come close to hitting him.

He rose slowly, hands up in the air. "I'm here to see Paul Clarke!" he shouted.

A man was standing in front of the house, holding a shotgun pointed directly at him. "Who the hell are you?"

"I'm Rick Hoffman. Lenny's son."

"Oh, Jesus." The man lowered the shotgun. He approached Rick. He was wearing a green-and-black plaid woolen shirt. "We've got a serious home invasion problem around here. Some meth heads live down the road, and they've got a black Suburban just like yours. Can't be too careful. The downside of living way out in the boonies is nobody can hear you scream."

42

Rick took a few steps and shook the old man's hand.

"Rick Hoffman. I know I should have called first, but I couldn't find your phone number."

"Paul Clarke," the old man said. "It's been years, right? How's Pop? Is he—?"

"He's okay," Rick said. "You know he had a stroke, right?"

Clarke nodded. "I can't really visit him. I don't know if your dad ever explained."

Rick shook his head. "I need to ask you some questions, if you don't mind."

"Come on in."

Clarke's house was low-ceilinged and looked very old, with small windows and wide-board plank floors. It was dark and warrenlike and smelled everywhere of wood smoke. Clarke took him through a few sparsely furnished rooms to a room with a large fireplace and a couple of mismatched sofas and chairs, which looked like the place where Clarke spent most of his time. Rick remembered this room, the crackling fire, the comfortable sofas where they'd curl up and read while Clarke and his father talked in Clarke's study.

"Did you drive up from Boston?" Clarke asked as he knelt by the fireplace, balling up old newspaper.

"I did. I had no way of reaching you first. Dad's unable to speak, you might have heard—"

Clarke turned around, nodded. "Awful thing."

"And the phone number he had from twenty years ago didn't work."

"I understand. I'm not easy to find, and that's no accident."

Clarke seemed to be implying something, but Rick didn't probe. In a few minutes, Clarke had lit the newspaper, and the kindling had caught fire, and before long a fire was roaring.

"What can I get you to drink?" Clarke said. "Coffee? Tea? Scotch?"

"Scotch would be good." He wanted Clarke lubricated and voluble.

Clarke nodded and left the room, and then Rick heard the sound of water running from the nearby kitchen. He returned with two freshly washed tumblers of Scotch over ice. Clarke handed one to Rick. "I should have asked, you prefer it neat?"

"This is fine, thanks." It was not long after noon. He'd have to drive back this afternoon, which would now entail stopping at the Town Grounds and getting a couple of hits of caffeine to help him through the drive home. "I have some good memories of visiting you here when Dad took us. Do you still make maple syrup?"

"Oh, yes. Still a sugar maker. I've still got the old sugar shack. It's gotten a little fancier than it was when you kids used to come here, I'm sure—tubing and reverse osmosis and such. I only have about fifty acres here, so I'm a small-time producer. But it pays the bills, which aren't big."

Rick sat at one end of a sofa, and Clarke sat in an overstuffed armchair next to the sofa. The chair's upholstery was shabby and threadbare, and tufts of white stuffing stuck out of the holes in the arms. Clarke had taken off his green plaid overshirt. He was wearing green wide-wale corduroy pants and a muted brown plaid flannel shirt, and his silver hair looked freshly barbered.

"Were you aiming at me?" Rick said as he took a sip of Scotch.

"If I were aiming at you, Rick, I would have hit you. No, I was aiming for just over your head and a few inches to the right. Close enough to put the fear of God into you. And again, I'm sorry about that. I was too impulsive."

Rick smiled. "My fault for showing up unannounced. But I need to talk to you. You were, I think, one of Dad's closest friends. Maybe the closest. And I know he came to see you the week before his stroke."

Clarke nodded. Joan had called him "one of the scruffy people," but he could hardly have been less scruffy. He could have been a country gentleman in a Ralph Lauren magazine ad.

"His doctors now think he was hit—beaten, badly. They suspect his stroke was likely brought on by traumatic brain injury."

Clarke winced, ducked his head, then put a hand over his eyes. "Oh, dear. I'm not surprised. I'm just surprised they let him live. He expected to be killed."

"He did? Why?"

"Because your father had had a crisis of conscience. He wanted out of the life he'd fallen into. He couldn't go on anymore."

You didn't play by the rules . . .

"Why not?"

"Something disturbed him deeply. Something he was told to do."

"What was that?"

Clarke shook his head slowly. "He wanted to protect me. Keep me ignorant of the details. He thought the less I knew, the safer I'd be. He was a thoughtful man, your father was. All he'd say was that some people had been killed and he'd been ordered to cover something up about their deaths."

Rick thought of the little girl at the piano recital and knew his father had been moved as much as he had. Lenny had been told to pay off the surviving family members. It must have been part of a cover-up.

"Why did he drive up here? Did he come to talk it over with you, was that why he came?"

"I think that was part of it, yes. But I think it was mostly to get my help."

"In what?"

"He wanted my help in doing what he helped me do, back in the day." Clarke gave him an intent look.

Rick shook his head. "To do what?"

"He never told you . . . about me?"

"What about you?"

"Oh, Lordy. He wanted to disappear. Same way I did."

43

L enny was ordered to cover something up, and he couldn't go
through with it. So he knew he had no choice but to get out, to quit
his life and set up a new one. I'm sorry, I thought he'd told you and your
sister. He was planning to. Maybe he never got a chance."

"How was he planning to 'quit' his life? What does that mean, exactly?"

"He'd begun to accumulate his assets—to gather cash, enough to buy
him a new identity and a new life, and leave some for you and—your
sister's name was Wendy, perhaps?"

Rick nodded. He wondered how much Clarke knew about the cash,
how much there was. "But where'd he get the cash?"

"He was paid very well by one of his clients—the one he'd become
fearful of—and he always lived modestly. And on top of that, to be
honest, I think he skimmed money off of the cash he'd amassed for this
client. He wasn't troubled by the morality of it, I have to say. He called it
'stealing from thieves.'"

"How could he disappear?"

"The same way I did. You do know that Clarke isn't my real name, don't you?"

"No."

"So you don't know . . . Your dad stood by me when no one else would."

"Stood by you how?"

"Lenny was a hero. Back in the day, he'd take cases no other lawyer would take. Like mine. My real name is Herbert Antholis. You might have heard the name . . . ?"

Rick shook his head. "I don't think so. Should I know who you are?"

Clarke—Antholis?—tipped his head and gave that crooked half smile that Rick remembered well. "Those days are long gone, I guess, and just as well. I used to be a member of the Weather Underground. Back in the days before that was a weather website. We were student radicals. We all had copies of Mao's little red book, and we were convinced that old Chairman Mao was right, that political power grows out of a gun.

"Well, we were protesting the US bombing of Hanoi in 1972—we were planning to break into an army recruiting center in downtown Boston and steal records. But I was the low man on the totem pole, and what I didn't know, what they didn't tell me, was that my comrades were actually planning to set off a pipe bomb there. I was driving the car, and my job was to wait for my comrades to come back and then hightail it out of there. Only later did I find out that an army sergeant, the guy who ran the recruiting center, was killed when the bomb went off. A father of four kids. That wasn't part of the plan at all. No one told me. But after we were arrested and charged, it didn't make a difference that I was at the bottom of the totem pole. A grand jury indicted me, and the district attorney was going for the maximum sentence he could get—life in prison. I mean, I drove the getaway car, so I knew I was culpable. I deserved some kind of prison sentence. But not life. Your father took my case and he believed in me. He worked his butt off. But he knew I could never get a fair trial. I said to your dad, 'What are my odds?' and he said, 'Frankly, they're bad.' I told him I'd have to make a run for it, go underground like some of my Weather Underground comrades did. He said, 'Do you know what kind of position that puts me in?' But he helped me anyway. It was a lot easier to disappear back in the early seventies. I got some fake papers made and moved to rural New Hampshire and set up a new life. No one knows, not my neighbors or my friends in town. They just know me as a sugar maker."

"I had no idea about any of this."

"It was a lot more complicated for your father to disappear back in — 1995, was it? '96?"

"'96." Rick was astonished at Antholis's account. This was a Lenny Hoffman he didn't recognize.

"He had to set up a ghost address, and I think he was working on getting a driver's license in another name. But mostly, the thing is, you have to live on cash. Which is surprisingly not all that hard to do."

"Who did he tell? Just you? Or did he tell Joan as well?"

"Joan, his secretary? No way. Joan was always a problem for him. I don't know why he never fired her."

"What? She seems as loyal as they come."

"He never told you? Remember during the busing crisis in Boston when there was all that violence? The courts ordered that black kids be bused to white schools and white kids be bused to black schools. . . . There was this black teenager who was charged with stoning cars. Lenny represented him pro bono. He didn't think the kid was guilty. Well, Joan's uncle was badly hurt during all that madness—he was hit with a cinder block or some such outside a housing project in Roxbury. Wielded by another black teenager. I think Joan never forgave him for agreeing to represent that black kid."

"But I don't understand," he said. "I thought Dad represented strip clubs and such. His clients all came out of the Combat Zone."

"That's how he ended up, sure. But that wasn't how he started. That wasn't what Lenny wanted to be. Your father saw himself as a First Amendment lawyer. That was something he deeply cared about. I mean, this wasn't the sort of pro bono work that partners at big law firms get points for taking on. This was a cause for him. A life. But then he had kids and he knew he needed a reliable way to make a living."

Rick couldn't help but marvel at the old Leonard Hoffman, the man he never knew. "So what changed?" he said. "How could someone like that become someone like, well, my dad?" But he knew what Antholis was going to say, and he dreaded it.

"Look in the mirror, Rick," Antholis said.

44

By the time he arrived at his latest hotel, the DoubleTree Suites on Soldiers Field Road in Boston, he was exhausted. It was dark and cold and he'd had to battle rush-hour traffic getting back to the city from New Hampshire. Yet he was too keyed up to sleep. He poured a Scotch from the minibar and tried watching television for a while, but nothing held his interest.

He could think of nothing else besides what he'd learned in New Hampshire, from his father's old friend. He was still stunned.

His father had been planning to disappear, to become a fugitive, and only a stroke had interfered with his plan. He wanted out of the life he'd made for himself, a life of deceit and payoffs and bribes—a life that had become dangerous and repulsive to him.

The Lenny Hoffman that Herbert Antholis knew was a hero, plain and simple. He'd defended outcasts and rejects; he'd defended people who had no one else to defend them. Yes, he'd taken on work he disliked in order to support a family. He'd sold out. But in the end he did the right thing—the brave thing. He refused to cover up the cause of the accident that killed a family.

He marveled at the deception that was "Paul Clarke," a.k.a. Herbert Antholis. Rick wanted to call his sister and tell her what he'd discovered about the mysterious man who'd introduced them to maple syrup on snow—she'd be equally blown away—but he couldn't risk being distracted now.

He was tired, not just from the long day, the booze, and all that driving, but from having to run and hide. He was tired of his desperate, nomadic existence, having to change hotels every other night, always having to look behind him. The fortune he'd uncovered—or, was it, more accurately, the *mis*fortune?—had plunged him into a world of danger similar to what his father must have confronted. Part of him was tempted to give up, to throw in the towel, to stop running. But what would that entail, exactly? Was it even possible?

The people who'd been coming after him showed no signs of stopping. At least now he had some idea why. If Herbert Antholis was right, a part of that 3.4 million was skimmed—stolen, to put it simply—from Alex Pappas or from whoever his clients were.

Who was Pappas's client? Maybe the solution, the thing that would make him safe, was as simple as figuring out who the client was and making a deal, giving back part of the cash. That was one approach. Figure out what they wanted and give it to them.

But there was another approach. Call it the confrontation option. Investigate, figure out who the client or clients were, and confront them with proof of their crime, of their role in covering up the real cause of the accident that killed the Cabreras. Maybe confronting them would flush them out, keep them at bay.

Maybe.

He opened his laptop. The problem was, he knew very little. He had only a few threads to pull at. Start with the meat-packing plant in South Boston where he'd been taken to be tortured—and would certainly have been, would have been maimed or worse, had the guys from the demo crew not tracked him there.

Who owned the place?

The sign on the front of the warehouse where he'd been taken had said B&H PACKING, 36 NEWMARKET SQ.

Newmarket Square was an area where a lot of wholesalers were located—seafood dealers, fruit-and-vegetable vendors, and the like—just off the Southeast Expressway and near the Mass Turnpike. He Googled B&H Packing on Newmarket Square and came up with only a rudimentary, temporary website. There was a slogan—"Quality purveyors to fine restaurants in the Greater Boston area"—and then just a line: "New website coming." A few more Google attempts yielded not much more. It was a low-profile wholesale meat-packing company, that was all. No owner listed anywhere. Whoever owned the place had to be directly connected to the Irish gang that had abducted him twice.

But that seemed to be a dead end.

Then what about Donegall Charitable Trust, which, according to Joan Breslin, paid for his father's nursing home? That was, he knew, more than 120,000 dollars a year. Not cheap. This was another dangling thread. He Googled it, as he'd done before, only to have Google reply:

No results found for "Donegall Charitable Trust"

Charities, he knew, had to file with the Internal Revenue Service. There had to be some information to dig up. But unless Joan Breslin had lied about the name—which was a possibility—it didn't seem to exist.

A dead end.

So then there was the biggest, fattest target: Who built the Ted Williams Tunnel? That was easy. Google yielded a number of companies. The project manager was the mammoth construction firm Bechtel/Parsons Brinckerhoff. But then a name jumped out at him: Donegall Construction Company.

That was the link. Donegall Construction.

It didn't take long to determine that Donegall Construction was out of business.

So what did that mean?

Two points determined a line. Never mind if both points remained out of focus. An out-of-business construction company and a below-the-radar charitable trust. With enough digging, he would connect the two. He was confident in his ability to do just that.

But there was an easier way in. A name in the file of notes Monica had given him.

The name of the cop who had signed the accident report. If there had been a cover-up, the police officer who'd been on the scene would know the truth. He had a name—Police Sergeant Walter Conklin. He'd been a police sergeant twenty years ago. Odds were, he was still alive. Also that he was retired.

There was a handful of Walter Conklins in the country. In Massachusetts, only one. But he lived in Marblehead, which was a wealthy town full of yacht clubs. Not a place where cops lived. A Google search for that Walter Conklin pulled up a few articles about some local controversy over a windmill off the Marblehead coast. There'd been a public hearing at Marblehead city hall, standing room only, at which local residents voiced their opinions on putting a nearly four-hundred-foot wind turbine off Tinker's Island, within view of Marblehead. "Over my dead body," said local resident Walter Conklin.

When Rick went on Google Maps, he did a double take. Conklin's house was not just in Marblehead but on Marblehead Neck, a peninsula where some of the town's biggest houses were located. His house was directly on the water. No wonder he didn't want his view marred by a few giant windmills. Rick shifted to Google Street View and found a sprawling shingle-style house on Ocean Avenue. He went on Zillow.com and pulled up Conklin's house. It was valued at 2.9 million dollars.

A retired Boston policeman living in a three-million-dollar house on Marblehead Neck?

Something was very wrong.

He checked his watch. It wasn't too late to make a call.

"Walter Conklin?"

"Who's asking?" a gruff voice answered.

"Rick Hoffman with *Back Bay* magazine in Boston. I'm doing a piece on the windmill controversy up in Marblehead. Looks like they want to put some awfully big, butt-ugly windmill right in your front yard. I was wondering whether you might be willing to talk a bit about it."

"Hell, yeah, I want to talk about it. If the board of selectmen thinks—"

"I'll be in Marblehead tomorrow midday and would love to come by and see your view and do an interview."

"Absolutely," Conklin said. "It would be my pleasure."

45

He was at City Archives when they opened, holding a box from a high-end bakery in Harvard Square.

"I hope that's not from the Tastee again," Marie Gamache said. "Because that would be cruel and unusual."

He handed her the box. "Raisin-pecan morning buns and carrot cake muffins. Both gluten-free."

"Interesting," she said. She opened the box. "Definitely promising. You are too nice to me."

"Only when I'm being unreasonable." He'd e-mailed her last night and asked for an appointment first thing in the morning. But that wasn't the tough ask. He asked to see the city's Transportation Department archives, specifically the repair records for a specific time period in 1996. Since 9/11, for some reason, these records weren't open to the general public. But access could be arranged with special permission.

"It's no big deal," Marie said. She indicated a steel trolley that held gray file boxes. "If you know the right people. Have fun."

Rick had a theory. Eighteen years ago there'd been an accident in the

Ted Williams Tunnel. A bad accident, bad enough for three people to be killed. The tunnel was closed to traffic for at least part of the next day, according to the newspaper. Standard operating procedure: The damaged car would be left there long enough for an accident reconstruction team to map out what happened. Only then would the car be towed away and the tunnel reopened to traffic.

Both westbound lanes closed for a day or so. That was in the public record. A huge hassle for drivers.

But Rick was convinced there would be something else. There had to be some sort of record of the work done. He was hoping to find a document proving that there'd been a grease slick or a problem with the asphalt. Something. After two hours of searching through tedious files, his eyelids were like sandpaper. He was about to give up when something caught his eye.

It was a memorandum on Donegall Construction letterhead to the secretary of transportation. "Replace fallen NuArt fluorescent light fixture" was its subject line.

He read it over several times. A ceiling-mounted fluorescent light fixture in the Ted Williams Tunnel had fallen. It had been replaced the day after the accident that killed the Cabreras.

A light fixture?

He imagined a flimsy glass fluorescent tube dropping from the ceiling and couldn't see what that had to do with causing an accident. He found a computer at one of the workstations provided for archives users, went online. Fairly quickly he discovered that the light fixtures used in the Ted Williams ranged from 80 pounds to 110 pounds. They were attached by means of bolts and epoxy adhesive.

Eighty pounds fell. On what? What if it fell on a car? He imagined the impact, the spider-webbed windshield. The blinded driver, the panic.

The car spinning out of control.

It was as simple as that. Now he understood what happened, what had caused the accident. Now it made sense. But nothing about a falling light fixture had been reported in the press. Somehow it had been covered up.

He had a pretty good idea how that might have happened.

He needed to take a few notes. He reached into his pockets. All he had was his wallet and, for some reason, Andrea Messina's business card. He smiled. He'd been thinking about her and about how awful their dinner had been. Then remembered he'd brought one of his old reporter's notebooks, long and thin and spiral-bound on the top, for his interview with Conklin later that morning. He wanted it to look like a real interview.

He opened the notebook and took notes. Now he knew exactly what he had to ask the ex-cop.

At the end of the afternoon he stopped by Clayton Street and found Jeff there, sweeping up with one hand. His other hand held his phone to his ear. "All right, cool," he said. "Got it. That's no problem. All right, later."

Jeff flipped the phone closed, and it tumbled to the floor. "Shit," he said, reaching over to retrieve it. He held it up in the air triumphantly. It was an old-model Nokia flip phone. "Takes a licking and keeps on ticking." He flipped it open and closed a few times. "Oldie but goodie. Doesn't talk to you and tell you what time the movie starts, but drop it and the screen doesn't shatter."

"True."

"What's up, boss?"

"Got a minute?"

Jeff shrugged. "Sure."

"I need your help on something. You know anybody who used to work on the Big Dig?"

"The Big Dig?" He chuckled. "Oh, sure. A lot."

"Let me tell you a story." He gave Jeff the briefest possible summary of what he'd been investigating. As he finished up, he said, "There must have been a dozen workers on site there to replace that light fixture. Subcontractors. Electricians and lighting specialists and epoxy guys and all that."

"Boston's a small town," Jeff said. "I should at least know someone who knows someone. I got a couple ideas; let me ask around and get back to you."

"Thanks. And do me a favor—be discreet about why you're asking, okay?"

Jeff paused a moment. Warily, he said, "Do my best."

"Some people out there don't want anyone asking questions."

46

Marblehead was a half hour's drive from Boston, mostly up 1A, along the coast. It was a town usually called "charming," its harbor one of the best on the eastern seaboard, allowing the chamber of commerce to call Marblehead "the yachting capital of America."

It was not the sort of town to which cops tended to retire.

Rick had been to houses bigger and grander than Walter Conklin's waterfront estate. But not many. And none of them belonged to retired police officers.

As he drove up he was dazzled by the light reflecting on the water, the bright white paint of the house, the emerald of the lawn. The house was situated on a bluff overlooking the ocean. It had to have water views from almost every room in the house. He parked in the circular drive beside a champagne Mercedes sedan. There was a long walk to the house. The place had absolute privacy. No neighbors to be seen.

Walter Conklin looked like a retired captain of industry, maybe a retired admiral. His full head of white hair was carefully combed back. He wore a white polo shirt under a soft blue lamb's wool sweater, tan slacks, and moccasins. His ruddy face spoke of long afternoons spent sailing off his private beach. His handshake was unnecessarily firm.

"No problem finding me?"

His accent, however, was pure unadulterated Southie.

"Easy. Right up 1A. Beautiful setting."

"Thank you."

A slender woman in a tennis dress materialized from the hallway behind him. Her blond-gray hair was pulled back with a lime-green headband. She looked easily fifteen years younger than Conklin. "Lunch at one at the club?" She, too, had a working-class Boston accent, though Rick couldn't quite place it. She kissed her husband on the cheek, gave Rick a wary glance before sliding out the front door.

The décor was Grand Hyatt tasteful. "My wife made coffee," Conklin said. "How do you take it?"

"I'm fine."

"Then I'll help myself." He led the way to a spacious kitchen—granite island, cherrywood cabinets, built-in ovens—and poured himself a mug of coffee from a Krups machine on the island. He went over to a banquette against the window next to a round wooden kitchen table and sat, gesturing to Rick to join him. Then he took a sip and looked at Rick over the rim. "So what's your take on the wind farm gonna be?"

"Actually, I'd be more interested to hear *your* take." He took out one of his old reporter's notebooks and a pen and started jotting.

"You have any idea how big that thing is?" Conklin said. "It's taller than the Statue of Liberty. It's taller than the Zakim Bridge. I mean, each blade is like the width of a football field, you know that?"

"You've got a gorgeous view of the Atlantic here. How do you feel about what a windmill would do to your view?"

"The view? That ain't the half of it. These things make a hell of a racket. I read a website about it. They disturb sleep and cause irritability. It's like a jet engine hovering over you."

"'A jet engine'... that's good."

"Plus, when it's freezing they throw off shards of ice. And they kill birds."

Rick nodded, pretending to take notes, as he planned how he was going to segue to the tunnel accident.

"Yeah, it's an unholy monstrosity." Conklin paused and gave a twist of a smile. "But I have a feeling you didn't really come here to talk about windmills, did you, Rick?"

"Excuse me?"

"I'm not exactly a *Back Bay* reader, but they never commissioned an article about the Tinker's Island windmill. Not their kind of thing. Now, if someone wanted to put one of these wind turbines in Boston Common, maybe they'd do something." Conklin's eyes glittered. He took a sip of coffee.

Rick felt a surge of adrenaline, a pulse of anxiety. "I've changed my mind about coffee."

"Help yourself," Conklin said casually. "The mugs are right there. Cream in the fridge."

Rick took an earthenware mug from a spindle by the coffee machine and poured himself a cup of coffee, and by the time he took a sip he'd thought of a response. "They usually have no idea what I'm working on until I turn it in." He sat down at one of the uncomfortable ladder-back chairs around the table.

"Uh-huh. They also say you're no longer on staff there."

All the years in retirement fell away, and Conklin was a cop again, talking to a perp in an interrogation room. He stared at Rick with a zookeeper look.

"Busted," Rick said. "You know what, you're right. I'm actually interested in asking you about something else, and I apologize for coming here under false pretenses. I'm actually working on something a little more interesting. A story about an accident eighteen years ago in the Ted Williams Tunnel where a family was killed."

"I have no idea what you're talking about."

"You know exactly what I'm talking about. You were a patrol officer. You signed the incident report."

"You know how much shit I had to deal with in my twenty years on the force? How many years ago was that?"

"Eighteen years ago."

"Come on."

"Well, I have a fairly good working theory of what happened. You were driving by or else got the call on the radio and you discovered a grisly accident scene. You saw a car that was badly smashed up. Then you saw what had happened. You saw that a light fixture had dropped from the ceiling and crashed into the car's windshield. And that's when you made a really smart decision."

Conklin was no longer meeting Rick's eyes. He seemed deflated, maybe hostile, but hard to read.

"Because you're a smart guy," Rick went on, "you realized you'd just found something really valuable. Something that might be worth a hell of a lot of money to the company that had just got finished building the tunnel. You probably even had friends who'd been hired by Donegall Construction. So you knew who to call. And that was a call that made you a rich man."

Gears were turning in the ex-cop's mind. Maybe he was trying to decide whether to break almost two decades of silence.

"You knew that Donegall Construction really wouldn't want it known what caused this accident. Because that would expose them to some really bad publicity and, who knows, maybe a hundred-million-dollar lawsuit? You figured out that that light fixture would be worth a hell of a lot of money to them." Rick paused, smiled. "But only if you put it away somewhere. Made sure it wasn't found by any other cops or state troopers or accident investigators. So you put it away somewhere. Like the trunk of your car."

Conklin was still looking off into the distance. Rick tried to measure whether his conjecture was hitting home, whether he'd got it substantially right. But the man remained unreadable.

"My guess is, you made a really good deal with them. Maybe even millions of dollars. Because it was worth it to Donegall Construction. Given how much they'd be on the hook for if anyone found out about the fallen light fixture, that was pocket change to them."

"It was blocking traffic," Conklin said finally. "I wasn't gonna leave it there."

"Of course not." Rick had seen moments like this before, where the interview takes a sudden turn. The hostile corporate CEO abruptly decides what the hell, why not fess up? But it was important now to lock Conklin in to a confirmation.

Rick leaned in and said deliberately, "Look, the story's going to come out, one way or another. Your best hope is to make sure it's a version of events that's . . ." *Favorable to you,* he thought, but he said, "accurate as you recall it. This interview can be entirely off the record, if you prefer.

Nobody needs to know that we spoke. You see, I just want to know the truth. That's all."

Rick looked into Conklin's eyes, and this time the old cop returned his gaze. Conklin pursed his lips and looked as if he'd just swallowed something unpleasant. There was a long beat of silence.

"Get the hell out of my house," he said.

47

Conklin's already ruddy face had turned dark, and his eyes twinkled with moisture. There was something in his expression very close to hatred.

Rick was about to speak, to attempt to talk the man down with some combination of wheedling and threat, when Conklin jabbed a fat finger in the air close to Rick's nose and said, with teeth bared, "Get the fuck out of here this instant before I make you."

There was no more reasoning with him. Anyway, Rick had gotten what he'd come for. He stood up, the ladder-back chair crashing to the kitchen floor behind him. He picked up the chair and slid it neatly against the table. Then he left the kitchen and headed down the hallway to the front door, his footsteps loud in the silence.

He descended the steps of the gray-painted wraparound porch, his heart thudding. The air was salty and the sun was so bright he had to blink a few times before his eyes adjusted. When he was a good ways down the long driveway, he heard a noise behind him. There was a scuffing sound, like a shoe against gravel, and he turned his head and for a fraction of a second he saw something in his peripheral vision: a person.

Then something walloped his upper back with such force it sent him sprawling to the ground. He heard a cracking sound on impact and wondered if it was a bone. After a brief moment of nothing, a supernova of pain exploded in his upper back, of a magnitude he'd never experienced before. Needles of pain were shooting down his arms, his hands, and radiating down to his lower back. His right cheek had scraped against the asphalt, but that hurt was insignificant. *What the hell?* He looked up, saw a guy looming over him, holding a baseball bat, silhouetted against the bright sun.

"Leave it . . . the fuck . . . alone," the man said. It was the bouncer from Jugs, and the man clearly intended to kill him.

He scrambled to his feet, as the ground beneath him tilted, and he lunged unsteadily toward his car. He tried to run but for some reason he found himself moving slower than usual; maybe it was the pain that had gripped his back and shoulders.

The bouncer pulled the bat back and swung it hard at his face.

Rick watched it come at him, as if in slow motion, and he knew that the bat would derange his face as soon as it made contact, break his nose and cheekbone and probably other bones he didn't know he had. For a split second he considered contracting into a fetal position to protect himself. But at the last moment, as the bat came at him, he spun and flung out his hands to try to block the blow, try to grab the bat out of the guy's hands, but he managed only to have the fingers of his left hand crunch against the shank of the bat, slowing its speed and maybe altering its trajectory just enough so it cracked into his jaw. His field of vision exploded in a constellation of stars. His left arm flopped uselessly against his side and he screamed in pain. The bones in his left hand felt as if they'd shattered like glass.

He tasted the metallic tang of his own blood. A part of his brain, the project manager that was overseeing everything at a cool distance, wondered whether the bouncer intended to kill him or just inflict brain damage. Maybe he'd get hit on the side of his head and suffer a stroke, and he'd end up just like his father.

"*Hold on*," he huffed. "*Listen.*"

Or maybe he only thought he'd spoken these words aloud. His jaw felt broken and his mouth wasn't working.

"Leave it . . . the fuck . . . alone," the bouncer said again.

He tried to lift his arms to ward off the next blow, but he couldn't lift his left hand, and this time the bat connected with his trunk, slamming into his solar plexus, knocking the wind out of him, doubling him over. He couldn't breathe. For a brief instant he saw stars again. He crumpled to his knees. He gasped for air uselessly like a goldfish out of its bowl. Everything went quiet, and all he could hear was a high-pitched squeal, like feedback from a microphone. He collapsed into a ball.

But the man wasn't done yet.

The bat connected one more time, smashing into his right shoulder and his right ear, and somehow the starburst of pain was even worse, a crescendo of agony, and his field of vision went dark and he was gone.

48

He wasn't able to move.

"Stay still, sir," a voice said.

"No . . . no . . ." Rick moaned.

Someone was doing something to his left arm. He tried to pull his arm away but it wouldn't move. Then he remembered vaguely a baseball bat colliding with his hand and rendering it useless.

Someone else was jabbing something sharp, a pin or a needle of some kind, into his other arm. He was aware on some level that it hurt, but he was in such a world of pain that one more hurt barely registered.

A second voice, a woman's, said, "Say your name. What's your name?"

Rick Hoffman, he may have said, or maybe he only thought it.

"BP one hundred palp," said the first voice, a man's voice, high and nasal.

"Out . . . out . . ." Rick said. He was trapped in something, he now realized. Or on something. His entire body was frozen in place, and he struggled with all his strength to get free.

"Big poke again," said the woman.

"Ahh," Rick groaned.

"You get it?" the man said.

"He feels that," the woman said. "There's the flash. Good IV."

"Here's your liter," the man said.

Rick saw faces coming in and out of focus, in and out. "Run it wide," the woman said. "You still with me, sir?"

Rick moaned some more and tried to tell them to leave him the hell alone.

The faces were gone now, and he could see blue sky, and then it began to move, and he saw shadows and a dark shape of some sort and he didn't know where he was, somewhere inside now, not outside, and everything had gone dark, and he was gone.

A couple of people stood over him now. They wore yellow paper gowns. One of them said in a low, hoarse voice, "Gimme the story."

A familiar voice—a man's voice, high and nasal—said, "Thirtysomething male assault. Unwitnessed but the person who called 911 said something about 'bats.'"

Rick was moving, rolling. He passed through glass doors that slid open on his approach. One of the people in the yellow paper gowns, alongside, said, "Sir, what's your name, sir?"

Rick said his name again.

"What's he saying?"

"Been that way the whole time." The woman's voice from before. "GCS maybe ten. BP one hundred palp. Pulse 120s."

He finally understood he was in a hospital. He saw beds with patients lying in them, uniformed nurses ducking out of the way, then there was a tight turn and he was in a large space, bright and hectic, filled with people.

"Easy on my count." The low, hoarse male voice. "One—two—*three*."

He was lifted high up into the air, then down.

"No other medical history," the nasal voice said. "He's not talking much. We got a liter going."

Now he was aware of several people looming above him, men and women. They were making him dizzy. He let his eyes fall shut. Now all around him was a hubbub, yammering indistinct voices, and everything had gone dark.

A man's voice: "Field line in the right AC. Liter up."

A woman's voice: "Open your eyes, sir! Tell me your name."

Obediently, Rick opened his eyes. He said *Rick Hoffman* but what came out sounded more like *brick house*. His mouth wasn't working right. It hurt when he tried to speak.

"Sir, do you remember what happened?" the woman said.

Rick saw the woman's face, looked into her eyes. He tried to nod.

"Don't move, sir," a man said. "Got a second line, eighteen gauge left AC."

"Okay," the woman doctor said, "protecting his airway for now." She had a stethoscope in her ears and was putting the diaphragm end of it on his chest. Meanwhile someone was cutting his shirt open with a large pair of shears. "Bilateral symmetrical breath sounds." Her voice was low and husky.

A new voice now. Male. "On the monitor—BP 108 over 64, pulse 118, sats 92 percent."

"Good peripheral pulses all around," said another voice.

"Show me a thumbs-up," said the woman. "Give me a squeeze. . . ."

Rick tried to squeeze her finger, which she'd put in his left hand, but just moving it was ungodly painful.

"He's not following commands. Sir, can you wiggle your toes?"

Rick obediently wiggled his toes.

"Guess not," someone said.

The woman said, "Okay, two liters up, CBC and trauma panel."

"You want some fent?" a man asked.

Some piece of equipment rolled up alongside his bed. He felt something cold and gelatinous being squirted onto his chest.

"Fifty of fent to start," the woman said. "You still with me, sir? Open your mouth. Wide."

Something cold and metallic, he assumed it was a probe, was moving in small circles on his chest.

Rick obeyed, or thought he did. He moaned. His jaw was incredibly painful but only when he opened his mouth to breathe or talk. His chest and stomach ached terribly. He moaned again.

"No pericardial effusion, good cardiac motion," someone else said. A young man. "Multiple abrasions and bruises over the chest wall."

"Ahhh," Rick moaned. He gasped in pain.

"Sorry," said the young man. "Good sliding motion on the lungs, no pneumo."

"Got a big lac over the left parietal scalp," the husky-voiced woman said. "Stapler."

"No blood in Morison's pouch. Left paracolic gutter dry." The young guy.

The woman: "Let me have twenty of etomidate and 120 of succs ready in case we have to tube this guy."

"Already got it," a woman said.

The young guy: "He's pretty altered; you should tube him."

The woman: "Sir! Say your name."

Rick tried again to say his name, but this time it came out as *Off me*.

The woman: "Sir, I have to put a tube in your throat to protect you. Do you understand? We need to put you to sleep for now."

I don't want a tube in my throat, Rick tried to say. *That's totally unnecessary*.

"FAST is negative," said the young guy. "Call the scanner and let them know we have a tubed blunt head on the way."

Something glinted—a blade of some sort? The doctors and nurses seemed to shift position around the bed. A baby or a kid was crying nearby.

"RT here?" asked the woman.

"He's here," someone said.

Someone ran past with a heavy tread. He heard a hissing noise. Then somebody put a mask, loudly hissing, over his face.

"Sats going up ninety-six."

"Okay," the young male doctor said. "Push the etomidate, then the succs."

"I got your tube," the husky-voiced female doctor said. "You do C-spine."

"Okay."

"Drugs are in."

"Sir!" said the woman doctor. "Sir! You're going to feel sleepy now. Just relax, just go to . . ."

49

Andrea Messina is talking to him, looking more gorgeous than ever, backlit as if in a TV commercial for shampoo. But he doesn't understand what she's saying. He asks her to repeat it, but now she doesn't understand what *he's* saying, and he can't keep his eyes open, and when he opens them again, she's gone.

The next thing Rick was aware of was light, blindingly bright. He wondered if he'd died and gone to heaven, but he also felt as if he'd been hit by a truck—no, as if the truck had rolled over him and was still parked on top of his body—and he didn't think you could be in heaven and also be in a world of hurt.

Everything was bright and glary, and he realized he was only looking out of one eye. His left eye wouldn't open. He heard steady beeping and another sound, a strange sound that went *whoosh-click, whoosh-click, whoosh-click.* He heard a hubbub of loud voices as if he were in the middle of a crowd.

He coughed and realized something was in his throat, something big, and now he began to gag, to choke, and then he tried to breathe in, but it was like breathing through a straw, he could barely get any air, and he had to get that thing out of his throat or he'd choke to death. He was overcome by panic. He struggled, tried to get up, tried to rip this thing out of his throat, and then there was a loud beeping and he heard a woman's voice saying, "He's awake, he's bucking the vent."

"The doctor's right here," said another voice.

He couldn't clear his throat, couldn't stop choking.

"Okay, relax, relax, you're feeling the ventilator," a woman said. "You need to show me you can breathe on your own. I need you to breathe out and cough."

Rick, in full panic mode now, struggling with all his strength, managed to free one hand and reached up toward whatever the hell it was that was lodged in his throat.

"Mr. Hoffman, relax, you have a tube in your throat, you're on a ventilator, but—Mr. Hoffman, if you understand me, give me a thumbs-up, okay?"

Rick stuck his thumb up, with the only hand that seemed to be working, thinking, *There's your goddamned thumb, get this thing out of my throat,* but unable to say anything.

"Mr. Hoffman, take a nice breath in and out."

Rick tried to breathe in, but he could barely suck in any air.

"Okay, excellent," the woman said. "Now I want you to cough for me. Or push out really hard as if you're coughing. Make a big cough. On three, I want you to cough. One, two, and three—excellent." Rick coughed, though it felt more like he was gagging, he hacked and then caught his breath—and a moment later he was taking a deep, wonderful breath, and it was like coming up from the bottom of a pool; he gulped the air in and it was great. And then at almost the same instant, he felt a terrific stabbing pain in his chest.

"Good, there you go. Now spit."

And someone was holding a pink plastic bowl under his mouth and he spit out gobs of something and it felt terrific.

"Mr. Hoffman, I'm Dr. Castillo. You were intubated because they were worried you might not be able to protect your airway. Do you remember what happened?"

The doctor was out of focus. Rick blinked a few times and she began to swim into focus, but he was looking at her only with his right eye.

"Uh," he said.

"Your vital signs look good. Can you say your name?"

"Uh . . . Rick Hoffman," he said. His voice was hoarse and his throat hurt.

"Excellent. Now, it looks like somebody beat you up pretty good. Do you remember what happened?"

Rick just looked at the doctor, who was dark-haired and pretty and looked barely out of her teens. "Uh," he said. The room was white and dazzlingly bright and mostly out of focus.

He remembered the baseball bat and the guy with the shamrock tattoo swinging it at him, remembered shouting at the guy to stop. And the guy not stopping. He couldn't figure out how he got here, how he ended up in this hospital, wherever it was.

But why could he see out of only one eye? He reached up to touch his left eye, pulled it open, and he could see blurry shapes, and when he let go, his eye closed again.

"Well, you got banged up, quite a bit," the doctor said. "You've got a left lateral nondisplaced clavicle fracture—that's a collarbone fracture. Plus you've got some fractured ribs on your left side—posterior ribs three, four, and five on the left. The CT scan showed you have a fracture of your left cheekbone, a zygomatic arch fracture."

He took a deep breath and gasped as he felt the stabbing pain in his chest once again.

"Yeah, you're going to hurt a lot, pretty much all the time." She gave a low chuckle. "We've got you on some pain-killers but you may need some more, looks like. You've got some big bruises on your back and on your chest and over your left kidney. You had some blood in your urine, what we call hematuria, from the renal contusions."

Rick suddenly realized he felt a strange, unfamiliar sensation down there, and he reached down and felt it.

"Yeah," the doctor said, "you've got a tube down there, a Foley catheter, and we can get that out of you in a couple of minutes. Your urine's going to be pink for a little while. Oh, and it looks like you may have a sternal fracture—you got hit in the solar plexus. I don't know if you want to take a look." She handed him a mirror with a white plastic handle. "Maybe it's better if you don't."

He took the mirror. He wanted to see how bad he looked.

It was bad. He barely recognized the face in the mirror. One side of his face looked mostly normal, just some scrapes here and there, but the left side of his face was swollen and misshapen and eggplant purple. His left eye was shut and dome-shaped. He looked like a boxer after twelve rounds. Like a purple Pillsbury Doughboy. He put his hand to his face and pulled open his left eyelid again, just to make sure his left eye worked. It did. He moved his jaw up and down and was pleased to discover that worked. Gingerly he rolled his head back and forth on his neck a few times. It hurt, but it worked, too. He handed the mirror back to the doctor.

"Looks pretty bad, huh?" she said.

"Pretty bad."

293

"But really, I'd say you were lucky."

"Lucky." He laughed mordantly, which made his head hurt.

"I've seen a lot worse. You've got a lot of contusions, anterior and posterior, but apart from the rib fractures and the clavicle, you came out of this okay. You had a concussion, so we want to be careful about that. You're going to look pretty swollen for a week or so—you're going to have raccoon eyes for a while—and you're going to have a lot of pain."

"What pain meds am I on right now?"

"A fentanyl/Versed IV drip."

"It's no good. It's not working."

"We titrated the meds down until you woke up."

"Yeah, well, it hurts to breathe."

"It's going to be that way for a while. Everything's going to hurt. You'll feel like a pro football player the day after a big game. But we'll give you some pain meds for breakthrough pain. Oh, and stay out of fistfights. A concussed brain is a lot more likely to get a repeat concussion."

"Okay. Where am I, by the way? Mass General?"

"North Shore Regional Medical Center in Salem. I think the EMTs picked you up in Marblehead?"

He nodded, groaned. He wondered who called 911. Conklin? The bouncer, when he was finished working with his baseball bat?

"When can I get out of here?"

"Maybe later today when your friend comes back."

"My friend."

"Ms.—Messina, I think? Given your condition, I'm unwilling to release you except into somebody's custody."

"Andrea? I don't understand."

"Anyway, do you have your own doctor, Mr. Hoffman?"

"Doctor . . . yes, I think so."

"Good. You're going to have to follow up with your doctor or a trauma clinic. The staples will need to come out in a week."

"Did you say staples?"

"You got a pretty bad cut on your scalp. Also, there's some stitches to your left cheek. Those are absorbable, but you might want to get them out anyway."

Someone, a male voice, said, "Can I talk to him now, Doc?"

Rick saw a uniformed police officer enter the curtained-off area.

"I think he's good to talk now, don't you agree, Mr. Hoffman?"

"Talk to . . ."

"Mister, uh, Hoffman," the cop said, "I'm Detective Harrison. Can we talk for a minute?" He was young and overweight, with black hair and gray eyes and deep circles under his eyes.

"Sure, I guess so."

"All right, Mr. Hoffman," the doctor said, "I'll see if we can reach Ms. Messina." She tugged at a curtain and was gone.

"Mister Hoffman, who beat you up?"

"I don't . . . know."

He thought: *The bouncer at Jugs. What was his name again? Don't answer.*

"Lemme, lemme back up a second. Do you remember anything about the incident?"

"Just being beaten with a baseball bat. Everything else is kind of vague."

"But you don't know the person who attacked you?"

"Right, I don't."

"Can you describe him?"

"All I saw was the baseball bat."

"Do you have any idea why he beat you up like this?"

Rick tried to shake his head but it hurt too much. "No."

"Mr. Hoffman," the cop said, exasperated, "I can't help you if you don't tell me what you know. Are you afraid of this person, for some reason?"

"Take a look at me," Rick said. "Wouldn't you be?"

"You must have some idea who did it."

"No."

"It just came out of the blue. You were walking down the street and someone went after you with a baseball bat and beat the crap out of you."

Rick was silent.

"Here's my card," the detective said, handing it to Rick. "Just call and ask for Detective Harrison if you change your mind."

Rick nodded, and it hurt, but less than shaking his head.

Why was he refusing to tell the police? He had no idea. Maybe because it seemed pointless. The police weren't going to be able to do anything anyway.

A minute later he heard a woman's voice and the curtain parted and he saw Andrea.

"Rick, you're awake! What the hell happened? Who did this to you?"

He looked at her through his one open eye. He smiled, or tried to. She was wearing a green jewel-toned suit. Her honeyed brown hair fell to her shoulders in tangled waves. Her full lips, the lips that always looked slightly pursed, were parted. Her brown eyes, normally skeptical, were wide.

"They said your wallet is gone. Did you get held up and you tried to fight them off or something?"

"Something like that. Andi, why are you here?"

"Andi? No one's called me that in, like, twenty years."

"Old habits. Sorry."

"No, it's okay, it's just . . . someone took your wallet and the only thing you had on you was my business card for some reason so they must have assumed we were friends."

"Sorry about that."

"Don't. . . ." She smiled ruefully. "You're going to have to go home with me. Otherwise they won't let you out."

"That's okay, I'll be fine."

"Have you seen yourself? You look like . . . Raging Bull or something. Anyway, I've got plenty of room."

"I don't want you to do this, Andrea."

"As far as I can tell, you have two choices. Spend the next week in the North Shore Regional Medical Center in Salem or go home with me. As long as you don't mind sharing a house with an eight-year-old boy."

He closed his sole functioning eye, then opened it again. "Just for a day or so."

"Let me see what I can do about getting you discharged."

"Thanks."

"On the ride home you can tell me everything."

"Right," he said. The question was whether he could safely tell her anything at all.

50

He sat in the front passenger's seat of her Volvo station wagon. He could barely keep his eyes open. He wanted nothing more than to drift off in a narcotic haze.

"I hope you don't mind my getting you out of the hospital that quickly," Andrea said. "I've got to get back to my office."

"Happy to get out of that place. I couldn't sleep with all the beeping."

"I've got a big meeting this afternoon with a foundation that's interested in giving us a multimillion-dollar gift. So I have to be on my best behavior."

"That's why the fancy suit?"

"You got it." She signaled and sped up to pass a slow-moving truck. "Rick, what happened to you?"

"I . . . got mugged."

"Mugged?"

"I made the mistake of trying to fight the guy off."

A long silence followed. "You were mugged in Marblehead." She sounded dubious.

"Right."

Another pause. "Okay. So they took your wallet but they didn't take your iPhone."

"You can't use someone else's iPhone if it's locked with a code."

"Strange." She glanced in the rearview mirror, then back at the road. "You want to stop by your house and pick up some stuff?"

"My house?"

"Clothes, whatever."

"Oh, right. No, I'm not living there."

"Yeah, all that plaster dust . . . can't blame you. Where're you staying?"

He couldn't remember. There'd been so many hotels and B&Bs. "Oh, right, the DoubleTree. On Soldiers Field Road. But I'm okay for now."

"Think you'll be okay if I just drop you at home and leave you for a while?"

"I got my pain meds, I'm all set."

A couple of minutes later she said something he didn't quite get, and the next thing he knew they were pulling up to her house on Fayerweather Street.

Some time later—hours, probably, but he couldn't be sure—he awoke to find a pair of eyes staring at him from a few inches away.

"Wow," someone said. A kid's voice. Probably the owner of the staring pair of eyes.

It was a mop-headed boy wearing a Red Sox T-shirt. Rick lifted his head off the pillow, which hurt. Moving his head hurt. It wasn't just the physical act of moving his head, the muscles in his neck. That was bad enough, but then there was a headache from hell. His eyes felt as if there were needles sticking into them from behind.

"Gross," the kid said. "You look like Jabba the Hutt."

"Who are you?" he said.

"I'm Evan."

"Evan who's seven?"

"I'm eight now. I just had a birthday."

"Right, with all the Goldfish. How was your party?"

"Good."

"Get anything good?"

"I got Lego sets."

"Yeah? Which one?"

"AT-AT Walker from *Star Wars*."

"Cool. How come you're not in school?"

"I just got home."

"Where's your mom?"

"She's still at work. Most days she doesn't come home till six."

"She lets you go home from school on your own?"

"Grandma walks me home. Anyways, what happened to you? You look like a monster."

"Thank you. I had a disagreement with someone who had a baseball bat."

"Like a baseball player?"

"Not exactly. But he had a pretty good swing."

"Does it hurt?"

"Yep."

"Where? On your face?"

"Pretty much everywhere. Which reminds me it's probably time to take one of my happy pills. Also I need to use the bathroom. Evan, is there a bathroom around here?"

"Yes."

"Where?"

Evan pointed to the door.

"Got it." Rick tried to bend his knees, to lift his legs, but that apparently involved muscles in his lower back, which were too stiff and painful to move. They shot out warning daggers of pain.

"Can I help?" Evan said.

"I'll be okay." Eventually, Rick was able to get out of the bed by lifting the chenille bedspread and revolving his straight legs around and down. He was wearing hospital scrubs, which must have been put on him in the hospital. The clothes he'd been wearing when he was attacked had been given back to him in a plastic bag. They'd been cut up.

He limped, like a very old man, across the carpet into the hall and into the bathroom. There he discovered that it hurt to relieve himself—no doubt a result of the Foley catheter—and that his urine was pink. They'd warned him it might be pink because of the renal contusions: The bouncer from Jugs had walloped Rick's left kidney. They said the pink would go away.

When he came back to the guest room, Evan was still there waiting for him, sitting on the floor.

"You must really hurt," Evan said.

"At least I can walk," Rick said.

"Not really," Evan said. "Not so good."

Rick smiled. "True." He lowered himself to the carpet next to Evan, wincing and groaning.

"Grandma said you're a friend of Mommy's."

"We went to high school together." He reached around to the bedside table and found a pencil stamped GEOMETRY PARTNERS. "Wanna see a trick?"

"Yeah!"

He put his hands together as if he were praying and parked the pencil in the hollow at the base of his thumbs. His left hand wasn't quite working right, and it was radiating spasms of pain. But it was like riding a bicycle: You never forget how. His muscle memory compensated for the pain. He swiveled his left hand around and ended up with his hands flat on top of the pencil, thumbs hooked underneath. Fast and mystifying.

"Cool," Evan said, wide-eyed. "Let me try it."

But he was to discover that the truly cool thing about the pencil trick was when you tried it yourself and found it impossible to do.

"Wait," Evan said as he struggled with it. "Wait."

Rick watched benignly, patiently.

"Wait," Evan said again, slowly growing frustrated. "Wait. I can do it. *Argh!* Do it again!"

Rick took the pencil back, hooked his thumbs around it, rotated his hands smoothly, ending up with the backs of his hands up and the pencil gripped underneath.

"Can you do it slower?"

"Sure." Rick swiveled and twisted slowly.

Evan tried several times. "What's the trick?"

"There is no trick."

"Yes, there is. Can you show me how?"

"Sure." Rick took the pencil. "Start with your thumb crossing like this, okay?"

"Okay." Evan watched closely, mouth slightly ajar, mesmerized.

It took around five minutes to teach him, which was about how long it took Mr. Clarke a.k.a. Antholis to teach Rick years ago.

"I'm doing it!" Evan said excitedly. "I got it!"

"You got it."

"But there's no trick! I thought there was a trick, but there's no *trick*."

Rick laughed. "Want to know something, Evan? You're a lot smarter than I was when I was your age. You got it. The trick is, there's no trick."

"Hi, guys."

Rick looked up and saw Andrea standing at the door. She was holding a big balloon glass of red wine. He realized she'd been standing there for a minute or two, just watching.

"Hi, Mommy!" Evan said, springing to his feet. "Wanna see a trick?"

51

I'd offer you some wine," Andrea said a few minutes later, after Evan had gone back to his room to do his homework, "but I don't think it goes well with Vicodin."

"Probably not."

She sat on the bed. "Also, I don't think you'd be satisfied with this. It's not exactly DRC."

He looked at her, saw the barest trace of a smile. It took him a moment to remember the nickname for Domaine de la Romanée-Conti. "Why do I get the feeling you're giving me a hard time?"

She grinned. "I know, no fair with you in that condition."

She was as brimming with confidence as once she'd been insecure. She'd grown up. Maybe the years she spent in the blast furnace that was Goldman Sachs had annealed her. But all that newfound confidence didn't make her arrogant or obnoxious; it burnished her, gave her a glow, a vivacity she'd never had before. Or at least not that Rick had noticed.

"I deserve it." Consigning their grotesquely bad date to the realm of mockery felt like progress. He tried to get up off the carpet. "Could you give me a hand?" He reached out his left hand, then remembered and put out his right. She pulled, and he groaned as he got to his feet, his broken clavicle shimmering with pain. He sat on the edge of the bed next to her. "How'd it go with the big funder?"

"Could not have gone better. I think they're going to come through big-time. It's going to let us hire a bunch of new tutors and get iPads for all the kids, and . . . Hey, thanks for being so sweet to Evan."

"No problem. Seems like a cool kid."

"He is. He really is. Are you still in terrible pain?"

"I'm better," he lied. Even taking a breath hurt.

It had been a mistake to come home with her. But the painkillers had screwed up his judgment, sapped his will, made him far more compliant than usual. He hadn't been thinking clearly. For him to stay at Andrea's house was just putting her and her son at risk.

And since he'd recently taken another couple oxycodone tablets, everything was starting to slow down just a bit.

"Good. Listen. When we talked on the way home you said you got mugged and you tried to fight the attacker off."

"Right."

"Problem is, I don't believe that. You weren't mugged on the street in Marblehead. Sorry. You should have said Central Square. Dorchester, Roxbury maybe. Just not Marblehead."

He looked away.

"What really happened?"

He hesitated, then told her.

It took almost fifteen minutes, with Andrea breaking in several times for clarification. He spoke slowly because of the drugs he was on. When he was finished, she had tears in her eyes and she seemed angry. Neither of which he had expected.

"You don't think he meant to kill you, did he?"

"No more than they meant to kill my dad twenty years ago."

"Meaning—what? They wanted to leave you maimed?"

"Maybe they wanted to know where the money is. Also, I think it was meant to be a warning. He could easily have killed me if he'd wanted to."

"A warning." Her eyes flashed. "Warning you what?"

"To stop digging. To stop trying to uncover something they want to keep covered."

"And are you going to obey their warning?"

Rick exhaled slowly and was silent for a long while. "I don't know," he said truthfully.

"Do you know anybody in the police?"

He nodded. "I had a pretty good source at the FBI who's still there. But I don't have enough to take to the FBI. Not yet anyway."

"Okay. You said the guy who attacked you was the bouncer from that strip club."

"Right."

"The strip-club owner—you don't think he was behind the attack, do you?"

"No. The bouncer and the guys who abducted me, the guy with the shamrock tattoo—they're all part of the same gang. I think he gets assigned these guys as muscle."

"By who?"

"By what he calls 'the powers that be.' I think he's an old stoner who does what he's told. I don't think he knows who's pulling the strings."

"So who *is* pulling the strings? Who are the powers that be?"

"It's whoever's behind a defunct construction company called Donegall. And whoever's behind the Donegall Charitable Trust. But it's a dead end. And you can bet I looked. Remember, I used to be an investigative reporter."

"What do you mean, a dead end?"

"Donegall Construction is out of business. Went bankrupt."

"But bankrupt doesn't necessarily mean a dead end. Remember, I used to do troubled assets. There's tons of corporate records filed in a bankruptcy. There's a trustee and an agent of record—"

"From the stuff I've seen online, the agent of record is a shell company."

"Huh. Weird. What about the charity? Nonprofits have to file tax returns and such."

"I pulled up nothing on the Donegall Charitable Trust."

"Well, that I can help you with. I run a nonprofit. I know how these things work. Hold on."

She returned a few minutes later with a Dell laptop under her arm. She opened the laptop, wiped a few tendrils of hair back from her forehead, tucked them behind her right ear. He was beginning to float away, making it increasingly difficult to understand what she was saying.

"Okay, there's a couple of websites for nonprofits . . . one called GuideStar . . . and the Donegall Charitable . . . Oh, now, this is bizarre."

"What?"

She said something about "form 990" and "the IRS," then he subsided back into a black fog of exhaustion and opiates.

"Rick?" she said.

"I'm here."

"It's registered in Reno, Nevada. The address is a law firm I recognize. It's used as a home to millions of corporate addresses, limited liability corporations that want to disguise ownership. It's basically a post office box. A dead drop."

He didn't understand what she was getting at. A thought glimmered and vanished, like one of those transparent fish you can see only when it catches the light.

She said, "I've never heard of a nonprofit going under the radar like that. Someone's got something to hide and they're serious about it. What about this guy Alex Pappas?"

"Pappas?" he said thickly, and he tried hard to focus.

"He knows who's calling the shots."

"Pappas isn't . . . he won't . . ."

"There must be some way to get it out of him. Or to find out from him. He's our best way in."

He noticed that *our* but said nothing. His tentative grasp on what she was saying was slackening, and she began to speak nonsense. "Alex Pappas" and "meeting" and something else.

"Rick?"

He opened his eyes. "I'm here."

But when he opened his eyes again, she was gone.

He closed his eyes, and when he opened them once again, he looked at his watch. It took him some time to understand what time it was—his watch said nearly three o'clock, but was that in the afternoon? The shades in his room had been drawn, but he could see the darkness around their edges and he realized it was the middle of the night.

With some effort he managed to sit up in bed, and he reached over to the bedside table for his phone. It showed 19 percent battery life remaining. Slowly and deliberately he opened the Uber application and set the pickup location.

Fifteen minutes later he was in a cab, and on the way he got the phone call he'd long been dreading.

52

"Change of plans," Rick told the cab driver. "I'd like to go to the Alfred Becker nursing home in Brookline."

"Where?" The driver pulled over to the side and entered the Becker home in his smartphone's GPS.

Rick felt his heartbeat slow as he watched the traffic, the buildings they passed, and everything seemed remote and miniature. He was lost in thought. Twenty minutes later, though it seemed to be two or three, the cab pulled up to the circular drive in front of the Alfred Becker.

He got out gingerly and limped to the entrance, pushed the glass doors open with his right hand. The woman sitting at the front desk ignored him, as she ignored everybody. He signed in and walked down the broad main corridor, past the elevator, everything slower and unreal, as if in a dream.

When he reached his father's wing, he passed one of the nurses, Carolyn, who just looked at him with surprise as he passed. For a moment he forgot why, then he remembered what his face must look like. The beautiful Saint Lucian nurse, Jewel, with the fawnlike eyes, was lingering in front of the closed door to Lenny's room. "What happened to you, Mr. Rick?"

"I was in an accident, but I'm okay."

"It looks—very bad."

"It's not as bad as it looks."

She touched his arm and said, "I'm sorry about your father."

She opened the door. He was lying on his back. When Rick saw him, his stomach took a deep dive. He couldn't stop himself from exclaiming, in a small strangled voice, "Oh."

He hadn't expected Lenny's expression to be so serene, but it was. That angry expression seemed to have dissolved in death. His mouth gaped, just a little. His cataract-clouded eyes looked at nothing. Rick reached up with his good hand and pulled Lenny's eyelids closed. The skin was pale and waxy, translucent, and it felt slightly cool to the touch.

"Dad," he said. "I'm sorry."

"He die in his sleep, your father," Jewel said. "I come by and see him when my shift start, at midnight, and he was watching the TV. I come by again and ask him if he want to turn off the TV because it's so late and he didn't say nothin' but he was alive. I turn off the TV and his lamp and tuck him in and everything. When I look in at three tirty, he gone."

"He died in his sleep," Rick echoed, just to say something. "That's nice."

"I pronounce and tell doctor by phone. But we wait till you get here to call funeral home. Do you have funeral home to call?"

"Funeral home? Oh. Yeah, no. What's that big one, Orlonsky and Sons?" The big funeral home on Beacon Street in Brookline. He remembered driving past the Grecian columns, ORLONSKY & SONS MEMORIAL CHAPEL in black letters.

She nodded. "Orlonsky, yes, we call them. Your father—he was a very nice man, your father was."

"He was. What was—the cause of death?"

"I think the doctor will say cardiac failure. Maybe he was leaving here too much." It took him a while to understand what she meant. Finally he understood: Lenny's traveling to Charlestown and back as often as he did must have been stressful for him.

When Jewel left, Rick sat in the chair beside the bed and thought for a moment. He felt heavy-limbed and achy. The pain had come back. It was time for another pain pill, but he needed to stay alert a while longer.

Then he took out his phone and stepped into the hallway. On the West Coast it was three hours earlier: one in the morning. She might still be awake, but more likely she was asleep.

The phone rang six times before she answered.

"Wendy," he said. "How soon can you get back to Boston?"

Half an hour later—surprisingly quickly—someone from the funeral home came, a young guy in a dark crewneck sweater. He went to work at once, lowering the bed expertly, transferring the body to a rolling cot, covering the body with a quilt he had brought.

Rick didn't cry.

He'd been meaning to tell his dad how much he admired him, but it was too late.

53

By the time he was finished signing forms and doing paperwork for the death certificate and composing the death notice for the newspapers, it was five thirty in the morning. Lenny wasn't an organ donor. He believed that if the doctors found an organ donor card in your wallet, they didn't try as hard to save you. There was not much to sign.

Rick got a cab and went back to the DoubleTree. He was hobbling slowly. His pain had come roaring back. But he couldn't take a pill, not until he was settled someplace else.

He had one suitcase and a few clothes to pack, some toiletries in the bathroom, not much else.

He thought about his father's funeral. Who were Lenny's friends anymore? For almost twenty years he'd lived in a nursing home, unable to communicate. Most of his friends stopped coming by after a few months. There was Mr. Clarke/Herbert Antholis, but he couldn't appear in public. Lenny's secretary, Joan, whom his father had reason to distrust. Who else was there?

At a few minutes after six in the morning, his phone rang.

It was Andrea. "Rick, are you all right? Where'd you go? Was it something I said?"

He'd rehearsed a few answers but nothing seemed right. *I didn't want to trouble you* made him sound like a martyr. *I'm all recovered* sounded delusional.

"I'm okay," he said. "I thought it was better for you and Evan if I wasn't there."

"That's ridiculous. You're going to stay at some hotel—?"

"My father died."

"Ohh, Rick, I'm sorry. When did this—?"

"I got a call in the middle of the night. Heart failure."

"So that's why . . . What can I do?"

He didn't correct her. No reason for her to know he'd left before getting the call from the nursing home. "Nothing. Apologize to Evan for me. He was going to show me how to play *Minecraft*. Tell him another time."

Rick wanted to change hotels, because that had become his routine, but he couldn't. Since his wallet had been taken, he had no credit cards, no driver's license. The DoubleTree had his card on file, so he was okay until he checked out. By tomorrow he'd have replacement credit cards he could use.

He had around ten thousand dollars in cash left and was in no condition to go back to the storage unit for more, not until he felt stronger. Fortunately, he'd paid off all his credit cards, so after a few hours on the phone he had new credit card numbers he could use once they arrived.

He took a pain pill and slept for five hours.

By the time he'd awakened, the funeral home was open. He surveyed himself in the bathroom mirror as he washed up. The bruises on his face were starting to look less acute, less well defined, with green and yellow tints seeping around the edges. His left eye was still swollen, but much less than it had been. He no longer had a constant headache. He was starting to heal. But every time he moved, even to lift a cup of coffee, he felt the pain. It hurt when he coughed, grunted, or laughed. It was as if he were made of broken glass in a bag.

He took a cab to the funeral home and picked out a plain wooden casket, and still he didn't cry. The funeral director offered to bring in a rabbi to conduct the service the following day. Neither Rick nor his father was observant, but in the end, Rick decided that was what his father would have wanted. Better safe than sorry.

He went back to the hotel and slept some more until his cell phone ringing woke him up. He looked at the time on the phone. He'd been asleep for seven hours.

It was Wendy. She'd just arrived in Boston. She'd caught an Alaska Airlines flight from Bellingham—her least favorite airline, she made a point of saying—with a brief layover in Seattle. Rick told her he'd had a car accident a few days ago, was fine now, but needed his rest. He'd see her at the funeral tomorrow.

"Is Sarah with you?"

"No. She can't leave the restaurant." Rick had met Sarah exactly once, a couple of years ago, at their wedding.

"Hey, Rick? How'd he die?"

"They're saying cardiac failure."

"Maybe it's just as well. Ever since his stroke, his quality of life was pretty lousy."

"I guess."

He gave her the address of the funeral home and told her to be there at ten o'clock. The funeral started at eleven.

"Hey, Rick?"

"Yeah?"

"Know something weird?" Wendy said. "We're orphans now."

54

Jesus, Rick, what the hell happened to you?" Wendy said.

"I told you, I was in an accident."

"Yeah, but . . . you look like you were in a fistfight and you lost, bad."

Rick shrugged, then winced as his ribs shrieked with pain.

"I'd give you a hug, but I have a feeling that would hurt you."

"Yeah, please don't."

They were in the lobby of Orlonsky & Sons Memorial Chapel, which, with its green wall-to-wall carpeting and framed paintings of fruit, looked like a suburban living room, the formal room no one ever uses.

Wendy was small and pretty but she was becoming stout, with a large, almost maternal bosom. She had the same build as their mother, but in her early thirties she already looked like their mother did in her fifties. Her eyes were red-rimmed.

"I think I cried the whole way here," she said. "The guy in the seat next to me was getting nervous."

Rick nodded. He wasn't going to tell her he hadn't cried.

"So much easier for you living near him," she said. "At least you got

317

to see him once a week. Me, I had to suffer the guilt of not seeing him for months at a time. I almost asked you if you knew what his last words were, but then I remembered his last words were eighteen years ago."

The rabbi was young, too young to have the gravitas and authority his job required. He arrived a few minutes after they did, in a gust of cold wind. After introducing himself and saying he was sorry for their loss, he took them into a small anteroom next to where the service was being held—Rick could see the pine casket on a bier next to a floral arrangement—and talked them through the ceremony. "I didn't know your father, of course, but he sounds like he was a wonderful man."

"Yes," Wendy said.

I didn't know him either, Rick thought, but he said only, "He was."

The rabbi tore a small black ribbon and pinned it on to Wendy's lapel. Then he did the same with Rick. He said a prayer in Hebrew that Rick didn't understand. The rabbi said the torn black ribbon was meant to symbolize their loss, a tear in the fabric of the family's life.

They filed into the funeral chapel, where a smattering of people had gathered. He was surprised that anyone had shown up. Jeff Hollenbeck was there, in an awkwardly fitting gray suit he obviously didn't wear very often. Andrea Messina, which surprised him. (Holly was in Miami, though she wouldn't have appeared if she were in town.) Joan Breslin and her husband. The rest were people of around Lenny's age, friends of his, a few of whom looked vaguely familiar.

And, just entering the chapel, Alex Pappas.

55

Instead of taking his place in one of the two reserved seats in the front of the room next to Wendy, Rick immediately circled around to the back of the room, limping quickly, painfully. Pappas saw him approach and remained standing in place. He was wearing a black suit with a crisp white shirt and a silver tie.

"I'm sorry for your loss," Pappas said.

You goddamned son of a bitch, Rick thought. *What the hell are you doing here? Is this your victory lap?*

"Thank you for coming," Rick said.

The man had apparently arranged for the payment of eighteen years' worth of nursing home expenses. Yet was he responsible for the very injury that made that care necessary? Rick couldn't prove it.

Alex Pappas had known Lenny for decades, and Rick hadn't exactly been a great son. He had no right to throw the man out of the funeral home, no matter how much he wanted to. He had no right to chew the man out. Not yet, at least. His anger at seeing Pappas was built almost entirely on supposition.

"I'm here to pay my respects to a fellow member of the brotherhood," said Pappas. His eyes, magnified by his heavy horn-rimmed glasses, gazed steadily at Rick's.

"What, a fellow fixer?" Rick said contemptuously.

"You say that like you've just tasted shit," Pappas replied. "Well, let me tell you something: Nothing would happen in this world without men like your father. Because our world is too damn broken. Things fall apart, Rick. That's the way of the world. I don't care if it's the White House or the Kremlin or the Vatican or the goddamned Élysée Palace; nothing in this world happens without the guy behind the guy, the guy with the Rolodex, the guy who knows the secret password, the guy who gets the job done after the handshakes are over. Because the machinery's always breaking down and the gears need to be oiled and nothing moves without the guy in the engine room."

"And that's you," Rick said dubiously.

"What do you think Saint Paul was if not a goddamned fixer? He makes a few timely introductions to the Roman emperor Constantine, and next thing you know, a small-time first-century cult is a global religion. The only reason this goddamned broken world spins on its crooked axis is because fixers get up every morning and do what they do. And now let's see if we can't fix this situation of yours."

"Yeah, well, I don't need any more fixing from you."

"Hear me out first, Rick. I'd like to make you an offer."

"An offer." He could smell Pappas's peppery cologne.

"Yes. When we can speak in private, I have an offer that I think will interest you."

"We can speak right now."

"All right. I'll keep this brief. What happened to you"—he indicated with a spread hand—"should never have happened."

Rick couldn't restrain himself from saying, "Your thugs did a pretty good job on me. But you made the mistake of leaving me alive. And I don't give up."

"I'm sorry you think I had something to do with what happened to you. I did not. But I can guarantee this sort of thing will never happen again. I will see to it."

"That right?" Rick gave a chilly smile. He could hear the muted buzz of Pappas's BlackBerry.

"Absolutely. You may have heard all sorts of things about me, but one thing you'll never hear is that I break my word. My word is my bond. You have my personal guarantee that you will be left alone."

Rick knew there had to be a condition. He was convinced of it. "If what?"

"All I ask is that you step back."

"Step . . . back?"

"Your father left you a rather nice inheritance. Keep it. It's yours. Just halt your crusade, and I can assure you no further harm will come to you." He paused. "Are we clear?"

Rick glanced at him, then away. He didn't know how to reply.

"This is what your father would have wanted, Rick. He left you money so you and your sister could live comfortably. Not so that you would get hurt. This is why I'm making you this offer, and let us be clear, it's a one-time offer. In honor of your father. You've gotten what you wanted. You've *won*. Now, let's move on. Walk the path of peace, and others will, too."

Pappas stuck out his hand. "Do we have a deal?"

Rick thought: *Pappas is offering to buy me off, and why the hell not?*

His father was dead. There was no point to continuing. The battle was over.

It was, truth to tell, a relief.

"You know what the right thing is," Pappas said. "Just live your life."

After a few seconds, Rick nodded, then shook his hand. "Deal," he said.

56

He was safe now, he was pretty sure of it. As sure as he could be, anyway.

Despite Alex Pappas's pretense—that he was an innocent, an honest broker instead of a ringleader—Rick actually believed Pappas's assurances. They'd been attacking Rick because he persisted in digging up something they wanted to stay buried. If he stopped digging, he was no longer a threat.

Though who "they" were was still a mystery. "They" were whomever Pappas was working for. As long as they weren't coming after Rick, he didn't need to know who they were.

No longer did he need to keep moving from hotel to hotel. Then again, he had no home anyway. A hotel was the best he was going to do for a while. Maybe someday he'd get back together with Andrea, this time as two equals who'd each been through some hard times and emerged in the light. Maybe they'd buy a big-boned, rambling house together on Francis Ave in Cambridge.

Maybe not.

The point was, he had money now. No doubt three-million-plus dollars was pocket change to a rich person, to some hedge fund titan, but by Rick's lights it was a lot. If he shared it with his sister, which seemed only fair, that was still 1.7 million dollars. Maybe not a fortune, but it was enough to buy a future. And it took some of the sting out of that handshake with Pappas.

Anyway, it was all in how you looked at it, right? Maybe Pappas was right and Rick *had* won. The money was his to hold on to now, whosoever it originally was, whether it was clean or dirty or clean *and* dirty. The war was over. Lenny was dead, and there was no more reason to fight on.

Rick was feeling better, physically. It still hurt when he moved, or when he coughed, but not as acutely. His bruises were purpling. He did some errands. His replacement credit cards arrived. He went to the Department of Motor Vehicles to get a replacement driver's license. He thought briefly about checking out of the DoubleTree and into the Mandarin, or the Four Seasons, in the Back Bay. After all, he had more than three million bucks in storage. Why not live it up?

But that felt wasteful. The DoubleTree was perfectly fine.

He drove over to the storage unit. He was sure he was no longer being followed, but he couldn't give up the ingrained habit of scoping out the parking garage, looking in the rearview. No one, as far as he could tell, was following him. He unlocked the unit and took a few wads of cash, then he drove over to the old house. He had some debts to pay.

No one grabbed him, no one followed him. No one was there.

He was safe.

He took Marlon and Santiago aside, one by one, and handed each of them a thousand dollars in DoubleTree envelopes. "Thank you," he said. Was a thousand dollars too little? They'd saved his life after all. He owed them a lot more than that. True, they'd saved his life by accident; they were really intending to grab his money. But no matter how they came to it, they'd saved his life. That was the important thing.

Staring him up and down, Marlon said, "Somebody beat the shit out you. They finally catch up with you?"

"It had to happen eventually," Rick said.

"Yeah? Tell us who did it."

Rick shook his head. "It's over," he said.

They were hanging drywall. Marlon was measuring eight-by-four-foot sheets of drywall with a T-square, scoring them with a utility knife. Jeff was fastening the large cut squares of Sheetrock to the bare studs using a screw gun.

Rick waited for Jeff to finish screw-gunning a cut of Sheetrock. "You guys are really making progress."

"We should be wrapped up within the week," Jeff said. "There's this and some skim coating and painting and then the floors, and that's all she wrote."

"That's excellent," Rick said. He had no plans to ever move back in. As soon as it was finished, it would go on the market.

Before it sold, though, he'd have to go through it and remove any personal objects, anything of value. By now there couldn't be much left. Wendy had come with a moving van some years ago. He'd taken whatever was important to him, mostly some books from childhood and school. But Lenny's stuff remained. That was the most of it. There was clothing to give away, a couple of file cabinets to go through and mostly discard. He had a lot of old LPs, mostly sixties folk singers like Pete Seeger, the Weavers, Judy Collins. Hipsters collected LPs these days. He could probably unload some boxes at the *Back Bay* office in a matter of minutes. Though he'd probably hold on to the Judy Collins. Then there were his father's books, from his study, all of which had been moved down to the basement in boxes.

"Hey, Jeff, got a second?" Rick said.

"What's up?" Jeff said. "You okay?"

"Not as bad as it looks."

"You know who did it, don't you?"

Rick nodded. "Yeah, and that's why I wanted to tell you—forget what I told you about asking questions."

Jeff looked puzzled.

"About the Big Dig. I asked you to see if you might know someone . . . I'm just saying, don't."

"Okay, whatever you say," Jeff said. "Let me ask you something. How much you have this place insured for?"

Rick shook his head. "I don't know, maybe three hundred thousand?"

"It's already worth a lot more. You should boost the insurance to a million five."

"That much, huh? Wow."

"Do it right away, man."

"Okay, Jeff, thanks—I will."

He went downstairs to do a quick survey of possessions. On the way he passed through the kitchen. All the old pots and pans were still hanging on their hooks on the pegboard, coated with plaster dust like snow. He ran a finger over the cast-iron skillet. The plaster dust was stuck to the oil residue. That was the pan Lenny used to make salami and eggs for Rick's breakfast, several times a week, after Mom had died. Rick didn't particularly like salami and eggs, but he'd once made the mistake of praising it and Lenny kept making it for him.

The basement was filled with crap, with old toys Rick had once begged Lenny to buy for him, he just *had* to have. Things that were once of paramount importance, used once or twice, then discarded. Castaways of abandoned passions. Snowshoes. A mountain bike. The electric guitar, the drum set, the oil paints, the chemistry set. Rick didn't remember whether he ever thanked him.

He found the boxes labeled STUDY. Most of them contained law books. He had no idea whether they were dross or might have value. In one of the boxes he found a familiar-looking book: *Walden and Other Writings* by Henry David Thoreau, with a very sixties dust jacket, a curvy, groovy Peter Max–like font. Rick had often seen that book on his father's desk, open to one of Thoreau's little essays. Sometimes Lenny would read from it at night. He had loved Thoreau. He liked to quote one of Thoreau's maxims: "The mass of men lead lives of quiet desperation." Rick wondered whether his father had lived a life of quiet desperation. Probably so. At least he heard the beat of a different drummer, that was for sure.

Rick had once said something snotty, some kind of hurtful thing to Lenny, he didn't remember what he'd said, and he waited to see how his father would respond. Instead, Lenny seemed to will himself into silence. There was the intake of breath, then the pursed lips. The small shake of the head. Dad disliked conflict.

The weight of things unsaid: At first, it was light, like a dusting of snowflakes. In time, it grew heavy, like six feet of hard pack.

That Thoreau book Rick would hold on to, even though he never shared his father's enthusiasm for Thoreau. It was important to Lenny, so it was important to Rick.

He noticed his father's old computer and removed its cover. This he'd have to throw away. He plugged it in and started it up. It crunched and grunted and eventually the green letters appeared on the screen. He took one of the 5 1/4-inch floppies from a box and inserted it into the disk drive and waited for the directory to load up.

CORRESPONDENCE/BUSINESS one folder was labeled.

CORRESPONDENCE/PERSONAL was another.

He opened Correspondence/Personal. He felt strange doing this. He was rifling through his father's private letters. Did his death make that okay? Did you lose the right to privacy when you died?

Maybe. But still it felt like a violation. There were all sorts of letters to friends, from the days when people still wrote letters instead of dashing off e-mails. Most of the names he didn't know, or knew only vaguely.

Then his eye was drawn to one file name: Warren_Hinckley_letter .doc.

Warren Hinckley was the headmaster of the Linwood Academy. Why in the world had his father written to Headmaster Hinckley? Rick couldn't resist opening the file.

A document came up, green letters against the gray-black monitor.

Dear Mr. Hinckley:

I was dismayed to learn from our telephone conversation today that you are considering expelling my son from the Linwood Academy.

Rick stared in disbelief. He was almost expelled? That he'd never heard before. His father must have fought this battle without telling him. Heart pounding, he kept reading:

I am enormously proud of my son. What he did in publishing that article about Dr. Kirby's plagiarism took genuine courage. He didn't "play by the rules," as most people would have done. That much is true. Yes, he is required to submit each issue of the school newspaper to your office for pro forma approval. By not doing so—by publishing an article that exposed an egregious instance of plagiarism by a member of your faculty without running it by you first—he knowingly broke a minor school regulation and thereby put his future at risk. Publishing this article would get him in trouble and he knew it. But instead of being expelled, he should be commended for his adroit scholarship and his bravery.

Violating school protocol pales in importance next to the plagiarism carried out by an esteemed member of your faculty—who also happens to be your friend. In a school whose mission is to teach its students the right way to live, plagiarism is by far the graver offense.

My son broke the rules to achieve a greater good. He demonstrated a courage most people lack. He is a braver man than either of us. If the Linwood Academy expels my son, you can expect a lawsuit and all the attendant publicity that will not put the school in a flattering light.

Please do not teach your students to play by the rules when there are important principles at stake.

Sincerely,
Leonard J. Hoffman
Attorney at Law

Rick read the letter three times through, astonished. His father had gone to battle for him. Rick could feel a wetness on his face, and he tried to blink away the tears. How he'd misunderstood his father!

And as he thought about the father he never really knew, something inside him gave way, and finally he wept.

He wept for the man he'd lost. For the man he was only now beginning to know.

Rick went over to the Charles Hotel and retrieved his BMW from the parking garage. On his way back to the house something came over him and he deliberately made a wrong turn and soon he was on Mass Ave heading south through Boston. He drove aimlessly. He just wanted to drive. He found himself drawn, like iron filings to a magnet, to Geometry Partners, in Dorchester. The subconscious mind has aims of its own.

He was in front of the old brick warehouse that housed the Geometry Partners offices. A young Latino-looking teenage girl was coming down the front stairs of the main entrance.

The girl had pigtails and was talking excitedly to a boy around her age, which was probably fourteen. She grinned and he could see her big gap-toothed smile, and for an instant he thought she was Graciela Cabrera, the pianist in that old videotape.

The dead girl.

She looked just like Graciela.

Graciela, who had been killed along with her parents in that terrible accident in the Ted Williams Tunnel eighteen years ago. Graciela, whose death was the fault of sloppy construction and was covered up. Graciela, whose tragic, altogether unnecessary death had haunted Lenny Hoffman and caused him finally to rebel, to refuse to make a payoff. Lenny had refused to sell out. He couldn't do it.

Unlike Rick.

Of course, this young girl wasn't Graciela. Graciela would have now been thirty-two. A woman. Maybe a mother herself.

He felt his stomach turn to ice.

He wanted to keep all that money and just live his life. *I just want to live my life,* he thought, that glorious cliché.

But part of him was a mule-headed goddamn fool.

Stand down: That was the smart move. *Live your life. Move on.* He knew what the smart move was.

Suddenly, though, Rick wasn't feeling very smart.

57

Gloria Antunes, executive director of the Hyde Square Community Partnership, was polite but firm.

"Mr. Hoffman, I've already told you I have nothing to contribute." She wore a blue paisley scarf around her shoulders and the same large hoop earrings she'd been wearing the last time he saw her.

"Actually, you do," he said. "You are already part of my article. The question is how big a role will you play in it. That's up to you." He held a DVD in its case from the video duplication place on Newbury Street. She wouldn't know what was on that DVD—he'd had a copy made of the old VHS that Manuela Guzman, Graciela's piano teacher, had played for him. But he waved it like a prosecutor wagging a piece of evidence in court.

"I don't understand."

"Give me five minutes of your time and you will."

"I can give you two."

Rick shrugged and entered her office. He sat in front of her desk, and when she had taken her place behind the desk he handed her the DVD.

She took it. "And?" She cocked her head.

"Play this in your computer."

"What is it?"

But she inserted the DVD in the disk drive of her desktop.

When the video started to play, Rick narrated: "That's the little girl. Graciela Cabrera."

He saw it in her tear-flooded eyes. The tape had that effect on people. On him, on Lenny, and now on Gloria Antunes. The girl's awkwardness and her endearing, pure sweetness.

Rick continued, speaking over the audio. "At first you called for an investigation into the accident that killed the Cabreras. After your organization received a sizable gift from the Donegall Charitable Trust, you suddenly zipped up. I know this because my father was the one who arranged it."

That last sentence he was improvising, but he knew at once he'd guessed right. She had no idea what his father might have told Rick after all these years. And if she had been given a check by Pappas and not Lenny, she wouldn't know what might have happened behind the scenes.

"You knew this family. This girl. Didn't you?"

Gloria nodded. Her eyes looked red. She closed them. "A terrible thing."

"It must be so difficult."

"What must be so difficult?"

"To live with yourself. Knowing what happened to them."

When her tears began to flow, Rick knew he had reached her.

Whether it was the videotape or Rick's bluffing, his intimations that he knew for certain far more than he did, she finally broke down. She had lived with the guilt for eighteen years, the guilt of her silence. The Donegall Charitable Trust was still one of her main funders, but she had others now. That wasn't the case when it was just Gloria Antunes, community activist, before the Donegall trust had offered to fund the launch of her own organization.

Legally, she'd committed no crimes. But she was haunted. The responsibility she felt was a moral one, the weight of all those years of keeping her silence about what had really happened to the Cabrera family one night in a tunnel in Boston.

Now, finally, she was willing to speak on the record.

58

"I've reconsidered your offer," Rick said.

The sun was bright in Pappas's office, glinting off the objects on his desk, the brass shade of his desk lamp, the buttery silver of the picture frames. In the bright light, Pappas gave off one single impression: red. His face was permanently flushed, the skin enraged with spider webs of capillaries.

"*Reconsidered* my offer?" He said it with amusement, as if Rick had told him he was taking up mime: with a heavy underlining of irony, in scare quotes.

"My father was able to talk at the end, and he told me an interesting story. And now that he's gone I can safely write an article about it."

Pappas looked at him for a very long time. Then he grinned broadly. "Okay, Rick, I'll play. An article about what?"

"About how the Cabrera family was killed eighteen years ago."

"The who?"

"The Cabrera family."

He shrugged, shook his head. "And I'm supposed to know these people?"

335

"They were driving back from Logan Airport through the Ted Williams Tunnel in the middle of the night when something crashed down on their car. An eighty-pound light fixture, heavy enough to smash their windshield and temporarily blind them. And they were killed instantly."

"That's a sad story, Rick. But it's a sad story that happened twenty years ago. You need a hook. Why do our readers care about it today?"

"I'm thinking it'll be an interesting way to show how crisis management works. Because this was a crisis you 'managed' brilliantly. You managed it right into oblivion. You had to. Because if that story ever got out, your client, Donegall Construction, would have been destroyed. There would have been an enormous lawsuit. Criminal charges, too. And no more work for the city of Boston. A few million dollars was nothing to a construction company that could easily have faced a hundred million bucks in legal costs and maybe prison time for a couple of the players."

Pappas laughed, long and loudly. "Spectacular. You have a talent for fiction, did anyone ever tell you that? Have you ever considered a career as a novelist, now that your career as a journalist is, sadly, over? Your father started talking to you, Rick? He couldn't speak two goddamned words, the poor guy."

He must have a source inside the nursing home, Rick thought. One of the nurses, at least, was on his payroll. "But not just my dad. There's also a very brave woman, a community activist who's agreed to speak on the record for the first time."

"Rick, let me tell you a story. A Buddhist parable, actually."

Rick smiled back. Another one of Pappas's stories.

"Two traveling monks are about to cross a river. There's a young woman on the bank who says, 'Please, brother monks, can you carry me across? The river is too deep.' The young monk turns away. See, they're not allowed to touch a woman. But the older monk hoists her up on his shoulder and brings her over. The monks keep going, over hills and dales, and the whole time the younger monk is complaining, 'Why'd you do that? You know we're forbidden to touch a woman. What you did was a violation of our precepts.' And on and on, mile after mile. Won't shut up. Finally the older monk looks at him and says, 'I left that woman at the riverbank. Seems to me you're still carrying her?'"

Pappas's expression was almost kindly. "My point is, Rick, you need to let this go. For your own sake. Leave it at the riverbank, and get on with your life. I'm telling you this because your father was a man I respected, and I figure I owe him this much. You want to martyr yourself because of what you *imagine* might have *possibly* happened two decades ago? Who are you really helping at this point? Whose life are you saving? What good do you think could possibly result from this?"

"It's an important story," Rick said blandly.

Pappas abandoned all benevolent pretense. "You're not writing an article, Rick. I know you. You're still the weasel who'll sell out to the higher bidder. What are you angling for, Rick, a bigger payoff? You want another million so you can buy fancy duds and a fancy watch and you can impress another vacuous fashion model? And then why stop there? Why not keep coming back to the well, asking for more and more, right? Well, as I told you at your father's funeral, this was a one-time-only offer."

"And I'm turning it down. I'm going to publish this piece with or without your cooperation. But I'd rather have your side of it. I've already established that Donegall was a client of yours."

"Donegall Construction filed for bankruptcy two decades ago!"

"Accounting trickery. They're more active than ever." This last part, he knew, was just speculation. That was the part he needed Pappas to reveal, what Donegall Construction had become. "We know you were in contact with *The Boston Globe* after the accident. If there's anything about my account that's inaccurate, I'd like to hear it now. This is your chance."

For a moment Pappas looked as if he was seriously considering the proposition.

Then he spoke, shaking his head sorrowfully. "I gave you the golden ticket, my friend. I gave you my personal guarantee that all will be good. And now you come with this? You sit there in front of me, beat up and bloodied and bruised and hobbling like an old lady, and you tell me you want back in the game?"

"There's no game," Rick said. "I'm giving you an opportunity to go on the record. You can confirm or deny. What you tell me can affect what I write."

Pappas's smile was wide and bright. "This is my big chance, huh? No, actually, this is all history, and as the saying goes, history is written by the winners. And you, sir, are no winner. If the Confederate army had won the Battle of Gettysburg, you think we'd be celebrating Lincoln's birthday? Every event can be made to mean a dozen different things. But the ultimate reality is determined by the victor. Call it the reality principle. Your father—he had a healthy goddamned sense of reality. Shame you never learned anything from him."

Rick closed his notebook. "Thanks for your time." He got to his feet and went to the door.

"You know what your trouble is?" Pappas called out. "You never learned anything from your dad."

"Yeah?" Rick said at the doorway. "Maybe I learned too much."

59

"How'd it go?" asked Andrea. She was leaning back in an armchair in Rick's suite at the DoubleTree. She wore black jeans and a crisp white shirt and a pair of gray TOMS. She had no makeup on. Her hair was up, held back with a band. Her attitude made it clear that this was a business meeting at Rick's hotel, nothing more than that. But the way she was sitting in the chair was more casual than businesslike.

"About how I expected. He came back at me with threats and ridicule."

"How did you react?"

"He probably thought he scared me off. He's good at that. That's his thing."

"That's fine. Let him think what he wants to think."

He looked at his watch. "Probably a good time to get back there."

"It's been over an hour, right?"

He nodded and headed back out the door.

*   *   *

At the office tower where the Pappas Group was located, front-desk security wouldn't let Rick back into the elevator banks. They insisted on calling up to get verbal approval. Rick got on the phone.

"Alex Pappas, please. It's Rick Hoffman."

"I'm sorry, Mr. Hoffman, Mr. Pappas is out of the office."

"That's all right. I think I left something in his office. I'm right downstairs."

Three minutes later he was standing in the reception area of the Pappas Group. A woman in her fifties, thick at the waist, with coppery hair, came out and introduced herself as Pappas's administrative assistant, Barbara. He walked with her back to Pappas's office. "He just left for a meeting out of the office," Barbara said.

"This shouldn't take a minute," Rick said. "I'm pretty sure I left my phone there."

"I didn't see anything left behind."

He went to the overstuffed armchair where he'd been sitting. Sure enough, there it was, wedged between the seat cushion and the arm of the chair: Rick's iPhone.

"Oh, good," Barbara said, sounding relieved.

"This is something you hate to lose," Rick said, pocketing it.

"Oh, tell me about it," said Barbara. "I'd be totally sunk."

"Well, all's well that ends well," said Rick.

Not until he got to the elevator did he take out his phone and hit Stop on the recorder app. It said one hour and forty-six minutes. Then he opened the submenu that listed "voice memos," and he selected the most recent one. He hit Play and put it to his ear. He could hear Pappas's voice, distant but still audible.

"*Yeah, Barbara,*" Pappas said on the recording, "*I need to speak to Thomas Sculley. Can you get him on the phone?*"

A few seconds later his secretary's voice came on. "*Mr. Sculley, line one.*"

A moment later: "*Thomas,*" Pappas said. "*We've got a problem.*"

60

Andrea paled when she heard the first words of the recording.
"Thomas Sculley," she said. "My God."

Rick looked at her.

"You know the funder I had lunch with the other day, and I didn't want to jinx by naming?" she said. "That was Thomas Sculley."

Thomas Sculley was a major figure in Boston, a developer and builder whose Bay Group had transformed the Boston skyline. He was also a major philanthropist whose name was on several hospital wings and was a part owner of the Boston Red Sox. When Lenny had received TMS treatment, it had been at the Sculley Pavilion of Mass General Hospital. Rick had read all the Sculley profiles. He knew the basic outline of the story. Sculley had come to America from Ireland decades earlier *with just a shovel and a wheelbarrow,* as every single profile seemed to put it. And went from being a small-time house builder to one of the preeminent developers in the country. Sculley's firm was about to build the tallest skyscraper in Boston, on the site of the old Combat Zone.

"How long have you been in talks with them?"

"It's been super fast. Their foundation director contacted us, I don't know, two or three weeks ago."

"After our famous dinner at Madrigal?"

"A couple days after. You're thinking . . . ?" She tilted her head. "I don't know. It's a real coincidence, if not."

"Somehow I don't think that was a coincidence," Rick said.

She nodded, looking despondent. She was quiet for ten, twenty seconds. Then she took a breath. She nodded again, but this time she looked different. Resolved.

They listened to the recording a couple of times. The iPhone's battery was at zero, so they plugged it in to charge while they used it. They couldn't hear everything Pappas said. Only when he raised his voice for emphasis did his words become clear. But in truth they had all they needed. A name: Thomas Sculley.

The billionaire builder and philanthropist he was supposed to be writing about.

The conversation, conducted over speakerphone, went on for just a few minutes. Pappas arranged to meet Sculley at his State Street office. Then Pappas spoke to his admin on speaker and asked her to cancel his next two meetings.

"Are you serious about writing an article?" Andrea asked.

"Deadly."

She smiled. "This is the old Rick Hoffman," she said. "Fearless. I like it."

"It only looks that way."

"Then we need to prove that Sculley was connected to Donegall Construction. From what I've found, Sculley grew up in Belfast, Ireland, on a street named Donegall."

"So can you connect him to Donegall?"

"Well, look—locating hidden assets and liabilities is what I used to do. But it's a hell of a lot easier finding connections between two known entities than trying to find out what happened to one small firm like Donegall eighteen years ago. At least now I know how and where to start."

"Can you do it now?"

"You got it."

As she typed on her laptop, she called her son to say good night. Then Rick's phone rang. He recognized Jeff's number. He glanced at his watch: almost eight o'clock P.M.

"Jeff?"

"Yeah, Rick, listen. I'm still at your house. I—I got something for you."

"You've got something?" Rick wasn't sure what Jeff was talking about.

"About that thing you wanted me to look into. I'll be here for another half hour." There was a click and the line was dead.

Andrea was asking Evan whether he'd finished his homework, telling him he could stay up a little bit longer if he wanted to read some more of his Mike Lupica book.

When she hung up, Rick said, "I need to head over to the house."

61

The kitchen door was open, which meant Jeff was still here, though it was late. He could see light spilling into the stairwell to the second floor. Everything smelled strongly of some sort of solvent.

"Jeff?"

"Up here." Jeff's voice came from the floor above.

Rick climbed the stairs. The solvent smell got stronger.

"I'm up on the third," Jeff called out.

Jeff was in a corner of the hall next to Rick's old bedroom. Beside him was a short ladder beneath a large hole in the ceiling. He looked around. The Sheetrocking was done, ready for painting. There were several large buckets of some kind of fluid, a few of them filled with rags.

"This solvent from the floor guys?"

"Right. They're doing some stripping before the sanding. Look, I got something for you but first I wanted to show you something I found today." He seemed nervous.

"What's wrong?"

"You got a serious problem," Jeff said.

You have no idea, Rick thought. "What is it?" he said. "Something structural?"

"Over here." Jeff beckoned Rick over to the ladder. Five foot high, four rungs, positioned in the corner of the hallway right below the hole ripped into the ceiling. Rick could see the rafters, the old plaster. "Wanna get up there and take a look?"

Rick climbed the ladder, peered into the opening in the ceiling. It was dark and hard to make anything out. "What am I looking at?"

"There's some real termite damage in there."

Rick peered farther into the darkness. "Where?"

"It's all over," Jeff said, now close behind him.

"All over where?"

Jeff spoke quietly, in a tight, choked voice, as if he was having trouble saying the words. "See, Rick, I asked around like you wanted me to do, and I heard some really interesting stuff."

Rick wasn't tracking. Was Jeff still talking about termites?

"The hell of it is," Jeff went on, "if you'd been more generous from the start, their offer wouldn'ta looked so good to me, you asshole."

"What offer?"

At the very moment that Rick realized, it was a beat too late. Jeff held a length of two-by-four and swung it at him, at his torso.

Rick tried to duck, but standing on the top rung of the ladder he risked toppling and losing his balance.

The board crashed into his ribs and Rick shouted, "What the hell?" As he began to topple from the ladder, Jeff swung at him a second time.

Rick thought: *Not my head!*

And he heard the impact an instant before he felt it, felt the screaming pain in his forehead, tasted blood, and then nothing . . .

. . . When he came to, he was lying crumpled on his back, his nostrils full of smoke, and he coughed violently. For a moment he had no idea how he'd gotten where he was nor how long he'd been out.

He craned his head, looked around. Flames were crackling, leaping all around. The heat seared his skin. Tall licks of orange flame leaped and danced at this end of the hall, devouring the pristine walls, the floors, climbing the newly Sheetrocked walls, searing them black, curling the paper.

The house was on fire.

Rick got up unsteadily, swaying. Then came a *whump* as the fire discovered another bucket of solvent-soaked rags and traced its fingers of spill along the floor. The buckets of solvent, he realized, were the accelerant. They'd all been tipped over, feeding the ravenous flames.

How could this have happened?

Through the billowing black smoke he saw Jeff's back. Rick watched in astonishment. Jeff was kneeling, back turned toward him, a lighter in one hand, setting more of the solvent alight. Next to him was a trash barrel filled with detritus, lumber scraps and wads of paper. Jeff was taking stuff from the barrel to use for kindling.

Jeff wasn't just burning down the house he had spent weeks renovating. He was trying to kill Rick.

He meant to leave him to be burned alive.

Rick's heart was racing. He didn't fully understand what Jeff was doing and why, but that no longer mattered.

He launched himself at Jeff, knocking him over. The lighter dropped to the floor. Jeff's phone, clipped to his belt, went scuttling across the floor. Rick's knees were planted across Jeff's neck.

"They got to you, didn't they?" Rick screamed. "They fucking paid you off!"

Jeff reared up, swung a fist at Rick, hit the center of Rick's chest. "You greedy son of a bitch, you goddamned liar. You said there was forty thousand bucks there? More like three and a half million!"

Rick groaned but slammed his fist into Jeff's left ear.

Jeff was taller and probably stronger. He swung again, aiming for Rick's gut, but Rick torqued himself to one side and the blow landed on his shoulder. He was bruised everywhere and aching, but he was powered by a great surge of anger and adrenaline. Just as Jeff swarmed at him, Rick reached over and snatched a two-by-four out of the barrel. He swung it with all of his strength at Jeff's head. At the last instant Jeff turned so the plank cracked hard into the side of his face. Rick heard the impact, the crunch of bone.

"My eye!" Jeff screamed, flinging his hands to his face. Blood gouted down from his left eye socket.

But Rick didn't pause. He wound up and swung the board at Jeff again, crashing into the top of his head, and Jeff went down. A *whoosh* and another pile of solvent-soaked rags went up in flames.

Rick got up wobblingly to his feet. Fire was all around him now, on all sides of the hall, encroaching into the staircase that led down to the second floor. He noticed Jeff's phone on the floor and impulsively reached over and grabbed it. His own phone was charging back at the hotel, and he needed to call 911.

Jeff must have intended to light the fire and then leave by means of the staircase. But now it was too late. The flames had them surrounded.

He ran into the bedroom, where the fire hadn't yet reached, though the smoke had, and yanked open the window. A leap to the ground from the third floor would be dangerous. Below, instead of lawn, was the blacktop of the driveway.

Then he remembered the yew tree a few feet away from the window, wild and untrimmed. It wasn't directly below the window, but it was close. Years ago when his mother was still alive he used to sneak out of the house by leaning out the window and leaping at an angle so that he could catch a branch and somehow shinny to the blacktop. But back then he was a young teenager and more agile. Not weakened by a nearly fatal beating.

He inhaled, and his trachea was singed by the heat or the smoke. He was racked by a coughing fit. He turned around and saw that the fire was now roaring across the threshold of the doorway. It was moving faster than he'd expected; the solvent had nourished the fire. Plumes of flame blackened the white-painted door, crackling the old paint. His heart was hammering.

He wanted to go grab Jeff and pull him out, but the fire was too advanced. Trying to save Jeff would likely be his own death sentence. He turned back to the window. He knew this was the only way out. But what was once, to a teenager, an exciting challenge now looked dubious. He would have to launch himself out of the window, angling to the right, hoping to grab branches of the tree before slamming into the ground.

He pulled the phone out of his pocket. Maybe he should call 911 now, in case he hit the ground and lost consciousness again.

He opened Jeff's phone. It had a text message:

Job successfully completed?

He pressed the keys for 911. "Fire," he choked out. He could barely breathe. "Two eighty-four Clayton Street in Cambridge."

There wasn't time to say any more. He closed the phone and pocketed it. Then he turned back toward the open window. The nearest branches of the yew tree were fairly close, just a couple of feet below and three or four feet off to his right.

Jump or you'll burn alive.

Straight down was the driveway. The drop would probably kill him. If he jumped to the right and immediately grabbed at the branches . . .

He felt the fire roasting his back. He could hear it roaring behind him. Smoke billowed and rolled.

It was now or never.

He pulled himself up—harder than it used to be, and the pain nearly crippled him—and, pulse racing, he hurled himself forward. He felt the branches scrape against him and he grabbed with both hands. The branch in his left hand immediately snapped off. The one in his right held, though. It bent, and Rick grabbed with his left hand for a bigger branch closer to the tree's trunk. His hands were scratched and sliced but he managed to get hold of a sizable limb just as the branch in his right hand snapped. He fell, hanging on with only his left, dangling from the foliage, his body convulsing with pain, his arms trembling from the exertion. With his right he scrabbled desperately, finding only air, grabbed again and clutched another limb. Letting the branches scrape against his face and arms, he lowered himself, and then the limb in his left hand cracked and he plummeted.

He landed, hard, on the driveway, on his knees, but his fall was broken somewhat by the tree's foliage. It was painful, but nothing compared to what he'd recently had to endure.

He collapsed, breathed in and out, deeply, and he coughed and coughed. His throat felt as if it were burned. He coughed some more, finally gulped a deep breath, and waited for his head to stop swimming.

As soon as he could, he pulled out Jeff's phone and texted back one word: **Done.**

62

He staggered to his car, panting heavily. His throat was sore from the smoke and his eyes were stinging.

He had to leave before the fire trucks arrived.

The fire seemed to be localized on the third floor, but it was a wood-frame house and would go up quickly and easily. He heard sirens, which meant they'd be arriving momentarily. Maybe they could save the house.

He wondered if they could. He hoped so.

Andrea was in the hotel suite when he returned. "I think I've got it, the—" She saw him, took it in. "Shit, Rick, what happened to you? Are you okay?"

His face and hair were covered with black soot. He looked like a chimney sweep. He'd attracted double takes in the hotel lobby. "I need some new clothes."

"Where were you?"

"Never mind that. Tell me what you found."

"I need to show you. But where've you been?"

He told her some, then went into the bathroom, turned on the shower, and let it run. He came back out and began stripping off his smoke-saturated clothes. He did it without modesty; they had seen each other naked before. She didn't look away.

"You reek of smoke."

"Take me through what you've got."

She talked to him while he showered. "The key piece was B&H Packing, that meat-packing plant. Apparently, Sculley's Bay Group has a dozen subsidiaries and two of them have as their principal ownership a nonprofit entity called the Donegall Charitable Trust. Including a meat-packing plant in South Boston. So the paper trail points directly to Thomas Sculley."

"All right. That's great. That's great."

When he finished showering, he toweled off and he still smelled of smoke.

"Can you pull up the Cambridge Fire Department's Twitter feed?" he said.

By the time he was dressed, she called him over to her laptop.

CAMBRIDGE FIRE DEPT. @CAMBRIDGEMAFIRE

BREAKING: fire sweeps through west Cambridge house. Firefighters respond to 284 Clayton Street for a 2 alarm fire.

"*Sweeps through* means the fire wasn't contained, I assume," she said.

"I don't know. What about a body?"

353

As if the Cambridge Fire Department's Twitter feed could hear him, another tweet rolled down the page.

CAMBRIDGE FIRE DEPT. @CAMBRIDGEMAFIRE

2 alarm fire 284 Clayton Street sadly claims 1 life.

"He's dead."

"Who?"

"My old fr—neighbor. Jeff. He died in the fire."

"Oh my God."

"Wait. They're going to assume it's me who died in the fire. Until Jeff's body is identified."

"So that buys you time, doesn't it? How long could that take?"

He shrugged. "Maybe a day. Maybe less. I don't know."

She noticed his eyes were wet. "He tried to kill you. If you hadn't stopped him, that would have been your body in the house."

"Still. I killed a man."

"He torched your house and tried to kill you because they offered him a better deal than splitting the proceeds from the sale of your house."

"I need to get over to the FBI," he said.

63

This time he met Special Agent Donovan in the reception area of the FBI's Boston field office, on the sixth floor of 1 Center Plaza in the big ugly sixties building complex called Government Center.

"I can't take you back to the bullpen," Donovan said. "Should we go out for a cup of coffee?"

"No," Rick said. "This is official. Put me in an interview room."

Donovan sniffed. "You been camping?"

Rick surrendered his iPhone and his driver's license to the woman behind the glass, as required. Jeff's Nokia he held on to. "This is for you," he said, clapping it into Donovan's hand.

"What is it?"

"It's text messages and probably phone calls from the guy who hired Jeff Hollenbeck to kill me."

Inside the secure area, Donovan got Rick settled in a small room that had a small table and four chairs. There was nothing on the walls. Then he went off to hand the Nokia to a tech. He came back five minutes later with two cups of coffee. "I put cream in yours. I wasn't sure. That okay?"

"That's fine." Rick started to tell him about Jeff and the fire, but Donovan interrupted after a few minutes. "Hold on, Rick. We have to get a few procedural things clear first. If I'm opening a new case, I need to set up a preliminary investigation."

"This is attempted murder and arson. You should have enough evidence here to present a case to the US attorney's office and get the authority to make an arrest."

Donovan looked as if he was about to scoff and then thought better of it. He knew Rick well enough at least to know that he didn't make things up. They'd shared information in the past. They respected each other. "Let's hear what you have." There was a knock at the door. "That was fast," Donovan said. He got up and keyed the door open.

A thin, wan man in his forties, balding on top, nerd glasses, handed Donovan a sheet of paper. The tech knew his role in the organization and dressed the part. "Holy crap," Donovan said. "Thanks, John." He closed the door.

Still standing, he folded his arms. "This was fast for a couple of reasons. The Nokia flip phones download to Cellebrite in a matter of seconds. Also, this is a Sprint phone, and Sprint has a portal exclusively for law enforcement, so tracing the calls was fast."

"The texts?"

"They took precautions. The texts came from a spoofed number. It's easy to do and just about impossible to crack. Takes forever, anyway. Two phone calls came in from the same blocked number."

"What's 'holy crap'?"

"The number belongs to a guy we have a closed case on. One Emmet Boyle of Lynn, Mass. An Irish illegal."

He wondered if that was the guy with the shamrock tattoo. "A closed case?"

"Any number of reasons. Not enough evidence. Priorities. Who knows. But this is a bad guy."

"What do you have on him?"

"Unsubstantiated accusations of arson, murder for hire. He comes from Belfast, Ireland. Believed to be part of a gang of Irish immigrants formerly associated with the Provisional Irish Republican Army."

"The terrorists."

"One man's terrorist is another man's freedom fighter," Donovan said. He was Irish, too, Rick had to remind himself. The politics are fraught.

"But all that IRA stuff is done, I thought."

"The IRA ended its armed campaign a decade ago. Which left some fairly skilled killers looking for work."

Rick shook his head. "Meaning—what? They're contract killers?"

"Contract muscle."

"Hired by who?"

"If we had that, we'd have an open case."

"Where's the phone?"

"In the tech lab. It's evidence."

"Evidence for what?"

"I've got at least enough now for a preliminary investigation."

"Like I said, you have enough for an arrest. I need my phone back."

A line creased Donovan's brow. "What do you want, Rick—the phone or an FBI investigation?"

"The phone and an arrest. I didn't officially give the FBI the cell phone, so I'd like it back."

For a moment, it looked as if there'd be a standoff. But Donovan knew Rick was right. "I'll see what I can do."

He returned more than ten minutes later. There had probably been a discussion with a superior. Donovan handed Rick the phone. "You've got a text."

He opened the phone.

`Meet at 7 as arranged`

Rick's stomach clutched. They still thought he was Jeff, but he couldn't convincingly be Jeff if he didn't know the prior arrangements. After a moment he texted back: **Can't appear where I know anyone. Change meet to Dunkin Donuts South Boston.**

He held his breath waiting for a reply. It came a few minutes later.

`Which location?`

Relieved, he texted: **Old Colony Ave.**

64

The Dunkin' Donuts on Old Colony Avenue in Southie was perched in the middle of a big parking lot, which made it a useful place to meet. It was a busy street, another advantage. Or so he was told. Rick was no expert.

He sat in his rented Saturn parked within view of the entrance. He wore a Red Sox cap and was barely recognizable.

He watched the customers enter.

A teenage boy with a bad case of acne. A man in glasses and an ill-fitting blazer, who could have been an accountant. An overweight woman in her twenties wearing a pantsuit. He gave a second look to a man who looked as if he worked with his hands but decided he was probably a construction worker.

He had nothing but fragmentary memory to go on. A shamrock tattoo on the man's wrist and not much more. He'd seen that only close up. Leathery hands. But the man he was waiting to meet would be powerfully built and in his fifties or older, maybe closer to sixties. Rick was twenty minutes early but wouldn't have been surprised if the man—Shamrock, he'd call him—arrived early, too. He'd look around, probably make a circuit, before he got his coffee.

Then at five minutes before seven a man came striding purposefully along the sidewalk and up to the restaurant. There was little question this was Shamrock. A bull-necked man of around sixty with a hard look, wearing an expensive-looking black leather jacket and a gray tweed scally cap. He had a pug nose and a scowl and big hands. He looked like a tough SOB. He was chewing gum. The cap was the giveaway. It was a flat cap, a longshoreman's cap with a small brim. It might as well have been a neon sign with an arrow.

The man squinted and cast a glance around the exterior, then entered.

Rick got out of the car and, making sure Shamrock wasn't looking out, crossed the street.

Directly across the street was a dive bar. It had a green awning with a Guinness sign on it and a green-painted door. There were four or five customers in here. The ones at the bar looked like regulars. The window in the front door had a good view of the Dunkin' Donuts.

He texted Shamrock:

```
Saw someone I know in DD. Meet me in bar
across street.
```

He wondered if this change in plans would screw things up. He watched out the bar window.

But not a minute later Shamrock came striding out. It was hard to tell whether he was pissed off or that was his normal glower.

He crossed the street and entered the bar. His eyes shifted side to side. He must have known what Jeff looked like; they'd probably met before.

Rick sat in a booth near the bar.

Thirty seconds later Shamrock's eyes slid past Rick's face and kept moving.

An instant later his eyes slid back and alit on Rick's.

A moment of recognition, and then he smiled nastily.

He approached Rick's booth and slid in next to him. Rick could feel something poking into his side. The blood drained from his face.

Shamrock leaned in close and whispered into Rick's ear. Rick could smell the barbershop and feel Shamrock's humid breath.

"So it's the other fella's body in the house, not yours. Ballsy gobshite, I'll give you that. But stupid as shit."

Rick's pulse accelerated wildly. He knew this was it and that it could go any number of ways. He tried to look unafraid but couldn't help a slight twitching in his left eye muscle.

"Here's how we're going to play it, boyo," Shamrock whispered. "You and I are going to walk out of here nice and quiet. My nine millimeter's safety is off. I will not hesitate to put a bullet in your spine."

Rick swallowed, nodded.

The gun in Shamrock's windbreaker pocket was hard in Rick's ribs.

"Get up after me and if you try to fuck around, it'll be the last time."

Shamrock got up from the booth, and Rick slid out, light-headed, heart jackhammering.

Shamrock helped him out, grabbing hold of his elbow as he did so, yanking him roughly to his feet.

This was, Rick realized, the most foolish thing he'd ever done. Bravery was akin to stupidity. He was about to die. He looked around the bar frantically but kept going. Shamrock's arm was around his shoulder. They could have been two friends who'd had too much to drink.

Shamrock shoved the front door open and Rick felt a gust of cold air hit his face.

He took a breath, then said, blandly, "You're surrounded."

Shamrock laughed disdainfully.

Three men in blue FBI windbreakers seemed to materialize out of thin air. As they shouted, "FBI!," Rick dropped to the ground as he'd been instructed to do. He felt the sting of asphalt on his face.

Shamrock didn't even struggle. He knew there was no point.

As Rick got up, he caught Shamrock staring at him with burning hostility. "You goddamned son of a bitch," he said. "You don't know what you just did."

65

Rick was surprised—pleasantly—at how quickly he was able to write the exposé. He knew the subject matter well.

Still, it took him all night. He was powered by caffeine and outrage.

In the morning he e-mailed the piece to Dylan, the copy desk guy at *Back Bay*.

Half an hour later Rick's phone was ringing.

"Dylan."

"Dude, you're serious?"

"Absolutely."

"I post this, I could lose my job."

"Dylan, I wouldn't want to put you in a situation where you—"

"No, no," Dylan interrupted. "I put that in the plus column."

It had been one gaseous speech after another. The head of the Boston Redevelopment Authority boasting about the Olympian Tower—"the tallest structure in Boston at twelve hundred feet high and sixty-five

363

stories"—and the mayor had talked about "this gleaming silver tower on the site of what was once Boston's blighted Combat Zone." A brass band played a John Philip Sousa march. Confetti fluttered down over the VIPs, blasted high into the air from six confetti cannons. The TV lights barely made a difference on this bright sunny day.

Groundbreakings were deadly dull, no matter how much confetti you pumped in, whether you use a silver spade or gold. Everyone wanted to claim some piece of credit. Nobody really wanted to be there. No ground was actually broken. Everything was theater.

Thomas Sculley understood this instinctively. He'd had countless groundbreaking ceremonies for the buildings he had put up. So his remarks were blessedly brief.

The mayor of Boston had introduced Sculley, whom he called "a man of singularly philanthropic bent." Sculley, dressed in a beautiful blue suit, had taken the microphone and spoken just a few sentences.

"When I came to this country fifty-two years ago from Belfast with just a shovel and a wheelbarrow, I'd never in a million years have imagined that one day I'd be standing up on a stage with the mayor of Boston. I'd never have imagined people would someday be waiting just to hear the words come out of my mouth. Oh, wait. As my wife reminds me, they're not." Polite laughter. "So with no further ado, let's break ground for the greatest building in the greatest city on earth!"

Andrea hadn't been invited to the ceremony, but it took no more than a quick call to Sculley's office to wangle an invitation for her and a guest. After all, Geometry Partners was to be given office space in the new Olympian Tower. She was here to celebrate, too.

After the dignitaries had dug a few symbolic shovels of dirt, to wild applause, Andrea sidled up to the low stage. She was beautifully dressed in a white dress and looked poised, but Rick could see she was nervous. Of course she was.

Reporters thronged around the mayor. Sculley they largely left alone. Finally, Andrea found her moment. She slid up to Sculley and handed him a folded sheet of paper.

Rick watched intently as Sculley looked at the note wonderingly, grinned, then took out a pair of reading glasses from his suit pocket. His brow creased.

He read the note. It was only a few sentences. His eyes lifted from the page and met Andrea's. Then they scanned the crowd, squinting, right to left, then left to right.

And then his eyes found Rick.

Sculley's smile faded. His expression was dead, but Rick was sure that in Sculley's eyes he could detect something very close to fear.

66

Sculley led the way to a small white tent on one side of the stage where employees of the Bay Group were handing out glossy brochures on Olympian Tower to the media and prospective investors.

As he approached, a couple of the employees recognized him and sat up straight in their chairs. A young man got up with an awestruck smile. "Mr. Sculley, how can I help you?"

"Can I have this tent?" Sculley said.

It took a moment for his employees to understand that he wanted them to vacate the tent, but once they did, they moved quickly.

Andrea hung back. Sculley flashed her a smile and said, "Mr. Hoffman and I will have a little chat." She nodded and let the two men enter the now empty tent.

"Shall we have a seat?" Sculley said, indicating a small card table piled high with Bay Group brochures.

Rick shook his head. "This shouldn't take that long."

He was struck anew by how craggy Sculley's face was up close. He had the face of someone who'd done manual labor outdoors all his life, though he probably hadn't since he was in his twenties. He was now over seventy.

"You look rough, lad," Sculley said. He gestured toward the bruises on Rick's face. "Maybe you should take it easy, you know what I mean?"

"I'm fine," Rick said. "I'm alive."

"We never had that sit-down, you and I."

Rick smiled. "I get it now. You told Mort Ostrow you wanted the 'Rick Hoffman treatment' because you wanted to meet me in person. Size me up. And at the same time you had your thugs put a scare into me. Sort of a two-pronged approach. Because you're a check-every-box kinda guy."

Sculley shrugged.

"I think you knew my dad, didn't you?"

"I certainly did."

"You took care of his nursing home expenses for twenty years."

"And you've come to thank me?"

"Actually, I'm here because I've finally gotten around to that Thomas Sculley piece. But the story has shifted a bit since I started."

"Now, how do you mean?"

"My story details how you covered up the death of the Cabrera family in the Ted Williams Tunnel in 1996. How you paid people off—a policeman, the survivors, even a community activist—all to make sure nothing slowed down your progress."

Sculley's face was impassive. "What a grand story you've got there. A grand and fanciful story!"

"Not so fanciful. Fortunately, my dad left records of the payoffs he made for you."

"Mr. Hoffman!" he thundered with a joyous smile, as if Rick had told him a wonderful joke. "Now it sounds like you're threatening me! Shaking me down!"

"Not at all. I'm a journalist with a story to finish. Call it the 'Rick Hoffman treatment.'"

Sculley stared at him for a long moment. "Let me ask you something, Mr. Hoffman, and it's something I've always wanted to ask a journalist. What motivates you?" He squinted and tilted his head to one side. "Really, what motivates you? Why would you choose to be on the sidelines, watching the action? Why does a clever man such as yourself *choose* to be in the audience and not in the ring? This I've never understood."

Rick smiled. "When I was in college, a famous journalist came to give a talk, and one of the students asked him the very same question. What motivates you? And the journalist said, 'I'm just a guy who wants to know how the story ends.' I've always liked that answer."

"You're an odd duck, Mr. Hoffman."

"So let's talk about those payoffs."

Sculley snorted. "Payoffs? Do you know who had to be paid off to make the Big Dig happen? Everybody! Anyone with a complaint got bought off. The government bought air conditioners and soundproof windows, even new mattresses for homeowners in the North End who hated all the noise of the construction. Must have been ten thousand palms were greased. This is the way of the world, laddy. You didn't come here to ask about *that*."

"Then let me put it more pointedly. Your empire came with a body count. How the hell do you sleep at night?"

Sculley's face flushed. "Do you have any idea how that tunnel has transformed this city? Boston traffic used to be a joke, a national punch line. Driving through downtown at rush hour used to take half an hour. Now it takes three minutes. Traveling to the airport is seventy-five percent faster. The Big Dig was the largest and most complex and most technologically challenging construction project in the history of this country."

"That's what they say."

"Did a few poor souls die because of the Big Dig? Son, a hundred men died building the Hoover Dam. A thousand men died building the Erie Canal. Four hundred Chinamen died building the transcontinental railroad. How about the Panama Canal? One of the greatest engineering feats in history? *Thirty thousand* men died building it. Ambitious projects always cost lives, son. That's the truth. Have you ever visited the great pyramids of Giza?"

Rick shook his head.

"They'll take your breath away, they will. But nobody who sees them sheds tears for the thousands of men who died building them. A pharaoh had a vision, and that's what remains. His vision. Do you know what would happen if they tried to build the pyramids today? There'd be a goddamned environmental impact review and a board of grievances and we'd have nothing more than a shelf full of pretty blueprints. The world is full of small men who want to tie the great ones down."

A woman popped her head into the tent. Sculley held up a hand, palm out, and she immediately left.

"When small men get in the way of big things," Sculley went on, "which d'ya think must go?"

"Small men. Like my father, you mean?"

Anger flashed in Sculley's face. "That was a decision *he* made." Then he gave Rick a basilisk smile, a snake regarding a mouse. "Do you know what the difference is between a man like your father and a man like me?"

"Why don't you tell me," Rick said acidly.

"Small men are always waiting for their opportunity. Great men seize the opportunity. Great men say yes to life. They're not naysayers. Every day you face the decision—do you say yes or do you say no? Do you seize the opportunity? Your father left you three million dollars? The curse of the small bequest. Not enough money to do things with. Just enough money *not* to do things with. So the question for you is, What could you do with *thirty* million?"

"Just yesterday you tried to have me killed and now you're offering me thirty million dollars?"

"I think I'm good at taking the measure of a man, up close and face-to-face. You're ballsy. You're sharp. But the question is, do you have the kind of spirit that says yes to opportunity? Thirty million, a man with imagination can do a thing or two with that kind of coin. Dream a little, my son. You can do anything you want with it. Set up your own news-gathering organization. Buy your own office building. You can choose to be one of the big apes, or you can be a microscopic louse nestling in their pubes. Which will it be?"

He placed an arm on Rick's shoulder, his eyes boring in. "You know, there's a saying in my business: Those who can, build. Those who can't, criticize. So my question for you is, What kind of man are you? Do you want to be one of the big boys, the ones who build something great? Or the ones who just want to pull things down? Because it isn't too late for you. A new day, a new decision. You've got the chance to take the money, ride the whirlwind, and do something special. Will you take it. *Are you that man?*"

"Not really, no. I'm just the guy who wants to know how the story ends."

A man stepped into the tent and Sculley put out his palm again, eyes flashing with anger.

"I said, leave us," he barked.

The man didn't move.

Rick saw the man in the blue FBI windbreaker, Special Agent Donovan, standing at the tent's opening. Rick nodded and smiled and held up one finger, asking him to wait a minute.

"What the hell is this?" Sculley said. But he now seemed to understand. He turned and stared at Rick.

"I can't finish my piece without some sort of response from you," Rick said. "It's sort of a policy of mine." He took out his iPhone and unlocked it. "Otherwise, it's all ready to go. And I mean, go live."

Sculley's face had gone deep red. "I don't believe you."

"I'll just say that Mr. Sculley declined to comment."

Rick hit a phone number, and when Dylan from *Back Bay* answered, he said, "Just as I wrote, Mr. Sculley declined to comment. We're ready to rock 'n' roll, Dylan. Go for it."

"It's done," Dylan confirmed a few seconds later.

"If this is blackmail," Sculley said, "it'll never work. You wouldn't dare."

"I just did."

"Lad, you just sealed your own fate."

"*Your* fate, actually. And my friend in the windbreaker here is about to escort you to it."

The words came from Sculley in a rasp: "You'll never get what you want."

"Yeah, well, I think I just did. At least I know how your story ends. Because I wrote it myself."

371

One Year Later

A ndrea wasn't having any wine but wasn't ready to tell people why. Rick poured himself a plastic tumbler of wine from the box.

"I know it's not up to your lofty standards, Rick," she said.

He grinned. "Isn't there a statute of limitations on wine jokes?"

"As far as I'm concerned, you're still fair game."

The party was crowded with Geometry Partners staff and donors and potential donors. The occasion was the opening of Geometry Partners' new Somerville location, which was called the Leonard Hoffman House, underwritten by an anonymous gift of one million dollars. There were Geometry Partners posters on the wall (DO THE MATH; KNOW THE ANGLES; IT ALL ADDS UP).

Evan was buzzed on grape juice and cookies, and when he wasn't playing *Minecraft* he was careening through the party, knocking into guests, and spilling drinks.

Thomas Sculley was in federal prison and would be for another ten years. Eight with good behavior. Alex Pappas was in prison as well but would be out much sooner. He'd struck a plea bargain with

372

government prosecutors: an eighteen-month sentence in exchange for full cooperation. For spilling all. Rick wasn't surprised that Pappas had made a good deal for himself.

But he didn't particularly care. After the Thomas Sculley exposé was published and was picked up by forty news outlets, Rick found himself weighing several job offers, including one from a nonprofit public interest website that funded investigative journalism projects and another from *The Wall Street Journal*. Eventually he went with the investigative journalism website, which gave him the flexibility to do his pieces in Boston. His current project was an investigation into corruption in the process by which the FDA approved pharmaceuticals.

It felt peculiar becoming a father—a stepfather, actually—stepping into the role instead of being promoted to dadhood through the usual system. But at the same time it felt right.

The house on Clayton Street was too badly damaged to be salvageable. Rick split the insurance proceeds with Wendy. Between the cash left over, after the Geometry Partners grant, and his salary from the nonprofit, money wasn't a problem.

The reporter from *Back Bay* magazine approached them, a young woman named Lindsay who looked twelve, wearing a bulky cable-knit sweater and heavy tortoiseshell glasses. "Is now a good time to do this interview?" she said.

"Sure," said Andrea, "but maybe we should sit down a little later. There's a lot to get into in terms of our success rate, measured along a bunch of different axes, and—"

"You know what?" Lindsay said. "I only have nine hundred words so I'm not really going to be drilling down so much. It's kinda more of a lifestyle piece about one of Boston's Power Couples."

"Okay," Andrea said.

"Awesome. So you guys just got married, right?"

Andrea showed her the wedding ring. They'd done the deed only a month earlier, at city hall.

"So how do you guys do it all? That's what I want to know." She turned to Rick. "Your article on Thomas Sculley just won the George Polk Award for investigative journalism, right? And then there was your piece about kickbacks in the defense industry." Looking at Andrea, she said, "And you guys have a little kid and Geometry Partners has got to be more than a full-time job. Plus it's expanding so fast, right, with locations in Washington, DC, and New York City? How do you do it? What's the trick?"

Rick and Andrea exchanged glances.

"The trick is," Rick said, "there's no trick."

Acknowledgments

I'm grateful to a number of people for their generous help in researching this book. For help with various medical details: my brother Dr. Jonathan Finder; Dr. Amy Goldstein of Children's Hospital of Pittsburgh; Dr. Carl Kramer; Margaret Naeser, professor of neurology, Boston University School of Medicine; Eileen Hunsaker of the Aphasia Center at Massachusetts General Hospital Institute of Health Professions; Dr. Joan Camprodon; and especially Dr. Mark Morocco. For legal matters: Allen Smith and Nick Poser. On public relations: Doug Bailey and George Regan. On renovating the old family house: Bruce Irving; and Doug Hanna and Eileen Lester of S&H Construction.

On the Big Dig, Sean Murphy of *The Boston Globe* was a huge help; thanks as well to John Durrant of the American Society of Civil Engineers, Timothy Finley of Semke Forensic, and especially Gary Klein of Wiss, Janney, Elstner Associates. (Some particulars of this mammoth project were changed for fictional convenience.)

Eight-year-old Henry Buckley-Jones was a precocious and patient interviewee. Thanks as well to Harry "Skip" Brandon of Smith Brandon, Jay Groob of American Investigative Services, Lucia Rotelli, Bill Rehder, Bruce Holloway, and Declan Burke. For help with technological details:

Jeff Fischbach, Mark Spencer of Arsenal Experts and Kevin Murray. On forensic accounting, Eric Hines of the StoneTurn Group. Zachary Mider of Bloomberg News provided intriguing information on secretive non-profits. My gratitude once again to Clair Lamb, Karen Louie-Joyce, and the irreplaceable Claire Baldwin. At Dutton, my thanks to Amanda Walker, Christine Ball, Carrie Swetonic, Stephanie Kelly, and especially Ben Sevier. I'm grateful for the loving support of my wife, Michele Souda, and our daughter, Emma J. S. Finder. Thanks most of all to my agent, Dan Conaway of Writers House, and my brother Henry Finder.